New Eden

KISHORE TIPIRNENI

DEDICATION

For my wife Hiral and our three beautiful children Mira, Anjali, and Jalan.

ACKNOWLEDGMENTS

Thanks to William Hammett whose help was invaluable.
The cover illustrations for the book were created by Guillermo Herrera.

INTRODUCTION

For me, truly compelling science fiction must be based on actual science. As much as possible I have tried to be true to sound scientific principles throughout this novel. This introduction is a brief history of the scientific premise on which NEW EDEN is based. It is by no means necessary to read the introduction to understand the plot, and those not interested can skip to the first chapter.

In 1935, Albert Einstein, along with Boris Podolsky and Nathan Rosen, wrote a paper describing an apparent paradox in quantum mechanics. In this paper, later to be called the EPR paradox, they described how if Heisenberg's uncertainty principle and quantum mechanics were to be believed, then there can exist quantumly entangled particles that can transmit information between each other faster than the speed of light which violated Einstein's own theory of relativity. In fact, quantumly entangled particles seemed to have the ability to transmit information instantaneously even if they were on opposite sides of the universe. Einstein found this absurd and hence wrote the paper describing this paradox.

The following is a simplified explanation of the EPR paradox. The uncertainty principle and quantum mechanics dictates that the physical properties of some elementary particles can become entangled at a quantum level. For example, two particles could be created that are entangled for the property of spin. When two particles are entangled for spin, the first particle must have the opposite spin of the other particle, hence if one is spinning left to right, the other must spin right to left. However, immediately after the particles are created and before their spin is actually measured, the uncertainty principle dictates that the spin of each particle is indeterminate. In this state, called a superposition, each particle is actually spinning in both directions at the same time. This indeterminate state of these particles, no matter how strange it may seem, is a hallmark of quantum mechanics and the uncertainty principle. If these entangled particles are then separated by any distance and then one of the particle's spin is measured, its state is no longer indeterminate, and this particle chooses a definite direction of spin. But this act of measuring the direction of spin of the first particle automatically and instantaneously must cause its entangled twin to also go out of superposition and choose the opposite spin no matter how far away it is—even if it's at the opposite side of the universe. The paradox here is that the information that the first particle's spin has been measured and which direction it is spinning has to be transmitted to the other particle for it to be able to pick the opposite spin, but this information must be transmitted instantaneously which means that it travels faster than light which violates Einstein's theory of relativity which states that nothing can travel faster than light, not even information, hence the paradox.

Einstein did not believe that these particles were actually sending information faster than light. In fact, he called this interaction "spooky action at a distance." He instead believed that each particle, when it was created, contained pre-determined and unmeasurable information all along about which direction it would spin when measured, and that measuring a particle's spin simply presented to us this unknown information. In this way, no actual information was being transferred between these particles. For many years, this was the state of physics with some physicists believing that entangled particles are transmitting information instantaneously and some believing Einstein that the particles already contained this information from the beginning.

In 1964, nine years after Einstein's death, John Stewart Bell, a physicist from Northern Ireland, wrote a paper in which he outlined a method that uses mathematics and probability that could be used to settle this debate. The method outlined in this paper, later refined into a theorem called Bell's theorem, could be used to devise experiments that could unequivocally settle whether entangled particles contain hidden information or instantaneously transmit information.

At present, using Bell's theorem, many physicists have performed these experiments and the results are unequivocal. Einstein was wrong. Entangled particles do not contain hidden information and actually are able to transmit information instantaneously no matter how far apart they are. So, it has been proven that a single bit of information can be transmitted instantaneously at any distance by entangled particles, but this bit of information is not presently useful for meaningful communication since this single bit of information is random, and after transmission of this information, the entanglement of these particles becomes broken.

However, still the fact remains, physics has proven that the universe contains a mechanism that can transmit information instantaneously across any distance. The story of NEW EDEN is an example of the profound implications for humanity given this one single revelation in physics.

Chapter One
Dear Old Albert

"Einstein was wrong! Light is not the fastest thing in the universe—information is. And everything is information."

The audience of Wheeler Auditorium at UC Berkeley held its breath at the first words of the lecture delivered by Dr. Henry H. Bowman, professor of particle physics. Students and colleagues knew that he had a flare for the dramatic and that his research had been shrouded in secrecy for several years, but his opening statement seemed to be more than a little pretentious.

In his late sixties, Bowman was a man of average height with gray hair parted on the side and spilling over his ears and shirt collar. He wore a suit coat that was fashionably out of style thanks to velvet elbow patches, and his deck shoes were cracked and worn. He wandered around the stage, hands in the pockets of his faded blue jeans, as he continued.

"Don't get me wrong," the professor proclaimed, stopping to face his audience with a grin. "He didn't get *everything* wrong, of course, and he was dead right on one very important issue thanks to his famous thought experiment called the EPR Paradox. By the way, that's E for Einstein, P for Boris Podolsky, and R for Nathan Rosen—just to be clear, mind you, about who was also in on this revolutionary little brain game being played in the field of quantum mechanics in 1935. So, what did Einstein get right?"

Bowman paused, staring at his audience, most of them in shadow, almost as if expecting an answer. He laughed softly and rubbed his chin. "I suppose I'm getting ahead of myself, so let me back up."

The professor resumed his aimless walking, and though he was mic'd up, he seemed to be talking as much to himself at times as to his listeners.

"Einstein desired certainty. In the lab, he wanted the properties of

1

subatomic particles to be measured accurately each and every time. He wanted reality to be . . . well, real!"

Laughter rippled across the audience as a few heads turned to the people sitting next to them as if to say *We knew this was going to be weird, and we're not disappointed.*

"You see, Einstein wasn't buying into quantum mechanics, at least not the vision of it advanced by the Copenhagen interpretation cooked up by Neils Bohr or Werner Heisenberg. Quantum mechanics and the Heisenberg Uncertainty Principle had the audacity to say that if you identified the location of an electron, you couldn't simultaneously measure its momentum. If you measure its momentum, however, then *poof*—you couldn't identify its location. Poor little guy. It was a wanderer, a hobo with no place to rest or call home." Bowman paused for dramatic effect. "Bummer, right?" he said, raising his voice.

More laughter drifted over the audience.

"No, no, no, this was unacceptable to Albert, who said that God didn't play dice with the universe. He wanted logic and what is known as scientific realism. To say that he was offended by Heisenberg's Uncertainty Principle regarding our aforementioned electron with an identity crisis would be an understatement. He wanted certainty, and don't we all! When I was married, I always wanted to be able to predict what my wife was thinking, but my guesses were only accurate fifty percent of the time, like tossing a coin and calling heads or tails. Sooner or later you're going to be right, but you're still going to sleep on the couch fifty percent of the time. I'm divorced by the way."

This time the laughter was much louder. Professor Bowman was winning his audience over by degrees without even having arrived at his main topic for the afternoon.

"Well, if you don't buy what I'm selling today, I guess I can always do stand-up comedy. But pardon me. I digress. To point out an absurdity about quantum mechanics related to the Uncertainty Principle, Einstein conjured up his fabled EPR thought experiment. He imagined that two particles created at the same time and place are then moved far apart, even on opposite sides of the universe for the sake of argument. The pair is separated, like fighting spouses who have retreated to different rooms within their home. There is seemingly no communication, but there's the rub! Quantum mechanics dictated that these particles had to be able to communicate instantaneously with each other. They had to be *entangled* at a quantum level. Long story short, quantum mechanics maintained that a measurement made of one particle's spin would influence the other particle's spin no matter the distance between them. And here's the kicker, ladies and gentlemen. It would have to happen instantaneously."

Bowman snapped his fingers and pounded his right fist into the palm of his left hand for emphasis, making a loud cracking sound. The professor, knowing that he had a captive audience hanging on his every word, walked to a table, drank from a glass of water, and wiped his forehead with a handkerchief. "Sure is hot under these lights," he muttered.

The auditorium was all silence and expectation.

"But there was a problem. Instantaneous communication? This was heresy for Einstein who felt that nothing could travel faster than light. For Einstein, instantaneous communication was as unlikely as our feuding spouses reconciling their differences from two rooms that are so far apart that each can't hear the other's voice."

Bowman inhaled deeply and gazed down at his Top Siders as he paced. "Remember that nothing goes faster than the speed of light according to the theory of relativity. And yet *something* had to be communicated between the theoretical particles if quantum mechanics was going to be upheld and eventually proven. Otherwise, God was playing dice with the universe, and the cosmos wouldn't make much sense—at least not to Albert. Einstein concluded that there had to be variables hidden somewhere in these particles if the quantum world could be regarded as . . . *complete*, to use his own word. He just didn't believe in instantaneous communication, so he copped out, dear friends, and claimed that what was happening to these particles was something he termed—" Bowman made the air-quote gesture with his hands. "Spooky action at a distance."

Bowman suddenly stopped pacing, faced the audience—legs spread— and held out his arms, fingers splayed. "Boo! Spooky action!"

There was no laughter this time, for everyone in Wheeler Auditorium knew that the next shoe was going to drop any minute now.

Bowman resumed pacing the stage yet again and waved his right arm dismissively in the air.

"He didn't bother to tell us what that spooky action was for one simple reason: he had no flippin' idea. After all, quantum mechanics was violating his own theory of relativity, and maybe he didn't really want an answer even though he spent a good portion of his life trying to find one—bupkis, nada, zilch." Bowman cupped his hands around his mouth as if telling a secret. "He couldn't figure out his own riddle any more than he could find marital bliss. He was a womanizer, in case you didn't know."

Einstein's famous equation appeared on the elevated screen at the rear of the stage.

$$E = mc^2$$

Bowman stood still as he faced the audience, arms folded after motioning to the equation on the screen behind him.

"You're all familiar with Einstein's famous equation no doubt. It shows that matter and energy are different forms of the same thing and are interchangeable. Now I'll grant you that anything made of matter or energy can't travel faster than light, which is the cosmic speed limit according to the theory of relativity. I'll give that much to Albert. But what about something that contains no matter or energy? Something like data, like information? Why does it have to obey this speed limit? Well, yours truly has a few tricks up his sleeve," the professor announced, running fingers through his long, unkempt hair, "and at the risk of sounding immodest, information *is* something that can travel faster than the speed of light, and not just random information either. Real data *can* be transmitted instantaneously, and I have created something that can prove it."

A collective gasp escaped the throats of the crowd.

"It's called the . . . well, why don't I just show it to you now, huh? Would you like to see it?"

Bowman received a round of loud applause and a standing ovation before he could utter another word and show the world his creation, something that would profoundly alter the course of human history.

Chapter Two
Time, Space, and Kashmir

(one hour earlier)

Rachael Miller walked to the back of the line waiting to be admitted to Wheeler Auditorium to hear the brilliant, eccentric, and reclusive Dr. Henry Bowman hold forth on . . . well, she didn't know *what* the professor was going to talk about, but she was getting extra credit from one of her professors for attending. Judging by the length of the lines waiting to get in—there were three for as many entrances—other students at UC Berkeley had been given the same offer.

Rachael was five six, a slim, attractive brunette with deep brown eyes, high cheekbones, and straight dark brown hair that fell below her shoulders. At twenty years of age, she carried herself with the poise and confidence of someone much older.

"Looks like a packed house," she muttered while opening her shoulder bag to retrieve a mint.

Vinod Bhakti, a young man of Indian descent, early-twenties with brown eyes and close-cut hair, heard the remark and turned around to look at the woman directly behind him. He was six two, had a slim build, and wore a vintage Led Zeppelin tee shirt with white letters on a black background.

"Yeah, this line is ridiculous," he commented idly. "Hope it's worth the wait."

"Mint?" Rachael said, holding out the roll to the young man.

"Sure. Thanks."

"Do you know what Professor Bowman is speaking about?"

"Physics, I suppose," he said with a laugh. "I mean, what else is the dude gonna ramble about? I hear he and a post doc research assistant have virtually locked themselves away at some particle physics lab in a sub-basement here on campus. A friend of mine thinks he's discovered the nature of dark matter and energy, but I think he's full of it. Nobody's even close to figuring that out."

Rachael raised her eyebrows and tilted her head. "Yeah, that's a stretch alright. Bowman's not even a cosmologist."

"Are you a physics major?" Vinod inquired.

Rachael shook her head. "I'm still undeclared, but I'm mostly taking science courses and have a minor in journalism. An odd combination, I guess."

"So you're going to be a—"

"Yep, a science writer—possibly. I still haven't decided."

"Gonna write about today's lecture?"

"I write about everything." Rachael popped another mint in her mouth. "What about you? Physics major?"

"Information theory. It's a branch of computer science that deals with data compression, algorithmic theory, linguistics, math—just about everything, really. Light, energy, matter—everything in nature communicates with everything else."

"Not sure if I follow."

Vinod pointed to his right. "We see that oak tree over there because light is reflected from its bark and leaves to the rods and cones in our eyes and then to the visual cortex in our brains. So, the information that there's a tree over there is being transmitted to us by light."

"So light is just a form of information?"

"Light is a *conduit* for information. In fact, I plan on writing a dissertation one day proving that all life on Earth, human and non-human, is a computer of sorts. And to be *really* radical, all matter, animate and inanimate, is just information that is used by these computers."

Rachael looked perplexed. "Sounds radical alright."

"For me, the digital age started when the Earth evolved a few billion years ago. There's never been a time in the history of the universe when information wasn't being sent, received, stored, and retransmitted. You don't need silicon chips and a modem for that to happen."

"Hmmm. Interesting way to look at creation." Rachael's eyes glanced at the man's Led Zeppelin tee shirt. "And naturally music is one of the higher forms of communication?"

Vinod spread his arms wide, looked at the sky, and emphasized each word as he spoke. "Absolutely . . . the . . . most . . . *glorious* form of communication that there is, especially if you're talking classic rock even though music in geological structures—long story—goes back millions of years."

"So Zeppelin came late to the party then?"

"I guess, but so did the Beatles, Stones, AC-DC, Rush, and a hundred other great classic rock bands."

"What's your favorite Zeppelin song?" Rachel asked to pass the time since she saw that the line wasn't moving. "'Stairway to Heaven'?"

The man shrugged and moved his head left to right as if to indicate his indecision. "Eh . . . good choice, but it's too obvious a selection for me. I prefer 'Kashmir.'"

Rachael nodded. "Isn't that the one with a lyric about being a traveler in space and time?"

"Yes, it is!" Vinod exclaimed looking at her with a shocked expression. Very few kids of their generation appreciated classic rock as much as he did.

Vinod extended his hand as the line finally started to move. "Vinod Bhakti. Junior."

"Rachael Miller. Sophomore. Nice to meet you."

The students filed into the auditorium, and from above, they looked like a column of ants crawling into their mound.

Chapter Three
Red Rover, Red Rover

Rachael and Vinod stared at each other in the darkened auditorium, mouths hanging open in astonishment at Professor Bowman's last pronouncement.

"Damn," Vinod muttered. "Data that can travel faster than the speed of light? Next, the old geezer is gonna tell us that he's discovered the Unified Field Theory."

"He's certainly got *my* attention," Rachael said as the applause died down. "Faster than light? That's impossible."

"Quick. Take some notes. This man might become the most famous scientist in history over the course of the next hour."

Rachael pointed her index finger at her head. "I already am."

Vinod smiled and turned back towards the stage. The professor was riffing on information theory, and the young student was hungry for the next part of the presentation.

*   *   *

"It's time to get technical, but I'll try to make this as simple as possible," Bowman stated. "To me, baseball is still our national pastime. *Field of Dreams* got it right, so let's start with a little country hardball. Notice the screen, if you would. You can see two baseballs, and no, the picture isn't out of focus."

On the screen above the stage—twenty feet by forty feet— were two baseballs side by side. The balls seemed to be spinning, but their images were unclear since they appeared to be spinning both right to left and left to right at the same time.

"For the purposes of my demonstration," Bowman continued, "these baseballs represent two subatomic particles, and as you can see, they're both spinning in opposite directions at the same time. You see, when two entangled particles are first created, they don't have a definite direction of spin and can be thought of as spinning in both directions at the same time—something we physicists call a superposition. I guess that blurry image is what a batter sees when a ninety-eight mile an hour fast ball comes screaming at home plate in the ninth inning when the relief pitcher—the proverbial closer—is throwing heat. Let's see what happens when the two balls are separated."

The balls were now a few feet apart and connected by a short length of string.

Bowman faced his mesmerized audience. "The particles are maintaining a connection with each other even when separated because they're still connected at a quantum level, something we call quantum entanglement." Bowman paused for dramatic effect. "But do they have anything meaningful to say? Maybe . . ."

Everyone in the auditorium leaned forward in anticipation.

"Maybe they have more to tell each other than you think. It turns out that both baseballs were hit out of the park. Home runs. One landed in the left field bleachers, one landed in the right field bleachers. They're quite far apart, but they continue to maintain a connection with each other. Let's give this discussion a little clarity. Watch what happens when a spin measurement is made on the baseball on the left." Bowman looked up at the ceiling of Wheeler Auditorium. "Are you watching, Albert?"

The baseball on the left was now in sharp focus and spinning left to right.

"Voilà!" Bowman said. "It has picked a direction to spin and is transmitting information instantly to the other baseball as to which direction it's spinning. You see, measuring a particle's spin causes it to move out of superposition, pick a definite direction of spin, and communicate this information with its twin. The other particle also moves out of superposition and spins in the opposite direction to the first. This communication happens instantaneously and is the hallmark of quantum entanglement. You can see now that the baseball on the right is spinning in the opposite direction to the one on the left."

Heads pivoted to look at the other ball as if the audience was a single organism, a cell reacting to a photon of light.

Bowman threw his head back and laughed, clearly enjoying the way he was able to manipulate the crowd with a presentation that had been planned for over a year. "I assure you that this is not a case of misdirection. I'm a scientist, not a magician." He walked back to the center of the stage.

9

"It's all about information, people. Information, in its purest form, has no mass or energy, so it doesn't have to obey the theory of relativity and doesn't have to *travel* through space-time. It can *jump* to any point in space-time. The *information* that the first particle's spin was measured, as well as which direction it chose to spin, is transmitted instantaneously to the other particle, which then spins in the opposite direction."

"This guy is speaking my language," Vinod whispered to Rachael excitedly.

"The communication between entangled particles is unaffected by distance. One of our baseballs, for example, could have been hit into the Andromeda galaxy—that's steroids in baseball for ya—and the result would have been the same, so you'll have to take my word for it. For now, that is. I've got a kick-ass demonstration planned for you in just a few minutes. First, a few more words of explanation—a very few. Science should be kept simple during lectures. Ask any fifth-grade science teacher."

Bowman once again took a sip of water, wiped his forehead with a handkerchief, and then, placing his hands on his back, leaned backwards as if stretching. "Still damn hot under these lights," he said.

"There aren't that many lights above the stage," Rachael said softly. "What's he referring to?"

"He's in his sixties," Vinod replied. "Plus, he's pretty informal for a guy who's in the process of shattering particle physics as we know it. Just eccentric, I suppose."

"Ladies and gentlemen," Bowman said, "this is the essence of quantum entanglement and the idea of non-locality that is its corollary. It's actually been demonstrated on a small scale in the laboratory many times by researchers, but there's a hitch. Whenever the spin of one particle, or a baseball in this example, is measured and the resulting information is transmitted to its twin, the connection between them is broken. They can no longer communicate."

The string representing the connection between the balls on the screen disappeared.

"It turns out that our baseballs had a fleeting encounter, nothing more." Bowman shook his head and closed his eyes. "To mix my metaphors, have you ever flirted with someone across a crowded room at a cocktail party? You turn away, look back, and they're gone. The communication is broken." Bowman sighed and shook his head. "What a letdown, huh? I guess yours truly will have to be sent down to the minor leagues. I flirted with you—built up your expectations—and we're right back where we started—theory. My apologies."

For the first time since Bowman had appeared onstage, the audience seemed restless. Had they wasted their time on the musings of a dodgy professor who was telling them, in the final analysis, what they already knew from textbooks, namely that entangled particles don't stay entangled after a measurement is made? He'd entertained them with humor and histrionics, but if this was his bottom line, then the whole afternoon had been a waste of time. A dozen people got to their feet and began walking down the two aisles toward the rear of the facility.

Bowman, however, appeared unfazed.

"O ye of little faith," he said. "Professor Henry Bowman has no intention of playing triple-A ball for a farm team. Many years ago, I realized through mathematical computations that particle pairs can be created that are permanently entangled—artificially created particles that can never become unentangled and never lose their connection. After years of rigorous research and lab work, I've succeeded in creating a special type of subatomic particle that, when entangled and measured, *remains* entangled with its twin. Kinda like till death us do part. Our feuding spouses are now communicating with each other—are back on the same page, soul mates reading each other's minds and planning a trip to the Bahamas."

The people marching down the aisles froze in their tracks.

"I *thought* that might get your attention," Bowman said. "Now then, as I was about to say, I've named these subatomic particles spookyons. An appropriate name, wouldn't you say? I assure you that the entanglement of my spookyons is quite stable and would have made Einstein a convert. I guess I just have better lab equipment than he did."

Applause erupted as Bowman recaptured the attention of his audience with the audacious nature of his announcement.

"Thank you," Bowman said with a broad grin, looking like Will Rogers ready to do a rope trick. "But don't take *my* word for it. After you've seen the demonstration, you can pass the hat to take up a collection for my airfare to Stockholm so I can pick up my Nobel Prize. Like I said, spookyons are permanently entangled. You can measure the spin on one, and its twin will immediately spin the opposite direction and will do so until you stop measuring. But once you stop measuring, they both go back into superposition—back to spinning in both directions at once. So instead of just being able to send one random bit of information, we can use them to send an unlimited number of bits instantaneously across any distance."

The baseballs began to grow clear then blurry over and over again, mimicking continual measurements made on their spin. With each measurement, the spin was locked either right to left or left to right.

The enthusiasm in the auditorium was palpable. People whispered to each other, pointed at the screen, and took out their smart phones to record the event.

"Wait a second!" Bowman said, his right arm and index finger pointing at the screen. "*That's* not the demonstration! Just a graphic! I've just been warming up in the bullpen."

The baseballs disappeared, and their images were replaced by a picture of the red planet, Mars. The abrupt change of imagery caused the excitement in the auditorium to intensify further. What did a distant planet have to do with entanglement?

"Yes, that is indeed the red planet, and my demonstration will cover approximately 142,000,000 miles. Anyone out there still want to leave?"

The auditorium grew silent, and the aisles cleared.

"It's time to do some real science, so let me introduce my capable Ph.D. student, Joshua Andrews." Bowman squinted as if to pick out certain audience members. "Ladies, he's single."

A young man took the stage—tall, mid-twenties, and handsome— approached a table that was now visible thanks to an overhead light being switched on. Joshua lifted a black cloth covering the table like a magician's assistant, revealing a clear, hollow glass sphere that glowed an eerie shade of green. It was, appropriately enough, the size of a baseball. The top and bottom of the sphere were coated with thin metal plating, attached to which were numerous wire cables that ran to a table six feet away, where they connected to a gray metal box with dual joystick controls and other switches. The overhead screen switched to an extreme close-up shot of the mesmerizing glass orb.

"The inside of this glass sphere is a vacuum except for a single spookyon I created," Bowman boasted, "and it's entangled with another spookyon even as I speak. Since the spookyon is subatomic, it's much too small to be seen. The equipment connected to the sphere allows us to measure the spin of the enclosed spookyon. But where's Waldo? Where is its twin?"

"On Mars!" a brave soul from the audience shouted.

"Well, duh!" Bowman shouted back. "The image of Mars didn't appear on the screen for nothing! But let me be a bit more specific. Joshua, do your thing."

Joshua Andrews picked up the control and flicked one of the switches. The screen's image changed to a scene of rust-red rocks on the forbidding Martian desert.

"What you are seeing," Bowman explained, "is a live feed from the latest Mars Rover NASA launched last year and that landed on the planet's surface last week. The gurus at JPL don't have a clue that I've concealed another sphere containing a spookyon entangled with this one inside the orbiter that the rover uses to communicate with Earth. They must be crapping their pants about now because I've just hijacked their rover by replacing their communication channel with one that uses our spookyons. But I don't think they'll be locking me up once they see the rest of my demonstration."

Joshua stood sideways to the audience with the controller in his hand. He was excited to be able to finally reveal the work upon which his Ph.D. thesis would be based. He had his eyes glued to Professor Bowman and hung on his every word.

"The best is yet to come," Bowman announced. "I said that you're seeing a live feed from Mars, but how's that possible? The red planet is currently twelve light minutes away, so to send a signal to turn on the camera and then receive an actual video feed should take, round trip, twenty-four minutes. But this image has no time delay. It is indeed live! You see, one of my colleagues at the University of Arizona was commissioned by NASA to build the orbiter's communications array. When she told me of her project, I convinced her to conceal the second sphere in its com panel. Spooky action at a distance, ladies and gentlemen. Instantaneous communication with the Mars Rover thanks to a pair of entangled spookyons. Joshua, let's look at that large black rock ten feet away and slightly to the right."

The green sphere on the table glowed brighter as Joshua worked the joystick and nudged the rover ahead. The camera on the vehicle wobbled only slightly as it crawled ten feet ahead to the black rock.

Using the joystick, Joshua extended the rover's main arm, technically known as the Instrument Deployment Device—and lifted the rock from the Martian desert using what had been nicknamed a "space claw,"— essentially a robotic hand at the end of the IDD.

"On second thought, Joshua," Bowman said whimsically, "let's have a look at the orange rock on the left instead. Orange is the new black."

Joshua maneuvered the rover and its arm to retrieve the orange rock, lifting it to a position in front of the rover's camera lens.

"Can you imagine what this will mean to the muckety-mucks at NASA and JPL when they want to send commands to spacecraft exploring the outer planets of our solar system?" Bowman asked. "And one day to probes in interstellar space? No time delay. No tense, anxious waiting to see whether or not some robotic arm or solar panel on a spacecraft a billion miles away has deployed. No time lag between taking a picture of Pluto and receiving it in JPL's imaging center. All because of spookyons."

Bowman winced as if in pain and placed his hands on his lower back and closed his eyes before continuing. "And can you imagine other applications for spookyons? With a little imagination, what amazing communication systems might be built that will enable us to talk in real time with colonies on Mars or the moons of Jupiter and Saturn. But why stop there? Even—"

Perspiring heavily, Bowman took a step towards the table and his glass of water, but he didn't reach it. His chest heaved, and he collapsed on the stage floor.

"Henry!" Joshua cried out as he dropped the controller, rushed to the side of the professor, and knelt next to the motionless form. "Are you okay?" He stared at the audience. "Someone call 911!"

Bowman lifted his head and tried to prop himself on his elbow. He looked into Joshua's face hovering over him.

"Einstein was wrong," he said in a hoarse voice. "Everything . . . is . . . information."

Bowman collapsed a second time as the shocked audience looked at the ghastly scene. Joshua grasped Dr. Bowman's hand to afford him some comfort.

Rachael and Vinod looked at each other in disbelief. They said nothing.

Chapter Four
Your Not-So-Average Scientific American

(five years later)

The radio was on in the Toyota Prius as Rachael Miller drove through the gray, slick streets of Berkeley, California. The windshield wipers swished back and forth, removing fat raindrops from the windshield at a tempo that perfectly matched "Sweet Emotion" by Aerosmith. Vinod had been mildly shocked that Rachael, despite their five-year friendship, knew almost nothing about lead band member Steven Tyler. She had programmed a classic rock channel on her Sirius XM to rectify all problems related to her ongoing education in classic rock music although she occasionally switched to a classical station to listen to string quartets by Mozart, Bach, Haydn, and other composers. She loved the complex yet pleasing interplay among two violins, viola, and cello. To the discerning ear, the instruments were definitely communicating with each other.

The weather was apparently causing static as the words of "Sweet Emotion" began to cut in and out, so Rachael gave a voice command to the radio. "Alexa, change to CNN." It was time, she thought, to catch up on the news. The New Horizons spacecraft was currently taking images of a newly-discovered planetesimal at the edge of the Kuiper belt. She planned on writing an article on the two dozen known dwarf planets beyond the orbit of Pluto, and the spacecraft's latest discovery, Cassandra Prime, would be featured in her opening paragraph. She thought to herself that if New Horizons had been launched with a Bowman sphere, which was the name now given to the glass spheres that contain spookyons, the imaging team at JPL wouldn't have to wait the six hours it was taking to receive the spectacular images of the planetesimal made of ice, rock, and frozen gases. The news, however, matched the dreary day in terms of content.

"This is Dan Boyd with CNN, and our top story at this hour concerns the alarming Ebola outbreak in Malaysia. The World Health Organization estimates that the number of infected individuals has exceeded one thousand. Healthcare workers on the ground in Malaysia are having trouble stemming the outbreak since the most effective vaccine up until now, known as VSV-EBOV, is proving ineffective. Doctors with the CDC and WHO have issued joint statements that previously-recognized strains of the disease have obviously mutated and that no vaccine at present appears capable of halting the spread of the highly-infectious Ebola virus."

This was an article, Rachael thought, that she hoped her editor would not assign her. It was grim, to say the least, and travel restrictions to and from the Pacific Rim had already been in place for a month. Panic had not yet seized the populations of the United States or Western Europe, but Rachael knew that this could change quickly as the number of reported cases continued to mount.

She was about to request that Alexa find her classical station when she saw a sign through the mist ahead that indicated she had reached her destination: BOWMAN PARTICLE RESEARCH CENTER — UC BERKELEY.

Rachael swung the wheel hard right and pulled into the long, curving driveway that led to the parking lot of the research center. The center was a gleaming complex of glass and steel buildings with immaculate landscaping. She parked her car close to the main entrance. Grabbing her brown leather briefcase, she quickly opened the door of the gray Prius and, holding the briefcase over her head to shield her head from the rain, trotted to the front door and slipped into the atrium of the facility.

The receptionist, a woman with white hair pulled into a severe bun, sat behind a wide semicircular white counter, on top of which was a bronze nameplate that read CHARLOTTE LLOYD.

"Good afternoon," Rachael said, approaching the counter as she brushed strands of damp hair from her forehead. "I have an appointment to interview Dr. Joshua Andrews. I'm Rachael Miller with *Scientific American*."

"Yes, can I see your ID?" Charlotte said in a British accent, her gray eyes briefly surveying the sole visitor to the center that afternoon given the constant nature of the downpour outside.

Rachael handed her a driver's license which Charlotte verified and handed back. She then checked her computer screen before looking up at the twenty-five-year-old journalist.

"Yes, here you are. Your background check has already been completed and approved." Charlotte handed Rachael a visitors' badge which she attached to her blouse. "I'll walk you back. Please follow me, Ms. Miller."

British reserve and propriety are alive and well Rachael thought as she followed Charlotte Lloyd down a hall that led to a walkway with a floor-to-ceiling glass wall on the left, beads of rain cascading down its surface. Beyond was a luxurious green garden with high hedges that Rachael thought might be as much for privacy as they were for beauty.

"Have you met Dr. Andrews before?" Charlotte asked as they walked.

"No, but I saw him on stage at Dr. Henry Bowman's final lecture five years ago."

"Really now," Charlotte said, breaking stride and turning to face her visitor. "*The* lecture, I presume."

"Yes, I was an undergrad at Berkeley at the time."

Charlotte resumed walking, talking as she faced forward while Rachael followed. "You were quite lucky to see that live despite the tragic outcome for Professor Bowman. These things happen, though."

Stiff upper lip, Rachael thought. *Death indeed happens to us all.* She thought it odd that she'd seen no one else in any of the intersecting corridors. It was a large building, but it appeared empty. Did Dr. Joshua Andrews work by himself? A chill ran down Rachael's spine. A research center with no researchers—no bustle of activity. A lone woman sat in the atrium. Dead quiet in the hallways. The center seemed more like The Overlook Hotel in *The Shining* than a modern research facility.

A minute later, the two women arrived at an office with an open door, upon which were the words JOSHUA ANDREWS, Ph.D. — DIRECTOR.

Joshua was seated at a desk, his back to his visitors. On his left was a PC. To his right were stacks of disorganized papers and folders. A lab bench with electronic equipment was behind the desk and ran the entire length of the back wall. The two women walked into the office.

"Dr. Andrews, the reporter from *Scientific American* is here for your interview," Charlotte announced.

Andrews grumbled a barely audible response. "Huh? What moron scheduled an interview for today of all days?" Andrews asked without turning around. He typed feverishly at the keyboard of his desktop computer.

Exasperated, Charlotte shot Rachael an apologetic look before speaking. "Dr. Andrews, *you* were the one who approved this interview with me three months ago."

Joshua, his back still turned, replied, "Well, just tell him I'm not here. Tell him I'm busy."

Charlotte cleared her throat. "But I'm afraid that—"

"Or tell him that I have the afternoon off. It's a beautiful day outside, so just say I went for a hike to collect my thoughts."

"Dr. Andrews, it's a dismal, rainy day," Charlotte countered, "and I believe there's been a bit of a misunderstanding. First of all, the reporter is a *she* not a *he*, and when I told you she's here for their interview, I meant here, as in standing in this room."

"What? Oh, sorry, Charlotte. I was busy working on—" He paused mid-sentence and turned around to see the young and beautiful reporter in his doorway. There was an awkward silence finally broken by Joshua. "Terribly sorry, Miss—"

"It's Rachael Miller," Charlotte said with a small grin as she peered first at Joshua and then back at Rachael. "You two have a nice chat." Closing the door, the receptionist left Joshua and Rachael in their awkward silence.

"Uh, well, *that* was awkward . . . and entirely my fault. I mean . . . I don't usually, you know, greet people by saying . . . by saying what I said, and so . . ."

Rachael knew that Joshua was embarrassed and fumbling for a way to apologize. She also knew that the man she'd seen five years earlier kneeling next to the prostrate form of Henry Bowman had matured, had gotten even more handsome than she'd remembered. He was thirty now, she guessed, thirty-one tops. His brown hair was of average length and was parted neatly on the side, and his eyes—light brown—indicated both enthusiasm and gentleness. Rachael prided herself on her keen powers of observation, which she'd developed as someone who was always writing in her journal, always observing people, places, and things. Gazing at the flustered director, she thought she'd put him out of his self-imposed misery.

"Pleased to meet you, Dr. Andrews," she said, extending her hand as she walked towards Joshua. "Rachael Miller with *Scientific American*. And hey, I get it. I know you're busy, but I'm working on an article with a deadline."

Joshua felt considerably more at ease and took the hand of the lovely science writer. "Of course. Make yourself at home. Are you okay interviewing me while I work? And call me Josh by the way."

"That's fine—Josh."

Rachael grabbed a chair from across the room and wheeled it next to the lab bench where Joshua was sitting. Electronic equipment and computers took up almost every inch of the wide table, but the object that caught her attention was a Bowman sphere, identical to the one which the professor had used in his demonstration at Wheeler Auditorium. It wasn't glowing green—or any color. It was just a hollow glass sphere with metal contacts on the top and bottom.

"Mind if I record you?" she asked, pulling out a digital recorder from her briefcase. "It'll be faster than taking notes."

"No problem. Go for it."

Rachael switched on the recorder. "So it's been five years since the untimely death of Professor Henry Bowman from . . . what was it? I believe the medical term is a ruptured aortic aneurysm?"

"A ruptured abdominal aortic aneurysm," Joshua said. "Physicians call it a triple A for obvious reasons. It'd probably been growing inside him for years, but the docs figured that due to increased blood pressure from the excitement of the presentation, it picked that particular time to rupture."

"I see. Quite sad that he was presenting what was arguably one of the greatest discoveries of science and never lived to enjoy the accolades."

"Yeah, I really miss Henry. He was a brilliant man—and a bit of a character. Had a great sense of humor and a flare for the dramatic as evidenced by the presentation that he never got to finish."

Rachael nodded. "I was actually in the audience for that. He worked that audience like a professional entertainer."

"It was memorable alright. I suspect that a bulb burns brightest just before it burns out."

Rachael smiled and noticed that Joshua glanced in her direction and smiled every few seconds as he entered data into one of the computers next to the Bowman sphere. He wasn't so busy, she surmised, that he didn't have time to partially indulge in some of the social graces.

"Definitely true in Dr. Bowman's case," she stated. "And am I correct that it's been four years since the university finished this facility and put you in charge of carrying on his work?"

"You're correct."

"And is it also true that, in that time, you've been unable to create even a single additional pair of entangled spookyon particles?"

Nonplussed, Joshua ceased working and looked squarely at his interviewer. "Wow, you don't beat around the bush, do you?" His eyebrows were raised as he was clearly caught off guard by how fast she got to the point—indeed, a point of obvious frustration for the director of the Bowman Particle Research Center.

"Just trying to be efficient," she said, "plus I've read some of your academic papers on the progress of your work."

"Or lack thereof," he said with a bemused look on his face. "Sadly, you're right again. So far, we haven't been able to create another entangled spookyon pair. I think the university is getting frustrated with our team." He paused. "Um, that last part is off the record, okay?"

"Fair enough. But who is 'we'? I didn't see a soul as Ms. Lloyd escorted me back here. This place reminds me of a mausoleum."

Joshua laughed. "You don't miss a thing. I have very few assistants due to the sensitive nature of the research."

Rachael leaned forward, glancing at her recorder to make sure the green light was still on. "To what do you attribute the delay? Some critics are questioning the wisdom of putting someone as young as you in charge of the entire project, and I've also heard that the university board is starting to question the huge expense of building and maintaining this facility."

"Actually, we're getting very close—and that's on the record—but I don't think the university had much of a choice in putting me in charge after Henry's death. The university had given him lavish funding and wanted to capitalize on his work. I was the only one he'd ever really confided in when it came to the heart of his research. Henry was a fairly paranoid person, even to the point of not committing his lab notes to a hard drive or any kind of electronic device whatsoever for fear of them being hacked. He therefore wrote all of his notes in old-fashioned black and white notebooks. You know, the ones with the faux marble covers."

Rachael was intrigued by the concept of so much heady research being recorded on ruled paper via handwriting. It appealed to the writer in her— the journalist who enjoyed committing her own thoughts to paper via cursive.

"A man after my own heart," she declared. "I like the heft of paper and ink, and I enjoy the physical act of writing."

"Then you would've gotten along well with Henry. He was paranoid about someone stealing his research. When I once asked him about his notes only being in a notebook, he told me, 'You can't hack a piece of paper Joshua.' The problem is that he hid every single one—all three hundred notebooks—and nobody can find them."

"Three hundred?"

"Yes. One would think that the sheer number of books would make the search easy, but Henry was as shrewd as they come. For a man who could create entangled spookyons, hiding so many notebooks would be a piece of cake. For all I know, he hijacked another one of NASA's satellites, and they're orbiting the Earth. Then again, they may be here in Berkeley right under my nose."

"Still, you got the gig," Rachael remarked.

"I did indeed. All of the work toward my Ph.D. was geared towards Henry's quest for spookyons, so the mantle fell upon my shoulders. I knew his methodology and remembered the basic steps he used in creating spookyons. I'd made my own notes, which have been of enormous help, so here I am."

"But still no spooky action at a distance?" Rachael queried.

Joshua held the thumb and index finger of his left hand an inch apart. "Not even action at a *short* distance. In fact, no action at all." He shrugged, held out empty hands, and turned up the left side of his mouth in a gesture of *I got nothin'*.

Rachael smiled as the young director displayed both honesty and humor. "It can't be that bad, can it? No results at all?"

Joshua sighed. "We can create spookyons easily enough. The basic process Henry taught me was pretty solid and easy to remember. The problem is isolating and storing them in Bowman spheres."

"Like the one at Wheeler and aboard the Mars rover?"

"Exactly."

"What happened to that pair, by the way?"

"NASA claimed ownership since Henry had played fast and loose by essentially making the sphere a stowaway on their rover. They confiscated the sphere from the presentation as payment for hitching a ride to Mars. They're still using it to control the rover, but they want the technology to remain top secret for fear that a foreign power might try to weaponize such communication."

"That's bureaucrats for ya," Rachael said wryly.

Josh pointed his index finger at the reporter as if to say *You've got that right!*

"That must have been a huge setback."

"To say the least, but like I said, creating spookyons isn't the problem. It's not child's play, but I can do it. But Henry never taught me all of the intricacies of isolating them and then storing them in the spheres without some contamination. I've had several ideas over the past four years as to how Henry pulled it off, and I've come up with some promising techniques. But close only counts in horseshoes, so we always aim to be precise and achieve a dead ringer."

"Where exactly do things stand as we speak?" Rachael asked. "Your wording implies that you may have gotten that proverbial dead ringer."

Josh moved forward, folded his arms, and leaned against the lab table.

"You're good. *Very* good. You should have been a lawyer."

"Ick! Too dry!"

"And science isn't?"

"Not to me."

Joshua fell silent for almost a full minute as he stared across the room before looking over at Rachael. He was clearly weighing how much to tell her—how much he was willing to tell the entire scientific community, for that matter. At last he spoke.

"We get a good pair about once a month, which isn't a bad average. In fact, we're going to attempt to create a pair of spookyons this afternoon using a new isolation technique I came up with. I was just finishing attaching a spookyon detector to this sphere shortly before you arrived. The detector verifies that we have indeed created a pair of entangled spookyons. That's why I didn't want to take your interview. Lots of stuff going on today."

"I understand completely."

"If we get a pair, the next step is to use the detectors to see if they're entangled. As I've said, we haven't observed entanglement yet, and we're not sure why aside from contamination issues."

"Hmm. I'd love to watch you create these spookyons."

Josh remained silent as he rubbed his jaw and looked away momentarily. "There are security issues with allowing a reporter to watch our work."

"Look Josh, I've got an hour scheduled with you for this interview. Either we spend that here and delay your work, or we talk while I watch you create your spookyons."

Joshua stared at her, indecisive about what to do. Security was of utmost importance, but he found Rachael somewhat disarming.

"Well?" Rachael said waiting for a response. "Look, I know that you're under a lot of pressure from the university because of your lack of results. There are rumors that the university is considering cutting their losses and pulling the plug on this entire facility. I could be of help to you by taking some pressure off by writing an article showing the progress you've made and also stating that you're close to your goal. But in order to do this, I need to be *shown* that progress."

Joshua pondered the situation. He was keenly aware of the pressure being put on him to produce results. If Rachael was correct about the funding of the facility being in jeopardy, a positive news article would certainly help him. Besides, he could let her watch them create spookyons without revealing any critical details.

"Okay," he finally said. "I'm going to allow you to observe us make spookyons, but I must have final say in what you're allowed to present in your article. Everything else is strictly off limits. You're also going to have to turn off your recorder. Is that fair?"

"More than fair," Rachael replied as she switched off the recorder and returned it to her briefcase. "Lead the way, Herr Doctor."

Joshua carefully packed the sphere and detector in a black case lined with protective cushiony material. "Come on. Let's take a walk," he said, and the two left the office. "Do you consider yourself a lucky person?"

"I'm usually fairly lucky. Why do you ask? Are you superstitious?"

"Not usually, but the longer we go without creating entangled spookyons, the more superstitious I become."

The pair walked to an elevator at the end of a dimly lit corridor. Joshua placed his thumb on a pad against the wall to the right of the elevator door.

"Thumbprint recognized," said a female voice that Rachael suspected was computer-generated. "Dr. Joshua Andrews. Director. Access granted."

"Pretty secret," Rachael remarked as they advanced into the elevator.

"Wait until you see the man downstairs with the gun," Joshua said, pressing the button with B for "basement."

"You're kidding, right?"

Joshua stared at the closing doors, and the hairs on the back of Rachael's neck stood up as she realized that her host wasn't joking.

Chapter Five
The Donut

As Joshua and Rachael stepped from the elevator into the basement, the director turned to his right and greeted a security guard wearing a gray shirt and matching slacks. His sidearm was a standard issue .38 caliber revolver.

"Hey, Gordon," Joshua said. "Keeping busy?"

"Very funny, Dr. Andrews," the guard replied. "I stand here eight hours at a stretch and stare at your . . . toys."

"*Expensive* toys," Joshua corrected, patting the guard on the shoulder. "As always, I'm appreciative of your diligence."

"Follow me," Joshua told his companion as they walked slowly around a large circular corridor two stories high.

To the right was a control room, behind which sat technicians—casually dressed in jeans and tee shirts—as they consulted computer screens and large panels that resembled mixing boards in recording studios. On the left was a slowly-curving metal wall with hundreds of pipes, ducts, and insulated electrical cables, all running parallel to each other as they disappeared around the curves ahead. Some of the pipes had thermal shielding surrounding them, but Rachael could see condensate flowing down as a fine mist from the areas where the shielding had gaps. Whatever the pipes were transporting must have been extremely cold.

"What exactly am I looking at?" Rachael asked looking at the curved metal wall to her left.

"A hollow metal donut fifty feet across. It's where we create spookyons. We created a pair last week, but they didn't survive because of contamination. A power cable blew out, and *poof*, the spookyons vanished. We use large amounts of energy to work our mojo in the cause of finding what may be one of the most elusive particles known to physics."

"I don't see any hollow metal donut," Rachael commented, perplexed.

"You can't see the forest for the trees. You're standing right next to it—a machine called a tokamak, which takes the shape of a torus."

Rachael was familiar with tokamaks. Invented in the 1940's by the Russians, they'd been used mainly in the quest to create nuclear fusion. The inside chamber of tokamaks was usually in the shape of a torus, or a hollow donut. Surrounding the torus were powerful electromagnets that created a magnetic field in the in the shape of the donut. The magnetic field in turn was used to contain plasma, a super-heated form of matter, which formed when atoms were heated to an extreme level. At these extreme temperatures, the electrons and nuclei of the atoms were stripped from each other, forming a cloud comprised of negatively-charged electrons and positively-charged nuclei. The plasma was so hot that the only way to contain and control it was to use magnetic fields.

Rachael slowly nodded in understanding. "Torus? A circle bent into three-dimensional space and hollow on the inside. Hence, a hollow donut shape. But aren't tokamaks what they're using to try to create nuclear fusion?"

"Correct." Joshua replied. "The tokamak uses powerful magnetic fields to create and confine superheated plasma in the shape of a torus. The entire tokamak is wrapped in field coils, both horizontally and vertically. That mist you see is condensate from the liquid helium pipes. The liquid helium is used to cool the coils that create the magnetic field. We need to cool them to the point of becoming superconductors."

Rachael knew that the plasma in most tokamaks consisted of heavy isotopes of hydrogen called deuterium and tritium. This plasma was superheated in an effort to get these hydrogen nuclei to collide and fuse in order to form helium. The fusion process released an enormous amount of energy and is what powered stars like the sun.

"I'm assuming that this is not a normal tokamak," Rachael said. "You're not trying to fuse hydrogen, are you?"

"No, we're not," Joshua replied. "We aren't interested in creating energy via fusion, but we need high energy plasma made with a specific combination of elements to create spookyons. This tokamak was created entirely for that purpose. This specific combination of elements is the fuel we use."

"Don't suppose you care to tell me what's in the fuel?" Rachel asked although she had little faith that Joshua was going to divulge such information.

"Absolutely off limits."

"Thought so. Then the collision of the nuclei in your secret fuel causes the creation of spookyons?"

"That, combined with high-energy pulses of laser light at a specific wavelength and specific angles of polarization. The wavelength, power level, and polarization angles of the lasers are also off limits, in case you're wondering."

As they continued their walk around the tokamak, Rachael noticed some wording painted in large letters on the curved outer wall.

EINSTEIN WAS WRONG. LIGHT IS NOT THE FASTEST THING IN THE UNIVERSE . . . INFORMATION IS.
AND EVERYTHING IS INFORMATION. – HENRY H. BOWMAN.

"From what I've read, tokamaks have been used for decades. How is it that nobody before Dr. Bowman came up with this process?" Rachael asked.

"It's a long story, but I'll condense it for you. When Henry was much younger, he worked at Princeton's PLT, or the Princeton Large Torus. It was while working at Princeton that Henry developed a keen understanding of the intricacies of high energy plasma. Everyone else was using the plasma in tokamaks to try to create nuclear fusion to generate energy, but Henry wanted to know what would happen in plasmas of other elements. He was kind of like a cook trying out different spices for his cooking. He noticed that when he used a specific combination of elements in his plasma, entangled particles were created that he couldn't identify. These particles were artificially created and not found in nature, but like all entangled particles, their entanglement collapsed after sending one bit of information. Henry realized through rigorous mathematical calculations that these artificial particles could be modified to produce permanent entanglement. For the next forty years, he strived to get the correct combination of elements in the plasma along with the correct laser parameters to create artificial but permanently entangled particles—spookyons. He finally succeeded just before his death."

"Wow, that story would make a great article in itself."

"When I took over his research after his death, I told the university that I had a request. There was no working tokamak at Berkeley at the time, and Henry and I had borrowed time on a tokamak in San Diego to create the spookyons that are controlling the Mars rover. The university built one here, along with the research center. They knew that the spookyons Henry found would turn science on its ear and become a goldmine for them. The scientific and practical applications are endless. The university poured a ton of money into this facility, and it's why they're putting a lot of pressure on me to get results."

The scientist and his guest had made almost a full circuit of the corridor surrounding the tokamak. They came to a door in the inner wall with a sign that read DECONTAMINATION above it. The door opened and a heavyset, young, Hispanic man walked out.

"Hey, Rodrigo. All set?" asked Joshua.

"All set, boss," the man replied with a thick Spanish accent. "The first sphere is in place."

Joshua introduced Rachel to his assistant. "Rodrigo, meet Rachael Miller. She's a reporter from *Scientific American* who's going to be observing today. Rachael, this is Rodrigo Torres. He's *my* Ph.D. student. Henry had me, and now I have Rodrigo."

"Que pasa?" Rachael asked.

Rodrigo replied in Spanish. "*Ah, you speak Spanish?*"

"*Four years in high school and one year in college. Does Dr. Andrews speak Spanish too?*"

"*Hardly a word. How'd you get him to let you down here? We don't get many visitors.*"

"*Let's say I gave him an offer he couldn't refuse.*"

Joshua looked back and forth at Rachael and Rodrigo, perplexed as to what they could be speaking about. It amazed him that even in a situation that would intimidate many people, Rachael was so poised and at ease.

"*Right,*" Rodrigo continued with a smile. "*Knowing the boss, you definitely must have made an impression on him.*"

"*I hope so.*"

"*Probably didn't hurt that you're a hot chick and not some stodgy old dude.*"

Many women would have been offended at such a crass and chauvinistic comment, but Rachael took it in stride. In her profession, she was accustomed to being around male scientists. "*Probably didn't hurt.*" She replied. "*Just curious—have you seen Joshua with many hot chicks?*"

"*Naw, he's too much of a nerd to know any hot chicks.*"

Rachael chuckled at the clandestine dig.

"What are you guys talking about?" Joshua finally asked.

"Baby chickens," Rachael replied as Rodrigo gave her a smile.

"What?" Joshua asked.

"Never mind," Rachael replied. "Inside joke."

"Nice meeting you Rachael," Rodrigo said as he started to walk away.

"Boss, I'll meet you at the control center."

Joshua turned to Rachael and asked, "Want to take a look inside the tokamak?"

"Sure."

"We need to install the sphere in this case inside the tokamak, but the inside is an ultra-clean environment," Joshua said as he opened the door. "We have to put on anti-dust gear and be decontaminated before we enter."

Inside the decontamination room, Joshua and Rachael donned white zip-up, anti-dust suits, as well as shoe and head covers, surgical masks, and gloves, leaving them with only the skin around their eyes exposed. They then walked through what appeared to Rachael to be a wind tunnel that was blowing a steady but strong breeze into their faces.

"The air flow blows away any remaining dust from us before we enter the tokamak," Joshua said with a voice muffled by his surgical mask.

On the other side of the tunnel was a small, round, metallic hatch that led into the tokamak. On either side of the hatch were large coils of wire interspersed with piping that vented the mist Rachael had seen outside. She surmised that these were the superconducting coils that created the magnetic field that containing the super-hot plasma.

Passing a technician also covered head-to-toe in the same anti-dust gear, Joshua stepped inside with the black case and turned to Rachael. "Pardon the cliché, but don't touch anything. The human body is surrounded by a small electromagnetic field, and these instruments are quite sensitive to it. Recalibrating the equipment can take hours."

"Got it," she said, taking Joshua's free hand as he led her inside. It reminded her of stepping through hatchways from one compartment to another aboard nuclear submarines, something she'd done on many occasions while pursuing a story.

The inside of the tokamak was the hollow donut-shaped room—the torus. The curved walls, ceiling, and floor were covered with thousands of gleaming metallic plates. Just ahead were two metallic cylinders set vertically in the floor, each with a circular lid in the open position. Rachael peered into the first cylinder and saw a Bowman sphere at its base. The second cylinder was empty. Joshua had Rachael hold the black case in her hands while he opened it and removed the other Bowman sphere, leaving the detector in the case. He then carefully placed the sphere into the empty cylinder. Looking closely at the spheres, Rachael noticed a small hole at the top of each glass sphere. Joshua closed the lids and sealed both cylinders. The lids were slightly funnel-shaped, with small circular holes in the center that lined up with the holes in the spheres.

"Okay, both spheres are in place," Joshua said as he closed the case and took it from Rachel. "Let's go to the control room. After we evacuate all of the air in here to create a vacuum in the torus, we're going to crank up old Hank here. We named the tokamak after Henry."

Rachael and Joshua exited through the portal. The technician at the opening sealed the hatch behind them.

*   *   *

Behind the thick protective glass of the gently-curving control room, Rachael took a seat at the rear while Joshua moved from station to station to check the status of the various equipment. Rodrigo sat at a computer terminal, munching from a bag of Doritos, his fingers orange from the flavoring. There were five other technicians in the room, each seated at a terminal. Multiple overhead video monitors displayed feeds from inside the tokamak. Most showed images of the torus, but two showed the spheres inside the cylinders. Monitors showing the spheres were captioned with SPHERE 0 and SHPERE 1.

"Atmosphere evacuation complete," a female technician announced. "Initiating magnetic containment."

The lights in the control room dimmed slightly for a second and then returned to normal brightness. Rachael guessed that a large electrical load had been put on the complex's power supply, which had taken a second to compensate for the extra amperage.

"Magnetic containment confirmed and stable," the technician announced. "Starting fuel injection."

The lights now dimmed permanently, with red flashing lights indicating that a test was imminent. The sounds in the torus—similar to a current of surging water—changed to loud rapid-fire clicks like those produced from the electromagnets in an MRI scanner.

Joshua turned to Rachael. "We're injecting the fuel, and the sound you hear through the speaker is plasma swirling through the tokamak. Our instruments tell us everything we need to know, but the actual machinery makes certain sounds when the experiment is proceeding as planned. The ear is a very discriminating instrument when it knows what to listen for."

The monitor showing the inside of the torus displayed an eerie purple glow in its center that seemed to be getting brighter. Rachael figured that this was the plasma. She also noticed that the spheres now glowed a dim orange. "Are the spheres getting hot?"

"Yes, but hopefully not too hot." Joshua replied. "Those cylinders they're in provide thermal shielding so that they don't melt."

"Boss, there's an imbalance in the electromagnetic field," Rodrigo interrupted.

"Maybe a power surge," Joshua replied. "Hopefully it will self-correct."

The control room suddenly lost power, and all consoles were black.

"Damn it!" a female technician complained. "I think the tokamak's fail safe just kicked in."

"Carajo!" Rodrigo exclaimed. "Boss, the temperature in the torus is way too high. It's in the danger zone for a coolant breach."

"Damn!" Joshua yelled. "If that liquid helium breaches into the torus, the whole thing could blow! Increase the fuel injection rate!"

Chapter Six
Heavy Metal

Rachael sat in the darkness, wondering if she was in danger. Beyond the thick glass windows of the control room, flashing red warning lights curved around the torus, interspersed with the words WARNING and OVER-TEMP. The faces of those at the work stations glowed red every five seconds before being enveloped by darkness again.

Unexpectedly, computer screens in the room came back to life, scrolling data on various functions of the reactor.

"Temperature stabilizing," Rodrigo stated.

"Not to worry," Joshua said calmly, his form a silhouette as the lights in the room returned to their previously dim settings. "Looks like increasing the fuel injection rate worked. The over-temp was probably a result of the electromagnetic field being temporarily out of alignment from a power fluctuation."

"If the plasma was too hot, why did you want to *increase* the fuel rate?" Rachael asked.

"The fuel starts out at room temperature and is heated in the tokamak to create the plasma," Joshua explained. "Adding more room temperature fuel will actually decrease the temperature of the plasma."

This made perfect sense to Rachael. It was similar to adding tap water to a boiling pot of water, causing the boiling to stop. Rachel was impressed by how quickly and confidently Joshua had handled a potentially disastrous situation.

Joshua turned back to his staff. "Status?"

All five technicians and Rodrigo relayed that operations were continuing within normal parameters.

"Hope we didn't scare you, Rachael," Joshua said without turning

31

around.

"No problem," Rachael replied. "My heart *always* beats in my throat. Was there really a chance that the tokamak would explode?"

"No chance of explosion, but definitely a chance of *implosion*. Remember that the inside of the torus is now a vacuum, and if there was some catastrophic structural failure, it would have imploded from the atmospheric pressure differential."

"What happens next?" Rachael asked.

"Now that we have stable plasma, we start pulsing it with the high energy laser."

"Laser warming up now," the female technician reported. "Pulses commencing in five seconds at two-second intervals."

On the monitor showing the inside of the torus, neon-blue laser light emanated from multiple sources. The lasers converged at a single point in the purple plasma cloud hovering over the cylinders. The lasers pulsed at two-second intervals.

"Those laser bursts into the plasma are creating spookyons?" Rachael asked.

"Hopefully," Joshua replied. "We have to wait up to ten minutes. That's how long the nuclei will remain stable and collide with each other. If a spookyon pair is created, magnetic fields in the torus will separate the spookyon pair and direct each to one of the cylinder lids. Spookyons are drawn to heavy metallic elements, and the lids sealing the tops of the cylinders are coated with a specific combination of heavy metals which should attract them. We're trying out a new combination today. Once they make contact with the lids, gravity should funnel them through the small hole at the top of the spheres." Joshua glanced to his rear. "Apparently spookyons like heavy metal."

"Sounds like a friend of mine," Rachael quipped.

"If we've created a pair, we'll know in short order."

"Good luck," Rachael said.

Joshua grinned and turned back to his monitors.

Rachael sat quietly as the technicians spoke to each other in soft voices. A green digital LED clock above a glass panel at the front of the room showed that four minutes had elapsed. At the five-minute mark, the room was silent, the technicians sitting back in their chairs, waiting with folded arms. After five minutes and thirty-two seconds had elapsed, a bright green circle appeared on three computer screens.

"Sphere 1, positive capture!" Rodrigo announced. "Starting laser sealing."

"Yes! We got one!" Joshua shouted while pumping a fist into the air. A new red laser beam was shining on the top of sphere 1. "We're using the red laser to seal the top of the sphere."

More tense minutes passed, and a second green circle appeared on the computer screens. "Sphere 0 positive capture," Rodrigo said. "Commencing laser sealing."

The technicians broke into a round of applause as a red laser glowed on the top of sphere 0.

"We have a pair of spookyons," Joshua announced excitedly as he accepted a high-five from Rodrigo.

"You sound like a proud father of twins," Rachael said.

"An apt analogy."

"Think they're going to be telepathic like some biological twins?"

"As in entangled? That's the million-dollar question. We rarely ever get this far. Most times we get no spookyons, and sometimes we only capture one. Only four percent of the time are we able to capture two, but none of the previous pairs were entangled." Joshua turned back to look at Rachael with a grin. "Definitely lucky today."

The sounds from the tokamak ceased.

"Powering down," a female technician said.

The LED clock had reset to zero and was now counting minutes and seconds again.

"When do you retrieve the spheres?" Rachael inquired.

"Not for twenty-four hours." Joshua headed toward Rachael and took a seat next to her. "First, we have to evacuate the plasma and then slowly allow the spheres to cool so that they don't crack from thermal contraction. Then we slowly re-pressurize the torus. The tokamak stays sealed for that long unless there's either contamination or degradation of the particles."

"Degradation?"

"Sometimes they disappear even when there's been no obvious sign of contamination," Joshua explained. "Not even Henry was entirely sure why they could just vanish, although his working theory was that they were ephemeral because they theoretically inhabit more than one physical reality at the same time."

"As in Heisenberg's Uncertainty Principle?" Rachael asked.

"Precisely."

"Then the sooner you measure them the better, right?"

"You would think so, but we've found that immediate measurement can also cause degradation during the first twenty-four hours. It's almost as if they have a mind of their own and want to acclimatize themselves to their new home."

"So if these guys like our universe, they may stick around for a while. Is that what you're saying?"

"Essentially, yes. Once they calm down, they stick around permanently and are very stable at that point. We've also found that moving them too soon can be risky. Relocating spookyons subjects them to a host of other particles, and since they have to be separated at a great distance before we can reliably test for entanglement, we like to wait twenty-four hours."

Rachael cocked her head. "What you're telling me is that once they're stabilized—accustomed to this universe—the interference doesn't bother them."

"That appears to be the case. Then again, Miss Miller, maybe they're just fans of heavy metal and want to listen to the complete playlist before being handled."

Rachael laughed. "Just educated guesses. Where does the test for entanglement occur?"

"In the bat cave," Joshua said nonchalantly.

"Oh, I'm *sure* it does, Mr. Wayne."

Joshua's expression didn't change.

"Seriously? The bat cave?"

"It's a nickname, of course, but it actually bears some resemblance to the one people saw at the movies. It's an abandoned mine about four hundred feet below us."

Joshua glanced at his wristwatch. "Well, Miss Miller, you wanted an hour and got quite a bit more. I take it that you have enough material for your article, so I'll call Charlotte and have her escort you to the front entrance. I'll be here all night to keep an eye on things."

Rachael was determined not to abandon what she considered a killer story for which she had only the opening paragraphs. Joshua Andrews had made the strategic mistake of whetting her appetite, and she wanted to learn more about spookyons—a lot more.

"Coffee?" she asked.

"Huh?"

"Doesn't seem like you have much more to do today, and I have a few questions I didn't get answered. Besides, if you're going to be here all night, you'll need a massive infusion of caffeine. My treat."

"You're pretty persistent, aren't you?"

"I learned a long time ago that being a little pushy is the only way to get a great story."

Joshua was surprised at his guest's chutzpah, and yet he admired it. One didn't go treasure hunting for subatomic particles that would change the destiny of humanity without a little audacity and attitude. "You're right about not much more for me to do today. You've got a little spooky action going on in your brain. Is it entangled?"

"Come to coffee with me and you'll find out," Rachael said with a smile.

"Go ahead boss," Rodrigo offered. "We've got this covered."

Joshua threw up his hands. "All right. Coffee it is."

*   *   *

The rain had not let up as Rachel and Joshua exited the front entrance of the center.

"Shit, it's raining," Joshua said looking at the gray sky.

"So?"

"I rode my Harley here."

"It's been raining all day. When did you arrive at the center?"

"What day is it?"

"Never mind. We'll take my car."

Rachael quickly tossed her briefcase onto the rear seat and climbed behind the wheel while Joshua rushed into the passenger seat to avoid getting too wet. The car sped off. Rachael thought that Joshua was almost a different person from the man she'd spoken to in the particle center. Without his lab coat on, he seemed more at ease. She also thought that he wore his untucked shirt and faded blue jeans well. As she drove through traffic, she knew that she needed to come up with more questions and witty banter—and fast.

Chapter Seven
Billions and Billions

"So what got you interested in particle physics?" Rachael asked, seated opposite Joshua in a booth at Yali's Cafe, a coffee house on the Berkeley campus. Because of the weather, the cafe only had a few individuals in the corners, faces hidden behind their MacBooks. Baristas polished chrome dispensers and set muffins in glass cases flanking the counter. The atmosphere was informal and intimate.

"Hard to say," Joshua replied, sipping a latte. "It was a matter of evolution. I was always good at math, and that led to my doing well in all of the sciences. I was especially good at chemistry, which deals with the bonding of various elements depending on their electron count, but going into chemistry—what was I going to do with such a major? Work for a pharmaceutical company? Wasn't for me. Over time, I became engrossed with particle physics and the work being done by super colliders. I couldn't help but wonder if there was such a thing as *the* smallest particle—the smallest building block of matter."

"And now we know, thanks to string theory, that maybe the smallest unit may not be matter at all, just vibrating loops of energy," Rachel commented.

"A lot of my colleagues went into string theory, but when I met Henry Bowman, who told me that he was working on entangled particles, it was game, set, and match. I knew in my gut that I had to follow his work. Einstein himself had thrown down the gauntlet with his EPR Paradox, and Henry wanted to solve the riddle."

"In the long run, he did," Rachael commented. "And on a macrocosmic scale that extended to the orbit of Mars."

"He was in it to win it. From the time he entered the field, he wanted to demonstrate entanglement beyond the confines of the laboratory. He'd read *The Tao of Physics* by Fritjof Capra."

"Hmm. That's way out there," Rachael replied. "Capra talked to Heisenberg about the manuscript before it was published. Turns out Heisenberg had worked on some of his equations while in India. Wasn't Capra part of those hippie physicists that were here at Berkeley?"

Joshua grinned and rubbed his jaw, which was covered by a five o'clock shadow. He knew of the group Rachael was talking about. They were infamous at Berkeley in the seventies, a group of physicists that called themselves the Fundamental Fysics Group and tried to make a connection between quantum mechanics and eastern mysticism.

"Yeah, he was part of that group. Those guys were out there all right. Henry never got into eastern mysticism like those guys and Heisenberg and Bohr, but he definitely felt that quantum theory would one day explain how the entire universe works, from subatomic particles to galaxies. If he could demonstrate that matter communicated with itself, he thought it might revolutionize how mankind regarded creation and the cosmos."

"In what way?" Rachael asked, taking a sip from her mocha.

"He never told anyone, not even me. Maybe he put his musings in one of his notebooks, but I haven't a clue as to what he thought the big picture was." Joshua took another sip of his latte. "We're getting pretty deep here. Let's change the subject."

"To what?"

"You."

"*I'm* the reporter, and I ask the questions," said Rachael, somewhat taken aback.

"I indulged you with this coffee break, so I get to break the rules and ask a few questions of my own."

"I guess that's fair. Shoot."

"Why did you become a science writer?"

Rachael leaned back against the pleated green leather of the booth. "I loved to read as a kid. I'd blown through *Hamlet*, *Jane Eyre*, and dozens of other classics before I graduated from middle school. In high school, I read the science fiction of Arthur C. Clarke. Everything he wrote. I loved the way Clarke tried to incorporate real and accurate science in his stories. By the time I was a junior, I wanted to be an astronomer. The first exoplanets had been discovered, and my mind was reeling."

"So how come you're not working at the Keck Observatory on Mauna Kea? Or at the VLA or Hat Creek looking for ET?"

"I started reading Carl Sagan's nonfiction books and realized that he was the liaison between science and the average guy on the street. He made science cool with all of his talk about billions and billions of stars, so I thought I'd write about science and have the best of both worlds."

"Very laudable," Joshua said, spreading his arms wide and resting them on the back of the booth.

A student of body language, Rachael knew that the young professor was relaxed, open, and receptive.

"I'm no Carl Sagan," she said, "but I do what I can."

"Astronomy, huh?" Joshua said with a faraway look in his eyes.

"I love it."

"Then I have a scoop for you. You can't write about it yet, at least not for a few years, but it's big. *Really* big."

"Do tell," Rachael said as she leaned forward, elbows on the table, her chin propped on the palm of her right hand.

"Ever hear of Project Breakthrough Starshot?" Joshua asked.

Rachael's eyes widened. "Hell yeah! Stephen Hawking proposed that a thousand small spacecraft the size of credit cards be launched from high earth orbit and powered by photon thrusters and laser beams. They could attain one fifth the speed of light and reach the Proxima Centauri system in twenty years, which is a blink of the eye when talking interstellar travel. Astronomers believe that Proxima Centauri b is an Earthlike planet orbiting the star in the habitable zone. But communication between all those spacecraft and Earth would take—"

"Would take a long time," Joshua interrupted, "unless they carried spookyons. The university is willing to partner with NASA and the Jet Propulsion Laboratory—for a hefty fee, of course. It's just as Henry envisioned in his final words onstage, when he was beginning to describe future applications for his discovery."

"Simply amazing," Rachael remarked. "Instant communication from Proxima Centauri."

Joshua's brows furrowed.

"What's the matter?" Rachael asked. "You'll be considered a hero, a pioneer."

"Once NASA gets in on the act, the military won't be far behind. That makes most academics cringe. The government has a way of appropriating technology it deems useful. But the whole thing is still on the drawing board, so it's one step at a time."

Rachael's hands were cupped around her mocha espresso as she gazed out the broad front window.

"Think anyone's out there?" she asked.

"I dunno. The rain's let up for the moment."

"No, silly. In the galaxy."

Joshua raised his head in understanding. "Probably not orbiting Proxima Centauri b, but as Mr. Sagan said, there are billions and billions of possibilities. With so many galaxies out there and so many stars in each galaxy, there *must* be other intelligent life. But on the other hand, there is the issue of the Fermi paradox."

Rachael was familiar with the Fermi paradox. Enrico Fermi was a physicist that had stated that if intelligent life existed beyond the solar system, then we should have already detected it. The current lack of evidence for intelligent extra-solar life led Fermi to conclude that it didn't exist outside the Earth.

"Despite the Fermi paradox," Joshua continued, "I feel that the universe is vast with billions of galaxies and that if life was able to establish itself here, it must have taken hold in other areas as well."

"I agree," Rachael said, refocusing her gaze on the dressed-down director across the table. "What time does the experiment resume?"

"About this time tomorrow. Wait—you've already got a pretty big scoop, Miss Miller. Getting greedy?"

"Yes, and it's Rachael."

Joshua sighed and cocked his head, a smile crossing his face. "I'm not going to get rid of you, am I?"

"Not tomorrow."

Joshua drained his latte. "Well, you've already seen the really secret stuff, so watching the testing should be no big deal. There's nothing really classified about the testing process. Come back around three o'clock. I'll make sure Charlotte is expecting you."

"Thanks. It means a lot. And I'll make sure to bring some luck with me."

"That we'll definitely need, and I'm expecting a glowing article from you about this process."

"Don't worry. It'll be more glowing than a Bowman sphere speaking to a Martian rover."

"Cute."

Joshua rode with Rachael back to the center, not quite sure what to make of the pert, intrepid reporter from *Scientific American*. As he returned to his office, he felt that he'd been manipulated by the young woman. Not that he was objecting, of course.

Chapter Eight
Handle with Care

Arriving at the Bowman Particle Research Center promptly at three o'clock, Rachael hurried through a second day of rain and opened the glass door of the atrium, where she was greeted by Charlotte Lloyd.

"Welcome back, Miss Miller," Charlotte said, this time with a warm smile as she stood and walked around the counter. "We'll go straight down to the tokamak facility."

On the walk to the tokamak, Rachael saw individuals, mostly young, walking through the building, though still not as many as would reasonably be expected to work at a large university research center. That changed quickly as she stepped off the elevator near the control room, for she was unprepared for what she saw. Two university security guards stood on each side of the elevator, and two more guarded the portal to the interior of the torus. A dozen technicians, all wearing white lab coats, hurried through the circular corridor, some entering the control room, some climbing into the torus, others checking digital readings displayed every few feet on the exterior of the tokamak's reaction chamber.

"We've had a busy day," Charlotte said, smiling at Rachael. "Why don't you wait for Dr. Andrews in the control room? I'm sure he'll be along any minute."

Rachael walked in and took the same seat as the day before as she watched personnel examining data on PC screens, printing hard copy readouts, and talking into microphones extending from their earpieces. Fifteen minutes elapsed before Joshua entered the room, the white tails of his lab coat flying behind him.

"Good to see you again!" he said enthusiastically to Rachael.

"What's going on? I didn't know you had a swarm of bees hidden in the bowels of the center."

Joshua raised both hands and wiggled his fingers. "No, just vampires that have come out of hiding. We scientists are a reclusive lot. All the technicians are resetting the tokamak for the next run. It's a long process."

Joshua sat down in a chair next to Rachael, staring at her with a Cheshire cat grin on his face.

"What's going on?" Rachael inquired. "You know something!"

"Um, maybe."

"You've made a *stable* pair of spookyons, didn't you? They're still in the spheres!"

Joshua's face beamed with pride. "Yes, and we're getting ready to take them to our testing sites to see if they're entangled."

"Sites? Plural?"

"Our first site is in the bat cave I mentioned, the deserted mine shaft that has been converted to an underground lab. The other site is in a mine shaft thirty miles away."

Joshua sat in a rolling chair adjacent to Rachael's. "Rodrigo retrieved sphere 0 from the torus about thirty minutes ago and is on his way to the remote test site. I'll be accompanying sphere 1 to the bat cave when Rodrigo is almost to his destination."

"How long before we leave?" Rachael asked.

"All that cool stuff yesterday really didn't give you enough material to write an article good enough to earn a Pulitzer for science writing—assuming there is such a thing?"

Rachael shook her head. "There are seven Pulitzers. One is for nonfiction. Hey, I didn't come back today to watch monitors and technicians. This is a three-ring circus, and I want to see what's going to happen in the center ring. And remember what's at stake here. My article may help keep this whole operation going. Besides, you told me that the test was straightforward and didn't constitute classified information."

"They're retrieving sphere 1 from the torus now," Joshua explained, amused at Rachael's persistence. "We'll head down to the bat cave as soon as we get it."

A few minutes later, a technician walked in carrying the black case that contained the sphere and detector and handed it to Joshua, who opened the case and carefully lifted the glass sphere to examine it.

"It looks fairly delicate," Rachael remarked.

"It is. We had to make the glass thick enough to hold the vacuum inside, but thin enough so that the detector could work. I'd say it's about as fragile as an iPhone screen."

"What happens if the glass breaks?"

"Game over," Joshua replied. "Remember that the inside of the sphere is a vacuum. If the glass breaks, the spookyon in it mixes with molecules of air in the atmosphere. Once that happens, there is *absolutely* no way of getting it back. It'd be gone forever. Definitely don't want that to happen. But the sphere is pretty protected when it's in this case. We've drop-tested the case with a sphere in it from twenty-five feet onto concrete. No breakage."

"That other black thing in the case is the detector?" Rachael asked, looking into the case.

"Yup."

The detector was a simple black rectangular base atop which sat a circular band just large enough to hold the sphere securely. It was not unlike a mantel clock in which the round wood holding the clock face tapers on each side to a flat base. The base scrolled into an enclosed black tube on one end, and a series of small digital LED lights were embedded in the round band. The detector was attached via multiple cables to the metal plating above and below the sphere. There was another cable that emanated from the detector, which Rachael surmised was used to interface with a computer. The main body of the device was made of a black alloy that Rachael couldn't identify, and the entire apparatus was only ten inches long and six inches wide.

"Put two long antennas on top—my grandmother called them rabbit ears—and it would look like an old VHF receiver that sat on top of televisions," Rachael said.

"That TV receiver, as you describe it, cost the university a quarter million dollars. It has to be small in order to be portable, but it admittedly does a fairly simple job. It detects spookyons and their spin in that black tube on its base, and LED lights turn the sphere different colors depending on what it measures."

Joshua gently placed the sphere back into the case. "Looks good."

"Rodrigo reports that he's almost to the other site," a technician announced while looking at a computer monitor.

"We should move down to the mine," Joshua said, turning to a male technician. "Alfred, make sure everything is ready in the bat cave."

The technician grimaced good-naturedly. "That joke's getting a little old, boss." He got up and left to check on the bat cave.

"His name's really not Alfred," Joshua said, turning towards Rachael.

"Yeah, I figured."

"That's all there is to it?" Rachael asked. "Pretty simple after all the hoopla surrounding creating that little guy."

"That hoopla may change Western civilization as radically as did the transistor or the silicon chip."

Rachael knew when she'd been bested. "Point taken."

A few minutes later, Joshua and Rachael stood before the gate of a freight elevator in the basement of the research center. The security guards would remain behind.

"We're going alone?" Rachael asked.

"No one else is needed. The testing is a very simple process of turning on the detectors and checking for communication. Probably going to be a letdown for you compared to yesterday's excitement."

"I'll be the judge of that."

The wide elevator arrived from below and a male technician stepped off and gave a thumbs-up, indicating that the bat cave was ready. Rachael and Joshua stepped onto the elevator.

"Going down," Joshua announced. "*Way* down."

Chapter Nine
The Bat Cave

Rachael was startled when she exited the freight elevator, which took almost two minutes to reach the bottom of the mine shaft. She expected to step into a high-tech environment with state-of-the-art equipment, blinking lights, consoles, and monitors. Instead, she observed only two desks sitting in the middle of a large cement floor with a single chair in front of one. Each desk had a computer on it, and one had a landline phone. There were no walls at all, just exposed jagged rock surrounding the space. Three other pieces of equipment were recessed in the black outcroppings, but they were dark and obviously not operational. The cave as yet had no built-in lighting sources, so four high intensity T5 laboratory task lights—each mounted on an eight-foot tall circular chrome stand—were positioned at the four corners of the adjacent tables.

"This is pretty sparse for an expensive, sequestered university lab," Rachael remarked. "I thought you said that it resembled the bat cave from the movies?"

Looking around, Joshua seemed perplexed. "Black rocks were *always* in the background of Hollywood shots for the cave. This is an old obsidian mine, which accounts for the black shiny surfaces of the rock faces. Hundreds of such mines extend westward from the Sierra Nevada Range. What's the matter? Not enough ambience for you?"

"But where are all the cool gadgets?"

Joshua pointed to the tables.

"C'mon." Rachael said, hands on hips. "There are two desks, each with a computer, and one desk has . . . a landline? Really? Not much of a bat cave."

Joshua was a little perturbed. The bat cave was his place of solace, somewhere he came to get away. Not many people were allowed in the mine, and he was irritated that this woman to whom he had granted a special privilege was criticizing it. As the director of the center, he was accustomed to everyone falling in line with his orders and being somewhat subservient. It amazed him that someone he had just met the day before had enough self-confidence to confront him. Even though he was perturbed, Rachael's self-confidence was definitely refreshing. Subconsciously, he also found it somewhat attractive.

"We have some portable equipment we occasionally bring down," Joshua replied somewhat defensively, "but when we test for entanglement, this is all we want or need. What's important is not what you *see*, but rather what the equipment we have on hand can actually *do*. I assure you that when we finally succeed, we'll have accomplished far more than catching the Joker or Penguin." He turned around and surveyed the black-walled mine. "And when we get entanglement on a regular basis, this area will undergo a great deal of development since it has so much natural insulation from . . . *everything*."

"You're the ringmaster," Rachael said, acquiescing as she folded her arms and winked. "I'm just a lady looking for a great story."

Joshua took a seat on the chair and started unpacking the sphere and detector. Rachael stood next to him in front of the other desk.

"Then this noir setting will surely suit your prose," Joshua commented as he continued his work. "I read some of your articles last night. Very impressive. I especially liked your pieces on chaos theory. Oh, by the way, I forgot to instruct you to put your cell phone on airplane mode. We can't have any interference when the test begins."

Rachael retrieved the phone from her briefcase and complied with the request. Joshua connected the interface cable from the detector to the computer on his desk. He then turned to his lone companion in the mine. "Did you bring more luck—as promised?"

"I got into your lab and managed to make it all the way down to the bat cave—such as it is," she said with a smile, verbally sparring with her host. "I'd say *that* was pretty lucky—and ingenious. Still feeling superstitious?"

"Only when it comes to spooky action at a distance. This whole quest doesn't represent the classic Newtonian model of physics. A lot of people think I'm operating on the lunatic fringe of science by looking for spookyons and that Henry's success, despite the stir it caused, was a fluke that will never be reproduced. So yeah, I'll take all the luck I can get."

Rachael appreciated the fact that Joshua was being very open with her.

Most scientists, especially men, were guarded and defensive, but Joshua was relaxed enough in her presence to reveal his vulnerabilities. "Not to worry," she replied. "I've got enough for both of us."

Rachael looked at the Bowman sphere on the table. "How come Tinker Bell isn't glowing?" she asked with a worried note in her voice.

"Tink is just fine," Joshua answered absentmindedly, his attention focused on placing the Bowman sphere into the detector. "It only glows when the detector is turned on." He continued working, running thin cables from the metal cap on top of the sphere to the detector. "There. All hooked up. The detector will now act as an interface module between the sphere and the computer."

"It's amazing that something so simple can detect entanglement," Rachael remarked.

"Looks that way, but the technology behind it is far from simple. Everything we accomplish in the torus counts for nothing if this little jewel doesn't function properly. That's why it came with such a hefty price tag." Joshua moved his chair directly in front of the computer. "Time to check on Rodrigo."

Joshua opened a video conferencing app on the computer, selected Rodrigo Torres from the contacts, and initiated the call. He waited almost a minute but got no answer. "Where the hell is he?" He tapped the floor nervously.

"Maybe he's lost. Maybe you need to put out the bat signal for him?" Rachael said jokingly.

Joshua found Rachael's remarks amusing. She was direct without being sarcastic, and he enjoyed the sense of humor of someone who was not only highly intelligent but well-versed in the sciences. And then there were her drop-dead good looks, which he was trying his best to ignore.

"Rodrigo's had enough time to reach the other mine by now," Joshua replied with mounting frustration. "Punctuality is not his strong suit."

"Don't worry," Rachael said, trying to reassure him. "If anything had gone wrong during transport, I'm sure he would have messaged you."

"True, but Rodrigo has . . . how shall I put it—some eccentricities."

*   *   *

Rodrigo walked quickly down a dark tunnel when he heard the video conferencing app ringing. His tee shirt, which read CAFÉ JUAREZ — BEST BURRITOS IN CHIHUAHUA, barely fit over his paunch and was stained with red sauce. Out of breath, he entered the remote mine shaft and hurried towards the computer. Holding a slice of cheese and pepperoni pizza in his left hand, he answered the call, Joshua's video stream starting to play on his computer. The director's face appeared on the screen, somewhat perturbed. Rachael was not in the frame.

"Hello," he said, barely able to get the word out as he chewed.

"Rodrigo, what the hell took you so long?" Joshua asked.

"Just grabbing some pizza," Rodrigo answered nonchalantly, his intonation sounding a great deal like Cheech Marin. "I wish you hadn't installed the kitchenette so far away in this godforsaken mine. It's not like I'm on the track team, ya know."

Joshua rolled his eyes. "Whatever—are you ready? I've just completed hooking up sphere 1."

"No, just got here boss. I still have to hook up the detector."

Joshua shot an exasperated look at Rodrigo. "C'mon man. Get with the program. I'll call you back in a couple of minutes. And damn it, make sure you're listening for my video call. We don't get a pair every day, you know."

Rodrigo chuckled as he chewed another piece of thick crust stuffed with mozzarella. "I got a pair all right or I wouldn't spend half my life in a mine shaft waiting for Batman to call."

The call ended.

"That's gratitude for ya," Rodrigo muttered as he put the pizza slice on a greasy paper plate and wiped his hands with a napkin. He sat at a long table, unpacked the detector and sphere from its case, and connected the detector to his computer. He then faced the screen and typed with a speed that surprised everyone who knew him.

As Joshua had noticed on several occasions, Rodrigo was more than a little sloppy, but not when it came to his scientific acumen. His brain, Joshua noted, worked with clockwork precision, which is why he alone was entrusted with sphere 0 when testing for entanglement.

*   *   *

"If he gets pizza grease on the equipment, I'll kill him," Joshua mumbled as he ended the video call. He sat back in his chair, arms folded, as he waited impatiently.

Rachael examined the detector. The glass was secured by small rubber clamps in the circular band on the base. She had looked up information on particle spin the night before. She learned that the term spin was somewhat of a misnomer since subatomic particles didn't actually rotate. Spin was only the name given to a certain property of how particles behaved in a magnetic field. Normal items, such as bar magnets, deflected to one side or the other when traveling through a separate magnetic field depending on how their poles were oriented to the field. The amount of deflection was correlated with how aligned the bar magnet's poles were with the magnetic field it traveled through. The more aligned they were, the less deflection they had. But the Stern-Gerlach Experiment showed that subatomic particles only deflected as if they were completely aligned with the field or completely opposite of it. For these particles, there were only two values, aligned and not aligned—with no range of values. This property of particles was named spin and, in the case of spookyons, the two values were termed left and right spin.

"So how does this detector work?" Rachael asked.

"By measuring the spookyon's spin using a magnetic field," Joshua explained. "When the detector is measuring, it checks to see how the spookyon is deflected by this field. The field is generated by magnets so incredibly small that they have to be manufactured under special magnification conditions almost identical to those used to create the circuitry in a silicon chip."

"Okay, but how does this measurement of the spookyon's spin allow you to send data?" Rachael asked.

"That's a bit more complex, but I'll try to explain," Joshua replied. "We use timing. For example, if we want to send one bit of information, we can define right spin as a zero and left spin as a one. Let's say Rodrigo wants to send me a one bit. When neither of our detectors is measuring spin, then both spookyons are in superposition and their spins are undefined. Are you with me so far?"

"If not, my parents wasted a lot of money on my dual major. Keep going."

"We send data at the bit level which means that the data is just a series of ones and zeros. If Rodrigo wants to send a one to me, he turns on his detector and measures the spin of his spookyon. There's a fifty-fifty chance it will be right or left spin. If it's right spin, which represents a zero, he simply stops measuring to return his spookyon to superposition and measures again. He repeats this process until his detector registers left spin, which is what he wants, and then locks his detector to measure continuously so that his spookyon will remain in left spin. Since his spookyon is locked on left spin, our spookyon here will be locked on right spin."

"Okay, I get it. Keep going."

"Now we simply use *our* detector to measure the spin of our particle multiple times. If all of the measurements result in right spin instead of being random, then we know that Rodrigo has locked in left spin and is sending us a one bit."

"But isn't there a small possibility that all of our measurements will come up right spin just by chance?" Rachael asked.

"Quite right," Joshua replied, "but the more times you measure, the probability of this happening is less and less. What I gave you is a simplified explanation. In reality, the detectors measure the spin millions of times per second and the LEDs in the detector illuminate the sphere depending on the results. It glows blue for right spin, yellow for left spin, and red if the measurements are random."

"In essence, red means that there's no entanglement of the spookyons?" Rachael said.

"Either that or Rodrigo doesn't have his detector locked to a certain spin."

"But I recall the sphere at Dr. Bowman's presentation glowing green. What does green mean?"

"Green means coordinated rapid data transmission. Spookyon transmission is half-duplex, which means that only one side can transmit at a time. Both parties cannot simultaneously send data. We use timing and coordination to allow data to be sent both ways, but not at the same time. Again, this coordination is extremely fast and is programmed into the detectors. Once the two detectors establish this synchronization and timing, they light the sphere green. At this point, the half-duplex communication becomes a moot point. We can send a lot of data extremely fast in both directions even though, at the subatomic level, only one spookyon is communicating to the other at a time."

"Since Rodrigo will have his detector locked on a certain direction of spin during the test, we want a sphere that glows either blue or yellow, right?" Rachael asked.

"Exactly."

"And red means there's no connection? No spooky action, no communication."

"Yes, red is the proverbial traffic light that brings the whole thing to a halt. No traffic, no communication. This is our fifty-eighth test for entanglement, by the way, and all we've seen is red."

"Do you know what caused the failures?"

Joshua sat back in his rolling chair with a slim black leather backrest, his fingers laced casually behind his head. "There could be a lot of different causes. Sometimes we capture a particle, but it's not a spookyon. Other times the sphere is empty to begin with, meaning that the tokamak registered a false positive during the capture procedure. Then there may be contamination and isolation issues, most likely from cosmic rays—they're passing through you, me, the Earth—everything—every minute of the day.

Or there could be breaches in the laser seals on the sphere, which allows air to leak in."

"Little bastards," Rachael interjected with wry humor. "They're very elusive, aren't they?"

Joshua managed a weak smile. "It's difficult to say why we keep failing, but this is the first time I've used a new isolation procedure, so I'm very hopeful this time around." He held up both hands and crossed his fingers. "I think Rodrigo should be ready by now."

Joshua called Rodrigo on the video conferencing app, and this time Rodrigo answered immediately. "You all set Rodrigo?"

"All set up, boss," Rodrigo replied.

"We're ready to rock and roll then. Note the time in your log, switch on your detector, and lock for left spin."

Thirty seconds elapsed without receiving a reply.

"Rodrigo, are you there, amigo?"

"Present, boss. The detector is locked and showing left spin. Sphere 0 is glowing a bright yellow. The computer confirms a total system lock for left spin."

"Great. I'm going to activate my detector now. Here's hoping that my sphere glows blue, indicating a right spin. After all, it's only our reputations riding on the line, right? Let's hope trial fifty-eight is the charm."

"Got your rabbit's foot, boss?"

Joshua smiled and turned to Rachael. "I've got a better good luck charm today, Rodrigo. *Much* better."

"Yeah? I'm betting that your good luck charm is five foot six," Rodrigo speculated.

Rachael moved so that she could be seen on the video feed. "Que pasa, Rodrigo?"

"*Thought so,*" Rodrigo replied in Spanish. "*You must be pretty good at what you do to make it all the way down to the bat cave.*"

"*I have my moments.*"

Thinking back to the previous conversation between Rachael and his assistant, Joshua blushed. "I think I'll need to learn some Spanish pretty soon." He pivoted his torso to face the keyboard on his computer. "Enough chatter, Rodrigo. Let's begin. Here we go. Switching on my detector . . . now!"

Chapter Ten
The Universal Language

All three of them were tense. Joshua's hand shook a little as he entered the keystrokes on the computer to turn the detector on, which made a few clicking sounds before producing a low, steady hum. Two loud crackling noises echoed in the mine shaft.

"Sounds like backyard bug zappers," Rachael observed.

"That was just a preliminary degaussing procedure to eliminate any random magnetic fields, which are present everywhere, even in these rocks, albeit it at extremely low levels. No stone left unturned."

The steady hum resumed.

"You up and running, doc?" Rodrigo asked. "Ready for the money shot?"

"Yep. Should be getting a reading almost any—"

Joshua's mouth dropped open. Speechless, he rolled his chair back a yard from the table as Rachael simultaneously took two steps backwards. The Bowman sphere was glowing—it was blue.

"Holy shit!" Joshua exclaimed. "It's working!" Eyes wide, his gaze was riveted on the blue sphere. "God, but it's a thing of beauty." He jumped up, spun around, clapped his hands, and grabbed Rachael by the shoulders. "It's working!" he repeated. "Blue!"

Rodrigo's voice sounded through the computer. "Say again, boss."

"It's blue, Rodrigo. Blue! I can't believe it! Well, I can believe it, but . . . I mean . . . hell, it's working!"

He wrapped his arms around Rachael and gave her a bear hug, lifting her an inch off the floor.

"Joshua?" Rachael said.

"What?"

"Bad news—I think. The sphere is glowing yellow now. It changed during your victory lap."

Joshua's heart sank. He released the young woman from his arms and crept closer to the sphere, leaning over as if he were a detective examining a small piece of evidence at a crime scene. His brows were knit as he shook his head in consternation.

"What the hell just happened?" he asked. "It's yellow now, Rodrigo. Did you do something different on your end? Did you unlock your detector?"

"Geez, gimme some credit, boss. This isn't my first rodeo. My detector is still locked and registering a left spin. Yellow, same as before."

Joshua backed away and folded his arms, wrapping his thumb and index finger around his chin and jaw in a pose of concentration. As he stared at the sphere intently, it changed yet again, now glowing red.

Joshua's hands fell limply to his sides. "Damn it! We have nothing— nothing at all. It's red now. Rodrigo, run a diagnostic on your equipment, please. Computer, interface, sphere integrity—everything."

Joshua sat and scooted his chair in front of the computer next to the detector and intently studied the screen. "I don't see anything unusual. Everything's as it should be. There's definitely a spookyon in that sphere, and there's no evidence of contamination."

"What's your best guess?" Rachael asked.

"To be honest, I think we're crapping out for the fifty-eighth time," he said with a heavy sigh. "There's obviously a malfunction somewhere. Or else—" He rubbed his eyes and placed his hands flat on his thighs as he tilted the chair back slightly, head cocked back as he gazed at the top of the mine. "Or else the science behind all this is flawed and Henry sent us on a fool's errand, though not willingly, of course. He fervently believed in his research. If only I had his damn notebooks." He shook his head defiantly. "No, Henry was right. I'm convinced of it. The Martian Rover proved it! Gotta be a malfunction."

"A malfunction in what?" Rachael pursued. "There's hardly any equipment down here."

"There has to be something wrong with the detector. Otherwise . . . I dunno." Joshua began typing on the keyboard in front of his screen.

"The diagnostic's complete," Rodrigo said. The voice emanating from the computer was subdued. "Nothing wrong over here. The detector is in perfect operating condition, and I'm still seeing a left spin. Constant yellow, boss."

A silence of several seconds was broken by an astonished Rachael. "Oh, my God! It's blue again. Did you run your own diagnostic here in the bat cave?"

"Of course," Joshua answered with irritation while doing a double-take at the sphere. "Everything checks out fine. Did you get that Rodrigo? It's back to . . . . No wait! It changed from blue to yellow *again*!"

"Madre Dios," Rodrigo said. "The damn thing is possessed."

"Is that your best scientific guess?" Joshua asked with exasperation in his voice.

The sphere reverted to red.

Joshua stared at the blinking sphere before speaking, his tone one of resignation. "That's it, folks. This is another failed test. Rodrigo, turn off your equipment. We're both going to have to analyze what happened today and crunch some serious numbers over the next week. No entanglement. We can't have this happen again. The university will pull the plug in a New York minute."

"Okay, the detector's off. Lo siento. Later, boss." Rodrigo ended the video call.

Rachael approached the table and, standing behind the scientist, softly put her hand on his shoulder. "I'm really sorry."

Joshua said nothing as he typed an account of the last several minutes into the computer. The clacking of the keys echoed off the black rocks. All else was silence.

"Uh, Josh," Rachael said, "you may want to take a look at this. The sphere is blue *again*."

Joshua and Rachael spent a minute staring at the sphere as it repeated its blue, yellow, red pattern at regular intervals.

"What can cause that?" Rachael asked. She bent forward, hands on her knees, as she stared at sphere 1.

"Absolutely nothing," Joshua replied. "It's violating the laws of physics unless we screwed up big time, which seems to be a distinct possibility. The damn thing is lighting up like a Christmas tree!" Joshua exclaimed, spellbound by the sphere's display of repeating colors. He checked the interface and then the computer before watching the sphere progress through its sequence of colors.

"Let's think this through," Rachael suggested, pacing the smooth, hard floor of the converted mine. "You said the colors blue and yellow indicate entanglement, correct?"

"That's true, but for a while, both spheres—ours and Rodrigo's—were yellow. That's impossible if they are entangled. If his sphere had a left spin, then ours would *have* to have a right spin to verify a link between the spookyons. That's the nature of the communication that happens with entanglement."

Rachael recalled Henry Bowman's presentation at Wheeler Auditorium and how the baseballs had opposite spins when their images became clear, representing entanglement.

"Then I see only one possibility," she remarked, "and it's courtesy of Sherlock Holmes. The spookyon here in the bat cave is entangled, but not with the one in Rodrigo's sphere."

"Not following. What are you getting at?"

"It's Holmes' famous theorem. When you've eliminated all other possibilities, that which remains, no matter how implausible, must be the truth. You said this can't happen, but it is."

Joshua rubbed his fingers through his hair as he considered Rachael's speculation. "It's theoretically possible, but any other particle it's entangled with would have to be locked down by a detector. Otherwise, the spin measurement of our particle would be totally random and show red only."

"Well, there *has* to be an explanation," Rachael said. "Science isn't random. There's always an explanation, no matter how implausible it may appear at first. Haven't other labs been working on spookyons ever since Henry's demonstration? Maybe this particle got entangled with another lab's by sheer dumb luck—a lab that is using a detector at this very moment."

"Can't happen," Joshua retorted tersely. "The particles have to be created at the exact place at the same time. It's how they get entangled in the first place, and it's why we create spookyons in pairs inside the tokamak."

Rachael felt deflated and out of ideas. "Just brainstorming." She wandered into the shadows several feet from the table, her body just a dark blue shadow. "Maybe it's time to bring down some members of your team. Some raw brain power to work the problem as they used to say in Mission Control at NASA."

Joshua shook his head. "No, not yet. I don't need a lot of competing voices filling my head right now." He looked from the sphere to the computer screen. "At least our eyes aren't deceiving us. The computer is registering the same cycle that we're seeing: blue, yellow, and red over and over again."

"And you've never seen this pattern before?"

"We've never seen a pattern—period."

"Well you've got one now, and it's not random. The sequence of colors isn't changing."

"Granted, but it's still the proverbial riddle wrapped in a mystery inside an enigma."

Rachael stared at the sphere before speaking again. The writer within her was doing what it had for a lifetime: observing with focus and concentration, looking for details, patterns, similarities, differences. "I just noticed something."

"What?"

"You said that you use timing to allow you to send data via spookyons, correct?"

"Yes."

"It seems to me that the timing of the colors isn't the same. It stays red the longest, yellow the shortest, and blue is in between. The color pattern is a constant, but the intervals at which they change are definitely not uniform."

The provocative statement snared Joshua's attention immediately. He looked at the sphere with curiosity for several seconds before turning back to the computer. "Damn strange but let me check something." He tapped a few keys and then invited Rachael to come closer and examine the screen.

Standing behind Joshua's chair, Rachael bent over and peered at the data.

"The computer has recorded all color cycles since the test began," Joshua stated. "Like you said, the time intervals aren't random. Good catch. They're repeating at specific time intervals. I asked the computer to display them for us."

The screen showed the following numbers.

blue: 10.1345 secs
yellow: 3.6159 secs
red: 14.9755 secs

blue: 11.3596 secs
yellow: 3.6159 secs
red: 14.9755 secs

blue: 11.3596 secs
yellow: 3.6159 secs
red: 14.9755 secs

blue: 11.3596 secs
yellow: 3.6159 secs
red: 14.9755 secs

The numbers corresponding to each color didn't vary by a single decimal place in all of the repetitions except the blue measurement on the first line. Joshua hit the scroll key, causing the computer to display the last one hundred sequences. They were all the same.

"I think that first blue data point is aberrant and should be disregarded," Joshua noted. "We may have turned the detector on mid-cycle and therefore the first blue value is shorter, but the rest are identical."

Rachael was surprised by the regularity of the numerical data. "Any way that the computer could have accidentally been programmed to do this?" Rachael asked.

"Not a chance. I'm the only one who has access to this computer—not even the team has my password—and I guarantee that I didn't program a version of Minecraft Rave Lights into it."

"What about the detector? Could anyone have changed its programming or circuitry?"

"If you're a conspiracy theorist, I guess it could have been sabotaged, but I'd vouch for everyone on the team. Their careers all have a lot riding on the success of this program. If we ever manage to create stable entanglement, my staff will become scientific rock stars overnight. They'll be able to write their own tickets."

Rachael stared at the pattern of numbers on the screen. She'd always been good at picking out correlations and patterns. "May I use the calculator on my phone?" Rachael asked. "I think I noticed something else."

"Go ahead. It won't emit any signal as long as it's in airplane mode, not that it matters anymore at this point."

Rachael produced the iPhone from her handbag and started hitting numbers on the screen while periodically glancing at the computer where the numbers were displayed. "As Alice said, curiouser and curiouser. You said that blue and yellow means we're receiving a signal, while red means we're not?"

"Right."

"We're definitely down the rabbit hole," Rachael said, narrowing her eyes. "When you add together the times for the blue and yellow, you get the time for the red—and to the exact decimal point. The time we're receiving equals the time we're not receiving. Can that be an accident?" For Rachael, the question was largely rhetorical.

"With *that* kind of mathematical precision?" Joshua replied. "Virtually impossible. The odds would be greater than winning the lottery."

"This is absolutely wild, so what do we do next?" Rachael asked. "I mean, we have a discernible pattern, which is what scientists live for."

Not one to ignore a challenge, Joshua closed his eyes again. What Rachael had said about equal parts transmitting and not transmitting triggered something in his thinking. After a moment, he held up his index finger, as if signaling that he had an idea. "Try dividing the blue time by the yellow time in your calculator. I want to see what the ratio is between the two."

"What are you expecting to find?"

"Indulge me."

Rachael performed the calculation and gasped. "You've got to be kidding me," she said, her eyes wide and glued to the small screen.

"What? What's the ratio?"

Rachael looked up, astonishment in her eyes as she turned the phone in her hand so that Joshua could see the results for himself. "It's pi. *Exactly.*"

"Pi? That can't be. You must have hit a wrong key. Do it again."

Rachael's heart started beating faster as she complied and held the phone screen before Joshua's eyes a second time.

"No, it's pi, Josh. And you're absolutely sure no natural phenomenon can cause this? Nature is full of unusual symmetries, such as fractals."

Joshua's heart also was beating quickly now. "Fractals faithfully duplicate geometric patterns on large and small scales, but this is about pure communication, not geometric patterns. No, nothing *natural* could cause this."

He paused, as if experiencing an epiphany, and turned to Rachael, nodding.

The words echoed in Rachael's mind. *Nothing natural could cause this.* "Then . . ." The impact of what Joshua had said suddenly struck her. "Are you telling me that some form of intelligence is trying to communicate with us using a spookyon?"

Joshua faced Rachael and spoke slowly and deliberately.

"I can't think of any other reasonable explanation," he said. "The repeating sequence of colors was to get our attention. It did—in a big way. It's communication, pure and simple. And I think I know what the red is for."

"Which is?"

"They—*someone*—is leaving us time to respond."

"You lost me."

Joshua typed as he spoke, his speech now accelerated, emotional. "Remember that entangled particles use half-duplex to communicate, which means they're connected, but only one party at a time can send data. In this case, only one particle at a time can communicate its binary information—

left or right, yellow or blue. Timing has to be factored in to allow two-way communication for both particles. It's exactly what Henry and I did when sending signals to the Martian Rover. The red is essentially a time when they're not sending." Joshua turned to look at Rachael. "They're leaving us time to send a reply."

Rachael raised her eyebrows. The implications of Joshua's last statement were slowly sinking in. "Whoever is on the other end of this long-distance call has refined the art of measurement to a high degree of sophistication in order to speak in mathematical constants that hinge on fractions of a second."

"No argument there."

"What kind of reply should we send?" Rachael asked.

"I have an idea. Get on the other computer over there and search the Internet for a mathematical constant."

"Which one?"

Joshua casually waved his hand in the air, his system coursing with adrenaline. "Doesn't matter. Something universal."

"Okay," Rachael said as she started typing on the other computer. "How about Avogadro's number, which is 6.022 times ten to the twenty-third? It's the number of atoms an element contains within a basic unit of measurement called a mole."

"No, we can't have exponents. Choose a simpler number—something between one and ten."

"You said *any* number," Rachael muttered under her breath as she resumed typing. "What about Euler's number, 2.71828?"

"Perfect! I'm programming the detector during its red phase to hold left spin for a certain time period, and then to hold right spin for a certain time period. If they divide the two time periods, they should come up with Euler's number. We're sending a reply."

"*They?* Who the hell are we talking to?"

"Beats the hell out of me, but we may be in the process of leapfrogging Project Breakthrough Starshot. My mouth is as dry as cotton." He paused to take a sip of bottled water. "Okay, here goes," he stated as he hit one last key.

The pattern of blue, yellow, and red ceased, replaced immediately by alternations between blue and yellow only.

"Whoa! That was awfully fast," Rachael commented, crossing her arms and placing her hands on opposite shoulders, as if trying to warm herself from a chill. "I know this sounds silly, but it feels like Halloween. It's dark down here, and I—I don't know—I feel like we're not alone, like that sphere is grinning at us like a jack-o-lantern. So why is the red gone?"

"Because we're now *transmitting* during the red time. But look—*their* timing has changed as well," Joshua said as he looked at his computer. "I believe Euler's number got their attention. Their blue is reading 9.2554 and yellow is 5.7201."

"I'm on it," Rachael said, entering the new numbers into the calculator on her phone. "The ratio between those two numbers is . . . 1.6180. Let me look it up." She went to the second computer and rapidly typed the ratio into a search engine. Though neither was consciously aware of it, Joshua and Rachael shared an enthusiasm and excitement that were in total sync.

"My God!" Rachael cried. "It's phi, the Golden Ratio, which correlates with the Fibonacci Sequence of 1, 2, 3, 5, 8, 13, 21—on and on. Add the two previous numbers to get the next. This is definitely a display of intelligence."

"Agreed. No phenomenon I'm aware of in nature could mimic this. It's not an aberration. No way."

"Who could they be?"

"I haven't a clue. Logically, it should be someone on Earth, but we've already ruled out that another lab's particle could be entangled with the spookyon in sphere 1. We created it, and nobody else could have been part of what we did in the tokamak. This goes beyond anything I learned in grad school or my post doc research with Henry. It's off the scale weird."

"What do we do now?" asked Rachael.

"I don't know," Joshua said staring at the constantly blinking sphere. "This is completely out of my league."

Rachael thought for a moment and then uncrossed her arms and approached the director. She intuitively sensed that her next suggestion was going to be summarily challenged.

"I know the perfect person for this. I have a friend who might be able to solve this riddle, or at least make sense of what we're seeing. This is right up his alley."

"What? You want to invite someone *else* down here?"

"No, I think we need to take the sphere and detector to *him*."

"No," Joshua shot back immediately. "I can't allow the sphere to be removed from this facility. It's too big a risk."

"I see where you're coming from," Rachael admitted, "but you're sitting on top of what might be the most important discovery in history. What if whoever is communicating with us decides to stop? This window of opportunity might close really fast."

Joshua appeared anguished at the question that was posed. His mind was racing. "As usual, your logic is disquieting but correct." Joshua stared blankly at the blinking sphere. "Alright then, but I hope your friend knows what he's doing—and is discreet. I'm putting a lot of trust in you, Rachael."

"I know, and I appreciate it. Let me give him a call." Rachael held her phone in her right hand. "Shit! Airplane mode."

"You wouldn't get a signal down here even if it wasn't on airplane mode. Use the landline," Joshua said pointing to the phone on his desk.

Rachael hurriedly picked up the landline and dialed her friend's number. A brief moment elapsed before someone answered.

"Vinod? It's Rachael. Hey, are you at home?" She paused. "Great, because I have something extraordinary to show you. Gonna blow your mind." She covered the mouthpiece with the palm of her hand and looked at Joshua. "We'll have to use *his* computers. He's an information theorist and created an algorithm that is perfect for this."

"Whatever," Joshua said as he began to disconnect the sphere from the detector. He was reluctant to admit it, but he knew that he had no choice. Time was of the essence.

"I'll be over in forty-five minutes," Rachael said. "Have your latest language algorithm ready. I'll explain later."

Rachael hung up and watched Joshua, who was now standing. "Why disconnect the sphere from the detector?"

"They have to be disconnected when they go in the case. Besides, whoever is communicating with us might change the sequence again, and we'd lose valuable data they're trying to send. Who knows where they're trying to take this conversation? If we disconnect the sphere from the detector, they might deduce that we're not transmitting or receiving. Might figure we're deciding what to do next—and they'd be right."

"Risky call, but okay."

Joshua was still shaking a little from nervous excitement. As he moved towards the carrying case with the sphere, he tripped on the leg of the nearest table, stumbled, and began to fall. His hands instinctively lifted higher in an effort to protect the sphere. The sphere, however, slipped from his grasp and was thrown into the air as he fell to the ground. For agonizing seconds, the glass sphere moved in an arc, heading for the floor. Rachael lunged forward and dropped to one knee, extending her right hand, and caught the orb.

"Oh my God!" Joshua exclaimed from the floor. "Nice save! It would have been all over if that sphere would've hit the floor."

"Definitely lucky," Rachael said. "You okay?"

Joshua got up from the floor. "Embarrassed, but okay."

Rachael handed the sphere to Joshua, who then positioned it and the detector snugly in the case before closing the lid.

"Ready?" Rachael asked.

"Yeah. I hope this guy is the best damn information theorist in the world. I'm taking a big risk here."

"Apparently less of a risk than just walking across the floor," Rachael said with a smile.

"Point taken."

"Vinod's the best. He's perfect for this job. Now let's haul ass."

Chapter Eleven
In the Beginning

Standing in the atrium, Rachael and Joshua saw that the rain was still slanting in silver lines across the campus. The parking lot was strewn with puddles where the elevation of the asphalt wasn't uniform, each one a mirror of the dull gray clouds overhead.

"So much for sunny California," Joshua said. "I feel like I'm living on the rain planet in *Star Wars*."

"The case is waterproof, right?" Rachael asked.

"Yeah, but I was hoping to ride my Harley today, but that looks like a no-go."

"My car again then," Rachael replied. "Let's make a run for it." She grabbed Joshua's hand, pulled him in the direction of the Prius, and broke into a sprint.

"Hop in," Rachael said, hitting the unlock button on her key. They hurried into the car and shut the doors. Rachael glanced at Joshua. "Wait—we may be talking to ET, and you were actually thinking of transporting the sphere on your motorcycle if the weather was dry?"

"I'm awfully good on a bike," Joshua replied with confidence. "But you're right, not my best idea."

"No Harleys or land speeders from *Star Wars* today—even if you're good at it."

Joshua buckled his seatbelt and thought that the very outgoing reporter had an answer for everything, usually laced with wit and insight. He'd only known her for two days, but he was starting to enjoy her company.

Rachael brushed away strands of wet hair with her left hand as she turned the key in the ignition with her right and pulled out of the parking lot. Joshua wiped the moisture from his face with the back of his hand, the case wedged between his feet in the passenger well. Rachael navigated through the Berkeley traffic and accelerated quickly as she steered toward the Interstate on-ramp. They both sat quietly, lost in their own thoughts of what had just transpired. Rachael finally broke the silence.

"Josh, I'm trying to figure out how the spookyon in that case could be entangled with some intelligence. How could this even be possible?"

"I have no idea," Joshua replied. "It's a mystery to me."

"You told me that Henry suspected spookyons existed because of a faint particle signature he noticed in other tokamaks," Rachael said as she eased the car up to a safe cruising speed of sixty miles an hour since they were now traversing the bay bridge, and the rain had grown heavier. She switched the wipers to high, but they still had difficulty clearing the heavy rain from the windshield.

"It's what spurred his quest for what he considered the Holy Grail of subatomic particles. And it's why there's a research center named after him. There's a granite block in front of the atrium with an engraving that looks like an oversized comma. The squiggle is a representation of the particle's signature, which became the logo for the center."

"Spookyons are artificial particles that you create in your tokamak, right?"

"That's right. Henry conjured them up with mathematical calculations from what he had observed. What's your point?"

"I'm wondering if there can be a *natural* source of spookyons. There are far greater energies in the universe—outright explosions—that cause nuclei to smash into one another. It logically follows that there could be natural phenomena that can create spookyons."

"I suppose," Joshua replied. "My thoughts never really went down that avenue since Henry focused on creating them in the lab. Even if natural sources of spookyons exist, the closest star, Proxima Centauri is twenty years away using Hawking's theoretical ideas. How would we ever have been able to capture some random spookyon in distant interstellar space?"

"Then make it a thought experiment," Rachael continued. "What kind of event would produce a spookyon if you could indeed magically reach out and grab one? Let's say the universe is your oyster, and all you have to do is be in the right location."

Joshua pondered her question for a while. "For starters, any natural event that could create spookyons would have to be one of cosmic proportions and yield enormous amounts of energy."

"Such as?" Rachael queried.

"I guess a nova or supernova could theoretically generate enough energy to create spookyons."

"But stars are mostly hydrogen and helium with only trace amounts of heavier elements. Don't you need heavy elements to create spookyons?" Rachael asked.

"Not necessarily," Joshua replied. "It depends on the energy level. According to Henry's calculations, the higher the energy level of the plasma, the less massive the nuclei have to be. We can only generate a relatively small level of energy in our plasma, so we have to use heavier elements. At the energy levels of a supernova, which also creates heavy elements, by the way, I suppose spookyons could form from lighter elements."

"So could our spookyon have been formed in a supernova?" Rachael asked.

"Possible, but highly unlikely," Joshua answered. "Supernovas are relatively rare events given that the average life of a star is quite long. Spookyons would be around, but not very plentiful, so it would be highly unlikely that we would capture one even if we had a mechanism to do so."

"But it's theoretically possible that they could be created naturally?"

"Yeah, but *everything* is theoretically possible if you appeal to quantum mechanics. It's the multiverse theory. Everything that can happen *does* happen. All possibilities branch off into infinite versions of reality. So yes— maybe there are naturally-occurring spookyons, but once again you're overlooking that spookyons have to be created at the same place and at the same time in order to become entangled. For there to be a significant number of entangled spookyons—enough, in fact, that we would *randomly* capture one—would mean that there has to be an enormous number of them. I don't think, given the rarity of supernovas, it would be probable that we would have captured one."

"In essence what you're saying is that we need a high-energy event that could simultaneously cause the production of a large number of spookyons," Rachael summarized.

"Correct, and only—" Joshua stopped as a thought entered his mind. His face became ashen, and his mouth was slightly agape. He turned and looked at Rachael and then the case on the floor of the automobile.

"And only *what?*" she asked.

Joshua didn't answer. His mind was occupied with an idea reverberating in his mind and what its repercussions might be.

"*What?* What is it?" Rachael asked again.

Joshua finally responded, "Only one thing would have almost endless energy, something that would account for the creation of entangled particles plentiful enough to be spread uniformly throughout the universe."

"What are you referring to? Quasars—the massive black holes at the center of galaxies?"

Joshua shook his head. "No, not things, plural. I'm talking about an event—a *single* event." He turned to look directly at Rachael. "The Big Bang."

For several seconds there was no sound in the car except raindrops hitting the windshield as the car's wipers rhythmically brushed them away. Rachael, processing her passenger's last statement, merely mouthed the words: *Big Bang.*

"Wait a minute," she said. "Are you telling me that spookyons may have been around since the beginning of the universe—that they may have been created by the Big Bang?"

Joshua nodded, hardly able to accept his own theory. "That's *exactly* what I'm saying," he said. "Hey, it was *your* thought experiment, and this is the only possible answer to your hypothetical question. I can't believe I'm saying this, but it kinda makes sense."

In her excitement, Rachael's foot depressed the accelerator, inching the car's speed to seventy. She gripped the wheel more tightly as her breathing quickened at the answer—both outrageous and bold—tendered by her companion.

"*How* does it make sense?" Rachael asked.

"Remember when I said that, at higher energy levels, spookyons could be created using smaller elements with smaller nuclei?" Joshua said with excitement in his voice.

"Yes."

"Well, it's not actually the nuclei that are required. It's the *protons* in the nuclei. But creating spookyons with only naked protons would require an extremely high energy level. Within the first few minutes of the Big Bang, protons and neutrons came into existence. At that point the entire universe was contained in a small space but also had an extreme amount of energy—enough possibly to allow naked protons to create spookyons."

"Josh," Rachael said in a whisper as the weight of what Joshua said was beginning to sink in, "the entire universe expanded from a single point. If what you're saying is true, then there are trillions—or a trillion trillion—spookyons permeating the universe, and their entanglement creates a cosmic communications network."

"I know."

"We're starting to sound a lot like those hippie scientists from the sixties."

Joshua couldn't suppress a laugh or the continued speculation about an endless number of spookyons existing in every corner of the cosmos. "Rachael, imagine if it's true."

"If it's true, Dr. Joshua Andrews is going to soon be giving his own lectures at Wheeler when he's not doing the talk show circuit. But something bothers me about all this. We've engaged in some pretty wild conjecture for the past fifteen minutes even though it seems to make sense and represents the only explanation for what we saw in the mine, but if it's true, then—"

Joshua anticipated what she was going to say next. "Then we didn't create the spookyon contained in this sphere in the tokamak at all."

Rachael nodded, her eyes on the Interstate as eighteen-wheelers blew past, sending large plumes of rain cascading onto the left side of the car and windshield. They were now traveling south on the 101 headed towards Palo Alto. The car drifted slightly to the left each time it was caught in the Venturi effect of a passing big rig. "You read my mind."

"I'm way ahead of you," Joshua said, growing more enthusiastic by the minute. "Yes, we just happened to trap a spookyon when the capture procedure was in progress."

"I'd call that winning at Galactic Powerball."

"Not really. Stay me with me on this and recall my basic assumption. If spookyons were created by the Big Bang, they would be plentiful in the universe and be distributed evenly throughout what is called the Picard Topology. In 1884, Emile Picard theorized that the cosmos was shaped like an elongated, expanding horn. Picture the main tube of a slide trombone, and you'll see what Picard was getting at. As the universe expanded, spookyons were evenly distributed through the end of its horn shape and in quantities that stagger the imagination. If that's correct, then it really isn't so farfetched that we captured one."

"But you're saying that one of these particles was free-floating through space and just happened to land in the sphere. The odds are still against us. Not trying to be a buzz kill, just attempting to play devil's advocate. What's the famous maxim governing science? Extraordinary claims call for extraordinary proof."

"I agree with you one hundred percent, but maybe the capture wasn't so random."

"How so?"

"Because we were actively trying to attract one, and I know with certainty that spookyons are attracted to heavy metals regardless of how they are created. Yes, we trapped a spookyon that's as old as the universe, but it was because we were *looking* for one with the right equipment. Until Henry came along, nobody believed in them and therefore there was no active search. After five years, however, my refined techniques have proven sound. The particle in sphere 1 gravitated towards the sphere because we were attracting it. Maybe the new formulation of the heavy metals in the container lids attracts spookyons created by the Big Bang."

"Quite convincing," Rachael conceded, shuddering. "It's almost too much to take in, but everything you've laid out *is* logical."

"*More* than logical," Joshua added. "Science indeed demands rigorous proof, but that's exactly what we may be in the process of finding—proof—if your friend's algorithm re-establishes contact."

"But only *if* the aliens, wherever they may be, are still transmitting," Rachael said. "Remember the WOW! signal that the Big Ear Antenna at Ohio State University found. It vanished after only a few seconds and was never detected again even though no one has ever been able to adequately explain it."

"But we've already got so much more than that. We have the sequence of color changes recorded on a hard drive, and it not only changed according to mathematical constants, but the sequence repeated over and over, unlike the WOW! signal. I mean, this blows SETI out of the water. All of a sudden, looking for extraterrestrials using radio telescopes seems archaic. No wonder we haven't found signals from intelligent life before. We've been searching the wrong medium. No intelligent species with the knowledge of spookyons would use radio transmission to communicate. Any truly advanced civilization would only use spookyons to communicate since there's no lag time of years, decades, or centuries in trying to open a dialogue with an intelligent species. In the space of minutes, they already sent multiple mathematical signals. It makes sense—*perfect* sense. We replied to the transmission, and I hope they're waiting for more."

"Remarkable," Rachael said. "I have a feeling you may be on to something, but we still need Vinod's help. I've got a gut feeling that the mathematical constants are only an introduction of sorts. Of course, you realize that if all this pans out, you're going to change mankind's understanding of its place in the universe. This could be the biggest discovery ever made in the annals of science. In all of human history, for that matter. In doing so, you might rattle some philosophical and theological cages. Are you prepared for the fallout?"

"You mean are *we* prepared for the fallout," Joshua replied turning to Rachael. "At this point, this is as much your discovery as it is mine."

Rachael looked towards Joshua with a slight grin on her face. He was definitely a refreshing change from the typical researcher she was accustomed to, most of whom were very protective of their work. Their careers, after all, depended on their research and the papers they published. The typical scientist was reluctant to share credit for an amazing discovery, but in what could be the most significant discovery in all of science, Joshua was freely willing to share this with her. She found his egalitarian attitude very refreshing.

"Galileo rattled some cages too," Joshua continued, "but scientists have an obligation to the truth. Sooner or later, Ptolemy was going to be supplanted by Copernicus, and those guys didn't have social media to spread the word."

Rachael glanced in her rearview mirror and saw that an eighteen-wheeler was drawing uncomfortably close to her rear bumper.

"Entanglement on a cosmic scale, not to mention universal communication," she said. "No wonder Einstein was freaked out by the very idea of entanglement, and it's going to freak out a lot more people if Vinod re-establishes contact."

"But what would—*will*—we tell each other?" Joshua wondered out loud.

Rachael, overwhelmed by the worldwide implications of the concepts they'd discussed, inhaled and let out a deep breath before chuckling. "We could start by saying it's a beautiful day in the neighborhood. You know—something non-threatening and benign."

"That's something else I've been turning over in my mind," Joshua said. "Whose galactic neighborhood are we even talking about? This intelligence could be in the Milky Way—maybe even close by—or in another galaxy altogether. Maybe even billions of light years away if my theory of the uniform spread of spookyons after the Big Bang is sound. That's a mindbender."

"The *real* mindbender is that we'll go a step further than SETI and be able to have meaningful communication with these beings in real time."

"That depends," Joshua asserted. "Swapping mathematical constants is one thing. It verifies that both civilizations have reached a certain technological level, but how do we turn math into a true exchange of information, such as ideas on culture, technology, and beliefs?"

"That's where Vinod comes in," Rachael replied. "He can not only help re-establish contact but create the basis for dialogue. His algorithm is that powerful."

Joshua's curiosity was piqued. "That's an incredible discovery in itself. How come he hasn't published it?"

Rachael slowed to sixty again since the rain had intensified further as they traveled south down the 101, the big rig still on her tail. She nevertheless remained calm and in control of the vehicle.

Joshua couldn't help but note that her cheeks had a rosy, youthful color. Maybe she was excited by the possibilities they were discussing, and then again maybe it was just makeup. The bat cave had been dark, and he'd been absorbed in the test earlier that afternoon. And he had, after all, been doing his level best not to keep staring at her. Either way, he was now sitting beside her and couldn't help being struck by her presence. Well, first things first, he told himself. They might be talking with ET, and he needed to retain his focus—if that was possible.

"Vinod works for a startup now," Rachael explained, "but right after college he did some volunteer work for SETI. As someone in information theory, he wasn't as much interested in finding a signal from outer space as much as what we would do if we ever got a signal. How would we establish communication? He wrote a computer algorithm that uses mathematical constants as a base to progress to language—that's the short version. He'll explain it in more detail when we get there."

"But how reliable is his algorithm? Are we his guinea pigs? You talk like this guy has been around the block and has proven technology. What's his track record?"

"He's shared a little with me," Rachael said, "although I think that, despite our long friendship, he knows I'm a reporter, and reporters like to quote anonymous sources. Still, he trusts me, and I'll tell you in confidence that his algorithm has been tested on artificial intelligence. Vinod's dropped some hints that AI is much farther along than anybody knows except for some tech gurus in Silicon Valley. And the government, of course. The military is always ahead of the technology curve."

The rain was still coming down in sheets. Joshua felt uneasy as Rachael navigated through the heavy rain with only an intermittent view of the road ahead. The wipers were on high, but they were having trouble keeping up with the deluge. Rachael, though, still seemed completely in control.

"I think you've got your article now," Joshua said. "That aside, Vinod may have to reveal the ultimate capabilities of his algorithm if he's going to help us."

"I've got enough for an entire *book*," Rachael said. "And you're right about the algorithm. This will test its potential to the max, and I don't see any way that he'll be able to keep this under his hat assuming we want to announce what we've found. We'll have to offer proof of whatever communication might ensue, even if it remains purely mathematical in content." Rachael glanced sideways for a split second. "You talked about

Vinod being discreet earlier. You're not contemplating sitting on a discovery of this magnitude, are you?"

Joshua was silent for several moments. "No," he said at last. "The creed at SETI has always been that any signal they received would be for all mankind. I think I'd have to follow the same protocol except . . ." His voice tailed away as he gazed vacantly out the passenger window at the impending nightfall. "We still haven't verified anything yet, and we're getting way ahead of ourselves. But assuming that the conversation continues, we don't know what this intelligence might tell us. Recall, if you will, that Stephen Hawking warned SETI against revealing anything about humanity."

"C'mon, Josh. This is too big to sit on. We already have evidence of communication even before Vinod runs the algorithm. Whatever the content of the communication, you have a moral obligation to go public. Sure, the intelligence is likely to be advanced, but so what? Maybe information travels faster than light, but not interstellar craft. It's not like anyone's going to drop in for a visit."

"That's true," Joshua replied staring out of the passenger window. "So how do you know Vinod? What's he like?"

"We actually met at Berkeley while in line waiting for Henry's lecture. He's a mixture of old school and new. Cool and geeky all at the same time. He's definitely got a unique personality though. A great guy overall."

"Sounds like our man, Rachael. Another good call."

"Journalism 101. Always think one step ahead."

"There's that spooky action in your brain again."

"Not too weird for ya?" Rachael asked. She glanced to her left. The big rig that had been tailgating was now trying to pass her. Its wheels were causing a constant spray onto the windshield.

"What's weird is that we're having this conversation at all. I woke up this morning hoping for entanglement in spookyons we created, not talking with intelligence that could be hiding anywhere in the known universe."

Looking at Joshua and then the case on the floor, Rachael laughed. "I wouldn't worry about using all your free minutes or roaming fees."

"Look out!" Joshua called.

The persistent eighteen-wheeler had finally made its move to get ahead of the Prius and was changing from the passing lane to the right-hand lane before fully clearing the front of the Toyota.

Rachael turned the wheel to the right as the rear end of the rig swung within a foot of the hood. The car skidded onto the shoulder of the Interstate, headed for a ravine.

Joshua looked with horror at the unfolding accident. His one thought was not for his own safety, but that the sphere in the case—a link to possible proof of extraterrestrial life—might break or end up buried in the mud after the Prius had made a few rolls before crashing. Would anyone look for it? More importantly, what would a state trooper do with it even if it were found?

Chapter Twelve
In-A-Gadda-Da-Vida

Rachael took her foot from the accelerator and steered left again, into the direction of the skid, as the eighteen-wheeler cleared the front of the vehicle. The Prius was now coasting straight down the narrow shoulder. She gently depressed the accelerator to give the front wheel drive needed traction and eased the car back onto the highway.

Joshua exhaled with relief, the case now in his lap as he'd instinctively clutched it and brought it out of the passenger well.

"That was a close one," he said. "Nice driving. How'd you know to do that?"

"It was mostly instinctual, but I once wrote an article on force vectors, mass, and acceleration," Rachael replied. "It's basic physics."

"I have a new respect for science writing," he said, relieved that nothing truly disastrous had happened.

Rachael relaxed in her seat as she continued to drive.

"Josh, I've been wondering about something. Where could this signal be coming from? Is there any way to find out?"

"Absolutely impossible," Joshua replied. "Unlike radio waves, entangled communication with particles has absolutely no directional component. There's no way to determine the source location of the signal. Also, given the fact that there is no signal loss with distance, and given that there are millions of galaxies out there, most likely this signal is not local in origin if you consider the size of the cosmos. Mathematically, the odds are against it."

"Interesting."

"Anyway, even if we wanted to find out *and* they wanted to tell us where they were, they couldn't do it."

"Why not?"

"Because we have no common point of reference. We'd need that in order to send location information. We have no idea where they are just as they have no idea where we are."

"Whew, that's a relief," Rachael said tongue in cheek. "It's good to know that no invasion fleet is on the way."

"Besides, even if they knew where we are and could travel at light speed, which I'm sure they can't, it would take millions or even billions of years to get here. But invasion?"

"Well, *you* were the one talking about *Star Wars.*"

"You have a habit of observing people very closely," Joshua noted. "Might make some people feel uncomfortable."

"Reporters are observant by nature—at least the good ones are—and you're right. It sometimes causes people to feel a little uneasy, as if they're under scrutiny, but it makes them cough up the truth faster. Journalism 102. Watch, wait, and record, which I've been doing every minute since you showed me the tokamak and the creation of a spookyon."

"Speaking of making things happen faster, when are we going to get to your friend's house? The intelligence controlling the other spookyon may have hung up on us."

"Almost there," Rachael replied. "Vinod lives in Palo Alto."

A short time later, Rachel arrived at a neighborhood in northern Palo Alto. She swung into the driveway of an average two-story suburban home.

"We're here," she said. "And for the record, your average Uber driver wouldn't have this kind of scientific connection."

"Don't rub it in. Yes, you're good luck, and yes, I'm glad I gave you the interview."

"Maybe things don't always happen by accident."

Joshua wondered what her last comment alluded to as the two walked to the front door.

*　　　　　*　　　　　*

Vinod answered the door promptly. He wore jeans and an AC-DC tee shirt with a cover image of their *High Voltage* album. "Rach, what's up? What was so urgent?"

Rachael introduced Joshua to Vinod. "Vinod, this is Dr. Joshua Andrews from the Bowman Particle Research Center."

"No introduction necessary. I recognize you from Professor Bowman's lecture. Come on in. Vinod Bhakti," he said, extending his hand.

"Thanks for agreeing to help us out on such short notice," Joshua said while shaking Vinod's hand.

Vinod led them through his home, which was strewn with old PCs, towers, electronic cables, books, and stacks of journal articles. They arrived shortly at his study at the rear of the house. The walls were decorated with posters for classic rock bands such as Metallica, Led Zeppelin, Van Halen, Jefferson Airplane, Pink Floyd, and dozens more. Some bore city names and tour dates as far back as the sixties and seventies. Two couches sat next to each other, forming a ninety-degree angle. Joshua placed the case on a coffee table in front of the couches. Near the back wall of the study was a large table with three computer monitors adjacent to each other, a single keyboard in front of the center screen. Behind the table were two floor-to-ceiling server racks filled with various servers and storage devices. Rachael and Joshua sat on one couch, Vinod on the other.

Joshua stared at the racks on the back wall. "Jesus, Vinod—you running your own data center from here?"

"Um," Vinod replied, "I work cyber security for a startup. I always feel that the best way to stop a hacker is to *be* a hacker."

"Dark web?" Joshua asked.

"Oh, definitely not!" Vinod replied. "That would be illegal."

Joshua got the gist of what Vinod was saying from the sarcastic tone of his voice.

"So Rach, why do you need my algorithm?" Vinod asked.

Rachael related everything that had taken place in the bat cave earlier in the day and summarized the conversation in the Prius. Joshua clarified some of the more technical issues involving the interface between the sphere, the module, and the computer. He grabbed a piece of paper and a ballpoint pen, quickly scribbled a few specs for the equipment that had been used and handed it to Vinod.

"Can you help us?" Joshua asked.

Vinod glanced at the paper, then at his visitors. "I'm being punked, right? Rach, I'm sorry for throwing you that surprise birthday party last year—I know you hate them—but this is a twisted way to get back at me." He grinned and sat back against the overstuffed cushion of his couch. "Let's just call it even."

"This is on the level," Rachael said, staring straight at her friend.

Vinod looked at Joshua, who had a stoic expression on his face. Vinod leaned forward again. "Holy crap. You're not kidding, are you? You really believe that you're having a chat with an intelligence somewhere in the universe using a spookyon in a Bowman sphere?"

"Yup," Rachael replied.

"And they're using mathematical constants?"

"Which is why we need *you*," Joshua asserted. "We can't go any farther with this. I thought I'd created the particle, but—"

"Yeah, I got it," Vinod said. "You think you snagged a spookyon created during the first instants of the Big Bang." He rubbed his hands together and puffed out his cheeks. "This is some heavy shit."

"Well?" Rachael said.

"Why not take the problem to the university?" Vinod asked. "They have a gazillion mathematicians and computer geeks who can write code."

Joshua was clearly tired and rubbed his hands across his face. Dark circles were appearing beneath his eyes from stress and lack of sleep. "Maybe they can write code, but from what Rachael has told me, your algorithm is fully operational and ready to run. Given the bureaucratic structure of a university, it might be weeks or months before we can proceed, assuming they don't hand the project off to a different department altogether. We need to make this happen tonight! Rachael has already reminded me that whoever is on the other end may not linger forever while waiting for a reply."

Vinod seemed receptive. "Bureaucrats are a bitch. I'll grant you that." He paused to consider Joshua's plight, but quickly broke into a broad smile. "No radio waves? I know a bunch of guys at the Hat Creek Observatory who would be green with envy. This is so cool!"

Joshua exhaled a sigh of relief. He'd apparently passed muster with the one man who was uniquely qualified to help him. Finding Vinod was nothing short of serendipity, and he began to believe that Rachael might literally be good luck. She'd materialized in the doorway of his office the day before, and he'd found success almost immediately, although in ways he couldn't have foreseen.

"Tell me more about your algorithm," Joshua requested. "How does it work?"

Vinod loved it when people asked about his work, and he gestured animatedly as he spoke with the enthusiasm of an inventor unveiling his latest marvel.

"It all flows from information theory," he began. "Like Professor Bowman said at Wheeler, information is the universe's stock in trade. *Everything* is information. So here's my premise. If two intelligent entities want to communicate, whether they're elephants or extraterrestrials, they have to have a common reference point. For an advanced intelligence, the most common starting point would be something science-related, probably mathematics since it's constant across the universe. No matter where you go, two plus two equals four."

"Makes sense," Joshua said. "Go on."

"Here's where it gets *really* interesting. Once you've established a reference point—in your case, a recognition of significant mathematical constants—you use that as a base to move to simple concepts such as basic mathematics and simple logic like yes and no, true and false. Once you have simple logic, you build from there using more complex ideas that you both would likely have in common, like the sciences. My algorithm progresses from simple mathematics and logic through the natural sciences, such as physics, chemistry, and biology, all the way to language."

"Is that really possible?" Joshua asked. "That's one hell of a leap."

"Like any algorithm, it's based on computer codes that determine a precise sequence of operations in order to calculate a function. By using subsets of various computational algorithms, it's able to process data until it reaches a level of automated reasoning as it moves through successive finite states. And you're right—it covers a diverse set of disciplines, but I've always operated on the assumption that all knowledge is related and builds upon itself. The really sophisticated part of my algorithm is how I use both variables and constants to interface with the next highest level of learning in order to jump from one subject to the next. It's a clever piece of code, if I say so myself."

"You mentioned biology, but their biology may be totally different than ours," Joshua pointed out, "so your algorithm could easily hit a dead end."

Vinod's smile grew even larger, demonstrating that he was clearly proud of his work. "That's the beauty of it. The algorithm may bypass biology altogether and take a different path. By the same token, it can account for different variables at any point during its progression. It can seek *alternate* biologies through a concept called modeling. It may model carbon-based life or jump to silicon-based biology, or at least a theoretical construct of it. Remember that information starts with output, or the sending of data. On the other end is input, or the assimilation of data. My particular algorithm is designed to accommodate how fast or slowly information is absorbed. If it hits a dead end, it simply tries a different route, sort of like a packet of data traversing the Internet. That's why the program is a combination of both deterministic and randomized algorithmic functions. It has a definite endpoint, which is language, but it's flexible enough to accommodate an almost infinite variety of variables along the way. It's this flexibility that allows it such an extraordinary ability to extrapolate information while not excluding its primary function of linguistic instruction."

"But language," Rachael said. "That's always been the part of your algorithm that's amazed me. Can you really teach these beings English?"

"Yes. The endpoint of my algorithm is always language. While it's running, variables continually point in the general direction of linguistics no matter what path it takes along the way."

Joshua scratched his head. "But language is so complex. In German, entire sentences equal a single noun in English. And think of the tens of thousands of characters in Chinese writing that express spoken language. Mathematics seems tame by comparison."

"You would think so, but it really isn't. If I know the basic elements of a language, such as the roots for various words, I can deduce etymology and vocabulary. If I add suffixes, prefixes, and possible combinations of word order, I can construct an entire syntax. And that, my friends, is language."

Joshua glanced at Rachael, as if seeking one final reassurance given the urgency and gravity of their need. Rachael nodded imperceptibly.

"So how long will it take for you to build an interface between our detector and your algorithm?" Joshua asked, feeling confident now that he'd heard the true potential of the algorithm and how it worked.

"I need to see what I'm connecting with. I take it that you have a Bowman sphere in the case."

"Yup," Joshua replied as he opened the case, took out the detector, and placed it on the table. "Actually, you'll need to connect to the detector, or interface module as we sometimes call it. The detector was specifically designed to interact with the sphere and the spookyon within it and allow for an interface with a computer."

Vinod whistled lowly. "Pretty cool gadget. Reminds me of an old VHF receiver for a TV."

"It's the second time today I've gotten that one," Joshua said. "It has a standard interface since it's designed to talk to the computers in my lab."

"What's the interface?" Vinod asked.

"Thunderbolt 3," Joshua replied.

"Lit," Vinod remarked. "Guess we don't have to worry about bandwidth."

The sound of "In-A-Gadda-Da-Vida" emanated from six wall-mounted speakers. The volume was cranked up to an almost deafening level.

"Layla!" Vinod shouted over the music. "Turn off music. Sorry, guys. I programmed the music to start before you called."

The music ceased immediately.

"Layla?" Rachael asked. "What happened to Alexa?"

Vinod pointed to a small black cylinder on the edge of his desk, its top glowing with a ring of orange light. "I modified Alexa. She was too slow and couldn't understand all of my voice commands, so I built my own version. Hey, did you know that the organist for Iron Butterfly was so drunk when he wrote that song that when his band mate asked him what the title was, he could only answer in slurred speech? The title was originally 'In the Garden of Eden,' but the words came out as 'In-A-Gadda-Da-Vida.' Cool trivia, huh?"

"Very interesting, Vinod," Rachael answered sarcastically. She was used to Vinod's ramblings about classic rock but really didn't have the patience for them now. "So, how long will it take for you to build the interface?"

Vinod dropped to one knee and closely inspected the module, ports, and LED lights. "What's the transmission protocol?" he asked. "That's the starting point for anything I do."

"It's half-duplex transmission," Joshua replied. "The entanglement of two spookyons allows for two-way communication, but only one particle can communicate at a time." Joshua gave the same explanation of spookyon spin detection to Vinod that he'd presented to Rachael earlier.

"Okay then, we need a workaround to tie into my algorithm, and that's certainly in my wheelhouse. I'm also going to have to rewrite the low-level IO drivers to accommodate Thunderbolt 3, but if this module can interface with your own computers, then I don't foresee any problems in using mine as long as some modifications are made. I'm guessing three hours to get the interface written."

A look of frustration crossed Joshua's face as he lowered his head and passed his hand across his scalp. "That's too long. Did you ever watch *Star Trek*?"

"Original series or *Next Generation*?"

"Original. Kirk always asked Scotty to cut the time in half since the *Enterprise* was usually in imminent danger. Can you shave some time off that estimate?"

Vinod crossed his arms and looked from the module to Joshua. "Give me two hours, but I'm going to need to work alone—no offense. Just me and the computers—and some music, of course. Also, I'm going to need your detector here with me."

"Alright, guess that'll have to do," Joshua said as he closed the case with the sphere still inside. He turned to Rachael. "Since Vinod wants some privacy, we have a couple of hours to kill. You hungry? Maybe we can grab some dinner."

"Sure," Rachael replied. "Vinod, do you have a recommendation for some place to eat close by?"

"There's a pretty good steakhouse about a mile from here." Vinod was already sitting at his desk, lines of code scrolling up the screen at what appeared to be superhuman speed.

"Um, I'm a vegetarian," Joshua announced.

"There's an Italian place two blocks from the steakhouse," Vinod said, his eyes remaining riveted to the screen as his fingers played across the keyboard. "Angelino's."

Rachael took out her phone and started looking up Angelino's. "You know you're in California when the Hindu guy suggests steak while the Christian guy is a vegetarian."

"Actually, I'm Jewish," Joshua corrected.

"I've mapped it," Rachael said, her index finger passing across the screen of her phone. "Twelve minutes away. Want anything Vinod?"

"Nah. I'm good. I need some mood music. Layla, play 'Come Sail Away' by Styx."

"That's our cue to leave," Rachael replied as music once again flowed from the several speakers placed around the room.

Joshua grabbed the case with the sphere, and the two headed for the front door. Outside, it was dark as the Prius backed out of the driveway. It was still raining.

Chapter Thirteen
Vinod's Theorem

Vinod remained seated at his desk after Joshua and Rachael left for Angelino's. At SETI, as well as the startup where he was now employed, he'd received the nickname King of Multitasking. His fertile mind always seemed to work on multiple projects at once, and his colleagues had concluded that it was his total immersion in information theory that accounted for his ability to mentally perform numerous tasks simultaneously without sacrificing the quality of what he termed his "mind mechanics." He claimed that the brain was the ultimate information machine, not that it wouldn't be improved upon one day with chip implants—interfacing the cerebral cortex directly with various digital devices—that had been in beta testing since 2006 with various tech companies in Silicon Valley.

Currently, as classic rock music filled his study, he was engrossed in writing code and thinking about the import of what Rachael and Joshua had told him moments earlier. Even while his fingers moved over the keyboard like a prodigy sitting at a Steinway, his lips mouthed the lyrics of each song that played.

Information was his bread and butter, but he'd had an abiding passion for astronomy since his youth—yet another reason why he'd formed a close friendship with Rachael so quickly after their happenstance meeting on the Berkeley campus—but his interest in the stars had been supplanted by how humans might be able to send messages across vast interstellar distances. Surely there was intelligent life seeded throughout the two trillion galaxies of the observable universe, and he regarded it as axiomatic that one day two alien races would want or need to talk to one another. Indeed, Vinod often dreamed of the treasure trove of information that could be downloaded from the databases of other civilizations, creating the fabled *Encyclopedia Galactica* described by science fiction writers for more than a century. He wanted to go much farther than SETI's goal of simply locating intelligence orbiting distant stars, and his personal motto in high school and college had been "Why go to a party if you didn't want to mingle, make new friends, and collect a few phone numbers?" Talking to ET was the ultimate mixer.

Earlier that evening, Rachael and Joshua had made an extraordinary contact, the kind he'd dreamed of for years when gazing into the night sky. His mind was reeling as to who was controlling the other entangled spookyon: where were they, what did they look like, how advanced were they, and, of course, did they have music? Music composition, after all, was based on mathematical constructs. If the aliens could boogie, what did *their* music sound like? And how amazing was it that the task of talking to sentient beings far distant from the shores of the blue and white marble called Earth had fallen to him? Amazing, he thought, but it was not totally unexpected that the opportunity had landed on his doorstep.

He'd written computer programs based on the premise that information of any kind automatically flowed in a direction where it could be accessed and acted upon in a meaningful way. Jung had termed the concept synchronicity, but Vinod had never read about a philosophical or psychological concept that he couldn't quantify, however obtuse his interpretation might look. He called the concept of meaningful information flow Vinod's Theorem, and it was based on the principle that all information was inherently intelligent regardless of the form it took. Critics had ridiculed him—not that he cared—by saying that it was dressed-up chaos theory, but they were dead wrong. His theorem was that all purposeful information was, by definition, intelligent, and therefore the opposite of intelligence was randomness—data that had no purpose. For this reason, he'd formed a corollary to his theorem: artificial intelligence was a *fait accompli*. In the end, the source of the intelligence, artificial or not, didn't matter. Sooner or later, information would start to combine and interact, and man would wake up one day to discover that his clever little digital devices, not so meek, had inherited the Earth. Most astronomers believed that contact with extraterrestrials would be with machine intelligence, not biological organisms.

As far as he was concerned, the existence of entangled spookyons totally validated his theorem. At least one kind of subatomic particle could communicate in a highly sophisticated manner, and if that wasn't proof of a naturally-occurring information network, then Ronnie Van Zant of Lynyrd Skynyrd hadn't written "Free Bird."

Communicating with extraterrestrials was way beyond cool. Hell, it was beyond comprehension itself, and yet here he was, about to interface his algorithm if all went well with a spookyon that would shatter mankind's beliefs about physics and life in the universe. As icing on the cake, it would corroborate years of his own research into information theory and prove beyond any reasonable doubt that communication was embedded in the fabric of the universe as intricately as a thread woven into a Medieval tapestry.

His sound system moved on to "Layla" by Derek and the Dominos. Layla was programmed to play its namesake at least once every four hours because . . . well, for obvious reasons to anyone who knew him. As lines of code appeared on his three computer screens, he pushed back his rolling desk chair and glanced at a bookshelf in the corner where a picture of *his* Derek had been placed in a silver frame. He still missed his cherished boyfriend, and the pain of losing him to a hang-gliding accident two years earlier was still palpable. One year younger than Vinod, Derek had had an upper-class British accent even though he'd grown up in Liverpool. They had met at SETI, where the two had made a bet as to when the first signal from intelligent life would be received from deep space. Derek had predicted that the signal would come on the narrow-width hydrogen band within ten years. Vinod hadn't bought into such an optimistic scenario, claiming that a conventional radio signal would *never* arrive since any extraterrestrial civilization would likely have advanced far beyond radio transmission technology soon after their atomic and digital ages, assuming they survived what mankind was now wrestling with: real estate wars that threatened to destroy the entire planet with nuclear weapons. If they were wise enough to master their technology, they would almost certainly have other ways of transmitting information that were infinitely more sophisticated than using radio telescopes.

Vinod and Derek decided that the winner of the bet would pay for a week-long vacation to the Bahamas. Vinod hadn't intended to wait the full ten years to see who won the wager, of course. He'd made hotel reservations and bought airline tickets to Nassau a few days before Derek's hang-gliding accident.

"It would have been a great getaway, dude," Vinod said wistfully while gazing at the photograph. "Sorry. I meant to say *Sir* Derek." The appellation had been used to tease his significant other about what Vinod regarded as his affectatious manner of speech even though he knew it was genuine since his parents were from London. "And I wish you were here for what might be my crowning achievement. You see, Rach brought this guy over who—" Vinod paused, choking back sentiment. "Never mind. Tell ya later. I'm on a deadline. But just between you and me, I would've won the bet."

Believing that no signal was forthcoming, Vinod had resigned from SETI, and as much as he'd respected his colleagues, it had been the right choice, for he could now devote his energy full-time to information theory and all of its various applications. The code that he was most partial to was the one his friends wanted to run that very night, an algorithm that would progress from mathematical constants to the ability, via language, to learn not just that aliens existed, but to discover their cultural identity, an aspiration that the astronomers at SETI dared not dream of. His heart was beating so fast that he got up, went to the kitchen, and grabbed a cold bottle of Dos Equis.

"I'm the most interesting man in the world," he said, twisting off the cap and taking a large swig, head tilted back, before returning to his study. "When aliens want to talk to someone on Earth, they speak *me*, Vinod Bhakti. You'll have to get over it, Zuckerberg. Your platform isn't the only one people use to network."

Vinod glanced at the screen as data continued to stream, waiting for the compiler to finish compiling his latest code.

As he drank his beer, his thoughts drifted to the young man Rachael had brought to his inner sanctum. Joshua Andrews seemed an affable enough young man, he thought. But Rachael was always so absorbed in her work that he wondered if she noticed how Joshua looked at her—and how often. Probably so since nothing escaped the scrutiny of one of the rising stars at *Scientific American*. She could have made far more money, he laughed, as a private investigator since her powers of observation and perception were unrivalled. She absorbed information almost as fast as the Bradley Cooper character in *Limitless*. If she ever married, heaven help the guy if he ran around on her since she'd discern it in a heartbeat—assuming he, Vinod, didn't kill the man first.

Vinod wanted to know more about the good doctor since he was very protective of Rachael, who he regarded as a little sister. After a five-year friendship, the depth of which he'd never experienced, he'd do anything for her. The task at hand was proof. She'd shown up at the door with an outrageous story and a man in tow who carried a glass sphere that he claimed had communicated with someone or something at an unknown location in the universe. It was something that he would expect to hear on Art Bell's late-night radio program *Dark Matter*, a cult broadcast for insomniacs, eccentrics, and lonely truck drivers who'd seen lights in the sky.

If Joshua would have shown up alone, Vinod would have slammed the door in his face. But if Rachael vouched for him, that was good enough for him.

It was back to work as Vinod instructed Layla to play *Long Distance Voyager* by the Moody Blues. It seemed entirely appropriate, both because of the album title and one of its tracks: "Veteran Cosmic Rocker." That was him, wasn't it?

He'd been hurriedly writing lines of code basic to any interface program, the kind of protocols necessary for a computer to connect to almost any external piece of hardware—screen, printer, keyboard, disk drives—the whole array of devices that could conceivably be called upon to receive communication from a conventional computer. Shooting a quick look at the digital clock on his screen, he saw forty minutes had passed, and he knew he would need to write more code specific to the detector, and quickly. But first he would have to connect the detector to his computer.

"Ya know," Vinod said with frustration, "the doc there could have told me how to hook this damn thing up before he went drooling out the door behind Rachael. Typical academic."

He inspected the detector and found the Thunderbolt 3 interface cable. There was no power cable connection on the detector, so he figured that the device must be bus-powered. "This thing looks expensive, so I hope I don't fry it," Vinod said aloud as he connected the cable to his computer. The LEDs on the detector cycled once through red, yellow, blue, and green and then went dark. *Must have run a boot-up self-check* he thought. Vinod checked the Thunderbolt bus on his computer and saw that a new device had been detected. The vendor name listed was BPRC – UCB and the device name was listed as PARTICLE SPIN DETECTOR. *Yup, that's the right device. Now I need low-level access.*

The detector communicated at the bit level. It used the spin direction of a spookyon to represents bits. Vinod would need direct access to the detection and the locking of bits in the detector in order to interface with his algorithm. He pulled up a pinout diagram for Thunderbolt 3 from an Internet search on his computer. The diagram showed that there were four high speed transmit pins, along with four high speed receive pins. He started testing the transmit pins one by one. When he signaled the second transmit pin, the detector lit up blue. *Nice, Found one.* Signaling the fourth transmit pin caused the detector to light up yellow. *Okay, got the second one.*

Having found the transmission pins, he started polling the reception pins. Again, pins two and four seemed to be live. When he had polled these, the LEDs glowed red. He figured that they were glowing red since there was no sphere in the detector, but if the sphere was in place, he could read data off of these pins. Now that he had low-level access to the detector, he needed to code a more efficient communication mode.

Vinod took a long sip of the Dos Equis and then exclaimed, "I need to teach these guys about packets."

The aliens were using timing of the spin changes to communicate. Vinod realized that time would continue to be a factor in their transmission protocol, but he needed to make a significant change. Presently, transmission and reception were given equal time. Each party had a defined amount of time in which they could send and receive information. Vinod knew that he needed to change this. His algorithm was created to teach the other party English, not to learn their language so therefore more data needed to be sent rather than being received. The easiest way to accomplish this was to use packets, small blocks of data with additional information at the beginning called headers, which indicated how many bits were in the packet.

Vinod decided that he would start by sending test packets of varying numbers of bits. The bits themselves would be sent at one bit for each time interval. The packets would only contain zeros except the first eight bits of the packet, which would be the packet header. The header was a number in binary that represented the total number of bits in the packet. *These beings must be intelligent enough to figure out this highly simplified packet structure.* He would continue to send the varying length packets until he got a response back in the same format. At this point, he would know that the aliens had understood his packet protocol.

Once the packet protocol was established, he would start shortening the time interval needed for each bit transmission in the packet in order to increase bandwidth. *I wonder how short I can make the time interval? What's the ultimate bandwidth of spookyons?* Finally, he would start increasing the size of the packet header such that the total length of the packet could be enlarged. With an eight-bit header, packets could be only 255 bits long. *Bits. Why bits? Surely I should be able to teach them about bytes.* He modified his code so that the number sent in the header represented the number of bits sent divided by eight, and he also made sure that the number of bits sent was always a multiple of eight. *There—now they should know about bytes.*

"Sometimes I simply amaze myself—not!" he exclaimed after he finished writing the packet protocol. "Now then, the final step is to interface the detector's low-level code with my algorithm."

After a few minutes, he seemed satisfied. "Okay. I think it's going to work. Vinod's Theorem rides again! Maybe."

The sphere was another piece of the puzzle altogether. The detector seemed to like his style of programming, but would the spookyon or the metal cap on top of the glass that held it? He noticed that there were nodes inside the circular band on the detector that obviously represented connection points to the sphere that fit snugly into the black rim. Hopefully, the sphere was synced perfectly with the detector—and why wouldn't it be? Vinod settled back and looked at his watch.

"One hour and forty-seven minutes. Engineering to bridge. Warp drive is online, captain. Wanna talk with some Vulcans . . . or will they be more like Klingons? Now that's unsettling." He finished his beer, placed the bottle on the table, and said, "Who the hell cares? They're extraterrestrials!"

He supposed Rachael and Joshua would be back soon. They were, after all, in a hurry to make a phone call.

Chapter Fourteen
Cairns

The rain had subsided to a steady drizzle when Rachael pulled into the small lot adjacent to Angelino's Italian Restaurant. Joshua carried the case with the sphere inside, which drew more than a few stares from the hostess and those waiting for a table, but he wasn't going to let a primordial particle created by the Big Bang—one with extraordinary capabilities—sit in an empty car while he ate dinner. Under normal circumstances, the sphere would have been confined to the Bowman Particle Research Center and protected by more than a few security protocols.

The restaurant was surprisingly busy given the constant rain inundating the area for two days, but Rachael and Joshua were shown to a table for two at the rear that afforded them some degree of privacy even though it was too close to the kitchen for Joshua's liking. There was, he claimed, too much foot traffic near the carrying case. The establishment nevertheless had more than its share of Old-World charm and atmosphere, unlike more modern Italian restaurants. The light was low, and the mandatory candles sat in small glass bowls on red tablecloths. The couple was given menus and glasses of red wine by Gianni, their waiter.

"Pretty nice place," Joshua remarked, glancing at the pictures on the walls. The renderings were rough but appealing sketches of St. Mark's Cathedral, the canals of Venice, the Vatican, the Leaning Tower of Pisa, and a stretch of the Amalfi Coast. "A bit stereotypical, though."

"Like I told you," Rachael said, "Vinod is a combination of old school and new. He's on the cutting edge of technology, but he likes vintage items. As you've already seen—and heard—he's passionate about classic rock, and he only collects vinyl albums. His taste in stores, clothes, restaurants, and the like is no different. I really like that about him. He doesn't blindly follow tradition. He's very much an individualist."

"Then I can see why the two of you get on so well," Joshua said as he nudged the case between his feet under the table, where he'd be able to feel it the entire time they were seated. "You're nothing if not an individualist."

"I'll take that as a compliment." Rachael casually surveyed her surroundings with a turn of her head. "A far cry from the bat cave and scientific instruments that, if the truth be told, are about as farfetched as anything I ever saw in a Batman film. Pretty nice place."

"This place is definitely retro, but I suppose we both needed a change in scenery and a chance to decompress for a while."

"Abbondanza," Rachael said, lifting her glass. "What shall we toast to?"

"I'd envisioned uncorking a bottle of champagne with my staff this evening after creating a pair of entangled spookyons, but that obviously didn't come to pass. I guess we have something far more significant to consider, however." He looked around guardedly at the surrounding tables, wary of those who might be able to overhear his remarks. "We just discovered alien life," he whispered. "How cool is that?"

"It's definitely been a wild ride for the past several hours," Rachael admitted.

"Say, why don't we raise a glass to Henry, without whom none of this would have come to pass?" Joshua suggested.

"To Henry," Rachael agreed. "God rest his soul."

"To Henry."

The pair touched glasses and sipped their chianti.

Joshua did a double-take. His eyes drifted to a small purple and red tattoo of a Byzantine cross on Rachael's right wrist. "So, are you a believer?" he asked.

"What do you mean?"

"I noticed the cross tattoo on your wrist."

Rachael lifted up her forearm and twisted it left and right so that the cross was more visible to both of them. "Not many people notice it."

"It's not just reporters who are observant," Joshua said. "You can't conduct good experiments without observing and recording data."

"Touché. And yes, I am indeed a believer. Does that surprise you?"

Joshua raised his eyebrows. "As a matter of fact, it does. I don't know many scientists—or science writers, for that matter—who are very religious these days. Quite the opposite, in fact."

"I suppose that's true. People like Sagan and Hawking were strict rationalists. So are Dawkins and deGrasse Tyson, and they speak for a large segment of the population."

Gianni—a thin young man with a black moustache—interrupted the conversation to take their orders. Rachael selected chicken cacciatore; Joshua chose pasta with marinara sauce.

"I assume then that you're *not* religious," Rachael said after their menus had been collected by Gianni.

"Not really. Disappointed?"

"People are who they are. I don't judge since that's in the instruction manual for believers."

Joshua, more relaxed than he'd been for the past two days, laughed at the allusion to the Bible.

"Speaking of religion," Rachael said, "how can someone with the last name of Andrews lay claim to being Jewish? There's got to be a story there somewhere."

"Not much of one, really. My dad was Christian—Protestant, to be exact, although he didn't attend church—and my mother was Jewish. She took her faith quite seriously, so my parents agreed to raise me Jewish. I was bar mitzvahed and everything, but I'm non-practicing. My mother is a fabulous person, and I respect her beliefs, but the Hebrew lessons with our rabbi were like a vaccination that didn't take."

"Then you're an atheist?" Rachael asked.

Joshua thought about the question as he watched the hostess seat a nearby couple while waiters and waitresses passed, large platters of food balanced on their upraised palms. In the background was the clanking sound of cutlery and glasses.

"Hmm. More of an agnostic, I'd say. As a scientist, I need proof of whatever lies beyond the here and now, assuming there *is* anything."

Rachael took a sip of wine, leaned forward, and clasped her hands on the table. "Agnostic? That's such a total copout."

Joshua was taken aback by the candor of his dinner companion despite his growing familiarity with her outspoken manner. "Really now. Why?"

Rachael looked at Joshua's soft brown eyes—they were very alluring—as she explained her statement. "Because atheists are firm in their belief that there's no God. Believers absolutely believe in God. Agnostics, on the other hand, sit on the fence, not wanting to make a decision either way."

"What's wrong with a little uncertainty?" Joshua asked.

"Personally, I think there's enough information out there to make an informed decision."

"You do get straight to the point as always," Joshua proclaimed with a grin. "So what about *you*?"

"Me? What *about* me?" Rachael picked up a breadstick from the brown basket on the table, snapped it in half, and took a bite while waiting for a reply.

"Yes, you—and that information you speak of. Do you believe that God created the world in seven days and all the rest of it—Noah's ark and Moses on Mount Sinai carrying around two giant stone tablets? And let's not forget Adam and Eve, who allegedly started the entire human race from only two sets of genes. Surely you don't believe that all of those things can possibly be true."

Rachael rolled her eyes. "No, I don't believe all those things are true—at least not literally. That's fundamentalism. Contemporary theologians believe that the Old Testament is genre fiction that was composed to teach lessons to the Hebrews of the time. More to the point, I definitely believe in science and evolution—and the Big Bang. Like Aquinas said, there has to be a first cause. Nevertheless, I don't believe that religion and science have to be mutually exclusive. I view God as an architect, not a magician with a magic wand."

Carrying their food slightly above his shoulder, Gianni appeared twenty minutes later and placed their orders on the table with a reminder that the plates might be hot. "Enjoy," he said.

"Vegetarian, huh?" Rachael commented.

"Yup."

"Sorry. I should have consulted you before ordering. You don't mind my eating chicken, do you?"

"Not at all. Like Gianni advised, enjoy your meal. I was raised in a mixed family. Plenty of tolerance. I'm a real mensch."

"Just out of curiosity, why are you a vegetarian?" Rachael asked. "Nothing in either Christianity or Judaism prescribes a meatless diet."

Joshua twirled his pasta with a fork expertly as he answered. "When I was eleven, I decided that I never wanted to eat anything that had a brain when it was alive. I guess it was the budding scientist in me. I'd been studying biology, and while cows and other animals that humans eat may not be able to solve the quadratic equation, they're still conscious of their environment. Some even display emotions. Dogs especially. They can sense the feelings of their owners."

"Consciousness? Emotion? Intuition? You're perilously close to invoking a religious concept," Rachael warned with humor, "but okay, I get it."

"So, let's get back to this creator thing," Joshua said. "It intrigues me. *Why* do you believe in God? I myself need tangible evidence. I just can't accept any kind of religious belief on blind faith. I think I gave the rabbi several nervous breakdowns with my unending questions. I need proof! It's mother's milk to a scientist."

"There's a great deal of proof, Josh. You just have to be willing to look for it."

Taking another sip of wine, Joshua looked directly at Rachael as he spoke. "It's a Catch-22. What constitutes proof? For believers, proof is so damn arbitrary and subjective, which means it may not be proof at all."

Rachael couldn't suppress a smile. "Remember, I'm as big an advocate of the scientific method as you, but proof is built on hypothesis."

"I've learned that many times over in the course of the past two days. And may I add that you'd make a formidable debater. In fact, we're having a robust debate right now."

"We're having a relaxing dinner with stimulating conversation," Rachael said, wrinkling her mouth in a good-natured frown. "Nothing more."

"Gimme a break. You were on the debating team in college, right?" Joshua asked.

"The captain," Rachael replied. "Now you were saying?"

With each passing hour, Joshua was learning that the knowledgeable reporter from *Scientific American*—a woman who didn't take no for an answer—was totally disarming. Her charm was mesmerizing.

"I was saying that I want to know why you believe in God. What proof do you have of his existence?"

"Like I said, there is proof of a creator if you're willing to look for it," Rachael replied, "but many scientists simply dismiss the *evidence* of a creator because they discount the *idea* of a creator."

"Not sure if I'm following."

"Let me explain by example." Rachael put down her fork and spoke directly to Joshua. "Have you ever been hiking in the woods and seen a tower made of rocks by the side of the trail?"

"Sure," Joshua replied, "people sometimes put those there to mark the trail. I believe they're called cairns."

"Yes, cairns," Rachael replied. "When you see a cairn on a trail, do you ask yourself what natural process could have caused the rocks to be stacked liked that or do you think someone must have put them there on purpose?"

"Obviously, someone put them there," Joshua replied.

"Why?"

"Because, it's too complex and ordered a structure to have happened randomly by chance."

"Exactly!" Rachael exclaimed happy to have gotten her point across. "I believe that there are cairns in nature that are too complex to be randomly formed by chance. They must have been created by someone, a creator."

"Really?" Joshua asked. "Like what?"

Rachael picked up her fork and made a three-word reply as she placed a bite of chicken in her mouth. "Like the cell."

"What?" Joshua was caught off guard by the brevity of the response. "Did you say cell—as in cells that make up biological organisms?"

"Exactly. Everything from amoebas to whales are made of cells. In fact, I have no problem whatsoever with evolution progressing from the first cell all the way to humans and their complex brains. Natural selection is one of the most sophisticated mechanisms I can imagine for creating sentient beings, and it all started with the cell."

"Is everything satisfactory?" Gianni asked, approaching the table, hands behind his back.

"The food's amazing," Rachael said. "I could use another glass of wine, please."

Joshua held up his finger, seconding the request.

"So you believe in evolution," he said, "and yet it's a purely scientific process. Where's the hand of God in survival of the fittest?"

Rachael sliced a piece of chicken and speared it with her fork as she contemplated her response.

"Try this out," she said. "I'll concede that with reproduction and natural selection, you can have evolution that can progress over billions of years to a human. Darwin got it right, but you *must* have reproduction in the first place for evolution to work. This reproduction not only has to copy the physical properties of an item, but also the information contained in the item. The cell is the basic unit of reproduction upon which evolution on Earth is based."

Joshua knew Rachael well enough by now to know when she was toying with him. Her pause had been calculated to make sure that he was hanging on her every word.

"But where did the cell come from?" she continued. "Even simple cells are highly complex. They have a cell membrane to contain them and genetic material with enzymes to unzip and replicate DNA, not to mention all of the structures needed for protein synthesis. They are highly complex entities. Did they just self-assemble from random organic molecules? Hardly. To me they are like cairns. They're too complex to have just randomly formed from natural forces."

Joshua put his knife and fork down while he contemplated what Rachael was saying. She was definitely making a rational argument. "You're perfectly aware that the cell, with both reproduction and genetic material self-organizing from organic molecules, is accepted scientific theory, right?"

Rachael sipped from her second glass of wine and held up the palm of her left hand. "Wait a second doc. History is littered with accepted scientific theories that were later proven wrong. You're saying that if you mix a soup of organic molecules in a glass and stir them up like Julia Child making a vinaigrette, you're going to randomly cook up a cell? That's some pretty amazing scientific cuisine. No one has ever been able to do it with science, and yet life has been around for almost four billion years. Again, *you* have no problem seeing a tower of rocks and deducing that some intelligence put them there, but you have an issue with something *much* more complex than a bunch of rocks, like the cell, and saying that intelligence didn't create it? It magically self-arranged itself randomly? Now who's the believer in magic forces here? Me or you?"

"You're oversimplifying matters, Rachael! You need the right atmosphere, temperature, chemistry, and a catalyst, such as a lightning strike. Early Earth was a violent planet with fierce storms."

Rachael dabbed the corner of her mouth with her napkin. "But you're just proving my point. You just added a number of complex variables to the equation for creating a cell—for life itself. The lightning bolt comes, and Dr. Frankenstein suddenly cries, 'It's alive!' Mary Shelley wrote a great novel, but it's long on suspense and short on believability. You're going through a lot of mental masturbation and conjuring up a lot of specific pre-conditions to try to justify the natural existence of cells while ignoring the possibility that the cell had a creator."

Rachael continued after taking a bite of her meal. "Let me ask you something. If during your presentation with the Martian rover, you had moved the rover and discovered some cairns on Mars, then what? Would you be looking for a natural cause, or would you be thinking there must have been some intelligence that created them?"

Joshua thought about the question for a moment. "That's a tough question," he finally replied. "Not sure what I'd think."

"That's my point exactly," Rachael said. "On Earth, you assume cairns are created by humans because you believe in the existence of humans on Earth, but on Mars you're not sure because you don't want to believe in alien intelligence. Pure science should not depend on pre-conceived notions or beliefs. I think that most scientists have a preconceived notion that there is no creator, so they ignore the potential evidence of one. In fact, did you know that after Edwin Hubble discovered the expansion of the universe, and after the Big Bang theory was proposed, many scientists rejected the theory outright because, to them, it smacked too much of creationism?"

Joshua wondered how to reply to the quick-witted woman sitting across from him. She could verbally parry and thrust with the best of them. "I did know about the initial resistance to the Big Bang theory, and I'll concede that a number of variables were needed to start evolution on Earth, but maybe chaos theory could account for how they combined. Random conditions produce non-random results. That was one of your best articles, by the way. I loved it."

Rachael was thoroughly enjoying the discussion. She disagreed with Joshua, but there was something compelling about his passion and enthusiasm. She'd interviewed countless other scientists, but never one so young and so sure of himself. He had a rare combination of confidence and playfulness. He also appreciated her wry humor and directness, which some men found threatening.

"Chaos theory?" she said. "It *almost* explains your point of view, but not quite. Even chaos theory dictates that there be some form of programming to initial conditions—conditions not unlike your random set of variables required for life. There needs to be some catalyst."

"And your catalyst is God?"

"Maybe, but let's return to the Big Bang for a moment. Where did the initial singularity come from? Where is the first cause, the programmer?"

Joshua appeared frustrated, and the look on his face was a gentle *Come on, you can't really be saying that.* "As you well know, the laws of physics don't apply inside of black holes, singularities, event horizons—or before the Big Bang."

"My point exactly, which is why I was captain of the debate team."

They both exploded in laughter as Joshua settled back in his chair and started drinking his second glass of wine. He was thoroughly enjoying the non-threatening give and take.

"Alright, I know where you're coming from," Joshua said, placing his napkin on the table, "but here's my point. What you're calling proof is conjecture. It's a . . . best guess in the absence of any concrete evidence."

"Au contraire," Rachael countered. "Why, just today we received more evidence of a creator, evidence that I find the most compelling yet."

Joshua looked perplexed. "Then I missed it. I'm clueless."

"Don't you find it awfully convenient that entangled spookyons were created by the Big Bang?"

"Amazing, perhaps, but convenient? No. Convenience is an emotional concept, not a scientific criterion."

Rachael smiled as if she'd just scored the crucial point in their discussion. "You asked me to bear with you several times while we were driving today. Now *you'll* have to bear with *me*. I'm going somewhere with this."

"I'm your captive audience. Hold forth."

"To begin with, we live in a universe that allows for intelligence to evolve. There may be many intelligent societies out there but each with a different level of intelligence."

Joshua nodded, "Okay."

"For the sake of argument, let's say that the aliens *are* more advanced than we are. Hawking himself claimed that they might not be so friendly. No little gray intergalactic beings zipping through the universe playing music as in *Close Encounters*. Maybe some are as mean and nasty as wolverines and live to conquer other races because their advanced technology gave them . . . oh, I don't know, delusions of grandeur from mastering their machines and the laws of nature. As the adage goes, absolute power corrupts absolutely. Is this science fiction? Maybe not. Time and again, science fiction has been an accurate predictor of the future."

"I'll stipulate that last point, but I'm still not seeing God in all this," Joshua said.

"If you were creating the universe, wouldn't you want to build a system in which intelligent beings could evolve to intelligence and then communicate with other intelligent beings without the fear and destruction that actual physical contact might entail?"

"You mean like a cosmic quarantine imposed by the enormous distances between stars?" Joshua asked.

"Exactly! So if you were to create the universe, you create it on the grandest of scales where nothing with mass or energy can travel faster than the speed of light. But information—that's different. From the moment of creation, you inject into the system an unbelievable communications network so that civilizations can speak to one another without fear of conquest."

"In other words, a communications network composed of entangled spookyons," Joshua said as he started to get the gist of Rachael's argument.

"It is, as the saying goes, a system elegant in its simplicity. Assuming that's what we've stumbled across, was this network a fluke, a random accident? No way. To me, it's another cairn, something too ordered and purposeful to be random. There has to be a programmer to assemble the random variables in just the right fashion. Otherwise—and I'll invoke a hallmark of science—entropy carries the day. Randomness. A total lack of organization."

Joshua looked away from the table momentarily and then back at Rachael. "I can neither prove nor disprove your hypothesis, Professor Miller, but I have to admit that it's compelling and well-constructed. It's quite interesting and certainly merits more thought."

"I guess we're two interesting people," Rachael said, raising her glass.

"I have to tell you, Rachael, that it's refreshing to have such stimulating, intellectual conversation for a change."

Rachael appeared puzzled. "Really? You have a brain trust back at the particle center. The cream of the intellectual crop. There have to be lots of people to have great discussions with."

"Yeah, but somehow I feel that they mostly just agree with whatever I propose. Maybe they're intimidated because I'm the director. The conversations are usually very one-sided and banal. But you, you're not intimidated at all which is refreshing. You also have some compelling opposing views which is also refreshing." Joshua looked up from his pasta. "Besides, no one at the lab certainly is as interesting to look at as you are."

"I do believe I've been paid a compliment," Rachael replied with a slight blush on her cheeks.

"Indeed you have. So tell me—did you win most of your debates?"

"Nah, I made that up. I was never on a debate team."

Joshua slapped his forehead with the palm of his hand. "You really had me going. Why on Earth did you tell me that?"

"Because it sounded awfully good and grabbed your attention. Reporters always have a few tricks up their sleeves."

They finished their meals and paid the bill. "I wonder what Vinod's up to," Rachael asked.

"Something good, I hope. The history of the human race may hinge on his algorithm. Let's find out." Joshua got up and retrieved the case.

"I hope that spookyon of yours has a call-waiting feature," Rachael said as she also got up from the table.

"Apparently *all* spookyons do. It's why we made contact. It's as if someone was waiting for our response."

"And maybe not by chance," Rachael added as she grabbed her purse and turned away before Joshua could reply.

They walked to the door, Joshua carrying the case and again drawing stares. He followed Rachael into the parking lot, blown away by their scintillating conversation. But this conversation would pale in comparison to the one they would soon be having.

Chapter Fifteen
Fat Pipe

Having finished his task earlier than expected, Vinod sat on one of the couches in his study while programming new music into Layla when the doorbell rang. He glanced at his smart phone since he'd installed a new security system that tied into his Android so that he could see who was at the door from anywhere in his home. Rachael and Joshua were right on time, so he pressed the keypad and spoke into the phone.

"Come on in guys. I'm in the study." He pressed another key to release the deadbolt.

Joshua had impressed him as a model of punctuality, and he hadn't been disappointed. There was obvious chemistry between the couple now proceeding down the hallway, but he thought that the particle physicist was a bit too uptight for Rachael. He'd always pictured her with a scientist, but one who was a rock climber or adventurist on the weekends—he and Rachael had been skydiving many times together—since she was an iconoclast and liked to push boundaries. Well, there was no accounting for taste—or the human heart.

"I thought you were racing against the clock," Joshua said, surprised to see Vinod studying classic album covers with his left leg draped over the arm of the couch.

"I was, but the clock lost. I finished the interface"—he looked at his wristwatch— "thirteen minutes ago. It appears to be successful."

"*Appears* to be?" Joshua said.

"Based on that barely legible piece of paper you left with me, I was able to create what I believe to be a stable link with the detector—assuming, that is, that the device's LED lights match what color the sphere is glowing."

"You actually managed to turn on the detector's lights?" Rachael asked.

"Hey, Rach, it's me—Vinod. Plus, I accessed information on the detector as well as its transmission and protocol pins thanks to some help from a Thunderbolt 3 pin-out diagram so that I'd know how to interface the algorithm."

"Hold on a minute," Joshua said, mildly alarmed. "You mean that you accessed the low-level detector firmware? I mean—" Joshua wasn't sure whether he should be pleasantly surprised or peeved that someone had violated his sensitive lab equipment. Had that really been necessary?

"Relax, dude. It wasn't that hard, and I was under the gun. I can't write an interface unless I know what the heck I'm interfacing with." He was on his second Dos Equis and lifted the bottle high in the air to drain the final ounce. "Don't worry. I don't think I did anything that could have fried your equipment or will cause the sphere to explode once it's in place. Looks like the detector's in good shape."

Fry? Explode? Joshua thought Vinod's speech to be too cavalier regardless of how much Rachael trusted him. Did he really understand the nature of what he and Rachael were attempting, or did he still think he was being punked and had been playing along?

"I was working on the assumption that if the detector can talk to my computer, and vice versa, then everything's cool. If they can't, then we can't dial in ET. I assume that the sphere and the detector are totally synced. Otherwise, my algorithm would hit serious configuration issues pretty fast."

"Josh, I think he's messing with you a little," Rachael said, elbowing the scientist. "He's a pretty savvy guy, and I'm sure the detector is okay." She shot Vinod an approving look tinged with the slightest hint of reprimand that only two close friends could interpret.

"The sphere and the detector are perfectly calibrated," Joshua assured the information theorist with a penchant for classic rock and disquieting informality.

Vinod got up, patted Joshua on the shoulder, and took a seat in front of the three monitors at the back of the room. Rachael and Joshua stood behind him looking at the monitors. "Rach's right. I tend to be informal, in case you haven't noticed. And I know the ramifications of this experiment, especially if we're successful. Let's put the sphere into the detector and light that sucker up. I'm ready to rock if you are."

Joshua gave Rachael another searching glance. *Are you sure this is safe?*

Rachael replied with a dismissive wave of her hand. "Time and tide. Let's do it."

Joshua opened the case and carefully installed the Bowman sphere in the circular band of the detector, clamping it in place and attaching wires from the detector to the metal cap on top of the glass. He double-checked the connections, took a cursory glance at the cables running from the detector to Vinod's computers, and stepped back. There was now a three-way hookup: sphere to detector to Vinod's computer that would run an algorithm that, if it performed as touted, was nothing less than a cyber version of the Rosetta Stone. "Okay, the sphere is installed onto the detector," he announced.

"Great," Vinod replied. "I'm going to power on the Thunderbolt 3 bus." Vinod typed some keys on his computer that caused the sphere to start glowing. "Pretty amazing," Vinod remarked as the sphere once again glowed blue and yellow over and over again. "And I'm not easy to impress when it comes to technology." He paused and looked at the black cylinder on the table.

In silence, the three figures watched the sphere in wonder as it repeated the same sequence and time intervals as before.

"Radically cool," Vinod said. "You really weren't kidding. A group of physicists from Princeton approached SETI back in 2017 about using quantum entanglement to communicate with aliens, but they weren't taken seriously. They were practically laughed out of the building. Anything else I should know before we start?"

Joshua shook his head nervously. "No."

"Okay then," Vinod continued. "Here's the game plan. The left screen will register the progress of the algorithm's function depending on how fast your distant friends can assimilate the data we'll send."

Vinod pointed to a horizontal timeline at the bottom of the monitor that ran the width of the screen, from ARITHMETIC CONSTANTS to SENTENCE STRUCTURE with multiple points in between marked by dots. A message at the top of the screen read PROGRESS: NOT INITIALIZED.

Vinod rubbed his hands together and lifted his hands above the keyboard like a pianist ready to play a concerto. The letters EXEC appeared on the screen as Vinod typed a brief command on the keyboard. "Is everybody ready?" he asked.

"Go for it," Joshua said, his tone steady and emotionless as he gazed at the monitor. Inwardly, he was more than a little anxious. A chill ran down his spine as he wondered what lay beyond the mathematical constants—if anything. He'd developed a certain level of confidence in Vinod—he was cautiously optimistic at this point—but the algorithm hadn't yet proven itself. If it worked, however, they were moments from changing history.

Rachael instinctively ran her hand over Joshua's back in a circle, whispering, "Calm down and let Vinod do his thing. The university would have taken months to decide to let you try this."

Vinod hit the RETURN key, starting the algorithm. All three waited, the breath suspended in their chests. Vinod was now all focus, all concentration as he awaited the results. He had high confidence in his algorithm, but he'd never expected it to undergo this kind of test. Indeed, it wasn't a dry run at all. This was a real-time application that had the potential to change how man viewed his place in the universe. If successful, the entire field of information theory might leap a hundred years into the future, not to mention the societal repercussions that might ripple across the globe. The lights of the sphere started flashing a faster pattern of yellow and blue.

The voice of Layla sounded unexpectedly. "It is time for movie *The Matrix*. Do you wish me to begin playback?"

"Layla, silence!" Vinod snapped.

Ten seconds passed, and nothing else seemed to be happening. No display on any of the monitors changed by so much as a single character.

"Is everything okay?" Joshua asked. "Shouldn't—"

"I think it's going through the packet protocol I developed," Vinod replied. "It wasn't part of my original algorithm, just something I did to speed up communication."

"Whoa, look at that," Vinod said, barely audible. "The sphere's blue-yellow sequence has accelerated considerably. The colors are changing faster and faster. If it ramps up even more, the sphere will be strobing like a disco joint from the seventies. Someone's in a hurry to communicate with you guys."

Rachael clasped her hands together chest-high. Joshua wondered if it were a mere gesture of anticipation or genuine prayer.

The sphere now started glowing green and was blinking at a slow steady rate.

"Jesus, It's green!" Joshua exclaimed.

"Sweet!" Vinod replied.

"They've established a bidirectional transmission protocol," Joshua remarked. He was becoming more impressed with Vinod's abilities by the second. "How did you this teach them about this Vinod?"

"I created a simple packet structure that de-emphasizes timing in the communication protocol," Vinod explained. "It looks like they get it. The bandwidth on this connection should significantly increase now."

A green arrow was now displayed on the timeline under ARITHMETIC CONSTANTS.

"So it's working?" Rachael asked.

"Oh, it's working alright. So far, so good. Right now they're working on the first step, arithmetic constants," Vinod said pointing to the green arrow on the monitor. "Theoretically, it could hit a snag at any of several junctures, but I think that depends on who we're talking with and not the algorithm itself."

"How long do you think this will take?" Joshua asked, trying to hide his impatience.

Vinod took a deep breath and exhaled. "That all depends. I originally designed the algorithm to function with radio waves. While I've always theorized that aliens would have progressed beyond radio transmissions—not a popular notion among some of the gurus at SETI—I had no idea what extraterrestrials might be using, so I was forced to make the algorithm compatible with existing technology that might be applied to talking with ET. That meant radio. I didn't think it likely that SETI would ever receive a radio signal, but I had to base my program on *something*."

"Then why design the algorithm at all?' Joshua asked. "Sounds like a waste of time given your doubts."

"Not entirely. SETI periodically runs simulations, programming computers to give them a false positive so they'll know how to proceed should they ever confirm that they have a bona fide signal. I was planning on testing this at their upstate headquarters in Mountain View when they had some down-time for maintenance."

"So how long?" Joshua repeated.

Vinod leaned back in his chair and scratched his head, eyes still focused on the timeline. "My original estimate based on beta testing with another computer was that it would take decades for the algorithm to run and be fully completed. It would, of course, depend on the distance to the star where aliens have been detected. If they aren't in the local neighborhood—let's say they're a hundred light years away—then the estimate is more like millennia even at the speed of light."

Joshua leaned forward, frustration etched on his features.

"Why didn't you tell me?" he asked. "I've been riding an adrenaline high for the past four hours, and now you're telling me that my great grandkids might see the results of what we're about to start?"

"Not to worry," Vinod said reassuringly. "Those estimates are based on light-speed communications. With instantaneous transmission via spookyons—not something I factored into this gem when I wrote it—the time will be drastically reduced. I estimate it should only take a few weeks. That's assuming that the aliens are at least as intelligent as we are, and they'd have to be if they're aware of quantum entanglement."

Joshua walked around the room anxiously before standing near the computers again. "Weeks? Seriously? Still too long. I'd need an entirely new grant from the university board to shift the focus of my research, and that could entail mountains of paperwork. I thought this was real-time transmission."

"It is," Vinod said, appearing somewhat annoyed, "How long did it take you to learn English? It didn't happen overnight, right? I can send aliens a linguistic database with relative ease, but how fast they learn it is completely out of my hands."

"Wait, guys," Rachael interjected. "We don't know anything about the aliens or how good they are at accepting and interpreting data. That's the big unknown here. We need to be patient and let the algorithm run its course. It's a little premature for predictions or expectations. We're in unknown territory."

"What *she* said," Vinod said.

"I know, I know," Joshua said with resignation. "It's just that the uncertainty and waiting is killing me."

"I totally get it," Vinod said. "You got thrown a pretty big curve ball this afternoon, and who the hell knows where the mound is."

The sound of a computerized *ding* came from speakers connected to Vinod's computer.

"I think it's a moot point, gentlemen," Rachael remarked with an almost flat affect. "Notice the progress bar."

The words PROGRESS: ARITHMETIC OPERATIONS were displayed, and the green arrow had progressed to the next dot. The lights on the storage devices in the server rack started blinking faster.

"Holy shit!" Vinod exclaimed. "They're already past the first milestone. Excellent!"

"Arithmetic operations?" Rachael noted. "As in addition, subtraction, and multiplication?"

"Basically," Vinod said, "although basic operations and logical operators can be a bit more advanced than that."

The sphere was blinking so rapidly that it was on the verge of displaying a solid color.

"What's with the sphere?" Rachael asked. "This is the fastest I've ever seen it cycle."

"Simulated full-duplex communication," Joshua explained. "The data flow is going back and forth at a tremendously high speed. Unbelievable."

"Believe it, dude," Vinod said. "These beings are putting on one hell of a show."

"This is far more incredible than anything we witnessed in the bat cave," Rachael observed. "And this certainly answers our concerns that they might sign off at some point if we didn't respond fast enough. It appears, just as we predicted at the restaurant, that they were waiting for us. Almost *eager* to re-establish contact. I don't know whether that's good or bad. Hard to interpret their intentions."

Another ding sounded.

"Look at the progress bar!" Vinod said, unable to suppress the widest of self-satisfied grins. "They're up to calculus already. These creatures go to school pretty fast. Even with instantaneous transmission, how can you jump from simple arithmetic to calculus in just sixty seconds? Even Einstein didn't learn that quickly. Who the hell is on the other end of this?"

Yet another ding was heard in the study, and a new progress report appeared on the screen.

"Check it out," Rachael said. "They've moved on to physics in pretty short order."

"Looks like they're ready to work their way through the natural sciences," Joshua said. "Vinod, the algorithm is working exactly as you predicted it would. Sorry for my caution, man. I never dreamed anything like this was possible even with spookyons. You've enabled us to take this kind of communication to the next level. When Rachael said you might be able to help, I never . . . well, I never imagined that you had something custom-made to solve our conundrum in the bat cave."

Mouth open as he stared at the screen, Vinod was too startled to reply. Another ding sounded from the computer, and the status now read PROGRESS: CHEMISTRY.

"Gotta be machine intelligence," he said at last. "*Has* to be. Only a machine could consume information this fast."

"Not necessarily," Joshua speculated. "Maybe their brains, or whatever organs they use to process information, are thousands of years—maybe millions—beyond the capabilities of the *human* brain. They may have organic neural networks that would make hard drives look primitive."

"Vinod, are you sure they're understanding all of this?" Rachael asked. "Maybe they're just downloading the information and are going to look at it later."

"Not possible," Vinod replied. "The algorithm is meant to be progressive in that it builds on the understanding of a previous segment to teach them the next segment. To ensure their understanding before the next segment is initiated, there are mini-tests built in, which must be passed before the algorithm progresses. They're definitely learning this material and at an incredible rate."

The sphere no longer flickered but was now a sold bright green as the data exchange continued to accelerate. The lights on the storage devices in the server racks were also on continuously, and cooling fans in the servers increased their speeds to handle the additional thermal load.

"Can the sphere handle this kind of speed?" Rachael asked.

"Absolutely," Joshua answered. "The spookyon is doing the heavy lifting and remember that it can be measured millions—if not billions—of times per second."

"Yeah, but they're sucking up information at a rate that nobody—not even an information theorist—could have predicted," Vinod pointed out. "What's the bandwidth of the sphere itself? Are you sure it can handle this load?"

"Don't really know the max," Joshua said tentatively. "Henry and I were limited by the nature of our equipment when we transmitted signals to the Martian Rover. Back then, the max bandwidth we achieved was about one terabit per second."

"Did you say *terabit?*" Vinod asked incredulously. "Damn! That's one fat pipe!"

"Fat pipe?" Rachael asked.

"It's slang for a high-speed communications network, which usually has one hell of a bandwidth," Vinod explained. "One terabit is pretty fat. And this? Who knows what the operational bandwidth might be given what we're seeing. I wouldn't believe any of this if I weren't sitting here watching it for myself."

A look of concern crossed Joshua's face as he looked from the computer screen to Vinod. "At one terabit, the sphere can definitely handle the bandwidth, but the data transfer might be limited by the drive speeds of your computers."

Vinod became defensive. "No way dude! These bad boys are all SSDs with a PCIe interface running RAID 10 storage. They can handle the data transfer rate."

"Are you two speaking a foreign language?" Rachael asked. "Or is this nerd-speak for mine is bigger than yours?"

Vinod clutched his chest and pulled out an imaginary dagger. "Rach, you *know* these are my babies. Show some mercy."

"I sometimes forget, papa," she said, touching his arm gently.

"Acronyms," Joshua explained. "It's about speed—flash disks, interfaces, disk striping, and the like. Anything to increase the amount of data and the rate at which it's transmitted. His babies, as he puts it, are thankfully fast. Screaming fast, in fact. I don't think that the algorithm could run on anything slower given the consumption rate."

A doubt suddenly popped into Joshua's mind that terrified him, something that he should have thought of before. "Vinod, please tell me that your computers are quarantined. They're not hacking the Internet or anything, are they?"

"Hacking? The Internet? Another insult!" Vinod replied, removing a second imaginary dagger from his chest. "My algorithm and computers don't need the Internet to work their mojo. Rest easy, doc. Both my computer and the storage devices are completely isolated. No external communications networks are involved." Vinod gave Joshua a thumbs-up.

After the next ding, the screen indicator showed PROGRESS: BIOLOGY. A new line of text appeared beneath the timeline: SUBCATEGORY: PROTEINS.

"Appears that they're going in a specific direction," Rachael said.
Ding.

"Very specific," Vinod reiterated. "Like I said earlier, the algorithm offers different pathways at almost every data point. And hey—look at the new subcategory. In a matter of seconds, they jumped to deoxyribonucleic acid. DNA, man. That's what I call looking at the details. If they're going into subcategories, it means we've piqued their curiosity bigtime."

"My God!" Joshua exclaimed. "They understand DNA? The double-helix?"

"If they can learn calculus, chemistry, and physics in such a short time, I don't see why not," Vinod replied.

"Then they know how a human being is made," Joshua stated. "A bit disconcerting."

Vinod laughed. "If they're *this* fast, who's to say they can't build one themselves?"

"And to think we were worried that this process might take too long," Rachael remarked. "They've condensed centuries and decades into minutes. But maybe we're giving away a little *too* much info."

Another ding sounded from the computer.

"Paydirt!" Vinod exclaimed. "It's a moot point, Rachael."

The onscreen indicators now read LANGUAGE and VOCABULARY respectively for category and subcategory.

"Damn and double damn!" Vinod said, unable to contain his emotion. "They made it all the way through to the final stage—language!"

Words rapidly appeared and disappeared at the very bottom of the screen until they changed so quickly that they were only a blur to the three figures huddled around the table.

"It was definitely English before the words became an unintelligible stream," Rachael said. "I'm positive. They now possess the lingua franca for communication if that's what they opt for."

"I don't believe what I'm seeing," Joshua said. "They're absorbing the entire English language in a matter of seconds. How is that even possible?"

Vinod seemed at a loss for words. At last he said, "I don't know, man. This is exactly what I programmed the algorithm to do—*exactly*—but this exceeds my expectations by several orders of magnitude. Maybe we're talking to alien computers." He paused as the thought suggested another possibility. "In fact, maybe the two sets of computers are working out a new algorithm of their own in order to communicate faster."

"Can they do that?" Rachael asked. "They're just computers!"

"Computers here on Earth talk to each other all the time," Vinod answered, "although not with this level of sophistication, so it wouldn't surprise me. They could be establishing a common language of their own. Who knows? We may get left out of the loop completely before this is over."

"Let's not jump to conclusions," Joshua warned. "Contact has been initiated, but there's been no conversation yet."

"That we know of," Rachael added with a cautionary note in her voice. "If it's machine intelligence on the other end, then maybe they've developed a simpatico that we can't detect."

Vinod, Joshua, and Rachael were getting apprehensive. What were they dealing with? A species that could absorb physics, chemistry, and biology in a matter of minutes? Rachael reached out and took Joshua's hand in hers. He turned to look at her as he squeezed, but her eyes were fixed on the screen, as if hypnotized by the constantly-changing text.

"I really do hope this is some kind of machine intelligence we're dealing with," Vinod said. "If any alien biology is capable of crunching data this fast, then it plain freaks me out. What's the analogy in all those sci-fi flicks we've watched over the years? They might be as far above us as we are above the ant."

Another ding caused Vinod to point to the screen with outstretched arm and index finger. He swallowed hard before speaking, as if he couldn't get the words out. "Look! They . . . they . . . made it to the final step."

The subcategory now read SENTENCE STRUCTURE.

There was one last ding.

The indicator arrow now pointed to PROCESS COMPLETED as the

drives to Vinod's computers stopped lighting up. The sphere was still glowing green, but not as brightly.

"Completed?" Joshua and Rachael said simultaneously.

"Whew!" Vinod said. "I thought we'd be here all night—maybe for a week on and off—but . . ." He had no words to finish his thought.

Joshua seemed to be in a daze. "Instantaneous communication—between stars, no less."

"Can we talk to them now?" Rachael asked.

An air of suspense—almost electric, like static electricity—filled the room, and no one answered for several seconds. It was Vinod who finally spoke.

"Theoretically, yes," he said. "I just need to open the com window."

Vinod pushed several keys, causing a black window to appear on the center screen, a blinking cursor waiting for words.

"Well?" Joshua said.

The screen remained black for an entire minute.

"C'mon!" Vinod urged. "C'mon!"

"Nothing," Rachael said. "Did they simply want to gain information about us with no intention of actually using it? Have they terminated the link? Maybe that's their gig—consuming information for a cosmic library. Perhaps we're totally insignificant to them. Maybe we really *are* just ants to them. A curiosity."

The screen remained an ominous black.

Vinod smacked his forehead with his palm as he thought of something he had forgotten. "Oops," he stated as he started typing on the keyboard. "I forgot to switch the source of the com window. I have it connected to the USB bus. I'm switching it to the Thunderbolt 3 bus—now."

At last, brief text appeared on the screen.

Rem: 'Sup? I'm Seth.

Chapter Sixteen
Live Stream

Joshua, Rachael, and Vinod took a moment to reflect about what was happening as they stared at the screen. There was no sophisticated message, no formal greeting, no dignified tone from the disembodied voice. The letters on the screen were from the English alphabet, but the abbreviation was unknown to Joshua or Rachael. They had made first contact with an alien intelligence, and yet someone or something was speaking to them using a spookyon—and with a most peculiar word, if that is indeed what it was. Eager to learn more about their collocutor, Rachael and Joshua grabbed two chairs and sat on either side of Vinod in front of the computer screen, shoulder to shoulder.

"What does 'sup' mean?" Rachael asked.

"Um . . ." Vinod began sheepishly, "I think it's short for what's up."

Joshua and Rachael glared at Vinod. "What dictionary did you send them?" Joshua asked.

"Webster's English Dictionary," Vinod replied hesitantly.

"And?" Rachael asked, knowing there was more to his answer than he was revealing since she could read his inflections instantly.

"The urban dictionary," he said with an innocent shrug.

"Nice job, Vinod!" Rachel said sarcastically. "First Neil Armstrong proclaims that we have one small step for man, one giant leap for mankind. Now, thanks to Vinod Bhakti, we have *sup* originating from alien intelligence. The history books may not treat you kindly."

"It seemed like a good idea at the time," Vinod said, ignoring the rebuff. "I mean, it's a spookyon, not the *2001* monolith."

Rachael turned her attention back to the screen. "What does REM mean on your display?" she asked.

"It's an abbreviation for remote," Vinod answered. "When we send information, the screen will display LOC, meaning local, but who the hell knows why he chose the handle Seth."

"What's done is done," Joshua said. "They're waiting for a response."

"What reply should we make?" Rachael asked.

"How about a simple greeting and our names," Joshua suggested. "Something simple, like you suggested earlier."

"Should I use 'sup' like he did, or just hello?" Vinod asked.

Irritated, Joshua glanced at Vinod. "How about you just say hello. Let's try to move this conversation a little more formal assuming your algorithm has the ability to go beyond the vernacular you sent."

"Your call," Vinod said as he typed. "And yes, they should be able to extrapolate variations on syntax. It's part of the program's learning feature."

Loc: Hello, Seth. There are three of us here. Joshua, Rachael, and Vinod.

Rachael and Joshua exchanged glances. Their names had just been transmitted across light years, although it was anybody's guess as to how far the actual distance might be since the concept of light years was irrelevant to quantum entanglement.

A reply was made immediately.

Rem: There are lots of us here. We're a collective, but you're speaking to Seth. I'm connected to the collective.

"A collective?" Joshua asked. "What the hell does *that* mean?"

"You're a Trekkie too, so think in terms of the Borg," Vinod offered. "If that's the case, let's hope that they're not mean, impersonal bastards waiting to assimilate the human race."

"I can't believe that Seth is his real name," Joshua said. "Is that something he came up with himself? You may have sent him the urban dictionary, but whoever we're talking to didn't grow up on the south side of Chicago."

"Only one way to find out," Vinod said, busily typing again.

Loc: Is Seth your actual name?

Rem: Naw, something I picked from the stuff you sent me. My real name's digital and wouldn't make much sense to you. We rap with each other digitally using the particles.

"Rap?" Joshua asked. "As in—"

"Yes, I think he means to communicate, as in he's *talking* to us," Rachael said as she glanced at Vinod. "Still using parts of the urban dictionary, I suppose."

"Thank God the *New York Times* isn't peering over our shoulders,"

Joshua said.

Rem: You got a name for the particles?

"No doubt he means the spookyons," Rachael surmised.

"Yeah, I didn't include the term spookyon with the science stuff I sent them," Vinod replied. "He gets straight to the point, but there's no secret on either end on how we're communicating. It's entanglement. Let's give him the nickname for the particle and see what he makes of it. It certainly wasn't in the urban dictionary."

Loc: We call them spookyons.

Rem: Spooky. Yeah, I'm down with it, though I don't know why you chose that word.

"Ask them when their spookyon was created," Joshua suggested. "No time for a history lesson on Einstein."

Loc: When was the spookyon that you are using to communicate with us created?

Rem: Its origin is primordial. Shortly after this universe began.

"My God," Rachael said in an excited voice. "It's like what we thought, Josh. There *were* spookyons created by the Big Bang. The universe has a built-in communications network!"

"He just confirmed what might have taken decades to prove," Joshua said.

The trio stared at the screen and tried to determine their next response. "Vinod, find out where they are. I want to know if they can tell us or not."

"Logical question," Vinod said," but I don't think they're going to say turn right at Orion. Let's give it a shot."

Loc: Where are you?

Rem: In your universe, but I can't be more specific. There's no common reference point between us. No way to tell you.

"I thought so," Joshua remarked. "They could be anywhere in the universe. By the same token, they have no way of knowing where *we* are, which means there's no way they could physically come here."

"That's a relief," Vinod replied. "No *Independence Day* scenario."

Joshua looked at Rachael, and they both recalled her theory of a creator making a universe in which communication was the norm rather than physical travel between the stars. He would have to give her musings more thought when he had time, but time was a luxury he might not have for a while.

"I want to know more about this collective Seth mentioned," Rachael remarked. "What's that about?"

"A collective is usually a group of individuals that are somehow connected," Vinod replied. "It refers to a hive mentality where individuality may or may not be present. For example, a beehive is a collective."

"Scary," Rachael said. "It's like science fiction."

"I'll try to scope out more details," Vinod said.

Loc: How large is your collective?

Rem: Over thirteen trillion individuals.

"Shit man! What the hell!" Vinod exclaimed. "Thirteen trillion. That's incredible!"

"Kind of scary, if you ask me," Rachael remarked feeling suddenly apprehensive. "Thank God they don't know where we are. Earth would be slightly outnumbered."

"I wonder," Joshua said, "if they're incredibly small. Standing five to six feet tall isn't a requirement for intelligence. Otherwise, they'd have a population crisis on their hands."

Loc: How does your collective work? How are you connected?

Rem: Each individual is connected via a spookyon to eight other individuals who in turn are connected to eight others. In this way, we're all connected. My thoughts flow to all of the individuals in the collective and theirs' to me, but I'm able to restrict this thought flow to myself or only other specific individuals if I want. Currently you are communicating to the entire collective. Any individual in the collective can restrict information flow or disconnect altogether, but only for limited periods of time.

"We got Seth to open up a little and give us some specifics," Joshua said. "This looks promising."

"Promising? Jesus man, they're using spookyons to speak to each other," Vinod said excitedly, "and we're live streaming to thirteen trillion of them from my study!"

"Not really surprising that they're using spookyons," Joshua replied, calmly assessing the situation, now very much the detached scientist. "As we've said all along, it's the fastest form of communication. No time lag. One thought or idea from one individual can instantly be transmitted across their whole collective." Joshua reflected for a moment. "This must also mean that they're able to create their own spookyon pairs to connect the individuals in their collective. Is it possible that they could have captured thirteen trillion primordial spookyons and their pairs? Seems unlikely."

"Who knows *what* they're capable of?" Vinod asked rhetorically. "They soaked up a lot of data very quickly."

"I think Seth was hinting that they can create their own spookyons when he labeled the one he's using to communicate with us as primordial, meaning created by the Big Bang," Rachael added. "They must have another way of describing spookyons that they created themselves."

As someone familiar with information theory, Vinod contemplated Seth's description of their collective. "The architecture of their collective is really remarkable. It's an amazing network if you think about it. Each individual is really a node that can inject information into the network but can also act as a *relay* on the network. And each node may be able to store information as well. Man, it's an unbelievably redundant and robust information distribution system. I wonder how Seth's connected to us. What's our interface to this collective?"

Loc: How are you communicating with us? What is your interface to the primordial spookyon?

Rem: Each individual in the collective also contains numerous other spookyons, primordial ones. We use them to send a carrier signal looking for other forms of intelligence. I'm lucky. My signal was found by you.

"There you go, bro," Vinod said. "Each one of these beings *does* have primordial spookyons." He looked up at Joshua. "They can harvest at least thirteen trillion spookyons created by the Big Bang as well as create their own. It suggests that they're a race of extraordinary capability. Master engineers perhaps."

"Vinod, Seth's showing some appreciation that we contacted him," Rachael said. "Let's reciprocate the gesture."

Joshua recalled Rachael's earlier reference to the affable Mr. Rogers and her suggestion that they exhibit a simple, nonthreatening gesture. He nodded his agreement.

Loc. We are also lucky to have made contact with you.

Rem: Thanks. Are you also a collective?

"Well, that's a tough one," Rachael remarked, pondering the question. Humans were definitely individuals, but with the advancements in communications, they were more and more becoming a collective, though not one with the sophistication of Seth's culture. "I guess we *are* kind of a collective. Even more so in the digital age. It's hard to stay off the grid unless you're a complete hermit."

Loc: Somewhat. We can communicate with other individuals and they to us, but this is not automatic. It's purposeful.

Rem: Purposeful. Does this mean that you can restrict the thought flow to certain members of your collective just as I can?

Loc: Precisely.

"It's good to know we have *something* in common," Joshua said with a laugh. "He's implied that they have at least some degree of individuality."

Rem: How many other individuals in your collective?

"Don't answer that!" Joshua exclaimed before Vinod started typing. "There's some information that I don't think we should divulge just yet. Revealing our social structure or our level of technological advancement could skew this conversation or, at the very least, produce a cosmic misunderstanding."

"I'm in total agreement," Rachael said. "It's our first date, so let's not rush the relationship."

"Okay," Vinod responded. "From now on, I'll type out a response but won't send it unless you two are cool with it. I've got an answer for our boy Seth, though," Vinod said as he typed away. "Short and ambiguous."

Loc: Numerous.

"Nice response, Vinod," Rachael said. "Ask Seth about life on other planets. It is, after all, what humans have been wondering since astronomy became a recognized science and the existence of planets was discovered by the Greeks and other ancient cultures."

Loc: Is there life on other planets besides yours?
Rem: Thousands more planets.

The trio stared in shock at the response on the screen. It consisted of only three words, but despite their brevity, they had completely displaced human understanding of mankind's place in the universe. Shocking as this information was at the moment, it would take months, if not years, for the implications of these words to sink in once the discovery of Seth's race was revealed, which was another matter altogether. Humanity would never be the same. They were not alone, but the trio's shock was interrupted by another message from Seth.

Rem: Is your collective all on one planet?

"Don't think we should answer that either," Joshua said, stepping back with a pensive look on his face.

"How about we answer their question with a question," Rachael suggested. "It's a standard ploy used by reporters."

Loc: Is your collective all on one planet?
Rem: No, thousands of planets.

"Shit!" Vinod exclaimed. "Is everyone else part of the collective besides us?"

"Didn't see *that* coming," Rachael said. "Space travel? Maybe truly advanced beings have mastered superluminal velocities if the collective has spread throughout whatever galaxy they inhabit. Maybe they've discovered physics that Einstein and mankind are unaware of. Or maybe they can travel through wormholes."

"Like an Einstein-Rosen bridge," Vinod chimed in.

"Not necessarily," Joshua said. "Recall your own theory, Rachael, of a cosmic quarantine built into creation. Perhaps these thousands of other worlds are only connected via spookyons."

"I never envisioned a network that large," Rachael said, "but I suppose it's only limited by the number of primordial spookyons, which may be almost unlimited in quantity."

Loc: Are all of the planets with life part of your collective?
Rem: No.
Loc: How many planets with life are part of your collective?
Rem: Can't tell you that. That information is redacted.

"Well, I guess there's some stuff Seth doesn't want to tell us either," Joshua said. "They can play it close to the vest too."

Another question arrived from Seth, one that was more personal in nature.

Rem: How many other individuals know about this conversation?
Loc: No others yet.
Rem: Have you made contact with life beyond your planet before?
Loc: No. You are our first.
Rem: Wow! Really? I'm honored to be your first contact. So happy to meet you!

"Very polite," Rachael remarked feeling a little more at ease. "But you two inadvertently revealed a lot about us by admitting that we've never made contact with anyone else outside of our solar system. Makes it sound like we're the new kids on the block—and maybe we are. That may hold some significance for them, be it for good or ill."

"Yeah," Joshua agreed. "We did let the cat out of the bag. But he seems to show emotion as well, so maybe he's just being friendly and is sincere in his response. He's almost human-like. Vinod, ask Seth how they know about DNA."

Loc: How do you understand deoxyribonucleic acid?
Rem: We are made of cells that use DNA. All organic life we know of is made from DNA or a derivative. I'm assuming that you are the same?

"Wow!" Rachael exclaimed. "They're made out of cells like us! And he said *all* life. He just answered the question posed by a few million scientists and biologists."

"Man, thousands of planets with life, and they're all based on DNA," Vinod remarked. "How's that possible? Given the size of the universe, I would have bet money that at least some intelligent life was based on other chemical elements and biological structures that we couldn't begin to fathom."

"A case of parallel evolution," Joshua remarked. "Many scientists think that all life must be carbon-based because of its unique bonding properties. It's really the only element that can form the complex molecules needed for life, like nucleic acids, which make up DNA. Since that's the likely scenario everywhere, I think it's safe to answer his query."

Loc: Yes, we are DNA-based.
Rem: Have you achieved self-determination?

"What the hell does *that* mean?" asked Vinod.

"It's both vague and philosophical," Rachael interjected.

"I don't know *what* it means," Joshua replied. "Are we still talking about DNA? Let's see if we can get him to narrow his question a bit."

Loc: Do not understand what you mean by self-determination.
Rem: Can you reorder your DNA sequence to change your physical properties?

"You've got to be shitting me," Vinod said. "What do I tell him?"

"The truth," Joshua said. "I think we need to press him on this issue."

Loc: No. Can you?
Rem: Yes.

"What the hell, man?" Vinod remarked. "They freakin' code their own DNA? That's some heavy shit!"

"Remarkable," Joshua commented under his breath. "Seth said that each individual in their collective contains many spookyons. If they can code their DNA and control cellular structure, their interface with these spookyons may be biologic in nature."

"Josh, what're you saying?" Rachael asked. "You think they have some biologic structures inside of themselves—maybe their very cells—capable of interfacing with spookyons?"

"I think so," Joshua replied. "Their technology might be biologically-based, especially if they can manipulate DNA sequences and create whatever biologic structures they want."

"Sounds like these beings are millions of years ahead of us," Rachael said.

Giving Rachael a somber look, Joshua turned to Vinod. "Try to find out more about their other technologies."

Loc: Besides self-determination, what other technologies do you possess?
Rem: Many more.

Loc: Like what?

Rem: Also redacted. We have strict rules not to divulge technology that you do not already possess. Doing so could destabilize your society and lead to its destruction. Destroying other sentient societies is strictly against our ethical rules.

"Whew, that's good to know," Vinod remarked. "Seth ain't out to destroy us. It's like the prime directive on Star Trek. No interference in the development of other cultures."

Loc: Understood.

Joshua felt uneasy. "Guys, I think we should end this conversation here. We're getting pretty deep, and I think we should consult some other people on exactly how to respond further. They don't know where we are, which is a big relief, but maybe we shouldn't keep playing twenty questions with him—or them."

"Agreed," Rachael said. "Small steps are in order."

Loc: We have to end this conversation now. We will contact you sometime later.

Rem: No problem. I'll wait for you. Peace out.

Joshua unplugged the detector from the computer, and the sphere stopped glowing.

"Holy shit, man," Vinod remarked. "That was some heavy stuff. Can't believe it! We just had a chat session with a freakin' alien! Maybe the early Internet and Instant Messages weren't so weird and archaic after all."

"What's our next step?" Rachael asked.

"I suppose we need to report this to someone," Joshua replied thoughtfully. We can't sit on this kind of information for very long. Plus he said he'll be waiting for us."

"Yeah, but who do we tell?" Vinod asked.

"I have no idea," Rachael answered. "My brain is fried right now. Too much stuff to process."

"I agree," Joshua said as he stood up and started disconnecting and packing the sphere and detector. "I think we should sleep on it and come at this fresh in the morning."

Vinod looked mildly shocked. "Sleep? Who can sleep after this?" he asked as he got up from his chair. "No, no, no. We just talked to aliens, man. Aliens! We made first contact and my algorithm worked! If that's not a reason to celebrate, I don't know what is."

"What're you talking about Vinod?" Rachael asked as she also got up from her chair. "This isn't *Animal House*. We can't even *begin* to take in what just happened. It's a sobering moment."

"Sober? Wrong! Man, it's Friday night and there's a classic rock band playing at the Rock Candy. I'm going, and you two are coming with me. We need to clear our heads."

"Clear our heads or *numb* our heads?" Rachael asked.

"Both," Vinod replied. "We'll kill two birds with one stone. We can sleep after a little self-administered anesthesia."

Rachael thought for a moment and turned to Joshua. "Not much more we're going to do tonight. I'm game if you are."

Joshua stared back and forth between Vinod and Rachael, who waited for a response. "Sure, why not? I think we could all use a break, plus I'm too wired to sleep anyway. I'd toss and turn all night, wondering about what happens next. I'll call the security team from the lab to pick up the sphere and take it back to the facility. But nobody's allowed to speak a word of this to anyone until we figure out what to do next. Okay?"

"Deal." Vinod stood up and gave the others a high-five. "Oh, it's on baby! It's on!"

Chapter Seventeen
Oh, What a Night

A team from the particle center retrieved the carrying case with the Bowman sphere, and although Joshua was reluctant to let it out of his sight, he knew that Vinod and Rachael were right: he needed a break, and the sphere and detector would be in good hands and protected by numerous safety measures at the center. He'd been hesitant to take it to Angelino's and toting it to the Rock Candy Dance Club was out of the question.

Rachael called an Uber since the words "party" and "numb" had been used together after their conversation with Seth had left them reeling. Joshua sat in front, Rachael in the back with Vinod who was moving his head front to back in time to the music like a mechanized bobble-head after he'd convinced the driver to tune the vehicle's radio to a classic rock station. He seemed particularly enthusiastic when David Bowie's "Space Oddity" came on.

"Major Tom," he said. "Now that's a name! Much cooler than Seth. I've been thinking that I need to upload rock's greatest hits for the collective. I'm sure they'd really dig it. It says a lot about the twentieth century as well as human culture in general."

"I won't argue the point," Rachael said, "but it's not going to happen. He chose Seth, and Seth he will remain. As for giving them classic rock, it might cause more confusion than enlightenment. What would they make of a title like 'Grow Some Funk of Your Own'?"

"I call it a meaningful cultural exchange," Vinod said with wry humor, "but whatever."

"Collective? Rock music? Are you guys modern-day hippies?" the driver asked. "Do you belong to a commune?"

"Uh, yeah," Joshua replied. "Trying to get off the grid. It's a modern

Woodstock thing."

The answer seemed to satisfy the driver, who asked no further questions.

Twenty minutes later, the trio were deposited in front of a three-story brick warehouse that had been converted to the Rock Candy Dance Club. Outside, the name of the establishment was written in bright script neon letters, orange and red, slanted at a forty-five-degree angle. The rain had finally stopped, but the streets were still wet.

"That's a really long line," Joshua said, eyeing patrons who were in a queue that extended to the end of the block and around the corner. "We won't get inside until after three, and that means the sun will be up when we leave. Remember that tomorrow we need to—"

"You worry too much, doc," Vinod said as he grabbed Rachael's hand and pulled her past the long line of people, many of whom looked resentful at the brashness of the young man and his friends. "I frequent this watering hole a lot, and I have a connection or two. The club has great music, by the way. Live bands *and* a DJ—a friend of mine—and that never hurts when one wants to . . . gain an advantage."

At the front of the line, a young man with blond hair pulled into a long ponytail motioned to Vinod and the others with a jerk of his head that they could go in—to the chagrin of those next in line.

"Thanks, dude," Vinod said, slipping the man a hundred-dollar bill as their hands brushed in a loose handshake. "Who's playing tonight?"

"New female band. Hearts of Glass. Not bad."

"Party!" Vinod cried as they entered. "We're getting bottle service tonight, and Joshua, my friend, you are definitely buying."

"Me? But this was *your* idea, and—"

Joshua's voice was quickly drowned out by loud music—a DJ was playing "Rubber Band Man" by the Spinners—and the ambient noise of the club, which was packed with dancers and people laughing, talking, and mingling.

The wooden support beams of the warehouse were covered with mirrors and panels of geometrically-shaped lights. The walls were black, although certain sections were covered by large rectangular light panels with amorphous, slowly-changing shapes, like fluids of different viscosity mixing together. Small spotlights on the ceiling were trained on the crowd but changed colors and were re-aimed every few minutes by a man standing next to the DJ in a loft on the right.

A hostess, a young woman with pink hair and a miniskirt—and obviously a friend of Vinod—escorted the party of three to a table in front of a padded U-shaped booth.

"Gray Goose and shot glasses, Star," Vinod said, "and keep 'em coming. Start us off with three beers to get us warmed up."

The music faded as Hearts of Glass took the stage, strapped on their guitars, and broke into their signature number, which was "Crushed by Your Love."

"Place has a nice vibe," Joshua said in a loud voice so as to be heard over the mounting decibels. "Nice call, Vinod."

Rachael shot him a look, surprised that he could have an opinion one way or the other about a night club. "How would *you* know? You're the mad, spooky scientist locked away in his lab day and night."

"I do have a life, you know. If you recall, I ride a Harley. All work and no play makes Josh a dull boy."

"The man has potential as a first-rate party animal after all, Rach," Vinod said with an approving look. "It's like my grandmother used to say." Sitting up straight and adopting a serious demeanor, he spoke with an Indian accent. "Beta, you must mark special occasions with a celebration. Rituals do not always need to be somber."

"Somehow I don't think that a night club with bottle service and loud music is what your grandmother had in mind," Rachael said.

"Obviously you've never met my grandmother."

As the evening wore on, they downed shots of vodka, and Vinod grew more talkative by the minute.

"Livin' the dream!" Vinod exclaimed, spreading his arms across the top of the booth. "Does it get any better than this? And to think we talked with Seth! Man, we have to go with the flow on that. No turning back. I'd like to download information from all thirteen trillion members of the collective. Might need more drives in my rack," he said with a laugh, "but think of what we'd learn. Maybe they've figured out the big picture."

"Speaking of going with the flow," Joshua said, "what do you guys think should be our next step?"

"I still don't know," Rachael replied. "I thought we were here to clear out heads so we could make a decision in the morning. Do we really have to talk shop?"

"I have the perfect idea," Vinod said, clearly buzzed as he took out his phone. "I'm gonna tweet this bad boy out right here and now. Why wait?"

Like a monster's claw from a horror movie, Rachael's hand grabbed the phone from Vinod and held it in front of her face.

"Hey, what're you—"

"No way you're going to share this with—" Rachael glanced quickly at the screen of her friend's phone. ". . . all seven of your followers." She deftly wedged the phone in a slim side compartment of her purse.

"But that's my phone!"

"Please keep that thing away from him," Joshua pleaded. "We had a deal that everything that happened would stay among us until we decided what to do next."

One of the spotlights played across the booth, turning from white to blue in the process.

"It's the mother ship," Vinod said, seeming to have forgotten that his cell phone had been confiscated. "I feel like I'm going to float right into the sky, just like those people at the end of *Cocoon*."

"Yeah, we had a deal," Rachael said, turning to Joshua, "before Vinod here took flight with Gray Goose."

"You're officially grounded, free bird," Joshua said.

"Oh, c'mon, guys. I'll behave. You don't think I'd really tweet this, do you?"

"You would in a heartbeat after enough shots," Rachael said.

"Okay, I'll get sherious."

Rachael shook her head at the slurred word. "Hey, how about we tell the people at SETI? They must have protocols for an event like this."

"I'm sure they do," Joshua said after their hostess brought them a new bottle and fresh glasses. "Their first protocol is to get verification of a signal and then call the media. For them, it's that simple. I think we have to be a lot more cautious. Besides, some of them are flaky. A bit sketch, if you know what I mean."

Taking another shot, Vinod looked at Joshua, his eyes out of focus. "Hey, those guys at SETI are awesome. They're my bros. They do cutting-edge science on a shoestring bucket—budget. Whatever. You know what I mean."

Joshua shook his head. "Not gonna happen. SETI is a private nonprofit organization. I'm thinking something more official." He leaned over to be heard above the music, which was now a song by Hearts of Glass called "Main Street Psycho." He took a shot and looked from Vinod to Rachael. "I have a contact at NASA—top man. We became friends when they started using the spookyon Henry created to control the Martian Rover. I think he'd be really open to what we've accomplished and would know what higher-ups we should contact."

"NASA?" Vinod said, his voice raised. Suddenly, he seemed more alert. "No way! They're government man! You can't trust the feds, dude. It's like getting in bed with the devil. They'll take the spookyon, sphere, and detector, and we'll never talk with Seth again. Look how they behaved after Henry Bowman died. The spookyon on Mars was suddenly *their* property. Bad move."

Vinod burped before anyone could respond as he put one hand on the table and began to leverage himself from the cushioned backrest. "Gotta take a leak, but definitely eighty-six the entire government idea."

He staggered away like any drunk in a bar doing his level best to walk in a regular fashion but failing. Several people slapped the palm of his hand as he passed their tables, and shouts of "Vinod!" erupted. He downed more shots as he paused briefly to chat with friends along the way.

The entire club turned red thanks to the man standing next to the DJ. The band was performing the last song of its set, "Shades of Sunset."

"Vinod is seriously trashed," Joshua observed.

"I can't deny that he likes to party," Rachael admitted. "Works hard, plays hard. It's his personal creed."

"If he clears his mind any more than he's already done, he's going to wipe it clean, like a data purge on a PC's hard drive."

Rachael, who was surprisingly lucid after her shots, just laughed. "Nah, he'll be alright. He's a great guy. As you've seen, he's smart as a whip. One of the most creative people I've ever seen even when it comes to having a good time. Tonight? Maybe a little *too* creative."

"You speak of him affectionately," Joshua said. "Were the two of you ever . . . you know?"

"Me and Vinod? Heaven's no. He's more like a big brother to me. He's the one who gave me the final nudge to become a science writer. I was undeclared when I met him. He told me that according to some postulate in information theory, combining writing with science would work synergistically."

Joshua nodded, now understanding why Rachael was able to finish Vinod's sentence when he was talking about his indoctrination into the appreciation of all things related to classic rock.

"He said it had to do with the quantification of the interaction between two variables," Rachael explained.

"In your case, that meant science and writing."

"Right. My gut was already telling me to do it, but Vinod has a way of reducing most things to some kind of equation or theorem, and the whole synergy thing made sense. If I had a dollar for every time he used the word quantification, I'd be rich. He can be quite convincing . . . when he's not totally hammered or immersed in his music. Besides, I think Vinod would be more interested in you than me for a romantic encounter."

Joshua nodded, indicating that the meaning of her message was received.

The DJ was back in control as the band put down their guitars and left the elevated stage to take a break between sets. The first song up was Journey's "Don't Stop Believin'."

Rachael, looking ecstatic, threw her arms into the air and cried, "I positively *love* this song. Come on! Let's dance!"

Joshua crossed his hands back and forth in front of each other, signaling no. "I don't dance. Ever."

"I insist," Rachael said, getting to her feet.

"My dancing is not a pretty sight. I'd embarrass us both."

"Nonsense. Nobody's watching us. Even if they were, the constantly-changing light patterns level the playing field. *Everybody* looks good. Geek out and have some fun."

Joshua reluctantly rose to his feet as Rachael tugged on his left wrist and pulled him onto the dance floor with such force that he slid the last two feet of the way. They were in the center of the floor, and Rachael's hips started to sway as her hands and feet moved rhythmically to the music. Joshua awkwardly shuffled around on his feet, jostled by nearby dancers. Spotlights played across the floor, illuminating the faces of Joshua and Rachael every few seconds.

Rachael was into the song, lip-syncing the lyrics with feeling, her eyes half-closed, her head moving back and forth, causing her silky brown hair to swing in an arc that Joshua found quite sensual. Her hand held an invisible microphone which she held to her mouth as she sang the first verse.

Joshua knew the song, and in an effort to deflect attention from his dancing, he picked up where Rachael had left off. He, too, held an invisible microphone to his mouth as he sang the next verse. Joshua played air guitar for the middle riff, the forefinger and thumb of his right hand pressed together as if holding a pick and matching the down-strokes of the song's beat. His face was scrunched into a snarl as if he were a lead guitarist feeling the music.

The awkwardness for Joshua had worn off, and he and Rachael were now doing the same moves as they lip-synced together.

Rachael leaned close to Joshua as the song faded so as to be heard. "I thought you couldn't dance."

"I can't. I'm simply ricocheting off the people around me. Random movement, but I can lip sync with the best of 'em."

Rachael found the answer hilarious and was inspired even more both by the spirit of the music and the enthusiasm of her dance partner.

"No," she said. "You're Batman, and you've been holding out on me, Bruce Wayne."

They continued dancing, moving closer to one another as the song segued into "December 1963" by the Four Seasons.

Rachael resumed lip syncing as Joshua played air piano for the iconic chords of the intro. She sang the first verse.

As before, Joshua picked up the next verse.

As the song changed to "I Melt with You" by Modern English, the pair danced still closer and with less movement, each maintaining eye contact with the other as their proximity became more important than the music. If Vinod had been observing, he would have commented that information of the most intimate nature was definitely being exchanged between the two.

As Joshua grew more uninhibited with each passing second, Rachael saw a man who was a tolerably good dancer—and getting better with each move—although she wondered if he was drawing inspiration from the music, the liquor, or her. Then it dawned on her. He was singing specifically to *her*. He seemed oblivious to everyone else despite the throng pressing on all sides. It was hard to believe that this was the same serious-minded researcher who had tried to shoo her away a day and a half earlier.

Only Joshua was now lip syncing, totally infatuated with his dance partner. He continued singing to her as if they were alone on the dance floor. He had lost all of his inhibitions.

Rachael looked at Joshua, who stared back. Her head swayed left and right, and her feet barely moved as their faces were inches apart. A spotlight from above found them and paused for a few seconds, but they didn't notice that they were being highlighted or that the crowd was applauding them. Joshua leaned forward and kissed Rachael deeply as the light moved to a different couple. As the kiss ended, Rachael simply stared into Joshua's face who stared back at her with a slight smile.

The song over, Joshua led Rachael back to the table, her hand in his.

"Wow. What a day!" she proclaimed, out of breath.

"Oh, what a night," Joshua retorted without missing a beat.

"You catch on mighty fast."

He gave her a glancing kiss, and she smiled without averting her gaze from the surprising young scientist. The evening had taken a pleasant turn, one that was not in the least unwelcome.

Rachael's trance-like mood was broken as she looked around and noticed that they were alone in the booth. "Oh, my God! Where's Vinod? We've been dancing for a while, and he should have been back by now."

"Who knows?" Joshua replied. "He marches to the beat of a different drummer, and it's a big club. Maybe he's making the rounds. He seems to know a lot of people here."

"But it's not like him to just wander off, especially in the shape he's in."

Rolling his eyes, Joshua slowly got to his feet. "I better check on him. Maybe he's worshipping the porcelain god." He took a credit card out of his wallet and handed it to Rachael. "Can you close out the tab?"

*   *   *

The restroom was clean and bright, and white tiles of different shapes and sizes lined the walls. It was as upscale as the rest of the club.

"Vinod?" Joshua called, his voice an echo in a space large enough to accommodate numerous patrons.

An attendant dressed in black shirt, slacks, and tie cleared his throat. "I believe the gentleman you're looking for is in the first stall," he said, pointing to his left with surprising decorum and lack of emotion.

"Vinod!" Joshua exclaimed as he opened the white stall door. "What the hell happened to you, as if I can't guess? You're absolutely shitfaced."

Vinod was sitting on the toilet, fully dressed. His upper torso was slumped over, head resting in his hands.

"We gotta get you home, man. You're in seriously bad shape."

Vinod looked up at Joshua with a half-smile on his face. "All of science and English in . . . just a few . . . minutes. It's nothing short of in . . . edible."

"Yeah, yeah, I know."

With great effort, Joshua picked up Vinod's body, which lurched forward against his own, knocking him back

"This isn't going to be easy," Joshua muttered.

"Do you need help, sir?" the attendant asked.

"No, thanks."

Joshua draped Vinod's left arm over his shoulder. "One step at a time, okay?"

"Instantaneous commiseration," Vinod stammered.

"Not far from wrong," Joshua said. The attendant opened the door as the two men exited the restroom.

"Not a pretty sight," Rachael said when she saw her friends approaching.

"The party is officially over," Joshua remarked.

"The tab is closed. I'll call an Uber."

Rachael placed herself on the other side of Vinod to help guide her very inebriated friend to the door.

In the Uber, Joshua sat in front, Vinod slumped onto Rachael's lap in the back. She repeatedly nudged him into a sitting position, urging him to "Keep it together for a few more minutes and you'll be home."

Vinod didn't seem to hear the voice of his friend. "Aliens, man," he repeated again and again. "We talked with freakin' aliens."

The driver, a man of Indian origin, looked in the rearview mirror briefly, his curiosity piqued.

"What is he saying?" he asked with a thick Indian accent.

"Uh, nothing," Rachael replied. "As you can see, the guy's wasted, and earlier in the evening we were talking about our favorite movies. His favorite film is *Aliens*."

"Oh, I thought he said he'd been *speaking* to aliens," the driver countered.

"Yeah, well, he's seen the movie so many times that he recites the dialogue, complete with commentary."

Joshua glanced at Rachael, appreciative of her quick response.

"Oh, *Aliens*," said the driver. "I know that one." He turned to Joshua and said, "Hey, Vasquez, have you ever been mistaken for a man?"

Joshua replied without hesitation. "No, have you?"

The driver gave Joshua a high five.

I'm surrounded by nerds, Rachael thought to herself.

At Vinod's house, Rachael and Joshua tugged on Vinod's tall body until he was braced between them and standing unsteadily on the sidewalk as the Uber drove away.

"Where's his bedroom?" Joshua asked after they entered through the front door.

"Must be upstairs."

Joshua groaned as he looked at the climb ahead of them.

Getting Vinod up the staircase proved far more difficult than merely moving him horizontally, which had been hard enough. They counted "One, two, *three!*" with each step in order to coax Vinod upstairs. Finally, they reached the bedroom, which, not surprisingly, was plastered with more posters of classic rock bands. The star man from the band Rush was displayed on a poster above the headboard.

"That's certainly appropriate," Joshua said as he glanced at the poster and deposited the limp body onto the queen-size bed as gently as possible.

As Joshua tried to get Vinod's body into a supine position, Rachael got a trashcan from the bathroom and placed it next to the bed. "At some point during the night, he's going to need this." She then pulled Vinod's cell phone from her purse and set it on the nightstand.

"Let's go," Joshua said. "This is more intense than a workout at the gym."

"Let's roll him on his side so he doesn't choke when the time comes," Rachael advised.

Vinod briefly opened his eyes. "Thanks, guys. Wow. Aliens."

He then fell asleep.

Outside, after Rachael locked the front door, Joshua said, "That was a lot of work. I think the combination of the night air and lugging Vinod around has sobered me up—somewhat."

"Somewhat being the operative word," Rachael said.

"Hey, I'm sharp as a tack."

"Famous last words."

"No, the famous last words tonight are that Vinod may be a brilliant information theorist, but he's one sloppy drunk."

"Don't forget that the sloppy drunk wrote an algorithm that enabled us to talk with Seth. No Vinod, no first contact."

"You continue to get the last word in. But hey, you happen to be right. We owe him a lot."

"And soon the world will too depending on what we decide to do about our long distance chat with Seth."

They both stood next to each other awkwardly.

"Well, I guess this is goodnight," Joshua said, looking at the sidewalk, hands in his pockets.

Rachael lowered her head and put her hands on her hips. "How far away do you live?"

"Huh? Oh, my house is maybe forty-five minutes away. In Berkeley."

"Aren't you forgetting something?"

"Nope."

"Are you sure?"

Joshua reflected a moment before saying, "Damn! My Harley's back at the lab. Can you gimme a lift to the lab so I can ride home? Or I can take an Uber back to the lab if you're too tired."

Rachael shook her head. "No way, Mr. Sharp As A Tack. You may not be falling-down drunk like Vinod, but you're still pretty buzzed."

"And you're not?"

"I took it a lot easier on the Gray Goose than you guys. Or maybe it's my Irish ancestry. I've been told I have a hollow wooden leg. My condo is only a few minutes away, so get in. You're not riding your Harley anywhere tonight. You can crash at my place."

Joshua grinned. "Well . . . if you insist."

He got into the passenger seat, although it took him a full minute to fasten his seatbelt because he couldn't find the latch receptacle between the seat and the console in the center of the Prius.

The car pulled out of the driveway and headed down the street until its taillights disappeared in the darkness.

Chapter Eighteen
No More Words

Arriving at her condo, Rachael killed the motor and got out of the driver's side as Joshua stood next to the vehicle, waiting for the woman he'd so passionately kissed at the club. She pressed her key, causing the car's lights to flash as the door was locked, and he followed her along the curving walk to the front door and into the hallway, where she took a left and veered into the kitchen.

"Make yourself at home," she said. "Be back in a sec."

Joshua was tired and needed to lie down, so he searched for a couch in Rachael's home. He headed down the hallway and saw an office littered with stacks of legal pads, digital recorders, flash drives, Post-It notes, and science magazines. A PC screen and laptop sat on her desk which was flanked by a small table holding a printer. Enlarged and framed was a selfie she'd obviously taken with Neil deGrasse Tyson, director of the Hayden Planetarium.

"Wow," he said to himself. "Busy lady."

He then turned right and saw two couches in the living room, one longer than the other. On the end table between the couches he saw a framed picture of Rachael and Vinod, which he picked up to examine more closely. They were standing on the campus of Berkeley with the Campanile in the background. Rachael had on a Cal tee shirt, and Vinod wore a Pink Floyd *The Wall* tee shirt. *Does this guy wear anything else but rock tee shirts?* He replaced the picture and picked up another. It was a photograph of a young boy and girl with their arms around each other, smiling widely at the camera. The kids were not more than ten years old, and Joshua recognized the girl as a very young Rachael but had no idea who the boy was.

Next to the pictures was a Bluetooth speaker. Joshua pushed the pairing button on the device and paired it to his phone. He lay down on the couch and browsed the music library on his phone.

Meanwhile, Rachael dropped her keys and the day's mail on the kitchen countertop before opening the refrigerator door and taking out a carton of orange juice. Pouring a tall glass and taking a long sip, she thought she'd never tasted anything sweeter in her life. She realized that the alcohol had left her dehydrated.

"Hey, Josh!" she called. "Want some juice? Water? Anything?"

There was no reply.

"Josh?"

She walked into her spare bedroom, which she used as an office. She preferred order and neatness, but she'd never been able to tame the clutter since she was always working on multiple articles at any given time.

"Josh?"

She walked down the hall, stopped, and saw Joshua lying on her couch. She thought his unshaven face was rugged and appealing in the muted light of the single floor lamp of the room.

"I'm beat," he said. "I guess I really did have more to drink than I thought. You were right. I couldn't have handled the Harley tonight. Thanks for looking out for me."

Rachael sat on the smaller couch and stared at Joshua blankly. Myriad thoughts coursed through her mind—spookyons, aliens, dancing, and the kiss that she and Joshua had shared on the dance floor.

"Anything the matter?" Joshua asked.

"Just reflecting," Rachael answered.

"This is definitely a day I'll never forget."

"Me neither," Rachael replied. She saw that Joshua was just a little too tall to fit on the couch. "You don't look very comfortable."

"It's fine. I'll be okay."

That was not entirely the response she had hoped for. "Okay," she sighed. "Let me get you a blanket and pillow."

Joshua stared at her as she walked to the bedroom. He selected a song from his music library on his phone, "You'll Accompany Me" from Bob Seger, and started playing it. A minute later, Rachael emerged from her bedroom empty-handed.

"No spare blankets?" Joshua asked.

Rachael didn't say a word. Instead she grasped Joshua's hand and led him to her bedroom. The music wafted to the bedroom from the living room. Joshua sat down on the bed and smiled as Rachael sat next to him, slipped her arm around his waist, and lay her head on his shoulder. He was about to speak when she silenced him by putting her index finger vertically across his lips.

"How did you know that I love this song?" she asked.

"I didn't. Just how I'm feeling at the moment."

"You *are* a romantic, aren't you Dr. Andrews?"

"Only with the right person." Joshua appeared reflective as he stared into Rachael's eyes. "We did have a real moment at the club, didn't we? I mean, that wasn't my imagination, was it? It wasn't just the Gray Goose and the music, right?"

"No, it wasn't the Gray Goose or the music. It was spooky action at *no* distance," Rachael answered, poking her index finger at his chest. She repeated the phrase more slowly, playfully jabbing him to punctuate each word. "Spooky . . . action . . . at . . . no . . . distance."

"So we're entangled?"

"Not yet, but the night's not over."

Joshua pulled her body close, kissed her cheeks, and then her lips as they reclined and began to make out. After several minutes, the song finished, and Joshua ceased his amorous activity and sat up to better see the woman he was in bed with. He used spread fingers as a comb to straighten his tousled hair.

"You're incredible," he said. "I've never met anyone like you."

"Come on, Josh," she said, catching her breath and brushing hair from her eyes. "You can do better than that. I've heard better dialogue on a soap opera while waiting in a doctor's office."

"I forgot," Joshua said with a small eye roll. "You're a writer."

"That's right, and you just interrupted an intense scene we were collaborating on."

A serious look replaced the smile on his face as he traced her lips lightly with his index finger. "You're beautiful, intelligent, and self-confident." He spoke the words quietly but seriously. "I find that to be a combination very hard to resist."

"That's a little better." Rachael closed her eyes as Joshua stroked her hair. "And you don't have to resist."

Joshua slid his arm behind Rachael's neck and pulled her to his lips. They fell into each other's arms. A few minutes later, the lights were dimmed, and no more words were spoken.

Chapter Nineteen
Black SUVs

Joshua awoke the next morning to an empty bed as he took a few moments to get his bearings. Propping himself on his elbows, he squinted because of the light seeping through levered blinds and looked at the side of the bed where Rachael had fallen asleep a few hours earlier. He touched the pillow and smiled, reflecting on how the lyrics of a few songs had moved them from friends to lovers in a matter of hours.

He heard the shower running in Rachael's bathroom, a sound both pleasing and intimate. He glanced at the clock on the nightstand, which read 7:50 a.m., and reclined again, his hands laced behind his head. He usually rose at five to jog and get to the lab early. Listening to the running water, he thought of entering the bathroom, but reconsidered since he wasn't sure where their relationship was headed. The chemistry between him and Rachael had developed quickly—*some things move faster than the speed of light*, he thought—although it had felt natural and unforced. Still, he didn't want to be presumptuous. Instead, he got up and dressed, his mind still brain-fogged from downing shots at the Rock Candy. He'd been more than a little buzzed at the club, and it occurred to him that if *he* felt this groggy, then Vinod must be all but comatose.

"Gotta get some coffee," he said aloud to himself, swinging his feet over the edge of the bed. "The neurotransmitters aren't firing yet at full strength."

He shuffled into Rachael's kitchen and found a Keurig coffee machine. He scrounged around the cabinets, found a dark roast—the perfect prescription for what ailed him, he thought—placed it in the machine, and started it up. The sound was music to his ears—still ringing from the much louder music of the dance club. After the machine finished, he sat down at the round kitchen table—a natural wood finish—with his mug of coffee, the side of which had the slogan SCIENTISTS MAKE DISCOVERIES—WRITERS MAKE THEIR REPUTATIONS. The caffeine and humor rapidly brushed away the cobwebs.

Glancing at the Keurig, its simple black configuration caused the image of the Bowman sphere nesting in the interface module—a simple process of association—to flash through his mind, and he was suddenly focused on the critical decision he and Rachael would make in the next few hours as to how to present their discovery to the world. His focus was short-lived, however.

Barefoot, Rachael walked in, dressed in jeans and a blouse, a towel wrapped around her head. Joshua thought she looked as beautiful as ever even in casual clothes, and his eye was drawn to the slight wiggle in her hip thanks to the contour of her faded jeans. He was now fully awake as he watched Rachael's lithe form move about the kitchen.

"Good morning," she said with a smile.

"Good morning. I hope you don't mind that I helped myself to some of your coffee."

"Of course not," Rachael replied, "although the latte is more expensive if you want another cup. The tip jar is on the counter, by the way."

"So now you're a barista?"

"Only when I'm not helping to discover extraterrestrial life." Rachael made herself a cup and sat next to Joshua, both hands folded around the cup. "This is my home, silly, not a bed and breakfast. You don't need to ask for permission."

"Got it," Joshua said. "Anyway, that was really amazing—what happened yesterday, that is."

"Which part?" Rachael asked with a bemused expression. "Talking with aliens, dancing at the Rock Candy, or spending the night with me? Choose your answer carefully."

"All three," Joshua replied with a smile before turning to face her. "Listen, Rachael, I know we only met a couple of days ago, but believe me, this is not the norm for me. I'm not the kind of guy who's into one-night stands. All of yesterday, including last night, was special for me. As Vinod might say, I felt a kind of synergy with you by my side. What I'm saying is that I really have strong feelings towards you, and well, I just wanted you to know that."

The warmth of Rachael's smile was highlighted by the morning sun streaming through the window over the kitchen sink.

She's beautiful. Poetry in motion. God—another cliché! I've fallen hard.

"I appreciate the candor. Does it surprise you that the feelings are mutual?" Rachael reached out and covered Joshua's hand with hers as they drank their morning caffeine.

"I was hoping you'd say that. I've felt a connection since we met, no spookyons required."

Many incredible events had transpired over the past two days, but meeting Joshua had impacted Rachael the most. She leaned closer to him, her shoulder touching his arm. It felt natural that they should be sitting together after all they'd been through the day before. And their emotional connection on the dance floor had been unanticipated but electric. She thought back to her conversation with Joshua about God and how things don't happen by random chance. Like Joshua, she felt they were destined to be sitting next to each other at this moment, which was, of course, a most unscientific way to view things.

But it's what I believe. We met for a reason, and I'm really into this guy after just forty-eight hours.

"Have you made a decision on what we should do next about making further contact with Seth?" she asked.

"Yeah. I still believe we should call Robert Langdon. He's the director of NASA that I alluded to last night. What do you think?"

"If you feel that you can trust him, then I think that would be the best choice. Unless you think notifying the university might be a better option. I presume they own the spookyon."

Joshua sipped his coffee, giving the suggestion some thought.

"They technically own my work, but we captured a primordial particle by accident, and the ensuing dialogue with Seth was not part of my research grant or what I was hired to do at the lab. This is my own discovery. *Our* discovery. This is too big an event to get mired in academic bureaucracy and wrangling."

"The board isn't going to be happy. It will surely invoke ownership regardless. There could be some *legal* wrangling."

"I can't see them circumventing NASA, and even if they claim the discovery as theirs, universities give credit to their faculty members all the time. Besides, they wouldn't dare throw me under the bus or it would reflect badly on them. I'll give them a ton of good publicity, and their alums will fill their coffers pretty fast."

"I agree. Langdon it is."

"Good. I'll call him now. I want you here with me when I talk to him. He needs to know all the details, including who was there when Seth came through. I want complete transparency."

Joshua took out his phone, dialed the director, and placed his phone on speaker so Rachael could hear the conversation. He placed the phone on the table, waiting for an answer.

"Hello," Robert Langdon said when the call was put through. His tone of voice was low and businesslike.

"Good morning, Robert. This is Joshua Andrews."

"Dr. Andrews, how are things going?" The director's voice was now cordial and enthusiastic. "Any progress on creating spookyons in that underground hideaway of yours?"

Joshua paused, took a deep breath, and looked at Rachael for moral support. "That's what I wanted to talk to you about. I'm here with Rachael Miller, who's a reporter with *Scientific American,* and we have something very exciting to share with you."

"Hello, Mr. Langdon," Rachael said. "Nice to meet you."

"Hi, Miss Miller. I'm a big fan of yours. I've read many of your articles, in fact. Very impressive work. You write with accuracy and clarity, but also have a stylistic flare. If you ever leave journalism, you'd make a great public relations director here at NASA given your communication skills and knowledge of science."

The director of NASA knew of her? "Thank you. I'm flattered." Taken aback, she looked at Joshua and mouthed three words: *A job offer?*

"What's this exciting news you two have to share with me?" Langdon asked. "Got some entangled spookyons?"

"Yes and no," Joshua replied slowly. "But it's much bigger than that."

"Bigger? In what way?"

Joshua and Rachael relayed the happenings of the last couple of days, including the creation of the spheres, receiving the signal in the bat cave, the running of Vinod's algorithm, and a summary of their conversation with Seth, although they omitted specific scientific details, such as the aliens' ability to engineer DNA. Joshua didn't want to put the director on information overload, and he thought too many details—shape-shifting aliens, for one—might result in his account being relegated to the category of science fiction.

When they had finished, Langdon, on the verge of shock, said nothing for several seconds. The story was unbelievable, but he knew that Joshua was not one to kid around. He knew that no matter how outrageous the story sounded—primordial spookyons and an algorithm to teach English to aliens were especially difficult to swallow—they were telling the truth.

"My God, you have a penchant for understatement," Langdon said. "Exciting? To say the least! Congratulations, you two. You've actually made first contact with an alien species. I never thought it would happen in my lifetime."

"Thanks," Joshua said, grateful that the director hadn't laughed out loud or hung up on him. "We weren't sure what to do next, but we thought contacting you made sense."

Joshua heaved a sigh of relief as he held Rachael's hand.

"Well, I'm glad you did. I assure you that calling me was the right thing to do. A lot of scientists, eager for recognition, would have put this on social media immediately."

Joshua declined to provide details as to how Vinod had been seconds away from doing just that. It would do nothing to bolster the director's confidence in the three.

There was another pause on the line, and Joshua grew paranoid. Was Robert routing the call to others? Recording it? He thought he heard the faintest clicking sound on the other end of the line. Vinod's words of warning were already echoing in his mind.

"Uh . . . who else knows about this?" Langdon continued. The last words were added with caution, giving Joshua yet another reason to be suspicious.

"No one," Joshua replied. "Just Rachael, Vinod, and myself."

"No one at the Bowman Particle Research Center? Or at the university?"

"Just us three. The university had nothing to do with it."

There was another pause on the line, this one longer than the first.

"That's good," Langdon said. "Very good. You may not know this because it's not public information, but we actually have protocols in place at NASA on what to do in case of first contact. They've been on the books for years. Where is the Bowman sphere presently?"

"It's back at the lab," Joshua said, "although we're not there now. We're in Palo Alto, but we'll be heading to the lab shortly."

"Okay, I need to make some phone calls, but stay the course. Don't tell anyone else about this, as tempting as it might seem. Something like this has to be . . ." He didn't finish his sentence. "I'll contact you soon with the next steps. Truly amazing, guys, and once again—congratulations."

"Steps?" Rachael asked. "Can you be a little more specific?"

"Unfortunately, not at this time."

"Sounds good," Joshua replied, signaling to Rachael that she shouldn't ask any further questions. "We'll wait to hear back from you." He ended the call, feeling relieved that he'd finally been able to share the dramatic news with someone he deemed trustworthy.

"Why can't he tell us what he's going to do?" Rachael asked, clearly bothered. "And did you notice his hesitation towards the end of the call?"

"Yes, but I don't think he wanted to describe NASA's protocols for such an extraordinary discovery over a non-secure line. I was concerned too, but in retrospect, I think he was as overwhelmed as we were yesterday and didn't know quite how to respond." Joshua thought for a moment, as if trying to convince himself of his own answer. "Yes, we had to tell someone, and if I were Robert Langdon, I'd be very careful about what I said over the phone."

Rachael took a deep breath and considered the response. "Okay, makes sense. Sounds like we really blindsided him, though."

"Of course we did. There's no easy way to break such an extraordinary discovery. We'll just have to wait and see what he comes up with."

Joshua and Rachael finished their morning coffees, and Joshua grabbed both cups, rinsed them in the sink, and sat back down next to Rachael. "Now then—you almost ready?" he asked. "I'd like to get back to the lab and get out of these clothes."

"Sure," Rachael replied. "Let me fix my hair."

Joshua grabbed her hand before she could get up from the table. "Rachael, I'm so glad that I took your interview," he said as he leaned over to kiss her. "One of the best decisions I ever made. Sorry for being so grumpy that day."

"Not to worry. You made up for it on the dance floor—and in other ways."

The two days of rain had finally let up, and the sky was clear blue as Rachael drove Joshua back to the lab. As they made their way up the driveway of the Bowman Particle Research Center, they noticed three black SUVs parked near the entrance.

Joshua and Rachael glanced at each other simultaneously, a sinking feeling in their stomachs.

"Shit," Joshua uttered. "He didn't even bother to call us like he promised."

"Behold," Rachael said ominously. "The next steps."

*　　　*　　　*

Vinod was still passed out on his bed when he heard the doorbell ring. He picked up the phone from his nightstand to look at the time. 12:03 p.m. *Who the hell can that be?* he wondered. *Maybe if I just ignore whoever it is, they'll leave.*

He had no such luck. They pounded on the door, shouting something that Vinod couldn't make out. He checked the app on his phone that allowed him to view who was standing on his front porch. These were definitely not Jehovah's Witnesses. The doorbell rang again.

"Alright!" Vinod cried. "I'm coming, I'm coming!"

He got out of bed and noticed that he was still wearing the same clothes from the day before. It was then that he recalled the previous evening—Seth, the Bowman sphere, the Rock Candy Dance Club, and . . . he couldn't remember how he got home. He'd gone to use the bathroom, and everything after that was a blank.

"Damn," he said under his breath as the loud knocking continued. "Can't a guy nurse a hangover in peace?"

Still feeling the effects of the night's celebration, Vinod stumbled down the stairs and opened the door. His sleepiness quickly disappeared when he saw a man and a woman standing on the porch, each wearing a dark blue jacket with the letters FBI emblazoned on it in yellow letters. A black SUV was parked in his driveway.

"Vinod Bhakti?" the man asked.

"Yes." Vinod looked from the man to the woman, puzzled as to why they'd been so insistent in their knocking. Getting hammered wasn't a felony.

"I'm Agent Hargraves, and this is my partner, Agent Ramirez. We're with the FBI." The agents showed Vinod their credentials, although the computer engineer's vision was too blurry to see the photos IDs when he leaned over to examine them. "We have orders to bring you to our headquarters in San Francisco for questioning."

"Questioning for *what*?" Vinod asked, his mind racing, his voice strained. Vinod could think of numerous reasons the FBI might be interested in him—his online computer activity wasn't always above board—but nothing seemed so critical that agents would want to question him at the bureau's headquarters. He wasn't going to take any chances, though. As he'd told Joshua, he was more than a little suspicious of the feds—outright distrustful, in fact—but he wasn't going to foolishly challenge them even though he felt outraged at their intrusion.

"We have no idea what they want to talk to you about," agent Ramirez answered. "Our orders are to bring you in—immediately."

"Okay, hold on a sec," Vinod replied. "I've got to get my shoes." Vinod walked back to his study. "Layla, execute protocol D 3 L 3 T 3," he said loudly enough so that his trusty electronic assistant could hear, but not the two agents at his front door.

Layla replied, "Confirmed. Protocol D 3 L 3 T 3 execution in progress."

The lights on the storage devices in the server racks started blinking rapidly. Vinod put on a pair of sandals and headed for the front door. As he did so, he was aware for the first time that his head was throbbing, as if someone was using a jackhammer on the inside of his skull.

The agents seated Vinod in the rear of their black Suburban and drove to San Francisco, not saying a word as they neared the city.

"I don't suppose we can stop at a Starbuck's, huh?" Vinod said.

His request was greeted with silence.

"I'll take that as a no."

Once at headquarters, the agents escorted Vinod to an elevator, and the three rode to an upper-floor conference room that contained a large mahogany table with numerous leather chairs surrounding it. There was a set of windows on one wall that afforded a panoramic view of the San Francisco skyline and the Golden Gate Bridge. As he walked into the room, Vinod saw a couple of familiar faces seated at the table: Joshua and Rachel. He took a seat next to them, his expression begging for an explanation.

"Wait here," Agent Ramirez instructed. "Someone will be with you shortly." The agents left the room and closed the door.

"What the hell is going on!" Vinod exclaimed, nervous and agitated. "In the words of Dylan, I was knocked out loaded when those two goons started pounding on my door." He rubbed his temples. "My God, I'd kill for two aspirins."

"Don't really know why we're here," Rachael replied. "There were FBI agents waiting for us when Josh and I arrived at the lab this morning. They hurried us into an SUV and drove us here a couple of hours ago and haven't told us anything yet."

"What did you guys do?" Vinod asked. "Wait a minute. You didn't—"

"This morning we called Robert Langdon, the director of NASA, and told him about the sphere and Seth," Joshua confessed unapologetically. "Rachael and I were in agreement."

Vinod looked accusatorily at Joshua. "NASA? I *knew* that getting the government involved was a bad idea." Vinod momentarily rested his head on the polished surface of the conference table. "This whole thing is gonna get buried deeper than JFK's assassination. I don't know what hurts more— my head or you guys going to the government."

"Still better than *your* idea," Joshua countered, mimicking Vinod's swagger while sitting in the booth at the Rock Candy. "*I'm gonna tweet this bad boy out right here and now. Why wait?* Brilliant," he said sarcastically. "Besides, maybe this is all related to your dark web stuff. Rachael told me that you communicate with some pretty unsavory people online."

"No way, dude," Vinod said defensively and then paused. "Well, maybe I *occasionally* make contact with foreign sources through back channels in order to gather information, but that stuff is locked up tight. Besides, Layla is cleaning it up as we speak. But you—you make one call to NASA, and now we're stuck with all this cloak and dagger shit."

"Calm down, Vinod," Rachael replied. "We don't know what's going on yet. Let's wait and see what happens." Rachael glanced at Vinod's shirt. "Same clothes as yesterday, huh? You pull a rollover? You smell like the Rock Candy Dance Club."

"Those FBI agents were in kind of a hurry. Mulder and Scully there were quite insistent that we hit the bricks ASAP. Really didn't give me a chance to change," Vinod responded as he glanced at Joshua. "But it looks like Joshua's wearing the same clothes as well. You two want to explain that?"

Joshua looked at Rachael. "Well . . ."

He started to explain, but he was interrupted as the conference room door opened. Three people walked in, two men and a woman. One of the men was none other than Robert Langdon. The other man, who wore a khaki military uniform with dozens of medals covering the breast of his coat, carried a black case that Joshua recognized immediately. It was the case that contained the Bowman sphere.

Chapter Twenty
Deep Pockets

The three newcomers took seats at the table opposite the others. They said nothing as they eyed Joshua, Rachael, and Vinod while opening laptops each had placed on the conference table. Robert Langdon, tall and slender, wore a dark brown suit and tie. He was in his late fifties, with graying brown hair that was cut short and parted neatly to one side. The woman was African American, slender, and looked to be in her late forties. The man in the military uniform set the case with the sphere on the table just to his right so as not to obscure his view of the three young people sitting across from him. He appeared to be in his sixties, had a rugged, weathered face, and was Caucasian, with gray hair clipped into a military-style crew cut. His eyes were of such a pale blue color that it seemed to Rachael that they conveyed an absence of emotion.

"Where did you get that?" Joshua demanded, pointing to the case. His tone was angry as he leaned forward, motioning to the case.

"We picked it up from your lab this morning," the man in the military uniform replied dispassionately.

"I didn't authorize that," Joshua said. "How did you get it? My instructions to my team at the particle center were that it be locked in a security vault, so I assume you waltzed right in and appropriated it for the Pentagon?"

"We'll get to that in a moment," the woman replied. "I'm Dina Williams, White House chief of staff." She pointed to the uniformed man beside her. "This is General Mitchell Porter, chairman of the joint chiefs, and I believe you're familiar with Robert Langdon, director of NASA. We're already familiar with all three of you." Williams turned to the Porter. "Mitchell, any comments on their background checks?"

"Background checks?" Joshua repeated, looking from Williams to Porter.

"That's an invasion of my privacy," Vinod protested. "You have no right!"

Breathing fast, Joshua rubbed the stubble on his chin and assessed the figures staring at him, but his gaze came to rest squarely on the NASA director. He was getting a feeling that calling Langdon had been a mistake of major proportions. The director had sandbagged him with flattery and congratulations over the telephone. He'd known from the outset what his "next steps" would be and who he intended to call. Joshua felt that his friendship with the director, rooted in his work with Henry, had been betrayed.

"No, they came up clean," Porter replied tersely. "For the most part, that is." He glared at Vinod as he tapped the fingers of his right hand on the table. "There are some minor issues with Mr. Bhakti's usage of the Internet."

Like Joshua, Vinod was growing more concerned by the minute. He hated being in an FBI office in the first place, but now there was a general talking about background checks, which included his online activity. This was definitely outside his comfort zone.

"Examine my servers," Vinod said smugly. "They're clean."

"But your digital footprint is everywhere," Porter corrected. "Would you like me to tell the room about your dark web activities on Asian sites alone?"

"Someone want to explain what's going on?" Joshua asked.

"Certainly, Dr. Andrews," Williams replied. "First I want to start by congratulating all of you for making first contact with an outside intelligence. Obviously, you know the significance of this discovery, and I also wanted to thank you for having the foresight to contact someone at NASA without splashing this all over the Internet. You clearly have presence of mind, which correlates with your sterling reputation as a scientist."

Joshua gave a knowing glance at Vinod, who rolled his eyes.

"Congratulations to three people who've been taken into custody," Rachael said, as if setting the record straight.

"You're not under arrest," Williams continued, "but we need to get a handle on who else knows about this discovery. Besides the three of you, is anyone else aware of what transpired in the mine or at Mr. Bhakti's house?"

"No one else knows," Joshua replied. "I already made that clear to Robert—to Mr. Langdon."

The NASA director was busy taking notes on his laptop and paid no attention to Joshua's verbal slight.

"How about this Rodrigo Torres who works in your lab?" Williams asked. "Weren't you working with him when you made contact?"

"No, he was working in another mine with a different sphere and spookyon," Joshua answered, "but he doesn't know anything about our conversation with the aliens. We'd been unsuccessfully attempting to create a pair of entangled spookyons, and we ended the video call with him before we realized we'd made contact with alien intelligence. As far as he knows, it was just another failed test."

"That's fortunate," Williams continued. "So aside from you three, the people in this room, the president, and some very high-level officials in the government, no one else knows." Williams looked sternly around the room before she spoke again. "And we want to keep it that way."

Joshua, Rachael, and Vinod stared at Williams, their mouths agape as they processed what the chief of staff had said. Joshua was the first to speak.

"What!" Joshua exclaimed, obviously upset. "You've got to be freaking kidding me! *We* made the discovery, and yet we're not allowed to tell anyone?"

"That's correct," Williams replied. "We've determined that it's in the best interest of the country not to disclose any of this, at least until we have more information. Knowledge of alien intelligence has the potential to cause widespread panic and destabilize important social structures. It could even affect the economy by causing market volatility. There could be a massive sell-off by people who fear imminent invasion. The market responds to news cycles as much as it does to corporate portfolios."

"Man, I knew it!" Vinod said. "That's Orwellian doublespeak. Joshua, I told you that telling these government clowns was a bad idea. This is just horse shit!"

"We contacted NASA in order to receive help," Joshua said by way of clarification, "not to be dictated to."

"Ms. Williams," Rachael interjected, "are you saying that we're not allowed to tell anyone at all? No announcement, no write up, no press conference—nothing? It's my understanding that even SETI has protocols that would make such knowledge public."

"I assure you that none of their protocols will ever be carried out," Langdon stated. "The NSA has plans in place to close down their facility in Mountain View as soon as they try to go public should they ever receive a meaningful radio transmission."

"But this is a major scientific discovery," Rachael declared. "You have no right to keep it from the public."

"We have *every* right to do what's in the best interest of the country," Porter said. "*We* make policy, Ms. Miller, not you or your friends. If I may be blunt, you're not qualified to assess the ramifications of what has happened or its implications for national security."

"It was my idea to call NASA," Joshua admitted, glaring at Langdon. "I thought you guys would know the best way to announce this—nothing more. If I'd known that you were going to deep six it, I would've let Vinod tweet it out like he wanted. I agree that this news would cause a stir, but it belongs to everyone on the planet. Who's to say that it might not unite humanity in the long run by enabling it to see itself as a single life form and not hundreds of fragmented countries?"

"Is that your goal?" Porter asked indignantly. "A new world order?"

"That's not what I meant, general. You're putting words in my mouth."

"Look, I understand your frustration, and I realize the significance of this discovery," Langdon said, now playing the role of good cop. "Believe me when I tell you that we'll work through the science in painstaking detail, but we can't just unleash this on society without first knowing exactly what we are dealing with. National security must come first."

"National security?" Vinod said rhetorically. "That's bullshit! It's just an excuse for you guys to keep this to yourselves—a catch-phrase for anything the government wants to cover up."

"This isn't a cover-up," Williams said. "It's an abundance of caution to prevent mass hysteria and the kind of social disruptions I've already described." She paused to highlight her next words. "And the president is in complete agreement with me."

Porter, whose steely features were nowhere near as diplomatic as those of Langdon and Williams, gave Vinod a stern look and said, "National security is not bullshit, son! You science people have no idea what you're dealing with here. You make contact with an alien civilization far more advanced than us, and you want to just turn them loose on society? Hell no! Listen here—I've got enough of a security problem worrying about the panic we have with this Ebola outbreak. I definitely don't need more fear as a result of this alien crap."

Joshua couldn't contain himself. "Is that what we are to you, general? Science people? That's pretty condescending. And this isn't alien crap, as you put it, or we wouldn't be sitting here today, nor would you have confiscated the Bowman sphere."

Williams tried to tamp down flaring tempers. "Let's everyone remain calm and take a deep breath. Obviously, these are important decisions, and we're not going to rush into anything. What we need is more information. First, tell us what you've found out about the aliens. You've had just the one conversation with them, correct?"

"Right," Joshua answered. "Last night. We talked to someone named Seth, although that's not his real name, just one he picked from the data we sent. Their language is completely different from ours. They communicate using spookyons, and their names—their designations, if your will—are digital in nature."

"What information did you send them?" Langdon asked, leaning forward and appearing concerned. "How much do they know about us? Do they know where we are?"

"They have no common point of astronomical reference," Rachael said. "In other words, their night sky would bear no resemblance to our constellations or our catalog of stars and their positions. That's why this is so radically different from SETI, which could pinpoint the source of a radio signal. So the answer is no—they don't know where we are."

"Yet," Porter said.

"The stuff we sent them is mostly information they already knew," Vinod said. "Math and science. But to teach them language, they needed to know basic concepts about culture and history. Language doesn't exist in a vacuum, which is why it's the end point of my algorithm."

"What language was it?" Langdon asked. "Just English?"

"Yes, English," Vinod replied looking at Rachael and Joshua. "In both the formal and informal usage."

"What have you found out about them?" Williams asked, remaining even-tempered, as if she were the moderator of the discussion. "I assume you asked them questions. Was this Seth individual very forthcoming?"

"We did," Joshua said, "but Seth was as guarded as we were. What we did learn is that they've evolved very similar to the way life evolved on Earth. They're carbon-based organic creatures. They're also multi-cellular, just like we are. Likewise, their cell structure is based on DNA, but they exist as some kind of . . . collective." He paused, knowing that additional details were going to make the three government representatives very uncomfortable. "Seth, who is an individual in this collective, said that there are thousands of planets with life, but all life they know of is DNA- and cell-based. However, their physical form, I'm sure, is very different from ours."

"What do they look like?" Porter asked, retaining his stoic manner.

"Who knows, man?" Vinod replied. "We didn't ask Seth for a goddamn selfie."

"We think that evolution on their planet must have taken a very similar path to that on Earth," Rachael added, "just as Joshua implied."

"There's nothing unusual about that," Langdon commented. "Many scientists believe that any life in the universe has to be carbon-based and water soluble. It's really the only chemistry that works for life."

"Their knowledge of DNA, though, is very advanced," Joshua said. "In fact, they use DNA on an engineering level."

"Engineering?" Langdon said, clearly startled. "What do you mean by that?"

"They can manipulate DNA sequences and create whatever organisms they choose," Joshua explained. "The only critical difference between an acorn that grows into an oak tree and a fertilized egg that grows into a human is the DNA sequence—the sequence of nucleic acids in the double-helix. If I understood Seth correctly, they actually design living organisms and code the DNA sequences needed to grow what they've designed. In fact, I think they code the DNA for their own bodies as well. Seth called it self-determination. Their interaction with DNA is highly advanced."

"This shit sounds scarier by the minute," Porter added, a scowl on his face. "If they ever came here, we'd all be dead."

"I've already explained that they don't know where we are, and that it's physically impossible for them to come here," Rachael said. "Even if they did know where we are, and if they could travel at light speed, which I'm sure they can't, it'd probably take them thousands of years to get here, perhaps even millions or billions depending on what galaxy they live in. Remember that they can literally be located anywhere in the universe since our communication with them is instantaneous over unlimited distances using spookyons."

"Besides," Joshua added, "Seth said they have a moral obligation not to destroy other sentient societies."

"I don't trust a word of that garbage," Porter said. "We don't know at this stage whether the aliens are hostile or not." He turned to Williams. "That DNA stuff, though, could be very strategic for us if we could coax it from these creatures. Count on it." He rapped his knuckles on the table confidently for emphasis.

Vinod glared at Porter. "Typical military bullshit! You guys find out about new technology, and the first thing you think about is how to weaponize it." Vinod angled himself in his chair, elbow resting on the leather arm, as if trying to distance himself from people he detested. "You're a real piece of work, general."

"Hey, it doesn't matter," Joshua interrupted. "The aliens aren't going to give us their technology. That's completely off limits for them. Seth already told us that."

Porter grimaced, unconvinced of Joshua's reassurance.

"We're probably better off that they don't," Langdon said. "Introducing new technology into a society that's not ready for it could be destabilizing."

"Oh, for God's sake!" Porter bellowed, slapping his hand on the table. "Of course they're not going to give us a technological advantage—unless it might be a weapon *disguised* as technology. We'd never know the difference."

Joshua ignored the general's rant. "Yes, destabilization. That's the main reason Seth gave for why they won't give us information about technology that we don't already possess. He was very adamant on that point. Seth called that information 'redacted.'"

"But the reverse isn't true," Rachael added. "At their intelligence and technology levels, there's not much we can tell them about our technology that they don't already know. What they *don't* know is information that's specific to humans and life on this planet. I believe that's what they're most interested in learning about."

"I'm sure they are," Porter said, his composure regained. "It's called tactical advantage, Ms. Miller."

"Anything else you've found out?" Williams queried, attempting to steer the conversation back to her original question.

"Nope, that's about it," Joshua replied.

"Do you have a transcript of your conversation?" Williams asked.

"Yeah," Vinod replied reluctantly. "I could probably download it from my computer."

"Okay, we'll need that," Williams said. "All of it."

Vinod gave her a mock two-fingered salute.

Langdon turned to Joshua. "How is it that you were able to capture this particular spookyon, the one that's connected to them?"

"I don't really know," Joshua replied. "It may have been just dumb luck, but I was trying out a new isolation protocol with a specific combination of heavy elements in the container lids of the tokamak. Rachael and I believe that this specific combination may select for Big Bang spookyons and not the ones created in our lab."

"A solid hypothesis, Dina," Langdon said.

"Who else knows about the formulation of these lids?" Williams asked.

"Rodrigo does," Joshua said, "but he thinks that they didn't work, so he's not going to pay much attention to them."

"I don't want to take any chances," Williams said. "The last thing we need right now is for someone else to make contact with aliens—these or any others—without our knowing what we're dealing with. Dr. Andrews, I want you to destroy those lids and any information you have on them. Also, delete any electronically-stored notes on their creation."

"My notes are not stored electronically. Just written in my lab books." Joshua turned to Rachael. "You can't hack a piece of paper."

Vinod shook his head, frustrated with the direction of the conversation. "I can't believe this. Any more secrets you want us to hide? Hey, man, I got a thirty-two waist. You want us to secure that information too?"

Porter glared at Vinod. "How about you secure your mouth, or I'm going to come over there and secure it for you!"

Williams turned to the stone-faced general. "Mitchell, please take it down a notch. We're asking a lot of these people. Some frustration is warranted." She turned back to the group, her voice measured and restrained. "Okay, so we've formulated a preliminary plan on how to proceed."

Vinod was still agitated. "What do you mean *you've* formulated a plan? This is *our* discovery. We own this shit. You can't tell us what to do with it."

"That's where you're wrong," Williams said as she faced Joshua. "Dr. Andrews, you can correct me if I'm wrong, but your contract with UC Berkeley, your employer, specifically states that all discoveries made by you while working at the lab are the intellectual property of the university. Is that correct?"

"Here it comes," Rachael said under her breath. "I knew it."

"I remember reading that somewhere," Joshua replied, "but we didn't communicate by using a spookyon that I created. The university doesn't own particles created by the Big Bang, nor do they own Vinod's algorithm."

"But they own the sphere and detector that you used to communicate with the extraterrestrials," Williams pointed out. "And first contact was made in a mine that is university property during an experiment to communicate with another spookyon that you hoped was entangled with your own, which is the focus of your research."

Joshua sighed, conceding the point.

"I'm glad you agree," she said, "because it's a moot point. Just prior to this meeting, the United States government, specifically NASA, finalized the purchase of the Bowman Particle Research Center and its intellectual property from the university. That makes the sphere in this case the sole property of the United States government."

Joshua stared at Williams for a moment with wide eyes. "What did you just say? You bought the lab from UC Berkeley? How?"

"Joshua," Langdon interjected, "you may not be privy to this, but the university contacted NASA six months ago about purchasing the lab. Apparently, it was becoming too expensive for them to run. We were already in negotiations with them, but this matter with the sphere made things much more urgent for the government, not to mention lucrative for the university. The deal for NASA to purchase the lab was going to happen regardless."

Vinod couldn't control his anger. "This is total and absolute crap! You government guys are all the same. You're just going to turn this into another Roswell, aren't you?"

Rachael was also upset. "So you're cutting us out of the loop completely? It was our ingenuity that made contact with Seth possible."

"No, we're not cutting you out at all," Williams said. "In fact, quite the opposite. We want to minimize the number of people who know about this in order to keep a tight lid on it, but we need manpower. Since you three already know about the aliens and have needed skill sets, we want you to be part of the investigative teams that research the sphere and try to get more information out of our alien friends."

"No way, man," Vinod said, shaking his head. "It's gonna be a cold day in hell before you see me working for the government. You can count me out right now."

Williams paid Vinod no heed but continued calmly. "Of course, it would mean leaving your current jobs, which would be inconvenient for you, but we would need your loyalty and cooperation. That's why the government is willing to pay each of you an annual salary of five hundred thousand dollars, with a two-hundred-thousand-dollar signing bonus."

Vinod stared at Williams for a moment. "Damn!" he said. "Hell just got a bit colder."

"Robert is going to lead the scientific team, and Mitchell is going to be in charge of security," Williams stated.

"And don't you guys even think of breathing a word of this to anybody," Porter piped in. He turned to Vinod, "'Cause if you do, your ass'll be behind bars before you can tweet about it."

Joshua addressed Williams. "What happens to my colleagues in the lab and the quest for creating spookyons?"

"Nothing at the center will be affected," Williams replied. "As far as they're concerned, only the ownership of the lab will be changed. They'll continue their endeavors to create entangled spookyons, but any interaction with or knowledge of this sphere will be strictly off limits to them."

"Ms. Williams, it doesn't seem that we have much of a choice here," Rachael said.

"I'm afraid you're right." Williams leaned back in her chair, knowing she had the upper hand. "You don't. But you still get to be part of the team, and you'll be compensated well."

"It's really the opportunity of a lifetime," Langdon asserted. "You three, along with scientific teams, will be able to work on one of the most important discoveries in human history."

Joshua shrugged and looked at his friends, both of whom looked resigned to the task presented to them. "You're holding all the cards. I guess we're in."

Williams got up from the table. "Okay, I think we're finished here. Robert, grab the sphere. We've got a lot of work to do. We'll contact each of you about the next steps within a couple of days."

Next steps, Rachael thought. She'd heard those words before.

Langdon removed the case from the table, and he, Williams, and Porter left the room.

Joshua spoke first. "Well, that's not how I expected this to go. Not at all."

"Gross understatement, dude," Vinod said.

Rachael folded her arms and lowered her head, thoughtful. "It could be a lot worse. We're the only civilians who know, and we get to continue to communicate with Seth. I think Williams knows that we've already gained his trust, and she obviously seems to be running point for the operation. She knows they need us."

"Typical government for ya," Vinod remarked. "Be careful what you say, Rach. You know they gotta have this room bugged."

Joshua turned to Rachael. "Looks like we're going to be spending a lot more time together."

Rachel smiled at Joshua and slipped her fingers through his. "Looks that way," she said.

"What?" Vinod said, a look of disbelief crossing his features. "Are you two like a couple now or something?"

"I guess so," Rachael answered, still looking at Joshua.

"Definitely," Joshua replied.

"Why don't you two get a room already," Vinod said as he got up from the table. "This shit's grossing me out."

Chapter Twenty-One
The Other Red Planet

Robert Langdon jumped headlong into modifying parts of the Bowman Particle Research Center to make it into a facility where three teams could learn more about Seth and the aliens in a controlled environment. He had decided that the bat cave would be the ideal place to pursue their scientific inquiries since it had only one entrance, which made it easy to secure, a fact that greatly pleased General Porter and his security detail. There were two scientific teams and one personal team, the latter comprised of Joshua, Rachael, and Vinod, whose mission was to act as the main liaison with Seth. The purpose of the scientific teams was to glean as much scientific information as possible about Seth's planet and its inhabitants. Even though much of the early information was redacted, he had dropped tantalizing hints about the state of his planet's technology and the scope of life in the universe. The personal team was tasked with finding out more about Seth himself and maintaining his trust in an effort to learn more about his culture and the collective's history and values to the extent that they would allow it. In the words of Robert Langdon, Seth was the key to the entire operation.

The first step in the process, therefore, was to expand the space in the bat cave, which was easily accomplished by a secure team from the Army's Corps of Engineers digging out more of the rock that already made up its rough-hewn walls. Next, desks and chairs were added facing the front wall, which gave the main workspace the appearance of a conventional classroom. Each table had a built-in touchscreen that could interface with other equipment in the lab. Finally, the portable lights were replaced with permanent light fixtures that hung from the ceiling.

"I originally said that new equipment would eventually be brought

151

down here," Joshua told Rachael one day as they watched the bat cave's transformation proceed, "although I never dreamed it would happen this fast or be this complex—or for the reasons that this entire renovation is happening."

"Still not enough equipment to qualify for a real bat cave," Rachael joked.

"NASA is calling the shots," Joshua reminded her. "Sorry if we've disappointed you."

"A little jealous of what they're doing?" Rachael said.

"To be honest, yes. This was my inner sanctum."

"Like Superman's Fortress of Solitude. I've heard of mixed metaphors, but you're switching superheroes."

"Either way, it's so different from what I envisioned." Joshua squeezed her hand as they watched engineers install servers, computers, consoles, and the infrastructure to support them. "What's the quote? O brave new world?"

"Yes," Rachael answered. "From Shakespeare's *The Tempest*. 'O brave new world that has such people in it.' Seems appropriate since we're going to try to find out about a new planet and the creatures that live there."

The cover story at the particle center was that the government had invaded the bat cave so that Joshua, who was described as being on special assignment, could aid NASA in its ongoing research to use spookyons in order to control remote spacecraft. It was plausible and raised no eyebrows due to Joshua's previous experience with the Mars Rover. Langdon had been very thorough and convincing in his initial presentation to the staff as he told them that their original research would neither be halted nor interfered with, with Joshua still technically retaining his role in overseeing the quest to create entangled spookyons.

"So you and I aren't a team anymore?" Rodrigo asked Joshua one day.

"For the time being, Rodrigo, but someone has to be left to mind the store up top. Plus you got a promotion out of all this. You're now one of the chief researchers who *run* the experiments to create entangled spookyons. I'll be looking over your shoulder, but you can handle it." Joshua slapped him on the shoulder. "But buy a lab coat, for God's sake."

Rodrigo considered the answer. "True, amigo, but these people don't like my tee shirts, and they have strict rules on where food can be eaten. And lab coats don't flatter my impressive girth. But at least they gave me a raise. So what gives down in the bat cave? Talk to any other planetary spacecraft yet?"

"Nah. You know NASA. It's a huge agency. The big science down below is yet to come." The answer had been vague but truthful.

"Better you than me," Rodrigo had commented. "Too much paperwork. I'm a scientist, not a bureaucrat. The big science, as you put it, is happening in the tokamak."

Initial contact with Seth had been re-established to make sure the project would continue lest Seth move on to another planet to chat with, but the real science wasn't underway yet as engineers continued the conversion of the bat cave to a more conventional lab, complete with a few creature comforts. The conversation with Seth, as Rachael deemed it, bordered on "interstellar gossip" when the engineers weren't present.

The crucial role that the personal team would play earned the trio the right to visit the renovation anytime they wanted since they needed to be familiar with the equipment. Additionally, Vinod provided considerable input to the tech teams because of his computer engineering skills and his familiarity with the basics of how communication with the aliens took place. However, one system to which Vinod did not have access was the secure servers that would store the data from the project. Porter didn't want to give what he deemed a hacker access to these systems. The three were present during an early construction phase in the bat cave, observing the progress that had been achieved thus far.

"You weren't kidding when you said that the place has the feel of a schoolroom," Vinod told Joshua.

"It's appropriate I guess," Rachael said, "since we'll be learning from them while they'll be learning from us."

"Quite literally true," Joshua said. "Notice that a protective case that contains the Bowman sphere and detector has been inserted into the front wall that the chairs face. If you look closely, you'll see that the case has a clear, bulletproof panel so that the sphere is visible, but the sphere itself is secured in the case with an electronic lock that can only be opened with the thumbprint of either Langdon, Williams, or myself. It was Porter's idea, but I was fully on board with it. Without the spookyon, there's no project, and who knows when we'd trap another primordial particle or if it would be entangled with Seth's."

Vinod pointed to several cables running along the walls of the space. "A lot of the equipment is located in a secondary chamber that's been excavated so as to minimize the number of staff that will be here at any given time. Porter and Langdon told me it was for reasons of security and practicality. That's fine with me. The less feds around, the better."

Joshua motioned to a projector mounted on the ceiling and aimed at a large screen on the front wall above the case containing the sphere. "That will eventually provide full or split screen images of Earth and Seth's home world and interface with the touch screens on the desks. That is if we can get Porter to approve the sending and receiving of images."

"Speaking as a writer," Rachael said, "a picture really *will* be worth a thousand words. I can't begin to imagine what we'll see."

"Personally, I would have made it Imax quality," Vinod remarked. "Go big or go home, but I'm just a lowly servant being paid half a million dollars to help people speak to each other. But what's with all the audio and video equipment in here? It's everywhere. Is Big Brother watching?"

"I think that's a given," Joshua replied. "But there's a utilitarian value as well. No information will be inconsequential. Everything needs to be preserved for the purposes of both security and analysis. Video cameras and microphones have been added and will constantly record all happenings in the room. The recordings will be stored on secured servers in the ancillary chamber that Vinod referred to."

"Secure is the operative word," Vinod said. "I'll bet a hundred grand of my salary that nothing that happens in here will ever be announced to the public, at least in our lifetimes."

"That's my biggest concern," Rachael said. "I'm glad to be included on the project but keeping this from the world still seems wrong."

"I don't think any of us can predict what will happen in the future," Joshua said reassuringly. "My own feelings are that there are a lot of variables involved in this endeavor that no one, not even the government, can predict. As you're fond of saying Rachael, some things don't happen by random chance. Who knows what events lie in the months ahead?"

"I'm not a religious man," Vinod said, "but I hope you're right."

"Jurassic Park," Rachael said.

"What?" Joshua and Vinod said at the same time.

"My favorite part of the movie is when the main characters find out that the dinosaurs find a way to procreate despite the best efforts of the theme park owners to prevent it. General Porter is arrogant enough to think he can control everything, and maybe he can. But even though Seth is a long way from here, this dialog could take a lot of unforeseen turns, just as Josh said."

It was a sobering thought, and the three figures looked at one another without adding further comment.

*   *   *

All contact with Seth was highly scripted for security reasons—Langdon and Williams had insisted on it—and it was a full three months before the text interface developed by Vinod to communicate with Seth was upgraded to an audio interface. The audio interface itself was a compromise since the scientific team wanted a video interface while General Porter, who never let anyone forget that he was in charge of security, determined that too much information would be transmitted via video interface. After all, he reasoned, video was simply numerous frames of still pictures that were stitched together, and each frame contained an enormous amount of information—too much in his estimation.

"Why were the projector and screen even installed?" Joshua asked Langdon.

"For obvious reasons," the director replied, "which demonstrates that even I can get overruled by the Pentagon. They play hardball, Josh. Let's play it by ear. Maybe Porter will come around."

"The audio interface with Seth works just like an ordinary phone call," Vinod explained to the technical team after one of the early contacts with Seth, little more than a dry run for the equipment installed thus far in the bat cave. "We speak to him, and he talks back to us. Since the aliens communicate digitally, they have no voice or sounds even though they've designed themselves specifically for communication."

"I get the basics," one of the technicians said, "but I'll be stationed in the secondary chamber, so can you be a little more specific on your specs."

"No problem," said Vinod, who'd learned to keep his frustration in check by frequently checking his online bank account balance. "The sphere is connected to a digital-to-analog converter, which in turn is connected to speakers here in the bat cave. The timber and tone of his voice is now completely controlled by Seth. He picked a male human voice since he originally chose a male name for himself. His voice sounds completely human since it's not electronically generated."

"It's not what I or anyone on my team expected," the technician said. "We thought we'd be listening to something similar to the voice that came to be associated with Stephen Hawking when he was alive."

"Way more sophisticated than that," Vinod said. "Seth is *the* man—or at least he adopted that gender—and he can really do some amazing shit. Take a listen." He pointed to Joshua and Rachael, who sat in two of the chairs facing the screen.

"Hi, Seth?" Rachael said.

"Hey, guys," Seth replied, his voice sounding entirely human. "Good to hear from you. How's everything going?"

"Fine," Joshua answered. "And you?"

"We've never been better. I mean *I* haven't. I mean—well, you get the whole gig, right? That I'm part of the collective."

"Yeah, I get it," Joshua responded. "By the way, when we talk to you, do you cut yourself off from the collective for a period of time, or are we always talking to your entire species?"

"It varies, but I can't really tell you what goes into that decision-making process. It wouldn't make sense to you. I guess the best way to put it is that it depends what we're rapping about—or talking, right?—during any one of our conversations. Can you dig it?"

"Yes," Rachael said, laughing. "We can dig it just fine."

"Laughter," Seth said.

"Does your species laugh or have humor?" Joshua asked.

"Absolutely," Seth replied. "Laughter is actually a very intelligent trait. It takes a complex thought process to understand when something is humorous."

"Simply incredible," the technician said. "Are you sure this is digital intelligence?"

"As far as we can tell," Vinod replied. "I don't see how they could do what they claim they can without being digital in nature. Speaking as an information theorist, that is. If they're truly a collective, then they'd almost *have* to be digital."

*   *   *

The pace of learning about Seth and his alien friends was glacial by most standards, and Joshua complained in the fourth month that greater progress could and should be made. The conversations with Seth were cordial in nature, but the information flow was stunted by the limited audio communication despite the realistic sound of Seth's voice.

Joshua picked up the phone in his office and was connected to Langdon.

"Robert," Joshua said, "Seth is giving us precious little information, and what we do get is of a generic nature and always vague or heavily redacted. Everything is valuable, of course, but we need to take this to the next level. He's described what his DNA-based engineering can do, but it's all theoretical. Your own scientific teams stationed here are growing impatient, which I'm sure you're aware of. We need to up the ante and get some visuals. Seth is willing to comply, but Porter's being a real ass."

"I'm told by the science team that Seth has informed us that life is spread throughout the universe," Langdon contended. "That alone is worth a lot, isn't it?"

"Of course, but he won't tell us where that life is located. We also asked about the technological levels of these other species so we can measure them on the Kardashev scale, which evaluates a society based on its energy consumption and output, but Seth's only answer was that civilizations reflect numerous stages of technological development. We were interested in finding out if most alien species were more advanced than Earth—in other words, have humans come late to the party—but he's playing it close to the vest. Data analysis could increase exponentially if we had images to examine, but Porter has nixed the idea. He still doesn't believe that these beings won't hop in some rocket ship—his phrase, not mine—and pay us a visit. The man is positively paranoid."

Langdon was surprisingly receptive to the case Joshua was making. "The small number of people here at NASA who know about this tend to agree with you, Joshua. I'll see if I can get Dina to twist the general's arm a bit even if she has to go through the president."

"Thanks, Robert. I'd appreciate that."

Langdon was true to his word, and within forty-eight hours, an image interface had been reluctantly approved by Porter after receiving orders from the White House. The images, however, were to be restricted in number until an assessment could be made by the general's security team as to whether any particular image posed a security risk.

"Security risk my ass," was Vinod's observation. "This isn't a kid's game of I'll show you mine if you show me yours."

The image interface was established by the scientific personnel with, as usual, considerable help from Vinod. He had taught Seth the JPEG compression algorithm for images which was used for the image format.

Joshua, Rachael, and Vinod gathered in the bat cave, waiting for the first picture to be projected onto the screen. General Porter had insisted that he and his adjutant be there to personally evaluate the initial images—and shut them down if necessary.

"By the book," he asserted as he waited for the screen to come to life, glaring at the three members of the personal team, all of whom he still resented.

"Reminds me of waiting for the images from the Mars Rover that day in Wheeler Auditorium," Rachael said.

"Our first close encounter," Joshua said affectionately, "even though I didn't know you were there."

The screen displayed static for a few seconds and then resolved to clarity as everyone in the cave held his or her breath.

"Damn," Vinod said. "It's certainly not what I imagined."

The first image received from Seth was a high-altitude image of the collective's home world. It was a red planet dotted with millions of shallow fresh water lakes. There were no oceans, but there were white, wispy, water-based clouds high in its atmosphere. Upon analysis, it would later be determined that the mass of the planet was approximately one and a half times that of Earth. Its axis of rotation varied only two degrees from the plane that prescribed the body's orbit around its star—its ecliptic—which meant that there were no meaningful seasons on Seth's home world. It orbited its sun approximately every seven Earth years, but it rotated on its axis every twenty-two hours as measured by Terran time. Therefore, a year on the planet lasted much longer than on Earth, but its day was shorter. It was also learned that day and night had no meaning to Seth and the collective since they didn't sleep, which was a small revelation in itself.

"No sleep?" Porter inquired on one of his visits to the bat cave. "Another tactical advantage." He appeared smug and vindicated by his pronouncement.

By this time—several months into daily communications with Seth—Joshua, Rachael, and Vinod had learned to ignore the general's grim and at times bellicose manner and warnings.

One of the most noteworthy images from Seth had been a selfie. The staff in the bat cave was shocked to see his appearance since it was, as Vinod put it in his usual succinct, blunt manner, "Not much to look at." His body was spherical and colored a dark green, with multiple small appendages that the scientific team thought made him look like an enormous sea anemone.

"And to think people originally made fun of *Star Trek* and its bad costumes," Vinod said.

The image of Seth was set against a red dirt background, which reminded the scientists of a bacterial colony on a blood agar plate in a petri dish. This eventually prompted the scientific team to name Seth's planet Petri, and the occupants of the planet as petrins.

"The *other* red planet," Rachael commented, "only it's got life that looks like something we inoculate against with antibiotics. You're right, Vinod. Gene Roddenberry had it right all those years ago."

In later months, the teams learned that there were only three species of life on Petri, a shocking revelation to Langdon and exo-biologists at NASA, who had assumed that all planets where life had evolved would display a diversity of forms. The petrins had completely reformed the biology of their planet billions of years ago—an indication of just how long they had possessed advanced technology—in a process that Seth termed bioscaping.

"That certainly answers the basic question of how far above us they are," Rachael said.

The writer, on sabbatical from *Scientific American*, was allowed to take notes on a laptop provided by NASA even though General Porter had insisted at first that no information be committed to any electronic storage device since he feared valuable data on the aliens would be smuggled out of the mine using a flash drive. Langdon had persuaded him to change his position, stating that the team couldn't do its job without taking notes and recording their observations. NASA, he reassured the general, would always have access to their laptops.

Rachael, standing next to Joshua and Vinod, pointed to her head with her index finger, and both friends had seen and understood the gesture before. "Even if they take away my computer, they can't hack my brain," she said in a parody of Henry Bowman and his allusion to his three hundred lab notebooks.

*   *   *

The first species on Petri was the petrins themselves, the species to which Seth belonged. They were the size of adult pigs and were comprised almost entirely of structures that resembled neural cells. Their outer covering was made of cells that could absorb sunlight and generate energy, so they had no requirement to eat or take in nutrition. Petrins, however, were not mobile. They couldn't walk around their environment and, in fact, petrins had no sensory organs. They were deaf, dumb, and blind, a fact that caused Vinod to frequently wear his "Tommy—Pinball Wizard" tee shirt to work. The petrins were scattered throughout the temperate zone of Petri at the edges of numerous freshwater lakes. They used their appendages as straws that dipped into the water to replenish fluid loss in their bodies caused by evaporation. For these reasons, humans considered petrins to be more plant-like than animal-like, albeit highly intelligent plants.

Even though petrins were not mobile, they could change the shape of their semi-gelatinous bodies as their environment dictated. This, Joshua pointed out in discussions with the scientists on several occasions, was an aspect of their self-determination. When the environment was cooler, they became more spherical in order to preserve heat. When it was warmer, their bodies spread out like thick pancakes in order to radiate heat. Since there were no radical weather changes, their bodies only had to accommodate a narrow range of environmental changes.

"Gross looking dudes," Vinod remarked.

"Beauty is in the eye of the beholder," Dina Williams countered on one of her rare personal visits to the bat cave. "Didn't you ever watch the *Star Trek* episode 'Is There No Truth in Beauty?' An alien ambassador is brought aboard the *Enterprise*, one who is deemed so ugly that one glimpse of it drives humans insane."

"Damn, you got me there," Vinod admitted. "I would never have taken you for a Trekkie."

"I'm not, but my husband loves the reruns. Some of the shows have some interesting social commentary."

Vinod had gained a begrudging respect for the White House chief of staff. She'd been the main force, second only to Robert Langdon, in making sure that the teams coordinated with each other and were given as much as possible in accordance with General Porter's restrictions.

"Wouldn't you just like to kick him in the ass sometimes?" Vinod asked her.

"You're forgetting, Mr. Bhakti, that everything in this room is recorded. Besides, the general may be gruff, but he's a good officer and serves an important purpose."

"We'll have to agree to disagree on that point," Vinod said.

"You're doing a great job," Williams said. "Just remember that the automatic deposits into your bank accounts are always open to an ongoing review of your job performance."

"General Porter," Vinod said loudly to make sure his voice would be picked up by the recorders. "Hell of a guy."

For the first time since he'd known her, Vinod saw Williams crack a smile.

The second species of life on Petri consisted of numerous green trees that dotted the red landscape of the planet, offering a stark contrast of colors. To the human eye, they resembled coconut trees in that they had long gray trunks ending at the top with a burst of large green leaves. The leaves themselves resembled those of a banana plant, and under the leaves were large spherical pods that contained a milky-white nectar. Connected to the pods were hollow vines that dangled almost to the ground. The trees, which Joshua nicknamed nectar trees, had a singular purpose, which was to produce nectar as fuel for the final species on the planet.

To all teams, the final species was the most interesting. It was the only one that they considered as a true animal life form. They looked like enormous dark brown spiders the size of an elephant.

"Oh, my God!" Vinod exclaimed. "*They Came from Planet X*. It was a B movie from the 1950s. Man, truth really is stranger than fiction."

They had a central body, analogous to a spider's abdomen, from which emanated eight articulated legs, and their movement resembled that of a tarantula. Four snake-like appendages also originated on top of the central body. At the ends of these extremities were sensory organs. Each appendage ended in an eye, an organ that could hear, and olfactory receptors for smell. Due to the fact that their sensory organs could move freely through space on the ends of the appendages, the creatures had acute depth perception and spatial orientation. Not only could they accurately discern from which direction a sound was coming from, but they could also detect exactly where a smell originated. Despite their enormous sensory capability, however, they didn't have anything more than a rudimentary brain. Appropriately, the teams named these creatures arachnids.

The arachnid brain, despite being vestigial in nature, contained eight spookyons that were able to interface with petrins. In essence, the arachnids were the eyes, ears, and bodies of petrins even though the two species were not physically connected; they didn't need to be. A petrin could connect to the spookyon in an arachnid and "remote control" it as well as get input from its sensory organs. It was almost as if petrins and arachnids were one species in which the body of the organism was separated from the brain. Petrins could therefore explore their planet remotely via the arachnids. If the need ever arose for a petrin to be physically moved, an arachnid would be summoned and the petrin was scooped into a chamber located on the undersurface of the arachnid body. This feature was also used when the environment of petrins became too extreme for petrins to physically endure. They could be safely protected in the abdomen of an arachnid until the environmental danger had passed.

Any petrin could control any arachnid on the planet. While the eight spookyons in an arachnid brain were only directly connected to eight petrins, the dominant species of the planet had the ability to relay information through the collective by way of spookyons. In essence, this gave any petrin the ability to remotely control any arachnid on the planet. Petrins could instantaneously and virtually transport themselves to the other side of the planet by controlling arachnids no matter where they were located—another example of the sophisticated network of communication via spookyons.

When not being controlled by petrins, arachnids existed in a form of hibernation, which meant they didn't move independently of a spookyon connection with a petrin. When in hibernation, therefore, they would position themselves at the base of a nectar tree and slowly drink from the hollow vines, using small mouths at the front of their central bodies.

The nectar trees and the arachnids were clones of each other, possessing the exact same genetic makeup. Petrins, on the other hand, were genetically diverse from each other. This genetic diversity, although small enough that they wouldn't be considered different species, was sufficiently varied so that petrins, even though part of the collective, could retain some degree of individuality. Petrin culture was therefore a unique mix of individuality and communality, with individuals being able to disconnect from the collective for short periods of time even though no individual was allowed to remain apart from the community permanently. As Vinod put it during one of the debriefings, they were not permitted to "go rogue."

Since there were only three species of life on Petri, and because there was little environmental variation on the planet, the pictures from Petri transmitted by Seth became somewhat monotonous.

"Seen one, seen 'em all," Vinod said. "Who would have thought that extraterrestrial life could be so bland? I mean, we're not exactly looking at the *Star Wars* bar on the planet Tatooine."

"But fascinating and educational nevertheless," Joshua pointed out. "The symbiotic nature between petrins and arachnids is more than amazing. Symbiotic relationships exist on Earth in both the plant and animal kingdoms. Orchids are a perfect example, as are various kinds of fungi."

"And then there are corals and algae, as well as cleaner fish, like remora that attach themselves to sharks and whales," Langdon said after one of the lengthy transmissions as the personal team gave him their preliminary onsite report before official debriefing. "Our biologists will be able to study this for decades."

Despite the monotony of Petri, the pictures sent from Earth, with its enormous diversity of life and environmental habitats, were anything but monotonous for the petrins.

"Really interesting," Seth told his listeners on Earth. "We find your images to be pretty cool. You have a lot of environments over there. You must be a highly adaptable species to be able to exist in so many places."

"I'd say that's true," Joshua said.

The comment was made during a session when the general's adjutant was present. He swiped his thumb across his throat, indicating that Joshua was not to relay anything further about humanity's adaptability. "It could convey the wrong signal," he said.

"Such as?" Joshua said.

"Such as whether we could live on Petri, or whether the petrins could live on Earth."

Joshua sighed. "Remind the good general," he said, "that colonization isn't even a remote possibility."

"As I said, this is off limits," the adjutant reaffirmed. "If they extrapolate the information for themselves, that's another matter."

Vinod rolled his eyes. "Like they can't—or haven't—already done so. Hell, dude, they're a billion years ahead of us and have the computing power of thirteen trillion individuals. You think they can't put two and two together even from the limited pictures your boss allows us to transmit? Tell Porter to go back to basic training. All this rigorous screening of each and every pic we send is pointless and stupid."

The adjutant made no reply.

Vinod drove the point home with his trademark directness. "Just look at the quality of pictures the petrins are sending, and you'll see the disparity between their technology—and certainly their raw intelligence—and ours."

The latter statement was true. The images received from Seth were extremely high resolution, over one gigabyte in size even with JPEG compression. In fact, when technicians zoomed in on images showing the entirety of Petri, individual nectar trees could clearly be seen. When the image of Seth was magnified, the teams were able to see the cellular structure that made up his skin.

Seth alluded to the fact that petrins had colonized numerous other planets besides Petri, but the method as to how they had done so, as well as any other information about these planets, was redacted. The three teams wondered what petrin spaceships looked like and what mode of propulsion they used, but this information was not forthcoming from Seth. How the petrins had colonized other worlds was a complete mystery to the researchers.

"We can't reveal anything related to our technology," Seth said. "You know the drill."

"That's my damn point exactly," General Porter shouted at a monthly meeting with Langdon, Williams, and himself again sitting opposite Joshua, Rachael, and Vinod in the conference room of the particle center. "You've spouted all this talk about how they can't possibly come here, but how did they colonize thousands of planets? There's something they're not telling us."

"It's a valid point," Williams said. "How do creatures that resemble sea anemones travel across vast interstellar distances? They can't even travel across their own planet without help from arachnids. And we've yet to see any machinery."

"Because they're hiding it," Porter speculated.

"They've revealed aspects of their biological engineering," Langdon stated. "Why not tell us how they travel through space?"

Joshua shrugged. "I don't have an answer for that."

In point of fact, it was something that Joshua wondered about himself over the course of the next year, during which they'd learned the rudiments of petrin culture as the renovations of the bat cave were completed. He completely trusted the petrins, and Seth in particular. And while Seth was never hesitant to use the word "redacted," a fact everyone had grown accustomed to, Joshua had the feeling that something was being withheld for other reasons, something very important.

Chapter Twenty-Two
Session 103

Joshua drove his Harley-Davidson through the streets of Berkeley, Rachael sitting behind him, her chin on his shoulder, arms wrapped around his waist as her brunette hair, bunched into a ponytail, whipped in the morning wind from underneath her helmet. Rachael was exhilarated as the bike, Joshua, and she felt like a single mechanism traveling the road. At the end of the ride, Joshua downshifted as the bike eased up the driveway of the NASA BOWMAN PARTICLE RESEARCH CENTER. It had been almost a year since NASA had procured the center from the university.

Rachael felt content and at ease as she did almost every morning since she'd met Joshua. Their relationship had blossomed into one of true love, friendship, and mutual respect. Rachael had imparted to Joshua her love for the outdoors as evidenced by the frequent hikes they took through the forests close to Berkeley.

"Whew!" Rachael said. "Maybe this is what it feels like when petrins and arachnids travel together. It's like a symbiotic relationship!"

"Maybe I should teach you to ride one day," Joshua suggested as he dismounted and removed his helmet. "You seem to understand the Zen of riding a Harley."

"It's a great machine, but it pollutes the atmosphere," Rachael said, "but . . ."

"But what?"

"But it's also really kick-ass fun. And you weren't kidding. You're really good on that thing."

"That *thing* is a Harley-Davidson Street Bob—a bobber—and it has a Milwaukee-Eight 107 engine with one hundred and ten foot-pounds of engine torque. You went sky diving with Vinod, so why not push another envelope and learn to ride."

"Tempting," she said. Rachael looked at the handsome scientist and the Harley as she smoothed her hair. "Okay. Deal." They walked hand in hand towards the atrium.

"Good morning Dr. Andrews, Miss Miller," Charlotte said as she greeted the couple with a smile. She was seated at the counter in the atrium as usual.

"Good morning, Charlotte," Rachael replied as she and Joshua walked around her into the main corridor of the facility while Charlotte logged them in on her computer.

"She's always so formal," Rachael remarked after they had gotten out of earshot.

Joshua shrugged his shoulders and replied with a one-word answer, "British," as if that alone was a justification for her formality.

As they walked through the complex, they ran into Rodrigo, who was wearing an ill-fitting lab coat with a tee shirt underneath that read I EAT AT THE RESTAURANT AT THE EDGE OF THE UNIVERSE. He walked towards them eating a donut, its powdered sugar coating covering his fingers and a small portion around his mouth.

"Hey Rodrigo," Joshua said as he approached. "That's a new look for you."

"Hey, boss. Maybe they can force me to wear this coat, but I have a few tricks up my sleeve—and in my pocket." He produced a second donut from the right-side pocket. "The NASA people look at me all weird, but they don't know crap about the tokamak, so they usually steer clear of me."

"Don't let 'em get under your skin," Joshua advised.

"Mamacita, que pasa?" Rodrigo asked turning to Rachael.

Rachael replied in Spanish. "*What's up, Rodrigo? I see you've found your breakfast.*"

"*Breakfast of champions. So you still hanging out with this loser?*" he asked jokingly.

"*Yeah, our relationship does have its benefits,*" Rachael replied.

"*Oh yeah? Like what?*"

"*Like, I get to ride in the HOV lane when we come to work every day so we can avoid that Berkeley traffic.*"

"*Right,*" Rodrigo said with a chuckle.

Rachael held out her fists as if revving the handles on a motorcycle. "*He's going to teach me to ride.*"

"*Pretty cool. That'll make you a biker chick. I know a chopper shop where you can buy a mean black leather jacket.*"

"Hey, I really like the sound of that. Text me the name of the place."

"Come on," Joshua interrupted. "You two do know that it's rude to speak Spanish in front of someone who doesn't know the language, don't you?"

"Yes, we know, honey," Rachael replied as she turned to Joshua and patted his face. "That's why we're doing it."

"Boss, you coming down to the tokamak today?" Rodrigo asked

"Maybe later this afternoon," Joshua responded. "We've got some work to do in the bat cave this morning."

"I've tried to get down there to talk to you about the new lids, but ever since those NASA guys took over, they have the place locked up tighter than Fort Knox," Rodrigo remarked. "Say, what do you two do down there?"

"Well, if we told you, we'd have to kill you," Joshua replied. "And I don't want to do that just yet."

"Some of the staff think you're planning the first manned mission to Mars," Rodrigo said.

"No, it's more of a think tank down there."

Joshua knew his statement wasn't far off the mark.

"Right," Rodrigo remarked as he started to walk away. "You two have fun."

"I really hate feeding him half-truths," Joshua said after Rodrigo had turned the corner. "The guy deserves better."

"The entire world deserves the truth," Rachael said, "but Williams and the feds aren't going to let that happen. Hey, I've got to grab the laptop from my office. I'll meet you down there."

"Okay," Joshua said as he gave her a kiss on the cheek and walked away.

Joshua continued through the halls of the facility to the freight elevator that led to the bat cave. Gordon the security guard was there as usual, although Porter had installed electronic surveillance in the hallway leading to the elevator as well as the armed guards that Rodrigo had alluded to. At least Gordon now had a chair and a desk with a computer on it. Joshua had often wondered what he did to avoid getting bored sitting for hours at a time guarding the only entrance to the bat cave. He was sure some YouTube videos might be involved.

"Morning, Gordon," Joshua said as he placed his thumb on the thumbprint detector that activated the elevator. The doors opened, and he rode down for the two minutes it took to get to the redesigned bat cave.

As he exited the elevator, motion sensor lights illuminated the entirety of the converted mine. He took a seat at a chair in front of one of the desks and looked at the Bowman sphere encased in the front wall behind its bullet-proof glass, glowing its usual green color. While he still had issues with the way NASA and the federal government had handled the discovery of Seth and his civilization, he had to admit that the test facility had grown in size and scope beyond all expectations, and its new purpose always caused his heart to beat faster when he entered the space. The text on the overhead screen read CONNECTION: INACTIVE. He pushed a button on the desk's touch screen to unmute the mics, and text now read CONNECTION: ACTIVE.

"'Sup Seth," he said.

"'Sup, Josh." Seth's voice emanated from multiple speakers in the room. Since he didn't sleep, he continually monitored his connection with the humans and was always available for conversation.

Seth had figured out the difference between formal and informal English. It was a running joke between Joshua and Seth that the first word that humanity had received from an alien intelligence was "'sup." It was a point of some embarrassment for Seth which Joshua kiddingly rekindled each morning by addressing him with this same greeting.

"You're never going to let me live that down, are you?" Seth asked.

"Never."

"It was Vinod's fault. He didn't tell me the significance of the words in the dictionaries he sent. English is a very versatile language with many colorful idioms since I've now learned standard English as well as a part of my introduction to elements of art, history, literature, music, and anthropology. They've all been greatly redacted, and psychology and sociology have been omitted altogether, although I've gleaned much information on the latter two through our conversations."

Joshua hesitated. Porter had allowed military intelligence teams to vet and redact the liberal arts that Vinod had sent to Seth in subsequent transmissions. In the general's estimation, some disciplines exhibited too many human weaknesses and failings. Joshua felt that, given the petrins' raw computing power, Seth could probably extrapolate what had been omitted.

"Yes," Joshua said. "That's correct. We thought that certain elements of human culture might seem puzzling—even contradictory—and can be better conveyed gradually as we establish a broader foundation for our relationship." Joshua knew that he was parsing words and felt a tinge of hypocrisy given his own suspicions about Seth's redactions. "Sorry."

"No apology necessary. You have as much right to redact information as we do. This is, after all, your first contact."

"Glad you understand."

"I especially like poetry," Seth continued. "It renders communication in a very compressed, figurative manner. Some of it is highly efficient in conveying ideas in few words."

"It's like music to humans."

"I'm deaf, as you may recall, but I understand the mathematics of your diatonic scale. Some species communicate solely through music and would appreciate the nuances of Mozart."

"Does your planet have anything like poetry? I can't imagine poetry being digital in nature."

"Digital communication can be whatever we want it to be. English, for example. But no, we don't have poetry and never have. We had legends millennia ago, which are archived in the minds of the collective. They're more of a factual history of our planet and its development than anything else, but it has a mathematical cadence in its coding that is similar to what you call meter in poetry."

"Some human legends might be considered factual, although greatly embellished for dramatic effect."

"Like your fiction?" Seth said. "That puzzles me. Why do people on Earth go to the trouble of making up false scenarios? Why not simply record facts?"

Joshua sat back and stared at the sphere, wondering how he could answer the question in a manner that Seth would appreciate. This was exactly the kind of detail that the personal team was charged with handling.

"Fiction gives us pleasure, but more importantly, the greatest fiction conveys truths about the human condition. Many of our finest books seek to facilitate a better future for humanity by assessing its values and shared cultural experiences. Hopefully, good fiction tells the truth about what it means to be human."

There was a pause in the communication, and Joshua wondered if Seth's curiosity was especially piqued by the response or whether he was passing on the answer to others in the collective.

"Yes, truth and the future," Seth finally said. "Important concepts. Tell me, Josh—where do humans see themselves in the future? What are your planet's plans for the years ahead?"

Joshua scratched his head at the unanticipated question, which was of a far more speculative and philosophical nature than any that Seth usually posed.

"We don't really think that far ahead, Seth, at least not most of us. We do have a few visionary figures who talk about life centuries from now, but

KISHORE TIPIRNENI

most of us wake up every morning and manage life one day at a time with an eye as to what may happen next month or next year. In some cases we look to our old age, although most of us try to put that off. I think it's one of our shortcomings that we don't plan far enough ahead—an inherent flaw of our species—but it's a human characteristic."

Joshua knew that General Porter wouldn't approve of his admittance that humans were flawed creatures, but it was an honest answer and the only one that came to mind. Besides, given Seth's unexpected interest about the planet's future, he considered it important to delve into the issue. It was, after all, part of his mission.

"Why do you ask, Seth?"

"Curiosity. It's a natural question, don't you think?"

"Yes, it certainly is."

The exchange was the latest during which Joshua believed that Seth was getting at something more specific and that he was withholding the reason for asking a question.

"What about *your* species?" Joshua asked. "What does the collective see in its future?"

"I'm afraid that's redacted."

"Huh? Oh, wait. I get it. Your future is tied to your advanced technology, and you can't share that with us."

"I think that's a reasonable assumption."

He's being damned evasive, Joshua thought. Assumption? A simple yes or no would have sufficed.

"Are Vinod and Rachael with you?"

"No, just me down here right now," Joshua replied. "They should be here soon."

"Soooo?" Seth asked, drawing out the word as if Joshua should know what he was getting at.

"So *what*?" Joshua replied.

"So have you asked her yet?"

Joshua looked around the room to make sure no technician was standing in the corner before replying in a hushed voice. "No, I haven't asked her yet. You know that's just between you and me, right? I want it to be a surprise for her."

"Yeah, I know. That's why I made sure you were alone before I brought it up. When you ask her, you have to make sure to record the exact time down to the second for me."

"Why?"

"The collective has a wager going."

170

"Doesn't the collective have better things to do than betting on when Rachael and I get engaged?"

"Sure, but we find your courtship very interesting and entertaining. So much of your literature involves mating rituals and coupling."

"Glad we can be your sideshow," Joshua replied sarcastically. "What does the winner get? I know you don't have anything like money."

"Just notoriety, which is actually something valuable in a collective of over thirteen trillion individuals."

The response was almost comedic in its content, and yet it made perfect sense.

Joshua was amazed that a species that had evolved beyond emotions still, in Seth's own words, accessed them occasionally. And notoriety indicated pride. For all his vast intelligence, Seth at times struck Joshua as possessing an almost human temperament.

More importantly, though, he wondered if the collective's interest in mating rituals was related to Seth's question about where humanity saw itself in the future. After all, marriage and procreation always pointed in that direction. While Seth was adamant about not sharing technology, he had more than a passing curiosity about the destiny of human beings. But there was something even more unusual contained in Seth's remarks. The entire collective was fascinated with the mating of two specific individuals: Joshua Andrews and Rachael Miller. He knew better than to ask Seth outright what he was getting at, however. He was beginning to know in advance when Seth would be evasive and when he would not.

"Any progress on creating spookyons?" Seth asked, abruptly changing the subject.

"No, not yet," Joshua replied with a sigh. "You know, it would really help if you could give me a hint on what we're doing wrong." His voice was laced with good-natured sarcasm.

"No can do, Josh," Seth replied.

"Yeah, yeah, yeah," Joshua remarked. "I know. Your prime directive."

"Prime directive?"

"Reference TV show, 1960s, *Star Trek*," Joshua answered, knowing that Vinod had told him once that some of *Star Trek* had made it into the original information sent to Seth.

"Got it. Very apropos."

Joshua heard the elevator doors open and saw Rachael and Vinod walking towards him. Vinod was dressed in jeans and a U2 tee shirt with an album cover from their *Joshua Tree* album.

"Rachael and Vinod have graced us with their presence," Joshua announced.

"'Sup, Rach?" Seth asked. "'Sup Vinod."

While Vinod and Seth referred to Rachael as "Rach," Joshua had grown accustomed to referring to her by her full Christian name and stuck with it. Besides, "Rach" was too awkward to suit his own taste. The abbreviation, he thought, was more appropriate for a sibling or longtime friend. Rachael was the woman he'd fallen in love with, and Rachael, he decided, was who she would remain.

"Good morning, everyone," Rachael said as she and Vinod took seats on either side of Joshua.

Joshua glanced at Vinod's shirt. "Hey, you're wearing my tree."

"Yup. I hope you feel honored."

"You ready to start, Seth?" Rachael said as she opened her laptop.

"Sure," Seth replied. "You want to begin, or you want me to?"

"I've got some questions jotted down, so I'll go first," Rachael said.

"Fire away," came Seth's response.

"This is NASA session number 103," Rachael announced. "Rachael Miller, Dr. Joshua Andrews, and Vinod Bhakti present. Seth, first question. You've told us that there is intelligent life on other planets that is not of your species. Is there a way for us to talk to these other beings using our spookyon connection with you?"

"Yes, it's technically possible," Seth replied. "We can use two separate spookyon connections to relay data between you and another species, but our ethical rules prohibit this. You know, the prime directive and all."

"Prime directive?" Rachael asked.

"I had Seth reference *Star Trek* before you two walked in," Joshua explained.

"Sweet," Vinod remarked. "Prime directive. We'll make a Trekkie out of you yet, Seth."

"Got it," Rachael said. "Okay, next question. Why can't we speak to someone else in the collective besides you? It might give us a greater feel for the degree of individuality you said exists within the collective despite its connected structure."

"Well, as I told you when we first made contact, my thoughts flow to everyone else in the collective and theirs back to me, so it would be unnecessary. I've been assigned as your personal ambassador. It's how we do things."

"If that's the case," Joshua said, "then why don't you disconnect from the collective whenever you talk with the three of us. You could reconnect with the collective when you speak with the scientific teams. It would allow you to interact with us on a more personal level. One on one, so to speak."

"Or one on three," Seth corrected. "Yes, I can do that. I've now disconnected from the collective."

It always amazed the humans how Seth and the collective could make important decisions such as this in an instant. There was no need for a lengthy debate and decision making. The collective seemed to be a true democracy, with choices posed to all of its members and decided instantaneously.

Joshua typed a note on his laptop: It's how things are done. Seth made it sound as if contact with other civilizations was routine, and maybe it was for his planet after billions of years of looking for signals via spookyons. Still, the phrase stood out for him. Joshua suddenly felt as if his home world was nothing but a hillbilly planet in the backwaters of the universe. Earth was not a place that was in on the secret of *how things were done*. He wondered if any of the teams would ever come close to learning anything truly substantive about Petri. Would they have to wait a billion years? The idea was disconcerting.

The phrase bothered Joshua at a deeper level. It implied a standard protocol for the many contacts that the petrins made, but protocols for *what*? He was certain that he was missing something, but his ruminations were abruptly turned away by the sound of Seth's always-inquisitive voice.

"My turn?" Seth asked.

"Sure, go ahead," Rachael replied as she entered notes in her laptop.

"What is the status of your current viral outbreak?"

Joshua looked somberly at Vinod and Rachael before answering. "It's not good, Seth. It's not good at all. There are now forty-nine separate outbreaks, mostly located throughout Asia, the Middle East, and Africa. There are outbreaks in Europe and South America, and just two days ago new cases were discovered in the U.S. in Dallas."

"So you haven't been able to contain the spread?" Seth asked.

"No," Vinod replied. "None of the isolation techniques we've used in previous Ebola outbreaks seems to work. In fact, our scientists are not sure that this virus is even Ebola. Some of the symptoms are Ebola-like, but its transmission seems to be very different. The scientists still haven't been able to isolate and culture it in the lab which is really the first step in trying to formulate a treatment."

"Frankly, Seth," Rachael said, "many people are starting to panic, and in some areas lawlessness has ensued, which, as you can imagine, is counterproductive when you're trying to contain an outbreak. It's really scary."

"How many have died?" Seth asked, clearly interested in the factual aspects of the outbreak.

"Thousands," Joshua responded.

"Sorry to hear that," Seth replied. "Being an immortal species, death is not something we are accustomed to, though we have encountered it in other species."

"Unfortunately," Rachael said, "death is a part of human life. I learned that the hard way when I was ten."

Joshua turned to Rachael. He and Vinod knew what she was talking about but were surprised that she was prepared to reveal it to Seth. He reached out and grabbed Rachael's hand to offer comfort.

"What happened?" Seth asked.

Rachael sat silently. Over the past several months, she, Joshua, and Vinod had grown fond of Seth. He had become a friend rather than a research subject. Indeed, some of their conversations were characterized by a very personal tone. This was exactly what Robert Langdon had hoped for since the entire purpose of their team was to interact with Seth on a less technical level.

"When I was born, I had a twin brother," Rachael finally began. "His name was Richard. We were best buddies and did everything together. When he was nine, he was diagnosed with a type of cancer called Ewing's sarcoma. Despite the doctors' best efforts, he wasn't able to be cured, and Richard died when we were ten. It was a very traumatic time for me."

"I'm sorry to hear that," Seth replied. "Thank you for sharing this with me. Cancer is really a defect in the force that creates life."

"What do you mean by that?" Vinod asked.

"As you know, reproduction is an essential part of growth and evolution," Seth said. "But unrestricted reproduction leads to a loss of differentiation, whether you're talking about an organism or an entire society. This loss of differentiation ultimately causes the death of either the organism or a society. Cancer is the unrestricted reproduction of a cell and leads to the eventual destruction of the organism. We would consider your Ebola virus as a cancer as well, with the difference being that this form of cancer is metastatic outside the host, not just inside. But whether you're speaking about cancer from Ewing's sarcoma or Ebola, the culprit is still unrestricted reproduction. This is why we have strict rules on reproduction, especially on that of sentient organisms."

"What's your definition of sentient organisms?" Joshua asked, noting that Seth had segued into deep waters. And not for the first time, he had raised the issue of reproduction.

"We consider sentience not an absolute quality, but an accumulated quantity. Every organism has some level of sentience, but as they, or more specifically their brains, get more complex, their level of sentience increases. When we require an absolute definition of sentience, such as for our rules of reproduction, we have to pick an arbitrary point on this range."

"So for this reproduction rule, where do you draw that line?" Rachael asked. "What do you consider sentient?"

"I'd say it's somewhere between a bacterium and a human," Seth replied.

"Bro," Vinod said, "that's a pretty broad range."

"Not for us," Seth responded.

There were moments during their conversations with Seth when he would say something that caused the trio to consider the extreme dichotomy between humans and petrins, something that caused them to realize the awesome power and intelligence they were dealing with. This was one of those moments.

"Humble much?" Vinod remarked to break the tension.

"Not trying to brag," Seth responded. "Just providing you information."

"Well, I for one am glad that you consider humans sentient," Rachael said. She turned back to her laptop. "I have another question on my list. You've told us before that you are immortal. How does that work?"

"We are immortal in that we don't die," Seth replied. "We grow to our adult selves from a single cell much like humans do, but once we reach adulthood, our genetic pattern stops aging, unlike the pattern in humans. When humans get old and die, it's not because their cells have gotten older. It's because the pattern of what their cells *represent* gets older."

"Not sure if I follow that," Joshua remarked.

"The cells that make up our bodies die and are replaced just like yours, even in adulthood. In humans, however, this replacement of cells is done on a pattern that is continuously aging. In essence, it's the specific arrangement of your cells that defines you, and it's that arrangement that gets older. We simply stop our pattern from aging at adulthood through the process of bio-engineering. We are therefore immortal."

"You make it sound so simple," Rachael said.

"For us, it is. Again, not trying to brag. I'm simply trying to answer your question as accurately as possible."

"There has to be *some* death," Vinod remarked. "What if some crazy asteroid hits your planet and physically destroys some individuals?"

"Accidents like that do happen from time to time," Seth remarked, "but the pattern, the specific arrangement of our molecules and cells that define us, is backed up periodically as data. This data is stored in data nodes at multiple offsite locations on other planets. If some accident befalls one of our individuals, they are simply recreated using their last backup."

Joshua scribbled a note on a piece of paper and shoved it in front of Rachael. *For them it really is that simple.*

"Man," Vinod said, "it's the ultimate offsite backup. AWS would be proud. It's the cloud on steroids."

"We have strict rules, however, about the backup of sentient organisms," Seth continued. "There can be an unlimited number of backups stored as data, but only one copy of a particular sentient organism can be alive at any given time."

"In essence, are you saying that what defines an individual of your race is simply the data that defines its specific pattern?" Rachael asked.

"Yes," Seth replied. "We believe that what defines *any* organism, including humans, is the data of its specific pattern. In fact, we've found that the sentience of an organism is directly related to the amount of data needed to contain that organism's pattern. The more data that is required, the more sentient they are. It's a straightforward data-to-sentience ratio."

The trio sat in silence, reflecting on the implications of what Seth had told them. A simple question about the Ebola outbreak had spurred a discussion of life, death, and the definition of intelligence. Had this been Seth's intention from the beginning?

"It's very ethical that you allow only one copy of a sentient organism to live at any given time," Joshua said, "but what you describe almost sounds impersonal. Your individuality is determined by bits of data."

"That's what DNA is," Seth countered. "Bits of data. But DNA only constitutes a small amount of the total data needed to define an individual, especially a sentient one like a human. In humans, the majority of data is stored as neural connections in the brain."

"I understand," Joshua said, although he thought that there might be subtle differences between Seth's definition of individuality and his. "Very true."

"I have another question for you," Seth said.

"Okay," Vinod said. "Go for it."

"What is the human definition of death?"

The trio paused a moment before Joshua answered. "I guess we consider death to be when a living organism ceases to function."

"This is different from what we consider to be death," Seth said. "We consider death to be the loss of the last copy."

"The last copy?" Vinod asked.

"Let me explain by example," Seth said. "Your scientists have told me about a species of frog on your planet called the wood frog, which lives in cold climates. Apparently, during the winter months when the ground freezes, the frog becomes frozen along with its surroundings, but with the spring thaw, it unfreezes and returns to normal. When this frog is in its frozen state, would you consider it to be dead?"

"Probably not dead," Rachael answered. "I guess we would consider it to be in some kind of suspended state."

"Okay," Seth continued. "Now what if you were to take this frozen frog and then physically alter it such that its arrangement is not ordered as a frog but is random. What then?"

"What do you mean?" Vinod asked. "Like if we were to put it in a blender and chop it up into millions of pieces?"

"Exactly," Seth replied. "If you were chop up the frozen frog in a blender, would it be dead by your definition?"

"Yes," Joshua responded. "It would be dead." He felt as if he were being engaged in a Socratic dialog by one of his undergrad college professors.

"So what has actually changed in the frog to make it dead?" Seth asked rhetorically before answering his own question. "What has changed is that the specific arrangement of the molecules which made it a frog is no longer present. This arrangement has been randomized. The *information* that defines it to be a frog has been lost, but if the information is backed up in another location, the frog can be recreated. Only if there is no backup, and the last copy of the information is randomized, would we consider the frog to be dead. Therefore, we define death as the loss of the last copy of information for an organism."

"Interesting," Rachael remarked as she pondered what Seth had said.

A broad smile crossed Vinod's face. "Offsite storage, backup copies, immortality—I get it!"

"Once the last copy of *any* information is lost from the universe, it can't be easily recreated," Seth continued. "Joshua, you are experiencing this problem with the creation of your spookyons. Dr. Henry Bowman had information on how to create them when he was alive and had written data in his notebooks. There were two copies of this information, one in his brain and one in his notebooks. When he died, the copy in his brain was lost. When you couldn't find his notebooks, the second copy was essentially lost and therefore you have to recreate his research to retrieve his information. This is why the last copy is so important. When humans die, the last copy of them is gone from the universe and can't be recreated because there's no backup. This is why the death of a human is so devastating, just as Rachael described when talking about her brother."

"My God," Joshua said aloud to himself. "Henry was right. Information really is everything." He wondered if Henry had prophetically known exactly what Seth was talking about but had never lived to advance the ideas himself. Maybe there was a good deal more in his notebooks, wherever they might be, than information on creating spookyons.

"Personally, I think this all makes perfect sense," Vinod stated. "It's what the digital age is all about."

The group sat in silence as Rachael feverishly added notes to her laptop regarding Seth's stunning concept of death and its relation to his philosophy of individualism, sentient life, and "the last copy." As she typed, she thought of a new question, the answer to which might distill the weighty matters they were talking about to a brief, meaningful word. Besides being informative, it might greatly aid the debriefing sessions that followed all conversations.

"Seth, you've referred several times to the specific arrangement of molecules that defines an organism, but do you have a simple term for it?"

"Yes," Seth replied. "Life."

The trio exchanged puzzled glances.

"Care to elaborate on that?" Joshua asked. "That's a rather all-encompassing answer."

"It's supposed to be. We define life to be the specific pattern of elements that constitute a particular entity, and we define living as the execution of that for which that pattern is purposed. For example, the frozen frog has life because it retains the pattern or *information* of a frog, but it isn't living because it's not actually functioning as a frog. A frog that is unfrozen and jumping around has life and is also living because it's fulfilling the purpose of its pattern. A frozen, chopped-up frog has no life and therefore cannot be living. The antithesis of purposeful data or life is randomness. So randomizing the data and order that define an entity, like chopping up the frozen frog, causes it to be destroyed, but it's only *truly* destroyed when the last copy of this data is randomized."

Rachael thought that Seth's elaboration was both simple and elegant as she entered it into her laptop.

"I want to clarify a couple of more points about our definition of life," Seth stated. "First, life does not have to be based on organic molecules. We consider anything with purposeful complexity, no matter what it's made of, to contain life. For example, we would consider a book to contain life. It contains a specific arrangement of letters and words that defines its message.

If you were to randomize the arrangement of the words that make up a book, it would become meaningless. It's not the words that make a book important, it is the *arrangement* of these words. When someone is reading a book, we would consider it to be *living* since it is executing the purpose for which it was designed. For us, we make no distinction between a frozen frog and a book since they both contain life. The actual molecules that compose the life is irrelevant."

"So when someone is reading a book," Joshua said, "he's executing the purpose of the author, which is that the words take on meaning and come alive in the mind of the reader."

"Exactly," Seth said. "I'm glad you understand."

For Vinod, the information theorist and programmer, this made complete sense. An app's code, with a specific arrangement of bits that defined it, had life, and when it was running or executing its code, it was living. It reminded him of a drastic mistake he made in his early days in college. He had a computer coding project that took him a week to write, but since he didn't back up the project, he lost his work when the hard drive on his computer crashed. In Seth's words, he'd lost the last copy. He had no choice but to rewrite the code again, which was a lengthy and painstaking process.

The more Seth elucidated his ideas on life, the more Vinod felt a kinship with petrin culture. For the first time, it occurred to him that there was no such thing as AI. Intelligence either existed or it didn't regardless of the form it took. The ramifications of the alien's words were enormous.

"The final point I want to make about life is that it is a quantity, not a quality," Seth said. "We consider a frog and a human to both have life, but a human contains *more* life than a frog. The amount of data needed to back up a human is much larger than that needed for a frog. This amount of data has nothing to do with physical size. We consider a human to have more life than an elephant because the amount of data needed to back up a human is larger than that needed for an elephant. In humans, the majority of data—or life—is contained in their brains in the form of specific neural connections that define human thought and memory."

Rachael continued taking notes and had found the session to be particularly revealing, with Seth going into more detail than usual on core matters of petrin culture. For Vinod, Seth's definitions of life and living were profound, bordering on a religious experience. For Joshua, the ideas presented were as deep and complex as Rachael's spiritual beliefs, which still challenged him when he tried to analyze them.

"May I have another question?" Seth asked. "I guess it's more of a request than a question."

"Sure," Rachel replied. "Go ahead."

"I've been given much information about your world," Seth began, "but you can understand that it's not the same as being able to move around and experience it firsthand. I was wondering if I could be permitted to actually move around your planet to get a better understanding of it."

Rachael's fingers stopped typing, and there was silence in the bat cave.

Chapter Twenty-Three
Ambassador Andrews

The trio looked at each other in shock at Seth's extraordinary—and totally unexpected—request. How could Seth come to Earth or physically move around the planet without appendages? After all, he could not even move about his own planet without the help of arachnids.

Rachael had assured General Porter at their original debriefing after first contact that it would be impossible for Seth to journey to Earth given the vast distances between stars and galaxies and because nothing could travel faster than the speed of light. There was not even a remote possibility, she had said, that petrins would ever visit Earth. Now Seth was proposing that he physically move among them, although he hadn't revealed any details as to how he might accomplish this. Perhaps, they thought, he was going to finally reveal how his race traveled to other planets. Was it possible that petrins had learned how to move through wormholes and didn't need any advanced propulsion system to roam among the stars? Maybe, Joshua reasoned, this is what Seth had been reluctant to reveal and why he'd been evasive when answering so many questions. Whatever the case, all three members of the personal team worried that they'd lose all credibility with Langdon, Williams, and Porter given prior assurances that no physical contact was imminent.

"How could you accomplish this?" Joshua asked, his tone now more guarded than friendly. "You don't know where we are and, uh . . . to put it bluntly, you have no legs."

Seth was not offended by the remark.

"In my discussions with your scientific teams, I learned about the advancements you've made in robotics. They're quite impressive for your stage of development. I was wondering if you would allow me to remotely control an android so that I could move about your world and better experience its sights, sounds, colors, and physical features. I've enjoyed our many sessions together, but you have to admit that there are certain constraints with the present arrangement, and I'd like to learn more about Earth. What I propose is simply a more direct and personal interface. Interfacing with me is, after all, the mission for the three of you—what you call your personal team—is it not? To get to know me better as an individual? What better way to accomplish this than to have me stand in your midst, albeit in the virtual sense of the word?"

To Joshua, the proposal had been advanced with the precision of a well-delivered legal argument, and at face value it seemed eminently logical. He was also relieved that there was no Einstein-Rosen bridge in spacetime that would allow Seth to physically visit Earth.

Rachael looked sideways at Joshua and mouthed the words *General Porter.*

Joshua cleared his throat, not sure how to respond except in an honest and forthright manner. "There would be serious security concerns with something like that, Seth. I don't honestly think permission will be granted by others involved in the project."

Seth was undeterred. "I completely understand, and I would be willing to comply with whatever security restrictions you would implement. You and your superiors would be in total control the entire time."

Rachael reached for the mic control on the desk and pressed the mute button to silence all microphones in the room. "Look, we obviously can't do this. Seth doesn't even know that we're keeping his existence a secret from everyone on the planet—seven billion people. He may believe that these transmissions are being broadcast to everyone on Earth since we told him at Vinod's on that first night that our digital advancements have made us a collective of sorts. He might take great offense and think we've been deceiving him. And I doubt that Porter's security team would even consider this." She shook her head slowly. "It's simply not possible at this point."

Joshua leaned back in the desk and folded his arms, his brows creased. "But imagine how much more we could learn about Petri if Porter would allow it. As Seth pointed out, this is our mission, and the information we might learn could increase a hundredfold."

"Joshua predicted that nobody knew where this gig would lead," Vinod said. "He was right."

Rachael seemed confused. "This would be about Seth learning about *us,* not vice versa. He would gain large quantities of data about us while focus on the petrins might be considerably diminished."

"I suppose that's a possibility," Joshua said. "but if he were robotically present, we might be able to cajole him into revealing more about his planet and society than he normally would. It would be like leveling the playing field. The experience of being in human form might overwhelm him. For all we know, he'd open up *more*. Just because he's extremely advanced doesn't mean he's totally inflexible—or perfect."

Rachael touched Joshua on his arm. "Are you seriously considering this idea or just brainstorming?"

"Just trying to weigh the pros and cons of this decision."

"I think it's a great idea!" Vinod proclaimed enthusiastically. "Let's see how much he still wants to redact when he gets all touchy feely with us. He's asking for an intimate tactile and sensory experience depending on the sophistication of the android. Maybe the dude would go rogue on the collective and slip us some serious answers. For all we know, he could tell us what caused the Big Bang."

Rachael wasn't convinced.

"Perhaps the collective does this with *all* cultures they contact," she suggested. "I don't think he'd let his guard down or violate the ethics of the collective."

Seth's words echoed in Joshua's mind. *It's how things are done.* Maybe this was indeed a standard request.

"You may be right," Joshua said, "but sometimes you have to push the envelope, like skydiving with Vinod or learning to ride a Harley."

"I see what you're getting at," Rachael said, "but I don't think it's going to fly."

"Where's your unquenchable spirit of scientific curiosity?" Joshua asked.

"Now that's hitting below the belt," Rachael said, jabbing his arm playfully. "It's alive and well, thank you. I'm playing devil's advocate, and Porter is going to see Seth as the devil incarnate."

"I'm afraid she's right," Vinod remarked. "Porter is going to blow his top when he hears about this. That ought to be a fun part of the debriefing. I can already see the veins standing out on his forehead."

Joshua nodded. "It's probably a moot point given the fact that NASA is running this project and we're more or less consultants. Unmute the conversation, please. I need to give him an answer."

Rachael unmuted the mics.

"Seth, that's a pretty tall order," Joshua said. "I don't think the higher-ups are going to be able to grant your request, but we'll ask them for you."

"Thanks. I appreciate it."

Seth's last words seemed unusually polite—even formal—to both

Joshua and Rachael as the session was terminated. Joshua now felt certain that Seth had an agenda, although he wasn't willing to entertain the notion that it might be harmful to Earth, as Porter might assume. Allowing Seth to use robotics to directly interface with humans was an idea that came with a great many unknowns, but as a scientist, he was of the opinion that the benefits outweighed the risks, and the risks could definitely be controlled. Convincing Langdon, Williams, and Porter might be impossible, but he would honor his promise to Seth to present the request. The opportunity to have an alien standing in their midst was one that had to be considered.

*   *   *

Robert Langdon had a large corner office on the second floor of the particle center, with windows that offered a view of the immaculately manicured atrium below. He sat behind a desk that faced two couches. A large flat screen hung on the wall adjacent to the couches, and pictures of various spacecraft, manned and unmanned, adorned the other walls of the well-appointed office, with tall potted green plants in the corners. Joshua, Rachael, and Vinod entered and sat on the couch to the left of Langdon as he swiveled his brown leather chair with a high back away from a computer on a small side desk.

"Well, how'd the morning session go?" Robert asked routinely. "I was in the process of setting up our conference call."

All sessions were recorded, but after each one a debriefing was held so that the administrative team could receive a synopsis of the information exchange with Seth. Williams and Porter insisted on knowing on a day-to-day basis what had transpired in the bat cave.

"It was very interesting," Rachael remarked. "*Intense* might be a better way to describe it. We talked about sentience, immortality, and life and death, with some *Star Trek* thrown in."

"Yeah, Seth told us the meaning of life," Vinod stated matter-of-factly. "If you're into that sort of thing, that is."

"Really?" Langdon replied, somewhat startled. "Damn but that's intriguing. I definitely want to hear about his nuggets of wisdom. You can tell us the details during the call. My curiosity is most assuredly piqued."

"Seth did have a request for us, though," Joshua added.

"A request?" Robert asked, sensing hesitation in the scientist's voice. "What kind of request?"

"The dude wants us to build him an android that he would control remotely," Vinod answered. "Says he wants to be able to walk around and see more of our planet. I guess it's the alien version of wanting to visit Disneyworld. You know—Epcot and the World Showcase. You get to sample a little of everything."

Langdon, who was in the process of grabbing a cup of coffee on the side of his desk, froze and stared at the team. "You're kidding, right?"

"No," Joshua replied. "This was *his* request, and I assure you it wasn't prompted by anything we said."

"He wants to experience Earth firsthand is the way he put it," Vinod said by way of qualification.

"We all know that's a no-go, right?" Langdon said, eyebrows raised as he surveyed each member of the team for a reaction.

"Yes," Rachel replied. "We told him we didn't think it would be possible, but that we'd bring it up with you anyway."

Langdon's face showed consternation. "Remote control? What's he talking about?"

"He'd control the android through the spookyon connection," Joshua explained. "The robot would be our new interface with him. Robert, your own team of engineers told him of our advances in robotics. I strongly suspect that's what gave him the idea."

Langdon slapped his desk in anger. "This is just the type of thing we feared would happen. We give him one seemingly insignificant detail and he takes it in a direction that's totally unacceptable. And we'd have to disclose his existence to everyone on Earth if we granted his request."

"It's problematic, to say the least," Joshua admitted, "but we're simply relaying what Seth has asked for. I'm sure Porter will be apoplectic, but this is the gist of our daily report, and he'll have to live with it even though I don't anticipate getting his approval."

Langdon saw that digital numbers at the bottom of the screen in his office were counting down from thirty.

"I'm totally against this, Josh," he said, a stern expression on his face.

"I think we should at least discuss it before dismissing it out of hand," Joshua rebutted. "It presents an enormous opportunity to accelerate the learning curve."

Langdon appeared conflicted. "I don't even know if we should bring this up in the call," he said. "What's the point?"

"The session is already recorded," Joshua pointed out, "and I'm not going to lie in the debriefing. That will piss off Porter just as much."

The screen in Langdon's office was activated, with video feeds of Mitchell Porter and Dina Williams shown split screen on the monitor.

"Good afternoon, everyone," Williams said in an affable tone of voice. "It's a busy day here at the White House, so let's get started, shall we? First, is there anything new to report from this morning's session or is Seth still playing his cards close to the vest? I'm urging the president to have realistic expectations, but he feels we should be gaining more information."

Rachael gave a report of the morning's conversation with Seth, relating details given to Seth on the Ebola outbreak, Seth's claim of immortality, and his definitions of life and death.

The expression on Williams' face clearly indicated that she was taken aback. "Oh, is that all?" she said wryly. "It's Alien Philosophy 101. I'm not sure I buy into everything he told you, but our purpose is to gather information, not come to sweeping conclusions on the nature of existence."

"I think it's a load of crap," Porter said in his usual clipped manner. "For the sake of argument, however, let's assume that his race is indeed immortal and has all of these backup copies of themselves. I don't like it one damn bit. It means they can't be killed because of their redundant patterns stored at unknown locations. There's no way they could ever lose a war. They'd have unlimited troops."

"Nobody said anything about war, general," Rachael said.

"I get *paid* to think about it, young lady."

"Let's file this away for now," Williams suggested. "We're obviously not going to be able to interpret such wide-ranging data in a single debriefing. The bottom line is that it sounds like a very productive morning. Our data analysis team will have their hands full for a long time. Nice job, team. Anything else?"

Joshua shifted uneasily on the couch as the trio looked at the director.

"There's one more thing," Langdon said.

"What is it?" Williams asked.

"Seth has a request for us," Langdon replied. "He wants us to build an android that he can remotely control using the spookyon connection. He says he wants to be able to see more of our planet—in person, so to speak."

"What?" Porter exclaimed. "Is this a joke? No goddamn way that bastard's going to do anything close to that! That's an absolute veto on my part."

"Really?" Vinod asked with a straight face. "General, we told him you'd be okay with it."

Rachael turned to Vinod with a slight smile and shook her slightly-lowered head. During the past year, her friend had yet to give Porter the deference he was accustomed to receiving.

Porter's face grew red. "You'd better be shitting me, Bhakti, because if you're not . . ."

"He's kidding," Langdon interrupted. "They told him it was a no-go."

"That bastard Seth has got a lot of balls asking for something like this,"

Porter claimed. "I'm going to have my security team comb through everything that's been said in that damn cave of yours. If I find that Mr. Bhakti had anything to do with this, I'll make good on my promise to put his ass in prison."

"This request just came through?" Williams said.

"This morning," Rachael said. "Session 103."

"And what was the precise nature of your response?" Williams asked.

Joshua answered for the group. "I told him there were security issues attached to building an android body and that I seriously doubted his request would be honored."

"It was the correct response," she said, relieved. "No one involved in this project would consider it for a moment."

"Actually, I would like the issue to be debated," Joshua retorted.

"Really Dr. Andrews?" Williams said. "You think this idea has merits? I don't feel that there's much of a debate here. What do you think, Robert?"

"I only learned of it right before the conference began," Langdon confessed. "Personally, I'm against it, but Joshua has the right to be heard. Dina, he's not just a messenger boy. He's an integral part of this project."

"I disagree," Porter said. "He doesn't make policy. He's strictly a liaison, an ambassador. I don't have time for this BS."

"Yes, I'm an ambassador of sorts," Joshua said, "and so is Seth. It's my job to not only present his request to you, but to analyze it and look at its pros and cons. Yes, it's risky, but so was sending a man to the moon. This entire mission is fraught with unknowns, and today Seth made an unexpected request. But what did we expect? That everything was going to go according to *our* script? How can we summarily dismiss what he asked without even giving thought to the possible benefits?"

"There *are* none!" Porter said tersely.

"Let him speak," Williams said coldly. "Dr. Andrews, I'm affording you a professional courtesy, nothing more. This isn't going to happen."

"Everything we do here is risky," Joshua stated in an impassioned voice. "Right now Seth is nothing but a voice and an image on a screen—one, I might add, that is hard to relate to. Also, remember that he's deaf and blind. If he can experience the senses we have, or at least some facsimile of them, he might be willing to share more about his culture with us because a commonality would have been established—a fundamental understanding of what it means to be human. Maybe Seth the individual and not the collective would be of greater value than a human-sounding voice that can't relate to humanity beyond a certain point."

"Which is the way I want to keep it," Porter declared. "It's giving away the store. I was guaranteed that his species could never travel here, but isn't that exactly what we're talking about?'

"He has a point, Josh," Langdon said in a cautionary tone. "This is essentially no different than Seth stepping off a spacecraft."

"Of course I have a point," Porter reiterated. "His presence could wreak havoc on Earth, and I'm not talking about all of your sociological crap. He could destroy us if he wanted to. He's billions of years ahead of us. He would no doubt know how to use our own materials to build a single bomb that could wipe out every living being on the planet."

"Not if we did it the right way," Joshua replied. "Look, *we* would be building the android and could have complete control of its construction. We could also mandate that it be monitored by us at all times. We could also build in any security measures we wanted to, including the ability to switch it off anytime we wanted. If we decide to do this, we could build it with minimal risk."

"Besides," Rachael added, "just because humans have aggressive tendencies doesn't mean that petrins do as well. If they've survived for billions of years, they must have learned how to use technology peacefully and safely. Our own scientists have said as much for years when speculating about extraterrestrial intelligence."

"That's the first valid point I've heard thus far," Williams said, "although it doesn't change my decision. Dr. Andrews, who would provide the specs for this android?"

"I think that we would have final say on the specs, although with Seth's input."

"That would make all the difference in the world," Langdon pointed out. "If we built something according to only his designs, he might go well beyond anything our robotic engineers could construct. Such a device could be dangerous, even lethal."

"It could be the prelude to an invasion," Porter said.

"Wait a minute, people," Joshua said. "Seth is prohibited by his culture from introducing any new technology into our world. You're all ascribing sinister intentions to someone who has demonstrated nothing but cooperation and a posture of peace. I believe that his request was to use our *existing* technology to build the android, not give us new technology."

"I think I've heard enough," Williams said. "I agreed to let Dr. Andrews make his case, and we've done just that. But the risks are far too great. Assuming I or Director Langdon or General Porter were willing to entertain this request, which we're not, it's a matter that would have to be considered over a period of months, possibly even years. At this point, I can speak for all of us and say that the matter is closed for discussion. Dr. Andrews, you're going to have to find a way to break the news to Seth but let him down easy so that the future of the project isn't endangered. Thank you all."

The screen abruptly darkened and the teleconference was over.

"Vinod, why do you torture Mitchell like that?" Langdon asked. "You're a man who likes to throw gasoline on a fire."

"Because it's fun ruffling the old dude's feathers," Vinod answered. "He's so tightly wound and paranoid that it's easy to trigger him. Besides, I agree with Josh. We should give this android idea a try."

"That old dude, as you put it, is perfectly capable of making good on his threat to put you behind bars," Langdon said, deadly serious. "Tread carefully."

"Whatever," Vinod said, folding his arms defensively.

"Robert, I appreciate your allowing me to present my rationale for building the android," Joshua said. "I knew it was a longshot."

"Josh, you know I'm a scientist at heart," Langdon replied. "Even though I'm part of the bureaucracy, true science should not be about the suppression of ideas but entertaining *all* ideas and allowing everyone to weigh the merits. You make a compelling argument for this android, and I agree with you that we could conceivably build in the proper security protocols, but the fact that we're keeping Seth a secret from the rest of the world, negates any chance of constructing it at this point."

Chapter Twenty-Four
Breaking News

Joshua and Rachael once again mounted the Harley, with Rachael seated comfortably on the Bobber as if she'd been raised to ride. They had decided to take an extended lunch break after their morning session with Seth and had packed a picnic lunch to eat while hiking a trail at Tilden Regional Park in the hills above Berkeley. The pair came to the park frequently to hike familiar trails such as Nimitz Way or the area near Wildcat Creek. Eucalyptus, newly-planted sequoias, and native coastal scrub gave the park diversity and beauty, and the trails provided the perfect rural setting for the couple to detach from science and the weighty responsibility they'd been given. Joshua parked the bike close to a trail head, and they started their hike hand-in-hand along a wide, wooded path.

"I love the fact that you got me into hiking, not to mention that I find your hiking boots and shorts pretty sexy," Joshua remarked as they walked down a gentle incline bordered by fir trees. "You know, a lot of girls don't like roughing it with nature. They put on spandex and hop on the elliptical, but that's as far as it goes."

"Well, that's certainly not me," she said, brushing away dark green branches on the heavily-shaded trail. "I've always loved being outside, even when I was a little girl. Richard and I spent a lot of time outdoors and fancied ourselves intrepid explorers. And I still love being around all this natural beauty." She pointed to the crest of the Berkeley Hills in the west. "I feel connected to nature and myself when I'm here. It helps me stay grounded. As much as I love science, being outdoors helps me unplug and get off the grid once in a while." As she took in the splendor of the nature around her, she remarked, "I can definitely see why Seth would want to be out here with us. It'd be fun if we could show him all this. I guess it would be like him hiking through a hologram, but it would still be pretty realistic."

Joshua was coming to regard Rachael more and more as a Renaissance woman, and he couldn't imagine living without her. She was well-versed in science, the arts, and was always up for a challenge. Most of all, she loved to examine issues from every possible angle and seek unorthodox solutions.

"Yeah, he's going to be disappointed when we tell him that his android idea got nixed," he said. "His planet seems so sterile and uninteresting by comparison. The petrins could have bioengineered more diversity into their landscape, but since they're deaf and blind, why bother, even with the help of arachnids? They wouldn't be explorers in the true sense of the word since they themselves would have created everything. Disneyworld, to use Vinod's analogy, would hold little interest for me if I'd created it myself."

"I never looked at it that way," Rachael confessed, "but it's an interesting point. I wonder . . ." She gazed at a valley to her right as she thought of the petrins and their bland landscape. "I wonder if they live vicariously through the other species they contact, just as they use arachnids as their senses on Petri and need to encounter new worlds more directly. Perhaps the universe is a playground for such creatures. Seth's request may be that simple—and that benign."

"A plausible hypothesis," Joshua said, stepping over a clear creek only a foot wide. He was reminded of Seth's interest in the date of his and Rachael's engagement and their wager. *Maybe they do live vicariously through the species they encounter.* "And to think I've been suspicious of many of his statements. I've had the feeling for months that he and the collective are hiding something from us, but despite their superior intelligence and technological capabilities, maybe they crave the diversity that their planet lacks. Maybe they want emotional experiences a lot more than Seth lets on. The petrins have evolved into almost pure intelligence, and maybe that's not such a good thing."

"You may be onto something," Rachael said. "He claimed they like to access emotions occasionally for recreational purposes, but maybe it goes a lot deeper than that. Maybe being part of a collective stifles individuality up to a certain point. It's sounds boring, not to mention intrusive."

"That would explain a lot, not that we can use our conjectures to change the minds of Porter or Williams about the android. Langdon, on the other hand, might be a tough sell, but I get the feeling that he's secretly more intrigued with all of this than he lets on since he's not just a fed. He has the heart of an explorer."

"Yeah, I think he's more open-minded than the others. His job is to explore new worlds. Porter and Williams are political and military creatures by nature, but NASA has always fought the government and military for funding."

Joshua followed Rachael as the path narrowed, carrying a small basket as they neared a clearing that overlooked the valley. "I feel sorry for Seth," he said. "The government feels as though the petrins want to position a mother ship over the White House and recreate *Independence Day*. I don't see it that way."

"Seems like you and Seth are pretty chummy. Have you guys been hanging out and holding private sessions? I just may get jealous." She turned to watch Joshua as a small cooler with sodas and bottled water swung in her right hand.

"Yeah, I guess we are. He's seems to be a great guy—inasmuch as he's assigned himself that gender. He's funny, smart, and comes through as genuinely caring despite my occasional paranoia about his redactions. Strange that my best friend may be an alien on another planet."

"Best friend?" Rachael asked with a pained look.

"Well, second best friend," Joshua replied with a wink followed by a small peck on her cheek. "Don't worry. It's not like we would have hung out at a corner bar and had a few beers if he'd gotten his request for the android." He stopped and laughed. "Hey, maybe a drunk alien might cough up some secrets."

The allusion caused Rachael to think of the Rock Candy Dance Club and their first night together. "It's incredible that I show up for an interview, and we end up talking to aliens and falling in love in less than forty-eight hours," Rachael observed. "Are we in a Nicholas Sparks movie?"

Joshua nodded. "I know. What are the odds?" He elbowed Rachael as he drew alongside her.

"It's what I was telling you that day when we had coffee. Sometimes the long shot doesn't seem plausible."

"Like cells assembling themselves into life without any help—without a first cause, as you put it."

"I think that's a good example. And talking with Seth, for the record, hasn't changed my way of thinking. Quite the opposite."

"So what you're saying is that our meeting and becoming lovers wasn't an accident."

"I think I am." She smiled as they neared the clearing, the valley dipping below them. "It's what *Romeo and Juliet* is about. Two young people from the houses of Montague and Capulet are destined to fall in love."

Joshua cringed. "Hmm. Let's not go there. They were star-crossed lovers. Not a happy ending, if I recall Brit Lit 101 correctly."

"You do, but this is Berkeley, not Verona, Italy, and I intend to hold onto you, mister. We don't have to hide our relationship or worry about feuding families like Shakespeare's lovers."

Joshua kissed her on the lips. "No, our feuds are with NASA, the White House, and the Pentagon. A piece of cake, right? Which is not to say that Vinod wouldn't like to parry and thrust with Porter. Let's hope it never comes to that."

They'd arrived at the clearing and paused to look at the view.

"You're avoiding the issue," Rachael remarked. "Kinda like Seth does sometimes when he changes the subject abruptly or answers obliquely. What do you think of fate with a capital F on it?"

Joshua settled on the ground, legs crossed, the basket by his side as Rachael joined him under the shade of a long fir branch.

"God?" he said. "I've given it a lot of thought over the past year or so, but I still don't know. The existence of primordial spookyons might be evidence of a creator, but it's still circumstantial. It's speculative, just like your theory of cell assembly. Maybe we should ask Seth about the big picture. The petrins have had a few billion years to think about the idea of a creator."

Rachael shrugged. "It wouldn't make any difference to me whether Seth gave the idea a thumbs-up or a thumbs-down."

"Really?" Joshua said, caught off guard by Rachael's response. "Their input wouldn't sway you if they've come to a definite conclusion that no first cause was necessary for creation? Not even with all the intelligence of the collective at their disposal? Or with the input of thousands of other civilizations spread across the universe? Surely they've considered the existence of a superior being and have some kind of opinion for or against its existence."

Rachael shook her head. "No, I can't envision anything they might say that would affect my beliefs. They're pretty much baked into who Rachael Miller is."

"But they've achieved immortality," Joshua said. "Doesn't that count for anything?"

"No, not really. They found immortality by using science that was available to them thanks to the existing universe."

"I know what's coming. Who put the science there? Or the universe?"

"Right." She pointed her index finger at the left side of Joshua's chest. "Belief is something written on the heart, Josh. It's not digital and it doesn't have anything to do with backup copies or frozen frogs. What I have is an inner certitude, and as Henry Bowman might have put it, you can't hack that."

Joshua crossed his arms and laughed out loud. "I do believe Dr. Joshua Andrews and perhaps an entire civilization of thirteen trillion individuals has been bested by Rachael Miller's theological musings. You're pretty convincing."

"I have my moments," she said, leaning over to kiss Joshua. "Now I hope that the cucumber sandwiches are still fresh. No meat. Just veggies on whole grain bread."

"I'm sure they're fine, but—"

"What's up?"

Joshua glanced at his wrist as his Apple watch began to vibrate. He'd been leaning back, arms braced against the hard-packed dirt, but he sat up straight in order to look at the watch.

"A notification on my Apple watch," Joshua replied.

"What is it?"

Rachael opened the cooler and produced two bottles of chilled water as Joshua angled his wrist to better see the face of the watch.

"What's the matter?" Rachael asked, noting the concerned look on Joshua's face.

"It's a news alert from CNN." He read the headline, shut his eyes tightly, looked again, and took a deep breath. "I don't know about God or heaven, but all hell's about to break loose."

"Why?" The carefree smile vanished from Rachael's face.

Joshua didn't answer. He grabbed his cell phone and brought up the CNN app to get the full story signaled by the alert. "Good God no!"

"You're freaking me out. What gives? Is it about the Ebola outbreak?"

Joshua shook his head. "Scoot close and watch with me."

Rachael inched closer to Joshua as he opened the live stream from CNN, her head by his shoulder as she glanced at the phone screen.

"I repeat," a female voice said. "This is CNN breaking news. Contact has been established with aliens. An explosive new video obtained from an anonymous source shows what our science contributors have identified as a Bowman sphere at the NASA Bowman Particle Research Center in Berkeley, California. Our source tells us that NASA has been using it to communicate with extraterrestrial intelligence."

The accompanying video showed the interior of the bat cave with a scientific team conducting a routine session with Seth. A close-up shot of the sphere was seen as it brightly glowed its characteristic green color.

"How in the hell did anyone get that kind of footage?" Rachael asked, spellbound by the images. "Porter's video surveillance system is locked down as tightly as anyone in the world could make it."

"And there's no way anyone without clearance could have gotten into the bat cave," Joshua added.

The female news anchor on CNN, a young brunette with a white blouse and a dark skirt, answered Rachael's rhetorical question. "CNN has further confirmed that the video was obtained by a hacker who breached the servers at the particle center." The shot tightened as she spoke against a background that showed the entrance to the particle center. "Along with this video, these images were also obtained." The entrance of the center was replaced by pictures that Joshua and Rachael were well acquainted with, pictures that very few people had seen until now.

"These images purportedly show, respectively, the alien home world that researchers have been communicating with and one of the alien creatures."

The image of Seth was instantly recognizable to Joshua and Rachael.

Joshua's phone began to vibrate, and the text alert and call ringtones on Rachael's phone began to sound every few seconds.

"It's Langdon," she said. "Wait, it's Williams too."

"Make it all three," Joshua said. "Langdon, Williams, and Porter. They want to know where we are. We need to get back to the center ASAP."

"Need?" Rachael said. "I've been *ordered* back. Porter is not a happy man."

The anchor continued. "CNN has learned that messages are coming in from multiple nations and organizations, all demanding that the United States disclose whatever information it has on the aliens and that all knowledge acquired thus far, as well as the sphere, be shared with the governments of the world."

"Demand?" Joshua said.

"The world?" Rachael said.

Rachael and Joshua exchanged glances as they ran up the trail. They were both thinking the same thing: had Vinod gotten fed up with Porter and NASA and decided to tell the world about the petrins? Maybe, as Vinod himself was fond of saying, he'd gone rogue.

Chapter Twenty-Five
The Sixty-Million-Dollar Man

Joshua and Rachael hopped onto the Harley and rushed back to the lab, weaving in and out of traffic quickly given the gravity of their summons. They knew that the whole project might be in jeopardy, and the administrative team would no doubt want to find both the source of the hack as well as a remedy for it as soon as possible. Dealing with government bureaucracy and security measures was one thing; engaging in sensitive diplomatic relations with the nations of the world was quite another.

"That might be above our pay grade," Rachael said.

"That doesn't mean Porter won't put all teams on the hot seat," Joshua added. "I suspect he's mad as hell."

As they entered Langdon's office, Vinod was sitting on one of the couches, and a video conference with Porter and Williams was in progress on the monitor. They sat down on the couch next to Vinod as the irate voice of Porter demanded an explanation for the hack.

"God damn it!" Porter shouted. "How the hell did this happen? All security measures were formulated and implemented by the best IT personnel at the Pentagon."

"We're looking into it now," Langdon replied. "The server logs show definite evidence of a breach sometime yesterday. The IP Address of the hacker has been traced to somewhere in Russia, but proxy servers were used, so it may take time to track down the perpetrator. He—or they—could be anywhere in the world. The breach has been plugged, not that it's going to make much of a difference now. The cat's out of the bag. The entire world knows what we've been doing in the bat cave." His voice sounded resigned and weary.

"We're definitely in damage control mode," Williams said, "and I want all options on the table."

Porter, however, was more interested in assigning blame. "I'm thinking that whoever did this had some inside help," he stated, "and my prime suspect is sitting right there in that room with you."

"Hold on," Langdon retorted. "You don't know that for—"

"Screw you, Porter!" Vinod shouted, knowing the general was referring to him. "This is *your* fault—yours and your almighty team from the Pentagon. You're in charge of security, not me. If you'd put me in charge of securing those servers instead of your lame-ass, incompetent IT personnel, none of this would have happened. I wrote the algorithm that made communication with Seth possible, but I wasn't good enough for the United States government?"

"How did someone in a foreign country thousands of miles away know what was happening four hundred feet below the particle center?" Porter asked indignantly. "It *had* to be an inside job."

"Maybe a member of one of your own security teams leaked the information," Vinod shot back. "Washington has more leaks than an old faucet."

"Let's calm down and focus on solutions," Williams interrupted. "The importance of talking with extraterrestrials has been taken to a whole new level, and we can't treat the sphere like a football that's handed off from one player to another. We will, of course, conduct a full investigation of this hack and find who's responsible, but we have more immediate problems to deal with. The White House is getting bombarded with calls from foreign governments demanding equal time with the sphere. The United Nations General Assembly and the U.N. Security Council are in session, and countries are demanding a response from our U.N. ambassador."

"Screw 'em all," Porter replied. "We own this sphere, and it's tough shit for them. We have no obligations to foreign governments regarding private government research."

"How about we try to play the angle that the video and the pictures were a hoax," Langdon suggested, his tone optimistic. "We can just deny everything. Videos are faked all the time."

"I agree," Porter declared resolutely. "We haven't been able to create entangled spookyons since Henry Bowman's work, so we have plausible deniability."

"That's not going to work," Williams said. "The leaked images are extremely high resolution, with incredible detail that would be almost impossible to create on Earth. No one is going to believe this is a hoax— certainly not professional analysts in the military or intelligence communities. At this point, it's politically untenable for us to continue to keep this a secret and not provide at least *some* access to the sphere to outside entities. But I want to share it in a secure manner such that we continue to get *all* information gleaned from Seth. Otherwise, we'd face redactions from other countries as well as from the petrins."

"We can't just flippin' hand over the sphere to some foreign bastards," Porter said. "We have no idea how they'd apply information they received from the aliens. Sharing information could create global instability."

"I'm forced to agree," Joshua stated. "If the sphere breaks, or if whoever we give it to follows shoddy security protocols, it could be a disaster. Just imagine what would happen if the sphere was directly connected to the Internet. Seth would have access to unlimited information, much of it unflattering and downright confusing. He could nevertheless digest it in a few hours, and it would take our teams years to explain what it all means."

"Or we could discontinue the program altogether," Porter said, raising a finger and sitting forward in his chair. "We're not gathering any actionable intelligence, and some of the joint chiefs think the project is becoming a liability. If we break the sphere, our problem is solved."

"That's absurd," Joshua said. "Why don't you shut down SETI while you're at it since they expect to receive a meaningful signal within thirty years?"

"Is that all you're after?" Vinod asked, hardly able to contain his anger. "Actionable intelligence? Like I said from the beginning, you'd like nothing better than to weaponize what we learn from Seth."

"If that's true," Joshua said, "then maybe we *should* pull the plug. I'm not here to play war games, general."

"The program will continue at the president's insistence," Williams replied. "I understand all your concerns, but we need to figure out a way to give controlled access to Seth to other nations while maintaining complete control over the sphere. We also need to restrict the information flow into and out of the sphere like we've been doing with the audio interface. I'm open to suggestions."

Rachael had been quietly listening to the conversation and finally chimed in. "I have an idea that addresses all of the concerns that have been mentioned."

"What is it?" Williams asked.

"For God's sake," Porter said. "She's just a reporter."

"Hear her out, Mitchell," Williams advised. "It's not like we have viable options at the moment. I'm looking for nuance, not a binary decision of share or don't share."

"How about we build Seth his android?" Rachael said.

"How's that going to help?" Langdon asked. "I'm not following."

"Look, we can't just hand over the sphere to someone else," Rachael explained. "There's too much risk of it breaking or being used insecurely. But if the sphere were encased in an android, the risk of breakage would be minimized. As far as security is concerned, it would be much easier to control an android than an isolated sphere. We could demand that our own security teams be with him at all times. With Seth in android form, the only way anyone could interact with him would be verbally, not digitally. Nobody would be able to hack him, so to speak. The security team could record all conversations with him so that we would get a complete record of all information he gave to anyone. We could also shut him down anytime we felt the need to, meaning that the information flow to and from the sphere happens at our discretion."

The group pondered Rachael's idea for a few moments. Vinod expected Mitchell to launch into another tirade but was surprised by his response.

"If just keeping the sphere to ourselves isn't possible," Porter said, "then this android idea may be okay if we can build in the right security protocols. The android would essentially function like a firewall, one that *we* control and set the rules for."

"Robert, what do you think?" Williams asked.

"I'm open to this idea given our current circumstances," Langdon said. "The android body can become a secure protective case around the sphere to preserve its structural integrity. The fact that other nations can only interact with the sphere using speech limits the amount of information that Seth can send or receive, and we can monitor this communication down to the last syllable. It's not optimal, but given the current situation and the fact that we're not going to just hand over the sphere to anyone who demands it, it may be the best option. I also like the fact that we can monitor the android twenty-four-seven and shut it down anytime we wish. Only we should have control of that process, by the way." Langdon rubbed his chin thoughtfully. "I think it might work."

"Very well then," Williams remarked. "I'll have to get approval for this from the higher-ups, but I think we should start working on this right now. I don't know how much longer we can hold off on not allowing Seth to communicate with other countries given the furor that the CNN story has generated. Robert, I want you to assemble an engineering team and start thinking about how to build the android. Mitchell, I need you to come up with the security protocols according to the rules we've outlined today. We'll reconvene in a day or two to see if this is even feasible."

Rachael and Vinod were visibly pleased.

"Dr. Andrews," Williams said, "it looks like you may get your wish after all."

*   *   *

It took six and a half months to complete the construction of the android. Langdon's engineering team had worked tirelessly to manufacture the android as quickly as possible. They had been given a virtually unlimited budget, as well as some specifications from Seth himself. As all large projects go, it was slightly behind schedule and had cost almost sixty million dollars.

Early in the construction of the android, Seth had requested some videos of human motion, which were begrudgingly approved by Porter. Vinod taught Seth the MPEG protocol and sent some videos of basic human movements such as walking, sitting, and talking. After these were sent, Vinod sent Seth videos of more complex human movements such as running, sports activities, and even dancing. Finally, Seth was sent a movie to watch - *Hoosiers*.

The idea of sending Seth the film was proposed by Joshua. Seth had requested the videos of human movements to better mimic them. Joshua thought that sending an entire movie would give Seth more of an insight into human interactions as well as human speech patterns. Porter's team scrutinized the film in extreme detail, but in the end, there wasn't much secrecy portrayed in a film about a high school basketball team in the 1950s, so it was approved.

One month into the construction of the android, Rachael came to work sporting a sparkling piece of highly-compressed carbon on her ring finger. Joshua had asked her to marry him the night before, and she had immediately accepted. He'd told a waiter at Angelino's to hide the ring in tiramisu and had made sure to record the exact time that Rachael found the ring down to the second in order to honor Seth's request. It had been exactly one year to the day since they'd dined at Angelino's for the first time, the day they'd made first contact with Seth. Joshua joked to Rachael that he'd picked that particular day to pop the question so he'd have one less important date to remember. Despite their formal engagement, they hadn't yet set a date for their wedding.

When Rachael found out about the wager that the collective had about the timing of Joshua's proposal, she was initially annoyed. "You mean thirteen trillion other individuals knew before I did that we were going to get engaged?" she said. "Not very romantic, Josh." Her irritation was short-lived, though. She couldn't stay mad at Joshua for long because she was too much in love with him. Besides, she realized that no one on Earth had had a clue as to Joshua's intentions, which, in her estimation, classified the wager as a special circumstance.

They continued to hike and work closely together, but thoughts of the android under construction were never far from their minds.

"How long do you think the android will last?" Rachael asked Joshua. "We've totally neglected the possibility that Seth might want to hang around."

"Good question. Theoretically, the android could last for decades." He pointed at the diamond engagement ring. "I have a feeling that's going to last a lot longer."

"That's the right answer," Rachael said with a wink. "You're officially out of the dog house, but no more secret wagers with Seth."

*   *   *

After construction of the android was completed, everyone who had prior knowledge of the sphere was assembled in the bat cave, including Joshua, Rachael, Vinod, and the scientific teams. Dina Williams was there as well, but Porter and Langdon had not yet arrived. They had all gathered to witness the first activation of Seth the android. Since it had been built in secrecy—Porter had insisted on the smallest possible team for the assembly—not many of those gathered in the bat cave had actually seen it. Once the sphere was installed, android Seth would be switched on and open his eyes on planet Earth for the first time.

Rachael and Vinod stood next to each other in the bat cave, anxiously waiting for the android to arrive. She looked at Vinod's Styx "Mr. Roboto" tee shirt. "Nice choice," she remarked.

"You know I always dress for the occasion."

The elevator doors opened, and Langdon and Porter appeared with several technicians, who wheeled a dolly holding the android, which was covered by a gray cloth. They pushed the dolly to the front of the room and placed it in plain view, after which the android was lifted onto a small pedestal.

"Ladies and gentlemen, I present android Seth," Langdon announced as he removed the gray cloth and revealed the android to the anxiously waiting crowd, which erupted in applause.

"My God," Rachael remarked. "He looks entirely human. I can't tell he's an android at all."

Android Seth stood in front of them, eyes closed and wearing a tight-fitting plain tee shirt and jeans. His complexion was that of an African male. The choice of ethnicity had been a matter of much debate, with each country demanding that its race be represented. In the end, he was made African since the continent had been the place where humanity itself had its start. The android was young and muscular looking, its visible features perfect in every detail.

"Man, he's hot," Vinod remarked when he saw the android for the first time.

"Take is easy, Vinod," Rachael said. "Although he looks human, I don't think he's anatomically complete."

Seth himself had given considerable input on the construction of the android. There had been no technology used that wasn't already available, but its construction had been very complex. It had variable-speed servos and actuators that facilitated the human-like motion of all of his joints. It also had micro-actuators in its face that allowed for a full and complex range of facial expressions. Furthermore, it had auditory sensors in its ears, a speaker in its throat, and two ultra-hi-def cameras in its eyes that could be moved using micro actuators. On the sensory side, it possessed numerous pressure and position sensors, gyros, and accelerometers, but there was no brain, no CPU. The omission was at the request of Seth, who had insisted it wasn't needed. All of the actuators, motors, and sensors were connected to an interface module, which in turn was connected to the sphere. This meant that Seth directly controlled the android and the individual actuators. For Seth, the experience would not be much different than how he controlled an arachnid on his own planet. Even though the mechanical and sensory functions of the android had been rigorously tested, no one had seen the android in action since the sphere had not yet been installed within its frame.

In the bat cave, Porter explained the numerous security protocols for the android. The protocols were for the protection of Seth and the Bowman sphere, as well as for the security of all humans who would interact with the android.

As was decided months earlier, Seth would never be left alone. He would be accompanied at all times by a security team akin to his own secret service detail. The security team, however, was to stay in the background and not directly interact with him. Seth would always be accompanied by a team from the lab, which would consist of at least three members. It was decided that Joshua, Rachael, and Vinod would continue to be part of the personal team. Each member would be given specially modified Apple watches that would act as electronic tethers. A tether would only operate if worn on the wrist of the user it was specifically designed for, and Seth would require at least two of the watches to be within one hundred feet for him to be active. Each Apple watch also had a panic feature which, when activated, would cause Seth to immediately go into hibernation mode, causing disconnection between the Bowman sphere and Seth's body, rendering him completely inert.

Seth's power supply was electric, in the form of lithium ion batteries that were housed in the cavity of his abdomen. They would allow Seth to operate for sixteen hours before recharging, which could be accomplished with any standard AC outlet in eight hours on 110 volts or three hours on 220 volts. When plugged in, Seth would automatically go into hibernation mode. He couldn't be active when plugged in. Once hibernating, he could only be reactivated by a simultaneous activation signal sent from at least two of the tether watches.

The Bowman sphere inside Seth was well-protected and was located in his chest. It was encased in a pressure vessel that was bulletproof and pressure-rated for one hundred feet of depth in water. Pressure greater than this would cause the sphere to implode. The pressure vessel itself was locked electronically and could only be opened with the thumbprint of Joshua, Langdon, Porter, or Williams. Due to Seth's overall construction and the weight of the lithium ion batteries, he was very dense, with a weight exceeding three hundred and fifty pounds. He was waterproof but would sink like a stone in water. For this reason, Seth would never be allowed on a boat or over any water deeper than a hundred feet. Additionally, the vessel protected the sphere from shock and had been drop-tested from twenty-five feet onto concrete, with no breakage of a duplicate sphere.

Porter had decided that Seth would never be granted access to a computer terminal or any electronic device for the same reason that he would be denied Internet access. The risk of connecting with unauthorized parties was too great, and his access to information would be unfettered.

After Porter finished briefing everyone on the security protocols, Joshua was tasked with installing the Bowman sphere. The access for the sphere compartment was located in Seth's back, and a technician lifted the android's shirt so that Joshua could use his thumbprint to open the compartment. Joshua used his thumbprint a second time to open the case in the wall where the sphere was currently housed. He carefully removed the sphere from the case and installed it in the android, sealing the housing. Android Seth was now ready for startup. Joshua, Williams, Langdon, and Porter stood next him.

"Everyone ready?" Williams asked.

The assembly gave her a thumbs-up in unison as Porter's right hand clandestinely grasped a revolver holstered on his right hip.

"Okay, Robert and Joshua," Williams said, "use your watches to fire him up."

Langdon and Joshua held up their wrists simultaneously and entered the activation command on their watches as everyone in the room stared at Seth. Initially, the actuators around his face twitched, followed by twitching of the motors that powered his arms, legs, and fingers.

"What's happening?" Rachael asked.

"I think he's testing the connections to his motor and sensory functions," Vinod replied.

The twitching stopped in short order, and his eyes opened and looked about the room as his head turned robotically. He lifted his right hand awkwardly and moved his fingers through their arc of motion. Then his head started bobbing up and down.

"What's up with the head motion?" Joshua asked.

"Don't know," Langdon replied. "It's damn peculiar."

Seth jumped off the pedestal and started moving his entire body rhythmically. His movement was no longer robotic, but well-coordinated and smooth.

"What's going on?" Williams asked, becoming alarmed.

"I don't know," Langdon answered. "Maybe it's some kind of malfunction."

Porter drew his revolver and pointed it at the android.

"What the hell are you doing?" Joshua exclaimed.

"I'm going to have to put him down if he goes out of control," Porter replied.

"Don't!" Langdon shouted as he lifted his arm and put his finger on the panic switch of his watch. "I can shut him off if this continues."

"I don't believe what I'm seeing," Rachael said. "It looks like he's—"

Seth's movements became even more rhythmical, and it was obvious that they were intentional.

"It looks like he's dancing," Joshua said as his jaw dropped in disbelief.

Seth was definitely dancing. He did the moonwalk as the crowd let out an astonished and collective "Ohhhhh!" He then dropped to the floor and began to spin on his back in classic break dance fashion before stopping and staring at the group, his head resting on his hand, elbow on the floor.

"'Sup? I'm Seth," he said, looking up at the astonished faces around him.

"What the hell is the matter with you?" Joshua asked as Seth got up from the floor. "That ridiculous stunt almost caused a weapon discharge that could have damaged your android body."

"Why?"

"Because it scared people," Joshua replied bluntly.

Porter re-holstered his revolver slowly and remained silent.

"Sorry," Seth replied. "I wanted to make a memorable entrance. I also wanted to correct your preconceived notions of androids having robotic like motions. As you can see, my control of your technology can be quite graceful."

"How are you able to do . . . *that?*" Langdon queried.

"What do you mean?" Seth asked. "How I move with rhythm?" He did a little jig, hands on his hips, his feet moving nimbly despite his great weight.

"Yes," Langdon replied. "Rhythm, dancing."

"Inside my petrin body, I have a neural nest that functions something like your cerebellum," Seth replied. "It allows for the simultaneous and coordinated movement of numerous servos so that I can make my actions completely human-like. This is why I insisted that no CPU be installed. I'm able to directly control its servos."

The people in the bat cave stared in awe at Seth's face as he spoke. His lip movements and facial expressions were perfect. From his appearance to his unexpected movements after stepping from the pedestal, no one could distinguish him from an actual human. For the first time in human history, there was an alien human on Earth.

Chapter Twenty-Six
The 103 Club

Seth was confined to the lab for seventy-two hours at Porter's insistence. The alien's erratic behavior upon start-up had resulted in the general's usual combination of caution and paranoia. For the duration, Seth sat quietly looking at the lab and its equipment, security guards stationed near the elevator. Scientific teams continued to question him—they delved deeper into the geology and atmospheric conditions of Petri—and he seemed unperturbed that he'd not yet been able to interact more directly with the people of the Earth. He'd been informed that the waiting period was part of the security protocols, a statement that was largely true since Porter had the final say in such matters.

Porter's initial stance was that he wanted to cancel Seth's tour of foreign nations. On one of their teleconference calls, he remarked, "He's too unpredictable. Because of his exposure to the initial information Bhakti uploaded to him, the United States might be the subject of heavy ridicule for misrepresenting the values and culture of Earth. For God's sake, nobody's break-dancing in India or China. And who knows what kind of movements or speech he might come out with once he's abroad? He might cause an international incident."

"What did you expect?" Vinod asked. "We knew that Seth was familiar with the urban dictionary and certain kinds of music, plus he augmented our robotics. He was simply trying to fit in."

"That's not the way diplomacy works, Bhakti. Your algorithm was written irresponsibly."

As usual, Williams stepped in to soothe flaring tempers.

"We're not calling anything off, Mitchell," she said. "Not after a sixty-million-dollar price tag, plus the entire world is waiting to see him. It's estimated that more people may watch him leave the particle center on TV than watched Neil Armstrong walk on the moon. The president is adamant that we avert any kind of diplomatic blowback by refusing to let the android begin his tour."

"I follow orders," Porter countered, "but this has the makings of a freak show."

"We're moving forward," Williams said. "After the tour, he's all ours again, but it's best to get this over with."

"The band is together again!" Vinod cried out triumphantly. "We're going on the Android Seth Tour, complete with roadies."

"Someone had better tell Seth what's he's in for," Langdon suggested. "He's going to be inundated by personality types that he's unaccustomed to. All of our teams in the bat cave were carefully chosen and went through extensive training before interacting with him. We don't have the luxury of insisting that every world leader and scientist behave like we want them to or fall in line with existing protocols beyond a certain point. They've been briefed on basic guidelines that need to be followed, but unpredictability has been the hallmark of this entire project."

"It's a valid point," Rachael said. "Seth can learn a lot about Earth by meeting a broader sampling of humans, but he should be briefed first."

Joshua smiled. "I guess this is where the personal team earns its pay."

"Quite right," Williams said. "We're counting on you and your colleagues to keep things on track."

"The party's on!" Vinod said jubilantly when the teleconference was over.

"Behave yourself," Rachael said, "or you'll get us all in trouble."

"Me?" Vinod said with an innocent look on his face.

"Yes, you."

*   *   *

Seth was seated in the lab as usual when Joshua walked in. The android had been left under the watchful eye of the main security team charged with his safety—and with protecting others in case a malfunction occurred. They'd been given backup tether watches in the absence of the personal team, although Joshua, Rachael and Vinod had visited him since his activation in order to acclimatize him to being on Earth.

"'Sup Josh," Seth said, standing.

"Hi, Seth. Everything okay?"

"Yeah, I'm doing fine, and people have treated me very well, although they don't make a lot of jokes like you and Vinod do. I kind of like the informality of the personal team. Are we ready to leave the lab yet?"

"Sorry about the delay. General Porter wanted to have you observed because of your unexpected dance moves. I think the security teams expected something a little more robotic and mechanical despite the upgrades you gave to our engineers. Frankly, we didn't know what to expect. Are you getting impatient?"

"No, just curious, but I understand your precaution. I did, after all, agree to abide by all of your security protocols. I was just trying to be friendly, but I guess my behavior must have seemed a bit unorthodox."

"I'm glad you understand, and I have good news. You'll be leaving the lab shortly. Today, in fact."

Seth flashed a grin as normal as that displayed by any human being on the planet. "That's great! Robert Langdon has explained everything I need to know—the tether watches, security details, water restrictions, battery recharging—all phases of my operation and maintenance."

"And you're okay with all of it?"

"Of course. And I've made a long list of the places I'd like to see, assuming they're places that I'll be allowed to visit."

Joshua was impressed by Seth's compliance to all protocols relating to his android form and future movements across the Earth, which made it all the harder to broach a subject that the administrative and personal teams had discussed, a subject they believed was necessary to share with their alien visitor. There was no way that Seth could begin a tour of the world unless he knew heretofore classified information behind the initial one hundred and three sessions. Otherwise, he might think the personal team had been dishonest with him, and a lie would be a poor way to start this new phase of their relationship with the petrins.

"Seth, I have to level with you about something," Joshua began. "Your request, as you know, was originally deemed too dangerous to fulfill."

"And yet here I am. Your administrators obviously changed their minds. I admire the flexibility of their thinking."

"Well, there's more to it than that. A lot more. To be perfectly honest, no one on Earth knew of your existence except Vinod, Rachael, myself, and a small number of people in my government. Knowledge of our contact with Petri was kept a total secret from the rest of the world. The reasoning was that large segments of Earth's population might panic if they knew that extraterrestrials were real even though it has been the subject of much speculation and despite the fact that most informed minds with a scientific bent felt positive that intelligent life was abundant in the universe."

"Why would they panic?"

Joshua looked Seth squarely in the eyes. "Acquiring astronomical knowledge, the building of large telescopes, and our first ventures into space have all happened in the last four hundred years, which is a small amount of time compared to a civilization that's thousands of years old. In fact, our biggest advances in these areas have come in the last few decades. Believe it or not, many people thought for thousands of years that we were alone in the universe. Many of these people also thought that life elsewhere would contradict the belief by many humans in the existence of a creator, who we call God."

"I'm familiar with the concept from your literature."

"Also, some people in my government believed that sharing knowledge of you and your planet might be used by some nations for technological or military superiority since . . ." Joshua paused and rubbed his hand through his hair, feeling embarrassed that he had to make an apology that showed his race in such an unflattering light. "Since, as Vinod might put it, not all of our countries have their shit together. Your world, we assume, is united, but I'm afraid we're not, and we have much to learn."

"I appreciate your honesty, Josh. I've extrapolated much of what you're telling me from the limited database you've provided. You're not the only species we've contacted that has recently embarked on their scientific age." Seth smiled broadly. "You don't have to be ashamed of your world, Joshua. I understand what you're telling me. I am, after all, trying to learn about your planet just as you're attempting to learn about mine. What I can safely share with you is that each planet has many commonalities as well as many differences. Our policy is not to judge anyone."

Joshua heaved a huge sigh of relief.

"That's really good to know, Seth, since your own preferences for where you'd like to visit will have to be postponed."

"Why is that? Do I have to remain in the lab for more observation? If so, I'm perfectly willing to comply."

"The reason? We were *forced* to acquiesce to your request to house the sphere in an android body because news of your existence somehow leaked out. Someone hacked our computers. You know what that means, right?"

"Hacked? Yes."

"So the bottom line is that the only way we felt we could physically protect the sphere while simultaneously making sure that no government tried to interact with you for selfish purposes was to build the android and establish some ground rules for the people you're going to meet—the many foreign leaders and scientists we've promised will have access to the alien who calls himself Seth."

"Okay, I get it. The protocols make sense now. I really appreciate your being open with me about that. You're a true friend and a good representative of the very best Earth has to offer."

Joshua shrugged. "Gosh, I don't know about that since I'm a person who makes mistakes like anybody else, but we couldn't very well bring you on a tour and expose you to a lot of questions without telling why we were doing so. Anyway, I'm sorry we didn't tell you earlier. I personally would have liked to, but I was overruled."

Seth laughed for the first time since the sphere had been installed into his thoracic cavity. "We're still cool, bro. I still get to see a lot of your world and meet all kinds of different people."

"Yeah, although there will be many restrictions as to who has access to you. By the way, you might want to tone down the urban vernacular when you meet foreign leaders."

"No problem, but it's the persona I've adopted. Don't worry—I'll use my judgment. Speaking of idioms, I think the way humans might describe the situation is that the glass is half full, not half empty."

"Huh?"

"I'll get to sample the diversity of your world and its many cultures—within reason, of course. I think I'm going to enjoy that."

"Good. After the tour, I promise we'll take you on a private tour and address that list of places you mentioned."

Seth extended his right hand. "I believe it's called a handshake."

"That's correct," Joshua said, taking Seth's hand. He noted the cold rubbery feel of Seth's hand. Even though Seth was visually indistinguishable from a human, he certainly didn't feel like one. "So let's get started."

A security detail was waiting near the elevator. Joshua and Seth, escorted by Porter's security team, rode up to the particle center and joined Rachael, Vinod, and Langdon in the atrium. Android Seth was about to see the world.

*   *   *

Seth was first taken to the countries of Western Europe, where, as promised, he met scientists and leaders from the United Kingdom, France, Germany, Spain, Portugal, Italy, and Greece. He was introduced to kings, queens, presidents, chancellors, and prime ministers, all of whom wanted to be photographed with a man who had quickly attained celebrity status.

When formalities were finished in each country, Seth was handed over to a panel of scientists and scholars limited to five per nation. The meetings took place at undisclosed locations, and Seth was always accompanied by two members of the scientific team as well as members from Porter's security detail and the personal team. Photographs of Seth with the most important political leaders of the twenty-first century, however, were published in every media outlet in the world. Even though Seth's exact location was always unknown by the general population of any country he visited, crowds choked the thoroughfares of capital cities across Europe in the hopes of spotting his motorcade. The routes were never published ahead of time, but the crowds didn't care. They carried pictures and banners with Seth's name and picture, and many handmade signs said in bright letters HI SETH or THE EARTH WELCOMES YOU. A few people, allegedly concerned with Seth's welfare, carried signs that said FREE SETH FROM THE MEN IN BLACK.

Each team of scientists that questioned Seth was required to keep the results of their sessions private. Williams had determined that scientists could pool the knowledge they gained at a later date but only publish their findings after the accumulated information had been approved by an international panel chaired by the United States. The concern was that some countries might try to creatively spin the results of their sessions, claiming that Seth had been partial to their culture, values, or style of government. Joshua and Langdon had both agreed, noting that it would be too easy for cultural bias to skew the interpretations of even the most professional scientific teams.

Joshua noted in city after city that the questions posed by scientific teams—they were composed of sociologists, philosophers, and theologians, as well as people representing traditional scientific disciplines—were hopelessly redundant. Seth had expected diversity, and yet he was sequestered in rooms with Earth's finest minds, all of whom could only repeat the same queries again and again.

"Answers?" Joshua said in Paris. "Seth is giving them almost nothing."

Vinod thought that the situation was hilarious. "It should be called the Redaction Tour. If it were up to me, Seth would only have to do two things."

"Those being?"

"Sit down with information theorists since Seth's discovery, as well as petrin culture, is based on information and its transmission. If we want to get meaningful data from Seth, we need to speak the same language as the petrins. Assuming that's the way all advanced cultures evolve, why not get on the train now and get ahead of the learning curve?"

Joshua agreed. "People are giving Seth a lot of esoteric philosophical questions that he won't answer, but if we steered the conversation in the direction you suggest, I think he might be more forthcoming."

"But we're not in charge of the project," Vinod said. "Next time we discover alien intelligence, listen to your drunken friend Vinod. If I'd have tweeted our find, this may have all played out differently."

"Okay, okay. So we're on the Vinod Bhakti I Told You So Tour. What's the second thing you'd do?"

"Enroll Seth in my own music appreciation class. Rock and roll is the key to modern civilization."

"Naturally," Joshua replied with sarcasm. "He might even figure out the meaning of 'I Am the Walrus.'"

As Joshua had pointed out, a routine session featured the same questions with only minor variations in wording.

"What form of government do the petrins have?"

Seth's answer was uniform in every country he visited. "We don't have a government as you would define it. Our collective has a unique decision-making process that I'm not at liberty to discuss since it might influence your own governmental decision-making processes."

"Is nuclear power safe? How can we stop global warming? Is it possible to use cold fusion as a source of unlimited power?"

"I'm sorry, but I can't answer any of those questions," was Seth's normal response. "Humanity must solve its own problems. We're prohibited from interfering with your development in any way. Technological development on any planet happens in a linear fashion and altering that timeline can have serious negative consequences for a civilization."

"Can you explain that Seth?" was a frequent comeback from scientists. "Surely a small hint about some of these matters wouldn't hurt."

"You wouldn't allow your children to use firearms or drive automobiles because they're not yet ready, emotionally or physically, to handle those devices. It's no different for more sophisticated scientific developments."

A particle physicist in England challenged Seth on his answer. "But even adult humans sometimes have trouble with these devices, as well as many others. Could you at least give us some advice?"

Seth tilted his head and paused, although he was, in actuality, calculating a response. "I believe you have a city in Italy called Rome. Is that correct?"

"Yes, that's right," the physicist answered.

"It wasn't built in a day," Seth said with a disarming smile. "Technological development takes time."

Responses such as this caused the people he spoke with to applaud, smile, laugh, and nod their heads, adding to his status as a friendly alien ambassador with wisdom and a sense of humor. His reputation spread as a result of leaks that were considered benign on the part of those interviewing him. Surely, they reasoned, a few harmless anecdotes wouldn't cause any disruption in Earth's way of life.

Many of the questions posed to Seth were of a profoundly philosophical nature—age-old questions pondered by great thinkers for thousands of years.

"Is there a creator?"

"I can't influence your value system," Seth answered.

"How did the universe begin?"

"As your scientists have told you, it started with what you call the Big Bang."

"But why did the Big Bang happen?"

"That's really another way of asking me if there's a God. Sorry. Mum's the word."

What Seth was always willing to discuss, however, was the petrin definitions of intelligence, information, and life and death—all of the material that had made Session 103 so unique.

"Seth," Joshua asked as the tour entered Greece, "you're always willing to talk about intelligence, life and death, and backup copies, but don't these topics represent petrin values that could influence Earth?"

"I can see why you ask the question," Seth answered, "but the collective believes that we're discussing matters that are already being considered by your species. Your planet is now embarking on the digital age, and you're skilled in backing up information. And the concept of intelligence on Earth is as old as your philosophers, going all the way back to the ancient Romans and Greeks, and you've spent much time attempting to define what is intelligent and what isn't. As for death, you live with it every day, as do many other cultures. We've simply told you how we view all of these. The fact that we don't die may seem shocking, but it's simply because we're farther along in bioengineering and know how to make backup copies better than you do. Notice that we've never shared how we actually do that. And I'll add that no human is forced to accept what are merely our interpretations of these concepts."

"Point taken," Joshua admitted. "You and the collective have this well thought out, and I can't argue with your logic. But for humans, issues such as life and death are a part of what we call religion."

"I know," Seth remarked, "but you used the word 'part.' For petrins, all of your disciplines and fields of study long ago became what we simply call knowledge. Just as we're a collective, we don't view things as being separate, as you do. For us, all things are connected in various ways. All knowledge is holistic."

"Wow," Joshua said. "That's deep."

"Did I just blow your mind, bro?"

"Yeah, something like that."

This was one of Seth's major revelations, which Joshua quickly passed along to Rachael, Vinod, and the other teams. The idea that all knowledge was integrated into a single awareness of reality was one of the weightier concepts Seth had been willing to share. It made headlines in every online and hardcopy newspaper and magazine. Hindu, Buddhist, and Taoist leaders said they'd known this all along, and there was renewed interest in meditation and mysticism even though Seth refused to address the subject of religious beliefs.

*   *   *

The broader leaks from confidential interviews with Seth began when he was in Scandinavia. Newspapers across Europe ran headlines such as ANDROID SETH REVEALS MYSTERIES OF LIFE. He was allegedly providing answers to humanity's timeless questions as he spoke of petrin concepts of intelligence, information, and life and death. Indeed, these became the preferred topics of discussion at many international sessions, and if Seth wasn't going to directly address issues of God and the origins of the Big Bang, matters of life and death were deemed close enough since, as Joshua had correctly pointed out early in the tour, world religious beliefs usually revolved around such themes. Seth was all too glad to accommodate questions on these concepts and seemed eager to share the information from the now-fabled Session 103. In fact, #session103 trended very quickly on the Internet, and Twitter, Facebook, Instagram, and Pinterest all had pages devoted to Session 103. Those who belonged to any or all of these groups, or who had "liked" the various social media pages with "103" in their titles, rapidly became known as The 103 Club, or simply the "103ers."

"He sounds like a sixties hippie from Woodstock," Porter commented on more than one occasion. "I'm not interested in his Zen or his damned metaphysics. As long as he doesn't start spouting tactical or technological information, he can talk all he wants."

Langdon was a bit more concerned.

"Dina," he said during a teleconference, "he's becoming a rock star, and I don't think this 103 club business is healthy. Western religions ignore him since he doesn't mention God or the Bible, and evangelicals are up in arms and protesting his lack of Christian spirituality. He could cause great division."

"Robert," she said, "I think there's a limit to what we can do. I'd rather

214

the leaks hadn't happened, but if Porter isn't concerned, then neither am I."

"Hey, John Lennon said the Beatles thought they were bigger than Jesus," Vinod pointed out, "and the world didn't fall apart."

"I tend to agree," Williams said. "I think we should let this movement run its course. People will eventually lose interest."

"But larger and larger crowds are gathering at every city he visits," Langdon said. "Local police forces are being strained to the limit."

Rachael had again been sitting silently as the discussion progressed. Clearing her throat to gain attention, she hesitantly spoke up. "Uh, I think I have a solution for this."

"What is it?" Williams asked.

"Let's give him a Twitter account. Joshua and I will personally manage it since Seth isn't allowed to use any electronic device. People will have access to Seth from anywhere in the world. In keeping with security protocols, we'll tweet Seth's answers to a select group of screened questions as well as other information about Seth's movements and pronouncements. Porter's representatives can vet each and every tweet if they want. I feel that if people are given more information about him, they may feel less compelled to crowd the streets and look for him."

Porter gave his begrudging approval since he didn't like the cult status the alien had attained. "Popularity can become power," he warned, "but as long as he confines himself to his mystical babble, I'll give it a green light." He sternly urged Joshua and Rachael to screen questions carefully, and he forbade Vinod to have any input into the process unless Seth was commenting on "that crap that Bhakti calls music."

"That's fine with me," Vinod said later. "I guess Porter never listened to the lyrics of sixties rock music. I can think of worse things to discuss with petrins than peace and love."

In the days following the creation of an account under the name of SethTheAndroid, Twitter crashed after the first tweet of "'Sup?" since he acquired ten million followers in the first hour. When the social media giant was online again—Twitter quickly allocated additional server resources to handle the extra load—Seth's profile picture became iconic and was copied and put onto tee shirts and posters, and his image became the avatar for millions of his online devotees. He immediately received thousands of marriage proposals, requests to attend Star Wars and Star Trek conventions, and the offer of millions of dollars to endorse every kind of product one could think of. Scientists asked Seth to solve the Unified Field Theory, and physicians asked Seth for the cure to cancer and other diseases even though the news media had written extensively about petrin rules prohibiting the introduction of new science techniques into an existing culture.

Despite Seth's refusal to respond to any of these requests, doctors and physicians alike pleaded with the android to provide a cure for Ebola, and a small backlash was created by his refusal to help. People accused Seth of being cold and emotionless since the disease was spreading to more countries every day, and the number of deaths was now approaching one hundred thousand. Behind the scenes, the president had instructed Dina Williams to ask Seth to make an exception to the petrins' rule of noninterference for humanitarian reasons. She relayed the request, promising Seth that any help he might provide would be kept confidential and that no one would know where the cure had come from.

"I'd like to help, Ms. Williams," Seth said after the chief of staff flew halfway around the world to make the plea in person. "Many civilizations throughout the universe face a multitude of crises, but we've learned through the millennia that it is the knowledge, wisdom, and ingenuity of a species to solve these problems, especially very serious ones, that allows these species to grow and evolve. To skip any steps in the natural evolution of your planet's culture would be cheating you of the very means by which a civilization learns to thrive and become truly advanced."

"We respect your position on the matter," Williams countered, "but do you know how cold that sounds? Here on Earth, the greatest among us have learned that helping those who can't help themselves is a virtue. Evolution is very real, but we also believe that the acquisition of technology must be used to help others."

Seth stared at Williams for many seconds, and whether he was communicating with the collective or simply analyzing her question was unknown to the personal team, who were the only other members in the room when the request was made.

When Seth spoke at last, he said, "I think your philosophy of aid and compassion is admirable, but it applies only within the framework of the actions that your own species chooses to take. If you choose to help yourselves, then that is your decision. If you chose to harm people, that would be your decision as well."

Williams, despite her jetlag, pressed Seth further. "You mention evolution, but are you invoking Darwin's survival of the fittest? If so, then your lack of help might condemn an entire planet to extinction."

Seth nodded his head. "At present, the collective does not view your Ebola outbreak as an extinction event. It is affecting only a small percentage of your total population. We have a strong moral obligation to prevent extinction, but we don't see this as the case with your current outbreak. I know this is difficult to accept, but we can't change our philosophy of nonintervention even for heartbreaking cases such as this. I believe you've heard of the Butterfly Effect, a well-known phenomenon on your planet. A butterfly disturbs the air only slightly in one hemisphere but causes a tornado in another. It's a ripple effect that can cause severe changes in an ecosystem in a short period of time. The butterfly seems harmless, but the tornado can be devastating and take many lives. Curing Ebola may be beneficial in the short term, but the consequences can be harmful in other ways."

"This is all too theoretical when people are dying," Williams confessed.

"Let me give you another example," Seth continued. "You manufacture beneficial chemicals, but many are turned into substances that are harmful when ingested. They have unforeseen consequences, just like the flapping of a butterfly's wings."

"By that logic," Williams said, "any action may end up being harmful."

"That's quite true, but the collective wisdom of your own planet must govern what actions are taken, not the wisdom of Petri. Every planet is its own contained system. In fact, you have a branch of science called systems theory which states that any influence from an outside system can cause chaos, as in formal chaos theory. Petri is an outside system and must remain that way so that we don't unintentionally cause disaster for your planet. We can't endanger the Earth in an attempt to save it in the short term."

Vinod stood and approached Williams and Seth. "He's right. I know exactly what he's talking about."

Williams sighed wearily. "I do too. Put in those terms, it all makes abundant sense, but I had to ask. We're desperate, Seth."

"I understand. We've monitored the outbreak carefully and will continue to do so, and I hope you'll soon succeed in finding a cure."

*   *   *

There were those humans who didn't understand the science behind the Bowman sphere or spookyons or who simply thought it was all made-up nonsense. They believed that the announcement of Seth and the existence of extraterrestrials was a government hoax, a misinformation campaign worthy of the *X Files*. Others believed the news, but they became survivalists and doomsday preppers and sat outside their homes, trailers, or bunkers, drinking beer and waiting for an invasion to begin.

Most people, however, were genuinely excited by the news and even embraced the information, as redacted as it was, that Seth was providing. The 103 Club continued to grow thanks to social media. Surprisingly, the majority of those who joined the club were not fervent believers in existing religions. They were mostly those who had grown up in the information age. There were many atheists and agnostics, as well as scientists and engineers who viewed The 103 Club not as a religion, but as a belief system, one that made sense in a world increasingly dependent on information. The believers of established religions viewed the club as more of a cult. Some of the more fervent believers in the club sported tattoos of the number 103 on their bodies.

It came as no surprise to Joshua and Rachael when Vinod came to one of their meetings one morning with a new 103 tattoo on his left arm.

"Are you paying homage to your guru?" Rachael asked.

"Yup," Vinod replied.

Mitchel Porter's response on seeing the tattoo for the first time was more jaded. "Bhakti, I see that you've decided to have your IQ tattooed on your arm." Porter didn't care about the outpouring of enthusiasm since Seth's repetitive recounting of petrin ideas—the 103 garbage, as the general sarcastically called them—contained nothing related to technology except the vague mention of backup copies minus the instructions as to how humans could accomplish the same task.

Seth's definition of life as purposeful complexity sparked a vigorous discussion on his visit to Russia. During the scientific discussion, Rachael and Joshua in attendance, he was asked a question by a female scientist.

"Given your definition of life as information with purposeful complexity," she began, "what do you feel about the controversial topic of abortion."

"I can see both sides of the issue," Seth began. "First of all, there is no question that an abortion ends a human life, but petrins believe that life itself is not an absolute quantity but an accumulated quantity. For us there is not much difference between a fertilized egg that will eventually grow into a human and one that will eventually become a pig for example at the time that they are both embryos. However, the human will accumulate more life eventually than the pig. This will happen over many years in the form of intelligence, thoughts, and personality. Therefore, an adult human for us is much more valuable than an adult pig."

"Are you saying that you approve of the concept of abortion?" the scientist asked.

"I'm not saying any such thing," Seth replied. "It is up to humans to make the determination of where to draw their moral boundaries. I'm simply giving you a way to measure life that can be used to make those determinations."

The scientist pressed Seth further. "By your definition then, a newborn infant contains less life than an adult."

"Yes, that's true. But that by no means indicates that we support ending a newborn's life." Seth turned the tables on the scientist. "But I feel that you have also determined that a newborn may be less valuable than an adult."

"How so?" the scientist asked.

"What would you do if you had to make a life or death decision between a baby and an adult? Do those situations happen?"

"I can think of one such situation," Rachael said. "Sometimes there is an incompatibility between a fetus and the mother so that continuing the pregnancy would significantly jeopardize the life of the mother."

"In that situation, who's life do you choose?" Seth asked the scientist.

"It's a difficult decision," the scientist replied, "but I guess we would choose the life of the mother."

"As would we," Seth replied, "but we justify this decision using our definition of life. What is your rationale for choosing the life of the mother?"

After pondering the question for a while, she finally replied, "I don't think I can give you a specific rationale."

"It seems to me that you may already be using the petrin definition of life without knowing it."

The scientist had no response to Seth's last statement and moved on to a different topic.

The concepts in Session 103 had other unforeseen consequences. Thousands of wealthy individuals began to explore the possibility of cryonically freezing their bodies if they became gravely ill or if they died since Seth had created great interest in the topic of immortality. Was it possible, people wondered, to live forever by periodically freezing one's body whenever serious illness or prolonged age incapacitated individuals? Could it be done again and again, always to be cured as medicine advanced over time?

Keying on the concept of backup copies of one's "pattern," as Seth had termed it, others wanted to have their pattern preserved at life extension centers, a business enterprise that grew almost overnight in the hopes that human efforts at cloning might one day achieve enough refinement to make exact replicas of people over and over again. Seth had correctly pointed out during one of his scientific sessions, that cloning a human was akin to creating an identical twin but would not act as a true backup since the thoughts and memories would not be preserved. For this reason, other people wanted to go to the ultimate extreme of transferring their consciousness to computers in the same fashion as portrayed in the Johnny

Depp movie *Transcendence*. Startup companies in Silicon Valley sprouted quickly, all seeking to create digital machines—even robots—that could accept uploads of people's narrated or written life experiences, complete with photographs and home movies.

When asked about these efforts, Seth responded dispassionately by saying that humans were free to do whatever they wished with existing technology. When asked further if any of the efforts at extending life approximated how the petrins made backup copies of themselves, he said that his home world's techniques were well beyond Earth's present technology—and comprehension.

"I naturally can't share information on how we make backup copies," he said, "or how we learned to do so, but perhaps you may come up with methods that satisfy your own needs and desires."

When Seth made this pronouncement, the tour had moved through Russia and India and was now in Southeast Asia.

"People are missing the boat," Vinod told the personal team over dinner at a Saigon restaurant on a rare night off, with Seth in the hands of a security team equipped with tether watches. "Seth has told us unequivocally that his race uses bioengineering to produce backup copies and hence achieve immortality. It's all about boiling down the essence of individuals to the data that represents them and then storing that data. The petrins aren't using cryonics or artificial intelligence."

"Seth has inadvertently started people thinking about how short their lives are," Rachael said, "but in reality, that's nothing new."

"It's new for young and healthy people," Vinod pointed out. "People in our age group normally don't think about dying. Like Blue Oyster Cult sang, don't fear the reaper."

"Looks like Seth is changing that," Joshua said.

"Actually, there are those people who've been thinking about life extension for a while," Rachael said. "My uncle has been the director of one of those cryo facilities for many years."

"Wow, you never told me that," Joshua said, clearly startled. "Is that the one in Arizona?"

"Yes."

"I thought you told me he was a scientist," Joshua asked.

"He is," Rachael replied. "He's a scientist that runs a cryonics facility, and to be honest with you, I've been signed up for many years to be frozen there."

"What?" Joshua exclaimed. "You never told me that."

"I guess it never came up."

"Miller, you're a mystery wrapped up in an enigma," Joshua replied shaking his head. "I may never figure you out."

"Well, I'm sure Seth has been good for your uncle's business," Vinod remarked. "Hey, I gotta run and meet up with Langdon. We have the night shift with Seth." He pointed at his tether watch. "Apple. Don't leave home without it!"

After dinner, Joshua and Rachael strolled through a well-manicured Zen garden under a full moon.

"It's lovely here," Rachael said, taking Joshua's hand in hers. "I miss hiking. We're either on jets or in SUVs on our way to undisclosed locations."

Joshua kissed her lightly on the cheek as they continued walking along a white gravel path, passing under several mimosa trees that glowed a neon green from the effect of the bright moonlight. "It will be over soon. After China, it's back to the particle center."

"Yeah, and then on Seth's private personal tour," she said glumly.

"I'll insist on a few days down time," Joshua said.

They walked in silence for several minutes until Joshua spoke about recent events. "So what do you think of The 103 Club?" he asked.

"I think it's quasi-religious, and that's fine. Everybody has to find his or her own way, but nothing that's happened or been said has changed my mind about God. I assume that's what you're getting at."

Joshua laughed quietly. "You can read my mind. I like that, by the way. You've had insights into how and what I think since the day we met."

Rachael slipped her arm through Joshua's and snuggled closer to him as they advanced along the path. She raised her other arm in the air briefly, revealing the tattoo of the cross that Joshua had noted at Angelino's.

Joshua paused, faced Rachael, and put his hands on her shoulders. "You're remarkable, you know that? You're steadfast in your beliefs at a time when the world is questioning and doubting and struggling to imitate the petrins. I love that about you."

Rachael smiled as she gazed into Joshua's eyes. "For me, it's about faith. I love science as much as I ever did, and Seth has certainly seeded the world with some interesting morsels of information. But I believe in a different kind of immortality. I still maintain that natural science isn't going to prove a supernatural concept, although I believe that whatever power created all this . . ." She paused as she looked up at the moon and stars. "Whoever created all this left some equally tantalizing hints, just like the ones I described at Angelino's. That's enough for me."

"You're not afraid of death, are you?"

Rachael shook her head. "No."

"Then why did you sign up with your uncle's cryo facility? I still don't understand."

Rachael had a pained expression on her face. She hesitated for a moment before she answered. "It has to do with Richard."

"Your brother?"

"Yes. When my parents found out that his cancer was terminal, they were distraught. They felt that he was being cheated out of his life. He would never get to be an adult, experience love, or raise children. My uncle had just started at the cryo facility and suggested that Richard could be frozen so that sometime in the future he would be able to have those experiences and live a full life. My parents were open to the idea, but they were worried that if he was ever revived, none of the people he knew and loved would be around. Since he and I were so close, they scheduled both of us for freezing in the hope that we would have each other when revived. I was ten at the time, but they told me that after I was eighteen I could make my own decision on whether or not to continue the arrangement."

"I see," Joshua replied.

"To be honest with you, lately I've been considering canceling."

"Why?"

"Because of you," Rachael said looking directly at Joshua. "I don't know if I'd want to go through life without you."

"Don't worry, you're stuck with me for a long time," Joshua asserted. "I plan to live to a ripe old age."

"I wouldn't have it any other way."

They fell into each other's arms and kissed passionately before resuming their walk.

The following morning, Joshua was recalled to California. Rodrigo said that he needed help with the tokamak immediately, help that only Joshua could provide. He was on a plane that departed at sunrise.

*   *   *

As the tour started its last phase in Beijing, Langdon and Williams held a teleconference, with Porter en route to China to do one of his periodic inspections to make sure security protocols were being followed to the letter.

"I have to admit that the tour has gone exceptionally well," Langdon said, "although I fear that we stumbled into the very thing we wanted to avoid."

"Which is?" Williams asked.

"A contamination of culture."

"Seth doesn't seem to believe he's been responsible for any contamination, and that's always been his overriding concern and highest ethic," Williams said.

"I know. His mantra is that he never broaches subjects or scientific topics that we're not already aware of or are exploring ourselves, such as robotics. I suppose that's true enough, but I'm unsettled by all of the 103 business and that people are frantic to live forever. Haven't we seen the pollution of our belief systems after all is said and done?"

Williams didn't reply immediately as she pondered the question. "I think 'pollute' is a strong word in this context, Robert. I don't think any world religion has been contaminated inasmuch as Seth as done nothing to persuade anyone from abandoning their beliefs."

"Perhaps, but haven't many people done just that?"

"Not really. Some statistics came across my desk this morning which show that church attendance has risen for the first time in decades."

"Really?"

"Keep in mind that most people don't have the big bucks to freeze themselves or invest in expensive and unproven experiments in cloning or highly speculative attempts to integrate themselves with artificial intelligence. As Mitchell would say if he were present, a lot of New Age people have jumped on this 103 immortality bandwagon, but nobody's going to see results for decades. People want a quick fix, and they'll soon lose interest. But people without a lot of spare cash turned instead to their churches for some reassurance in the face of the unknown."

"I hadn't thought of it that way," Langdon said. "Makes sense."

"Meanwhile, people are still going to work and paying their mortgages and rooting for their favorite sports teams. Life goes on. Seth was true to his word. He didn't drop any hints about the big picture, and for all we know, the petrins don't know that either."

It was Langdon who now paused. "I'm not so sure about that, Dina. Surely they must have discovered some deeper meaning to the cosmos after a few billion years."

"Maybe so," Williams replied, "but tonight I'm playing bridge with a few senators' wives. I'm bringing the chips and dip."

Langdon laughed heartily. "You know how to put things in perspective. And yet the world will never be quite the same."

William's tone grew serious. "No, it won't, Robert. We're not alone, and now we know it."

The teleconference ended.

*   *   *

After Seth had returned to the NASA Bowman Particle Research Center, Joshua stood in the control room outside the tokamak as champagne was poured and Rodrigo gave him a bear hug.

"We did it!" Rodrigo proclaimed. "Entangled spookyons! And to think that highly-refined tungsten was the key to creating them."

"And a few minor adjustments to the container lids," Joshua added. "You did great work, Rodrigo. I'm proud of you."

Joshua led a round of applause for his assistant as more sparkling wine was poured. Rodrigo held up Joshua's arm and proclaimed, "Let's have another round of applause for the boss, who worked on this project for the past six and a half years."

Another round of applause and cheers followed before Joshua spoke. "I think one final toast is in order. To Henry Bowman."

"To Henry Bowman," the staff said with reverence.

After the celebration, Joshua rode the elevator to the bat cave.

"I suppose you've heard the news by now," Joshua said to Seth.

"About the spookyons? Yes, congratulations. Tungsten?"

"Yes, tungsten," Joshua replied with an exasperated look. "I don't mean to give you a hard time, my friend, but all you had to do was say one word—tungsten."

Seth smiled. "I knew you were close and that it was only a matter of time before you succeeded. Besides, if I'd given you the answer, what need would you have had for a celebration?"

Joshua, slightly tipsy, put his arm around Seth's shoulders. "Yeah, well, maybe next time I'm in a pinch, you can slip me a hint since we're buds."

Seth walked to his chair and sat, looking at Joshua. When he spoke, his voice seemed lower than usual, and his demeanor was serious. His face showed no signs of a smile, and his gaze was penetrating in a way that Joshua thought impossible for an android. The alien who claimed to love informality and jokes appeared deadly serious.

"It's the way things are done, Josh. It's the way things have *always* been done."

Joshua had heard this phrase before, but the words had taken on additional meaning and gravity. For the first time in months, Joshua was revisited by the feeling that Seth was withholding something. A shiver ran down his spine as he left the lab.

Chapter Twenty-Seven
Habitats

Joshua informed Seth and the administrative team that he, Rachael, and Vinod needed some rest after the world tour of android Seth. The six-week tour had been grueling, and as Rachael commented, it was easier for Seth to recharge his batteries while traveling than for the personal and security teams to get some sleep. With Seth back at the bat cave, the technical teams could take over for a week or more and resume questioning Seth about Petri, its science and culture, and whatever they could convince him to talk about given his predilection for redactions. Langdon hoped that his scientists would be able to extrapolate a certain amount of information based on Seth's data, most of which was rendered as generalizations. Porter even brought in three CIA agents skilled in interpreting intercepted data from foreign assets.

Joshua and Rachael resumed hiking and enjoying each other's company. During one hike, Joshua looked troubled as he sat on an outcropping of rock under a bright blue noonday sky.

"What's the matter?" Rachael asked. "We're supposed to be decompressing. Is Seth on your mind again?"

The couple had discussed Joshua's suspicions about a secret petrin agenda on several previous occasions, but neither could find a reason to doubt Seth's good will or integrity.

"Yeah," he said. "Sometimes he radically departs from his carefree persona and seems to be someone else entirely. It's unsettling."

"I've noticed that too, but what he displays is *only* a persona. As advanced as Vinod's algorithm is, Seth is still basing his personality on computer programming and approximating what he believes to be normal human behavior."

Joshua stared at the mountains in the distance. "You're probably right, but I can't shake the feeling that the petrins are holding something back from us, and I'm not referring to just redacted technology."

"What do you think it might be?"

"It's hard to even hazard a guess given that his society is billions of years ahead of ours. What if some of their ideas might be impossible for us to understand? Our teams may be incapable of getting at the heart of petrin culture."

Rachael leaned over and retied her hiking boots and pulled up her red socks before taking a sip of water from the plastic bottle in her backpack.

"Are you thinking of a scenario from *The Day the Earth Stood Still*?" she asked. "Michael Rennie's character comes to Earth and represents a peaceful, advanced civilization, but at the end of the movie, the other shoe drops. He knows humans are starting to venture into space and tells Earth's leaders to stop making war or else his planetary federation will open a can of whoop ass so that we don't contaminate the cosmos."

Joshua shook his head. "Maybe, although Seth has indicated in many sessions that they really don't want to interfere in how humans advance. But you're right. There's another shoe that's going to drop—I'm almost certain of it—and it's driving me crazy. Seth *is* like the Rennie character. Sooner or later, we're going to get the lecture. I just don't know what it's going to be about."

"Like we're all in kindergarten," Rachael said, "but sooner or later we graduate, and then teachers expect a lot more."

"Something like that."

"Sorry we made contact?"

Joshua thought for several seconds. "Nah. The scientist in me is too curious despite my foreboding. Besides, I'd never have gotten involved with you if we hadn't received mathematical messages that first day in the bat cave. It's what brought us together. Otherwise, you might have written your story and I'd never have seen you again."

Rachael kissed Joshua. "I love it when you talk like that."

"It was fate."

"Fate with a capital F?"

"Maybe." He took her hand and squeezed.

Rachael laughed as they resumed hiking. "I think you're coming around."

*   *   *

Joshua, Rachael, and Vinod were assembled in the lab and noticed that Seth had been reading a stack of books piled high next to his chair. The books given to him were vetted by the security team to make sure there was no content that they would consider off limits.

"Looks like you're big into books," Vinod remarked.

"Sure," Seth replied. "I wanted to see how humans have assimilated information for centuries. I could scan the pages quickly and read any book in a matter of minutes if I chose, but I wanted to savor the experience. That's why I'm here."

"But why not use a Kindle or iPad?" Vinod asked.

"Because he might like the heft of a book and the smell of paper and ink," Rachael interjected. "Like me."

"I do like the physical feel of a book," Seth said. "But you forget that I have no olfactory sensors. Besides, I have a restriction on electronic devices."

"Do you have any favorites?" Joshua asked.

"Plato and Aristotle had some provocative views on life and existence, which I can neither agree nor disagree with for obvious reasons. But it was enjoyable reading."

"Enjoyable?" Rachael said with a smile. "Except for philosophers, most people find it a bit dense. What else did you like?"

"Jane Austen. The heroines in all of her novels were in such a hurry to marry gentlemen of breeding. She provided many insights into human courtship. Was it that way with you, Rachael? Were you looking for a man of means, one who held a title?"

"Goodness no! I like Jane Austen too, although some of the customs she describes are a bit out of date. Still, I think I made a pretty good match with Joshua, as Austen would have put it." She slid her arm around his waist. "He's a keeper—and a gentleman."

Vinod frowned. "Gross. Too much PDA for me since you two got together. Austen wouldn't approve."

"PDA?" Seth said.

"Public display of affection," Joshua said. "Kissing, holding hands—stuff like that. So where to now, Seth? It's time to take you on a personal tour."

"Actually, I'd like to view more of your PDA, especially between you and Rachael. Your species devotes a great deal of time to talking and writing about mating rituals and procreation."

Vinod glanced at Rachael and Joshua before he remarked, "Awkward."

Joshua grinned, put his arm around Seth, and drew close to the android. "I'll have to teach you some of the nuances of human behavior, especially as they pertain to sexuality. It's complicated, even for us. The bottom line is that most humans regard mating as a very private act."

"I didn't realize that," Seth said. "Many cultures throughout the universe have mating rituals that are inherently public."

"I can think of a lot of rock songs and videos that talk about mating pretty explicitly," Vinod said. "And then there's always the Internet—"

Rachael elbowed Vinod hard in his side.

"I get it," Seth said. "Redacted information about mating. Okay, I have a second choice. I've gotten to see many humans on my trips around your world, albeit in a very formal setting. I'd like to see more of the diversity of life on your planet. How about somewhere where I can see more of the fauna?"

"Animals?" Joshua said. "Excellent choice."

"Perhaps we could board a jet and observe wildlife on an African savannah," Seth suggested. "Or the pampas of Argentina. Anywhere, really. Some of your animal species are quite beautiful and show an amazing ability to adapt to their environments."

"I think you're scheduled to go to South American and Africa on your next official outing to meet world leaders, but there's a simpler way to see a variety of animals," Joshua said. "We can take you to a zoo. Robert Langdon can arrange for an after-hours tour so you won't be mobbed. You're quite a celebrity."

"I'm accessing the term zoo. Yes, that will do nicely."

Joshua telephoned Langdon, and an hour later the trio and Seth rode the elevator to the atrium. This time, however, they walked toward a back entrance to avoid the pool of reporters permanently stationed in front of the particle center.

*   *   *

Seth and the personal team drove down the Interstate in Joshua's 1967 Chevy Impala convertible with the top up. Joshua and Rachael sat in front, with Vinod and Seth on the rear bench seat. A black Chevy Suburban carrying a security team followed the vintage automobile at a discreet distance.

"Damn, Josh," Vinod said. "This is one sweet ride. Heavy chassis and a great suspension system. If only that pushbutton radio could tune into the real rock and roll stations from the time period this gas guzzler was built, the effect would be complete. It's a freakin' time machine."

"Do you attempt to travel through time?" Seth asked.

"No, I was speaking figuratively. The car is old and considered a classic because it has been restored. It's what we call cherry. But hey, is time travel possible?"

"Classic. Cherry. I get it now. And another nice try, Vinod. About time travel, that is."

"You like classic rock, and I like classic cars," Joshua said. "I picked it up at a Barret Jackson auction. As for the radio, it doesn't get Sirius XM, so we're stuck with classic rock FM stations full of advertisements every four minutes."

Vinod belly-laughed. "Just like the sixties!" He looked back at the SUV following behind them. "Those government guys never leave us alone. They're about four car lengths back."

"It's for our protection," Rachael reminded him. "And Seth's too. We were followed all over Europe and Asia, so I'd think that you'd be used to it by now."

"Never. Big Brother is a pain in the—"

An eighteen-wheeler blared its horn as it passed another vehicle.

"In the ass," Seth said. "That's a common idiom, isn't it?"

"Yep," said Vinod. "They're a pain in the ass, but as Rachael said, probably necessary. At least they're not in the same car with us. All those black suits creep me out. They keep talking into their cufflinks and wristwatches."

"How much farther to the zoo?" Seth asked.

"About ten minutes," Joshua replied. "We'll get there with plenty of daylight left. You're going to enjoy it, Seth. When I was a kid, I loved it when my dad took me to the zoo. We'd stay for hours."

Rachael looked sideways. "I absolutely *hate* zoos."

"How come?" Joshua asked. "They're educational."

"Because I always feel that the animals are trapped there. It seems . . . unnatural."

"Do they have any say in whether they want to be held in captivity?" Seth asked.

"We can't communicate with animals," Vinod said. "Maybe a little with dolphins, whales, or chimpanzees, but otherwise we aren't able to bridge the gap. Animals communicate, but not in a language we can easily understand. Let me guess. On some planets, the main inhabitants communicate with most of the animals."

"Absolutely," Seth confirmed. "In many cases, the animals lie along a complex spectrum of evolution and intelligence and can talk to the dominate species. There's one planet on which the dominant species talks to an intermediate species which, in turn, communicates with the lower species."

"One big happy family," Vinod laughed as he began to hum "It's a Small World After All."

"I really like zoos," Joshua said, turning the conversation back to Rachael's concern. "Animals in modern zoos are treated well, get fed a perfect diet, and receive medical care they wouldn't receive in the wild. There's no pain or suffering in a zoo."

"I'm all for it," Vinod proclaimed. "They have the life. They can just chill and hang out. No stress from having to find food or the risk of getting eaten by some predator."

Rachael craned her neck to address Vinod more directly. "But they're still not free. I think if they *could* communicate with us and had a choice in the matter, they would want to roam about their natural habitats without restrictions. Maybe searching for food and avoiding predators is what makes them happy. It is, after all, exactly what they've evolved to do."

"I disagree," Joshua said. "As a matter of fact, we *need* zoos. They play a major role in protecting endangered species from extinction."

"Extinction that we humans are the major cause of," Rachael countered. "We have zoos and aquariums, and I'm not comfortable with the idea of keeping wild creatures in domestic settings. The orca whales at SeaWorld weren't healthy despite humane treatment. And since we can't talk with the animals like Dr. Doolittle, there's no way to know if they're happy or not. I think they'd be much happier roaming free."

"Hey, is this like the first fight for you guys?" Vinod asked, looking almost excited at the prospect. "Am I an eyewitness?"

"It's not a fight," Rachael said. "Call it a difference of opinion. That's something that's healthy in a loving relationship."

Vinod rolled his eyes. "Back to the lovey dovey shit."

"Is this a prerequisite for mating?" Seth queried. "An argument? That's often the way it is in Miss Austen's novels."

"Sometimes," Vinod said. "It's called makeup sex."

"Vinod, give it a rest," Joshua said.

"I nevertheless enjoyed the conversation about zoos," Seth said. "It gives me an interesting insight into human values and morality. Can you two have another difference of opinion so that I can continue to learn?"

"Not right now," Joshua said.

"I understand," Seth said. "More lovey dovey shit."

*   *   *

The personal team and Seth walked through a large portal constructed of forty-feet-high logs on either side, its enormous gates in the open position. A wooden logo in the shape of the continent of Africa hung from the crossbeam directly overhead. The words AFRICAN HABITAT were carved and painted in gold on the miniature continent. The team and android Seth walked along a winding curved deck of natural wood bordered by thickets of bamboo on either side until they reached a clearing. Beyond them, on the other side of a narrow stream and a wire fence, was a grassland several acres deep.

Rachael and Joshua donned sunglasses as the four stood and looked at the mock savannah before them. The security detail was positioned fifteen yards behind them, their hands crossed in front of them, feet apart. Giraffes, gazelles, zebras, and water buffaloes roamed lazily across the plain, most grazing, their tails swinging in the air to swat flies. After only a few moments, the zebras broke into a run and vanished into the haze on the far side of the habitat.

"Those are amazing animals," Seth commented. "They seem happy enough to me."

"What choice do they have?" Rachael asked rhetorically. "It's not like they can escape or ask to go back to their real homes."

"In the old days of zoos," Joshua said, "before habitats were the norm and animals were confined to cages, behavioral changes and illnesses were the telltale signs of what many zoologists claimed was literal depression in the specimens on exhibit. That's a thing of the past."

Rachael shuddered. "The very word specimen makes me uncomfortable. Prisoners in a penitentiary may appear docile, but it doesn't mean they want to be there."

"They seem to have accepted their situation," Seth observed. "They also seem to be coexisting peacefully despite their diversity."

"More than I can say for some countries," Vinod said, "but the peacefulness is probably due to the fact that the species you see are separated from the lions."

"The lions are the predators?" Seth said.

"Yup."

"I'd like to see them next."

A zoo guide who'd been instructed to stand some distance away motioned that they should follow him. The group walked past a second grassland area with rhinos and elephants.

"Quite majestic," Seth said upon seeing a male elephant in his habitat. "I can't say for certain whether or not he's happy since I can't directly communicate with him, but it's obvious that humans have great reverence for him."

"That much we can agree on," Rachael said, looping her arm through Joshua's.

"Problem solved," Vinod said. "Peace has broken out for the future Dr.

and Mrs. Andrews."

"Hey," Rachael remarked, "I haven't agreed to take his last name yet."

"Vinod," Joshua retorted irritatingly, "you have a way of causing trouble, don't you?"

"I'm sure Seth would love to hear this discussion between you two. Another point of contention between our PDA specialists."

"Well it's not going to happen," Joshua replied. "That's a private discussion for another day."

The four moved along a narrow path single file past a sign that read EXHIBIT UNDER CONSTRUCTION. Joshua, Rachael, and Vinod had walked several paces before noticing that Seth wasn't by their side. Turning quickly, they saw that he was kneeling down, the men in black a few yards behind him. One of the men was talking into his wrist, although he didn't seem concerned.

"What's he looking at?" Rachael asked.

"Let's find out," Joshua said as the group retraced its steps.

Seth, however, appeared to be staring intently at the dirt.

"Anything wrong?" Joshua asked. "Are your servos and actuators functioning properly?"

"Amazing creatures!" Seth said, ignoring Joshua's question. "Are these ants?"

Joshua and Rachael removed their sunglasses and squinted.

"Yes, they are," Rachael said as she knelt next to Seth. "They're not part of an exhibit, though. They occur naturally all around the planet wherever there's dirt."

Seth continued to examine the long trail of ants, which led into a clump of bushes a few feet away.

"Most interesting," he said. "They're quite small and yet they must have remarkable communication skills to move with such precision and stay in tight formation."

"They communicate by chemical signals," Vinod explained. "And yes, they're highly organized and sophisticated despite their small size. Believe it or not, entire models in systems theory have been based on the biological model of ants—and insects in general. Technology often mimics natural phenomena."

"Are they a collective then?" Seth asked.

"According to entomologists they are," Joshua said.

Seth stood. "I suppose I have a lot in common with them," he said with a smile, motioning to an ant hill under the branch of the nearest bush. "I suspect that I'm looking at their home and that this line represents individuals looking for food."

"Right on," Vinod said. "They have determination and purpose. They serve a queen ant, who is responsible for reproduction, the same as bees."

"So if this isn't an exhibit at the zoo, what is it?" Seth asked looking around.

"It's an area under construction," Joshua explained. "They're building a new exhibit here."

"What will happen to the ants during the construction?" Seth asked, a look of concern claiming his features.

Joshua shrugged. "Don't really know. I suppose this colony will be removed, intentionally or unintentionally, as construction of the exhibit continues. As Rachael pointed out, you can find them just about anywhere there's soil. They can become pretty bothersome and crawl up arms and legs and bite people. Whenever possible, they're exterminated by companies that deal in what we call pest control."

"And humans are morally okay with destroying their colonies?"

"Yeah, they're just ants," Vinod answered nonchalantly. "They're very lowly creatures from a human standpoint. Besides, it's only this colony that will be destroyed, not their entire species. They're plenty more like this to be found around the globe."

"They might evolve if you allowed them a stable niche," Seth noted. "All collectives are naturally capable of evolutionary advancement."

"It's been tried in science fiction films, where radiation zaps them and they take over the Earth," Vinod said. "No thanks. Geez, Seth. We bring you to a modern zoo and you become obsessed with lame-ass ants. Stay focused, dude. Gotta move on to the next attraction."

Seth straightened and smiled. "Of course. Sorry . . . dude."

The group continued on to the next exhibit. As Joshua walked behind Seth, who was looking down periodically to avoid stepping on any ants, his mind returned back to the concerns that he had shared with Rachael regarding Seth's secretiveness. It was reassuring for him to see Seth purposely trying to avoid killing ants. Whatever Seth was hiding, he didn't seem to have a penchant for destroying life, even life much less sophisticated than humans.

"I bet there are insect species spread throughout the galaxy," Vinod said, looking at Seth for a response.

Seth smiled. "Nice try."

They'd arrived at the lion exhibit.

"What beautiful creatures!" Seth exclaimed. "They look supremely confident."

"That's because they're apex predators," Vinod said. "King of the jungle and all that stuff."

"If you mixed the lions with the other animals you saw," Joshua noted, "there wouldn't be peaceful coexistence."

"I understand," Seth said. "They're carrying out the genetic destiny for which they're purposed."

"That's correct," Rachael said. "Just like you said in session 103."

Seth smiled. "Yes. Purpose."

*   *   *

On the way back to the lab, Rachael saw a golden opportunity to question Seth. "So what do you think of zoos now that you've seen one?" she asked.

"I was quite impressed," Seth replied. "Joshua was correct in that the animals are well-cared for and well-fed."

"But do they mind living in captivity?"

Seth turned and looked at her with a grin. "I don't want to start another disagreement between you and Joshua."

"Don't worry about that," Rachael said, pushing Seth for an answer. "You're being evasive. I think that's a question you can give us your opinion on."

"I'm not able to answer your query with certainty since I can't actually engage in a dialogue with them or ask them specific questions. I was able to cue on some visible signals, but I don't know what their preference might be."

"But what do *you* think about zoos?" Vinod asked, unwilling to let Seth off the hook. "Just asking for an opinion. You won't be influencing policy over whether or not zoos should exist, so you won't be interfering in our culture."

"When you put it like that, I would say that I agree with Joshua. Zoos preserve species in a compassionate way and prevent extinctions. Isn't that in the best interest of the animals? You're their caretakers—their parents, in a sense—and I think you're doing an admirable job."

"But is it *better* than living in the wild?" Rachael asked.

"It's neither better nor worse. Having zoos is simply the decision your species has made. The animals will thrive or not thrive depending on many variables that I couldn't possibly account for."

"So you're saying it's a value judgment," Joshua said.

"Yes."

"Like deciding to care for the ants or not," Rachael said.

"Yeah, I'd agree with that."

"You manage to be evasive even when you *do* answer questions," Vinod remarked.

"Just trying to be accurate, bro."

*   *   *

Back at the lab, Rachael sat in Joshua's office.

"What do you make of our trip to the zoo?" she asked. "Never a dull moment when hanging around an alien."

"I think it went okay," Joshua replied. "Like Vinod said, though, there are some things Seth just won't get pinned down on even when he's willing to respond. He'd make a great politician—a master of deflection. Ask him a hundred questions, and you'd probably get an approximate answer for everything, one that never commits him to a particular position."

"I think he was upset that we don't care for the ants," Rachael said. "It was very noticeable."

"Could be that he's partial to any kind of lifeform that demonstrates a collective mentality."

Rachael nodded. "Or his concern for the ants might be related to his belief that we're the caretakers of all other species on Earth and that we're not being good parents, as he put it. I can understand his viewpoint and might even agree with him were it not for the fact that I like to go on picnics without getting eaten alive by the little devils."

Joshua laughed as he sat back and laced his fingers behind his head. "And he agrees with *me*. Zoos aren't so bad. He seems to equate maintaining modern zoo habitats with being good parents, if I can read between the lines."

"Parenting is certainly a big responsibility," Rachael remarked reflecting on Joshua's last statement. "Do you want to have kids one day?"

"Of course," Joshua replied. "But you already knew that or you wouldn't have agreed to marry me."

"Correct."

"Do you want boys or girls?" Joshua asked. "And will they be writers or scientists?"

"Boys or girls—it doesn't matter as long as they're happy," Rachael replied with a dreamy expression on her face. "They can be whatever they want. That's also part of being a good parent. Knowing when to give them their freedom so they can evolve however they want."

"You're pretty smart."

"I have my moments."

Chapter Twenty-Eight
Bonding

Rachael popped into Joshua's office when she'd finished typing notes on the personal team's visit to the zoo. The team was expected to give daily reports on Seth's activities, which was now more time-consuming since interaction with the alien wasn't confined to audio and video sessions in the bat cave.

"Hungry?" she asked. "How about some pizza?"

"I'm famished. Let's grab Vinod and Seth. It would be a crime if Seth didn't interact with people having great food at a pizza parlor. He may naturally absorb sunshine for food, but let's show him how humans soak up grease, toppings, cheese sticks—the whole nine yards." Joshua adopted a serious tone, as if imitating a scholar. "It's a vital part of his education in human nutrition and cuisine."

"It's the least we can do for him after spending sixty million bucks to give him a body. I concur, Dr. Andrews."

The four piled into the Impala and rode through the dusk down a highway to a pizza restaurant with the name A Slice of Sicily. They were escorted to a red leather booth at the very rear, where Joshua and Rachael sat on one side, Vinod and Seth on the other. Joshua and Vinod ordered a beer, Rachael a glass of red wine. The security team that followed them to the restaurant took a table in clear view of the others.

"You look familiar, sir," the waiter said, staring at Seth. "Hey, aren't you that—"

Joshua put his fingers to his lips. "Shhh! We came here for a break, so if you don't mention that we're here, there's an overly-generous tip in it for you when we leave."

"Yes, sir!" said the waiter. "That works for me."

The waiter left, but not before giving Seth a thumbs-up. Seth returned the gesture, unsure of its meaning.

After looking at the menu, Joshua said, "There's an art to ordering pizza. Thin slice or deep dish? Meat or veggie toppings? And what combination of tomato sauce, cheese, onions, garlic, peppers—"

"To anchovy or not to anchovy!" Rachael chimed in. "That is the question."

"Or just get everything," Vinod said. "A combo supreme. Go big or go home."

"I didn't come across this ritual in my reading," Seth said.

"We're just messing with you a little," Vinod said. "We consume a variety of things. There aren't always as many decisions involved in day-to-day dining, but eating is not only necessary—it's a bonding experience, an opportunity for people to take time out from their day to share and enjoy each other's company."

"Since I get plugged in to recharge my batteries, I'll have to content myself to observe," Seth said.

"But you're sharing the experience," Joshua said. "That makes you part of the meal."

Seth flashed a smile that was almost childlike in quality. "Thanks, guys." He looked at a menu out of politeness and curiosity.

The waiter returned and took their order for two pizzas, one a combo and the other a veggie.

"So, Seth," Joshua said as he sipped his beer, "do you have any more questions about the zoo?"

"Not about the zoo, but on our way home from the zoo I saw some things I didn't understand."

"Such as?" Rachael said.

"There was a field with rows and rows of a single plant. Each had long, drooping green leaves. Do you know what it was?"

"Hmm," Joshua said, looking at his companions. "Got any ideas, guys?"

"I was listening to the radio," Vinod said. "Zoned out. Sorry."

"Got it!" Rachael said. "It was a corn field."

"I assume then," Seth said, "that humans planted the seeds for those plants—what you call agriculture."

"Right," Joshua said. "Collectively, the corn plants are called a crop. The corn was planted several months ago, and the farmers are waiting for it to grow into what we call full ears of corn." Joshua pulled out his phone and showed Seth a picture of corn on the cob. "It takes a while for the ear to develop, and different plants grow at different rates."

"In other words," Seth said, "you collect the plants when they're mature."

"Yes," Joshua said. "It's a very orderly, methodical process. Planting, watering, and fertilizing, and then when the plants are mature, they're cut and the ears are collected, something we call a harvest."

The waiter appeared, carrying a large round tray, on top of which were two pizzas. Setting them on an expanding aluminum tray stand next to booth, he carefully set the pizzas in front of his customers.

"Here you go," he said with a smile. "One veggie and one combo. Will there be anything else?"

"We're fine, thanks," Joshua said.

"Enjoy your meal," the waiter said as Seth gave him a thumbs-up, now believing it was part of the ritual of ordering and receiving food.

"Smells delicious," Vinod said.

"Mouth-watering," Rachael echoed.

Seth turned his head to look at the mouths of his three friends.

"Just an expression," Vinod explained. "It means the food smells and tastes good."

"It's pure heaven," Rachael said, pausing before looking up. "Uh, that's an expression too."

Seth watched as Rachael and Vinod each took a slice from the combo, while Joshua took a slice from the veggie.

"So you don't eat meat, Josh?" Seth asked.

"I'm a vegetarian," Joshua said. He explained how he'd decided years earlier not to consume anything that had ever had a brain when it was alive.

"But you and Rachael eat meat," Seth said, turning to Vinod.

"Yeah, we all set our own limits." He bit into the drooping slice he held in his hand.

"But what measure are you using to set those limits?" Seth asked. "It seems to me that you're using the petrin definition of life as your metric."

"How so?" Joshua asked.

"According to our definition of life, plants are less complex than animals and therefore contain less life. Joshua, you don't eat animals because you feel they are too complex to sacrifice for your consumption, but this really fits with our definition of life. You don't want to consume life above a certain complexity, whereas Vinod and Rachael are okay with eating more complex entities such as animals, but I'm sure they also have a limit on how complex an animal they would sacrifice."

"Definitely true," Rachael commented.

"You may be right bro," Vinod remarked. "Maybe that's the reason you have all those crazy 103ers following your every word. Me included. But you're definitely missing out on some great pizza."

"The solar energy we absorb from sunshine is very clean and efficient," Seth remarked. "It's all we require."

Vinod put his hand on Seth's shoulder. "No offense, dude, but it sounds really dull. Variety is the spice of life."

"But we accomplish what we're purposed for," Seth replied.

"We're purposed for a *lot* of things," Joshua said.

"I gathered as much from my reading back at the lab. Your species engages in many tasks. Wherever I've been, I've seen humans walking, driving, and working. It seems quite frenetic."

"That's very true," Rachael said. "Humans have many different vocations—purposes, if you will. But we also enjoy other things too, such as hobbies, eating, travel, and much more. They all give us purpose and pleasure, at least most of the time. Like Vinod said, variety is the key."

"Like sex and procreation?"

"Yes, those too," Rachael said.

"Do you need all these purposes to be happy?"

"Absolutely," Vinod said, struggling to swallow so he could talk. "And sometimes, doing nothing at all is an activity in itself."

"You mean just chillin', like the animals in the zoo?" Seth asked.

"You got it, bro. We love to be pampered. It's all part of being human."

"But planting seeds and harvesting is one of the most important tasks?"

"Right," Joshua said. "It enables us to eat. But after we finish our tasks—the harvest, if you will—we humans like to relax, just like Vinod said."

"Harvest and pleasure go together then?"

"You're catching on," Vinod said.

The three team members reached for more slices of pizza as the waiter brought a new round of beers and another glass of wine.

"There are other kinds of seed, though," Rachael said.

"For other crops?"

"Not in the conventional sense," she answered. "Seeds are also ideas that we plant as we educate our children in the hope that knowledge will grow and mature. Does that make sense to you?"

"Perfect sense. Children must learn and grow and one day . . . leave the nest. Is that the proper phrase?"

Rachael nodded. "Yes, you're a quick study."

Seth stared blankly at his companions as he watched them eat.

"Observing?" Vinod said.

"Yes. You seem most satisfied."

"Like I said, you don't know what you're missing."

"I have another question," Seth stated as the others continued eating. "We passed another field not far away from the corn. There were rectangular stones protruding vertically from the ground, all arranged in neat rows not dissimilar from the corn, although the spacing was different. Are they related to agriculture?"

"A field of stones?" Joshua said, puzzled.

Vinod laughed. "That gives new meaning to the saying 'grow a pair.'"

"I think he means the cemetery," Rachael said, shooting a chastising look at Vinod. "About three miles back."

"Yes, it's where we bury our dead bodies," Joshua said. "Remember that we're not immortal like you."

"Of course I remember, but don't you recycle the bodies?"

"Yes and no," Joshua answered. "They eventually decay and become part of the earth again."

"Ashes to ashes, dust to dust," Rachael interjected. "It's a saying we have that reminds us of our mortality."

"The process of decay takes much longer in modern times," Vinod said, "since bodies are buried in sturdy caskets that take longer to deteriorate than a human body. Also, cemeteries are well-cared for. On the other hand, some people are cremated and have their ashes sprinkled over the land or a body of water. I guess they get recycled pretty fast."

"Interesting. Their molecules are repurposed. But can't some body parts be used again?"

"Sometimes," Joshua said. "People can elect to donate their organs upon death assuming they're not damaged. The heart, liver, kidney, and other organs are transplanted into those who are ill. I guess it's a true form of recycling and maybe what you're getting at."

"It's certainly an efficient use of the human body and its parts," Seth Remarked, "and very compassionate. Are burial and cremation the only rituals you observe after someone dies?"

"Mostly," Vinod answered. "Some people get frozen, like Rachael intends to do."

"Yes, for your brother," Seth said. "That's compassionate as well."

"I told Josh that I'm thinking about canceling that," Rachael said.

Joshua put down his glass of beer and turned to Rachael. "No, you're not. I was going to tell you later, but I guess now is as good a time as any. I recently signed up at the same facility run by your uncle. I want you to honor the memory of Richard, and I'll be right there with you."

Rachael's eyes grew large with surprise and welled with tears as she leaned over and gave Joshua a hug. "Oh Josh, thank you so much. It means a lot to me. I love you."

"I love you too."

"Here we go again," Vinod said sarcastically. He began singing the chorus from "Leather and Lace" by Don Henley and Stevie Nicks.

"Damn, Vinod," Joshua interrupted. "For someone who likes music so much, you sure have a shitty voice. You're ruining that song for me."

Seth resumed the song in a clear, pleasing voice exhibiting perfect pitch. He sounded exactly like Don Henley singing the song, but it wasn't a recording.

The three members of the personal team exchanged astonished glances. Vinod then proceeded to put his arm around the android as the pair serenaded Joshua and Rachael with the song.

When Seth and Vinod finished their singing, Joshua and Rachael started clapping. Joshua's hand movements were slow and sarcastic; Rachael's were fast and showed genuine enthusiasm and appreciation.

"Gosh, thanks, guys," she said, wiping a single tear from her eye. "That was beautiful."

"More like beauty and the beast," Joshua added, looking from Seth to Vinod.

"So what do you want to see next Seth?" Joshua asked. "We promised you a personal tour, and there's a lot more to human behavior than eating pizza."

Seth seemed to have anticipated the question. "I'm curious about humans and their social interactions," he replied. "I've spoken to many humans in my travels, but the settings were very formal. I'd like to observe humans and interact with them in a more natural habitat."

"That might be hard to pull off given your celebrity status," Joshua said.

"General Porter might go ballistic," Rachael said.

Vinod appeared excited as he pushed away his plate and leaned forward, his elbows on the table. "I've got the perfect spot."

"Where?" Joshua asked.

"Vegas."

"Vegas?" Joshua asked.

"Humans in their natural habitat? Vegas."

"Are you out of your mind?" Joshua asked. "We're *not* going to Vegas. It's cheesy and crowded. Rachael's right. Porter will blow a fuse. Besides, Seth would get mobbed. Seth-o-mania."

"Not if we disguised him," Vinod replied, putting his arm around the android. "I think our boy Seth here would make a great rapper with the right outfit. He's got the moves, and I could tweak the urban dictionary a bit to be a bit more . . . urban."

"What's Vegas?" Seth asked.

"Are you serious, Vinod?" Rachael asked, ignoring Seth's question.

"Dead serious. Come on. It would be fun dressing him up."

"As a rapper?" Joshua asked.

"Yeah, we get him some clothes—perhaps a dreadlock wig—a gold chain, some sunglasses, and maybe even a gold grill for his teeth. We'd be all set."

"Maybe," Joshua replied, "but it still seems risky to me."

"Come on, Josh," Vinod said. "Where's your sense of adventure?"

"How about his voice?" Rachael asked. "His voice would be pretty recognizable given the amount of media coverage he's gotten."

"I can change my voice, bro," Seth replied in an exact copy of Vinod's voice. The others stared at him, mouths agape. "I can make it sound like anyone you want," he said in Rachael's voice.

"Stop that," Rachael said. "It's creeping me out."

"Is this one better?" Seth said in Joshua's voice.

"No," Joshua replied. "If this is going to work it's going to have be a unique voice that fits the persona."

"I can rustle up some rap videos from the Internet, and we could choose various sounds and mannerisms," Vinod suggested.

"You actually think you can get Porter to approve of this idea?" Rachael asked. "Disguising Seth as a rapper and taking him to Vegas?"

"Porter, the president wants you to approve this," Seth said with Dina Williams' voice.

Vinod chuckled. "That's hilarious dude. Spot on. Look, if we present this as Seth's request, which it is, and make sure the security goons stay close behind, they may go for it."

Joshua thought for a moment. "Maybe. I think we'll run it by Langdon first. We could also sell it as hiding Seth in plain sight, as the saying goes. Who would expect him to be in Las Vegas?"

Vinod clapped Seth on the shoulder. "We're going on a road trip, baby! Can you say it?"

Seth raised his eyebrows. "Say . . . ?"

"Road trip!"

"Road trip," Seth said, imitating Vinod's voice. "Baby. But you still haven't answered my question. What is Vegas?"

"The gambling capital of America," Joshua replied. "A place where most people go to get drunk, married, divorced, and lose large amounts of money to establishments called casinos."

"Sometimes all in the same day," Rachael added.

"I see," Seth said. "A lot of purposeful activity, just as we discussed. Fulfillment of tasks followed by chillin' and leisure activity. It sounds ideal."

"More leisure than anything else," Rachael said.

"A whole lot more," Joshua reiterated.

"Road trip, baby!" Seth repeated.

Chapter Twenty-Nine
Snake Eyes

Having asked Langdon about the possibility of taking Seth to Las Vegas, Joshua and the team were seated in his office, waiting for a teleconference with Williams and Porter. Langdon himself thought the road trip would be all right as long as security was modified so as not to stand out, but he was constrained to point out that the decision had to be unanimous among the administrative team.

As expected, Porter originally vetoed the idea, citing the many risks entailed in bringing android Seth into a populated area in which people were in extremely close proximity to each other.

"There are a million places you can take him," Porter said. "Let him see Yellowstone or take the harbor tour around the Statue of Liberty. Or take him for private visits to museums. He could hike in the Amazon and meet the remaining native tribes. All of those options would be safer, not to mention more educational. What can he possible learn from a trip to Las Vegas? Even more importantly, what can we expect to learn from *him*? You're ambassadors, for God's sake. Is showing Seth slot machines the best you can think of?"

"We kinda promised him," Vinod said.

"I don't see any harm in it as long as he's well disguised," Langdon said.

As usual, the decision fell to Williams.

"I'm going to overrule you on this, Mitchell," she said. "It wouldn't have been my first choice, but there are oddballs and Elvis impersonators on every corner in Vegas. I don't think anyone will notice Seth as long as the team provides him with the appropriate clothing. In the long run, Las Vegas is a part of who we are as a culture, albeit a small one. Games of chance are as old as humanity."

"Yes!" Vinod cried.

The right side of the screen went blank, Porter's face disappearing without further comment.

"Can I count on you three to be discreet?" Williams asked.

"Do you even have to ask?" Vinod said.

"Mr. Bhakti, you're the *only* reason I asked," Williams said before her image vanished also.

"Good luck," Langdon said. "This had better go off without a hitch."

"Thanks, Robert," Joshua said. "We'll take good care of Seth."

"Famous last words," Langdon said, unable to suppress a grin.

*   *   *

Joshua and Rachael were once again in the front seat of the vintage Chevy, Vinod and Seth in the back. The top was down this time as they drove through the desert headed to Las Vegas. The SUV carrying the security detail, now dressed in jeans and button-down shirts, trailed behind. Seth was unrecognizable in his rapper disguise as dreadlocks were blown backwards by the wind. The YouTube videos provided by Vinod allowed Seth to effortlessly adopt a rapper persona, including speech and gait.

As usual, Vinod had a rock tee shirt on. It was a cover from Loverboy's *Get Lucky* album.

"We need some tunes in here!" Vinod exclaimed over the din of rushing air.

"We're not going to be able to find any radio stations in the desert," Joshua shouted back. "Remember, this car only has FM."

"No problem," Vinod shouted back. "Just tune it to 107.5 and crank it up all the way. That's Radio Bhakti."

Rachael turned on the radio and tuned to the requested frequency. "Born to be Wild" by Steppenwolf blared from the speakers after she'd moved the dial through several stations marred by static.

"How'd you do that, Vinod?" Rachael asked.

"Simple," Vinod answered. "I connected an FM transmitter to my phone. Picked it up this morning before we left. An easy workaround for someone who knows a thing or two about interfaces. Can't go on a road trip without tunes."

The car drove through the white desert as the late evening sky turned shades of orange and violet.

The sun had fully set when they arrived in Vegas and cruised down Las Vegas Boulevard to show Seth the strip and the throng of people walking on either side. "Let's Go" from the Cars blared through the speakers of the convertible.

"Why they call this place sin city?" Seth asked. "Are they sinning right now?"

It amazed the group how Seth was able to change the syntax of his speech to match his current persona so easily.

"No, they're just taking in the sights like us—not sinning—but people are more uninhibited here and sometimes do things they wouldn't otherwise do," Joshua replied.

"It's why there's a saying that what happens in Vegas *stays* in Vegas," Rachael said.

"Think of it as a metropolitan black hole for naughty behavior," Vinod said.

"Naughty?" Seth said. "Ah, I see. They're jiggy with it. Like whoring and drinking. Shakespeare rapped about those behaviors in most of his rhymes. He was really fly."

"We've unleashed a monster," Rachael said.

"Josh," Vinod said, "let's hit up a casino. Seth can certainly observe humans closely in such a place. It'd be like Psychology 101. Besides, I'm feeling lucky."

"I don't know about that," Joshua said. "It might be *too* much interaction. They're really crowded, especially after nightfall."

"Then what are you gonna do? Take him to a show and a wedding chapel? Vegas has casinos, hotels, and more casinos."

"Vinod, I know how your brain works," Rachael said. "You're not thinking of using Seth to gamble, are you? He'd have an unfair advantage at the blackjack table. He'd be the best card counter Vegas has ever seen."

"Why not?" Vinod asked. "It'd be fun if the house didn't have the advantage for a change."

"No way," Joshua said. "We're not going to use Seth as our personal gambling computer. That would be cheating, and I'd feel like we'd be exploiting him."

"I wouldn't feel exploited by using my brain," Seth replied, "but what's card counting anyway?"

"It's keeping track of the numbers on each card in what's called a deck," Vinod replied, "It's definitely your game. Card counting is nothing more than using one's memory—hardly cheating, in my opinion—and you've got one hell of a memory."

"I'm down with it," Seth said.

"We're not going to do it," Rachael replied. "No way."

"You two are the killing the party," Vinod replied. "It's Vegas, for cryin' out loud! We gotta have some fun. How about a game of random chance like roulette or craps, where he doesn't have an advantage? You party poopers okay with that?"

Joshua glanced at Rachael before answering. "I guess that'd be okay."

"Fine," Rachael replied, donning sunglasses even though it was night. "I can't stand the gazillion lights, so let's get off the strip and do something."

Joshua parked the Impala, and they walked into a casino crowded with people. The main floor was lined with several dozen rows of slot machines, most of which emitted various electronic and musical sounds as their tumblers spun. A few people wore surgical masks, a result of the expanding concern regarding the Ebola outbreak even though no cases had been reported close to Las Vegas. The security team followed behind inconspicuously, although an acute observer would have noticed the deadpan expressions on their faces. No one paid any attention to the group that included an African American with dreds, sunglasses, and gold chains around his neck.

"Man, Seth's disguise is working great," Vinod commented. "No one recognizes him here."

"Small wonder," Joshua said, staring at cowboys in jeans, women in evening dresses, men in tuxedos, and old men in Bermuda shorts. "It's more bizarre than the *Star Wars* cantina."

As they progressed farther into the casino, Seth took in the sights: throngs of people crowded around gambling tables as they played poker, blackjack, roulette, and craps. Seth walked with swagger as a cheer erupted directly in front of them.

"What up with the cheering?" Seth asked.

"It's a craps table," Vinod replied. "Maybe it's getting hot, so let's check it out."

They arrived at the table, and fortunately there were four empty spaces available. Seth stood at the end of the table, with Rachael and Joshua to his right, Vinod to his left. Joshua, Rachael, and Vinod bought chips, some of which they gave to Seth.

"Start thinking of something else to do," Joshua told Rachael. "The house always wins, so we may end up at a show after all."

"What this game?" Seth asked, surveying the markings of the table while using his best rap jargon. "How it work?"

"It's a game of chance," Rachael answered with a sweeping gesture of her arm. "One of many."

"Don't worry, dude," Vinod said. "I'll explain it as we go along since the rules are endless."

The group made small bets, which they promptly lost as the dice made their way to Joshua. Vinod had Seth place a ten-dollar bet on the pass line, and Joshua rolled a six, which became the point. He then immediately rolled a seven, causing them to lose their bets, the stickman sweeping away the chips in one fluid motion.

"Nice job, dude," Vinod remarked sarcastically. "Worst roll ever."

"I don't get why the homeys like this game," Seth remarked. "Ain't no fun losin' bread."

Rachael passed on her turn with the dice. "I don't like losing the homeys' bread neither," she said, giving Seth a nod. "Some people become addicted to games of chance. It's an adrenaline rush for them."

The stickman at the table passed five dice to Seth.

"What I do?" Seth asked, his eyes concealed behind large, dark glasses.

"Don't worry, man," Vinod replied. "First, put ten dollars on the pass line and then pick any two of the five dice."

Seth picked up two of the dice and felt them in his hand, just as he'd seen other rollers do.

Vinod continued his on-the-fly tutoring. "Now you have to throw the dice to the other end of the table. You want to throw them in such a way so that when the dots on top of the dice are added up, they total a specific number."

"Which number?" Seth asked.

"It really doesn't matter too much on the come-out roll, but you want to avoid a two, three, or twelve. We lose with those."

"What number we win with?" Seth asked.

"On this roll, we win with a seven or eleven."

Seth took one die in each hand, threw them in the air, and caught them. He then rubbed his hand on the surface and edges of the table and tapped them gently.

"Come on!" shouted someone at the other end of the table. "Hurry up and roll."

"Cool it!" Vinod said. "It's his first time rolling. Seth, when you roll, make sure that both dice hit the raised back of the table before they come to a stop."

Seth placed the dice on the table in a specific orientation before picking them up with his right hand and throwing them with a sidearm motion. The dice rolled, bounced off the far side, and stopped, showing a four and three on top.

"Seven, winner," the stickman said.

Joshua, Rachael, and Vinod looked at Seth. Their heads moved in a smooth, simultaneous motion that almost appeared choreographed.

"It's what you wanted, right?" he asked.

"Yup," Vinod replied. "The dude definitely is lucky."

The dice were passed back to Seth. "Want a seven again?" he asked

"Naw," Vinod replied. "Let's make a point this time. Try to roll a four, five, six, eight, nine, or ten. Doesn't matter which one."

Seth threw the dice, which came up three and one.

"Four!" the stickman shouted. "Four's the point."

Those around the table placed their bets, quickly glancing at the new shooter and then the surface of the table, waiting for the roll.

"Should I add more dough?" Seth asked as he turned to Vinod. "Mo, bro?"

"Looks like that urban dictionary is getting some heavy usage tonight," Rachael commented with a sigh. "And hey, we don't need to have Seth lose money."

"I suspect it's part of the persona," Joshua said in her ear. "He is, after all, a rich rapper, right?"

"Just keep your bet on the pass line," Vinod advised, leaning close to Seth. "Leave the big betting to us. You have to roll a four again before you roll a seven."

"Another four?" Seth said. "Now?"

"Now would be good," Vinod replied, patting Seth on the back.

Seth threw the dice, which came up two and two, causing cheers to erupt from the gathering crowd.

"Four, winner," the stickman proclaimed.

"How can you possibly do that?" Rachael asked Seth.

"Do what?" Seth asked.

"Are you able to make the numbers come up like that on purpose?" She now suspected that craps was not a mere game of chance for Seth.

"Sure," Seth replied. "It's simple physics."

Rachael, Joshua, and Vinod stared at Seth in awe.

"Rachael," Vinod said, his eyes still staring at Seth, "don't disturb the physicist. He's on a roll."

On roll after roll, Seth hit the numbers Vinod fed him. An even larger crowd had drifted to the table, which erupted in louder cries of enthusiasm with each new roll. Vinod made sure to change the numbers up so as not to cause suspicion. Not surprisingly, however, the pit boss decided to observe the table and had the stickman change the dice on Seth numerous times, but to no avail. Seth's winning streak continued, stacks of chips piled high in front of each player at the table. A majority of casino patrons gravitated to the craps table, pressing against each other to see what all the commotion was about.

Vinod noticed that the pit boss was talking on his phone, after which an inconspicuous-looking man came up and stood beside Seth.

"Looks like they brought in a cooler," Vinod whispered to his friends.

"What a cooler?" Seth asked.

"A guy brought in by the casino who's supposed to throw you off your game," Vinod explained. "It's usually a stranger who attempts to break your concentration by his mere presence."

The cooler had no effect on Seth, however. He continued to hit roll after roll.

"I've never seen a roll like this," the pit boss stated in a businesslike manner devoid of the enthusiasm shared among the other observers.

A waitress brought free drinks to the players, which Joshua, Rachael, and Vinod gladly accepted. They were on their third round of drinks when Vinod remarked, "I can't believe this man. I think I've got over a hundred grand here."

"I still don't get this game," Seth remarked. "Why the casino giving y'all all them chips?"

"Don't worry, dude," Vinod replied, clearly buzzed. "I'll explain it later. You just keep doing your physics."

The remark caused the pit boss to stare long and hard at Vinod and the lucky rapper who claimed not to understand the very game he was using to crush the house.

Seth cleared another point, after which Vinod announced, "I gotta take a leak. Josh, watch my chips and tell Seth what to roll."

"I'll go with you," Rachael said.

The two left the table and headed towards the restrooms.

The stickman handed Seth the dice, who picked them up and prepared to roll. Joshua, also buzzed from the comps, suddenly had a disturbing thought. Looking in the direction in which Vinod and Rachael had disappeared, he shouted, "Vinod, Rachael—come back!"

It was too late. The electronic tether with Seth had been broken since there were less than two tether watches in range of the android. Seth's body stopped in mid-motion while throwing the dice, as if frozen. Off balance, he fell backwards onto the floor with a dull thud, causing his wig and sunglasses to fly off and land on the carpet. A dozen people rushed to his side, one of them shouting, "Oh, my God! It's that alien! It's Seth!"

Some patrons applauded, while others shrieked in alarm.

The security crew, flashing badges to both the gamblers and the pit boss, quickly ran in and cleared the crowd away from Seth's immobile body.

His lifeless eyes were fixed on the ceiling.

*   *   *

Rachael and Vinod returned to the crowd gathered around Seth, Joshua kneeling by his side.

"What happened?" Vinod asked.

"We screwed up," Joshua replied. "We forgot about his tether. You two left, and he got deactivated."

"Is he okay?" Rachael asked.

"I hope so," Joshua replied. "He didn't fall that far. Let's reactivate him."

Joshua and Vinod entered the activation signal on their Apple watches. Seth started to move his eyes and saw the faces above him. "What happened? I was about to make another point."

"Your tether got activated when both Rachael and Vinod left together," Joshua answered.

Seth got up from the floor to a round of applause. The pit boss from the table came up to the group. "I need to have a word with you."

*   *   *

The group walked around the casino, the throng held back by the security detail.

"No more incognito, I guess." Vinod said looking at the throng behind them.

"Josh, we should get Seth to a more private place," Rachael said. "This crowd looks like it's growing by the minute."

Exiting the casino, the group passed a club which was having karaoke night. Someone was singing "The Waiting" from Tom Petty.

"Great song," Vinod commented.

"What is that place?" Seth asked.

"It's karaoke," Vinod replied. "It's where ordinary people try to sing famous songs."

Seth was intrigued. "Can I try?" The crowd behind them had heard the request and erupted in applause. Vinod looked towards Joshua and Rachael.

"Why not?" Joshua commented. "His disguise is blown at this point."

The group went into the bar and took a table. The previously half-full establishment became standing room only as the crowd entered waiting to see Seth on stage.

"What should I sing?" Seth asked Vinod.

"It's Vegas," Vinod replied, "how about something from Elvis?"

"Can I hear the song before I sing it?"

Vinod took his phone out of his pocket and showed Seth a video of

251

Elvis performing a song. After the song had finished, he asked Seth, "All set?"

"Ready to rock."

Seth walked up onto the stage as the crowd let out a cheer. He looked over the crowd and pointed at Rachael and Joshua. "This song goes out to my two friends who have a burning love between them."

Seth started singing "Burning Love" with a voice that no one could distinguish from Elvis himself. His movements also mirrored those of the famous rock star better than any impersonator. Many in the crowd recorded videos of the performance on their phones, videos that would go viral over the following days. The crowd erupted into a thunderous applause as he finished the song.

"It's official," Vinod shouted to Rachael and Joshua over the cheers of the crowd. "He's a rock star."

*   *   *

The foursome sat around a table in the penthouse of the casino, eating food ordered from room service. Two-story high floor-to-ceiling windows offered them a birds-eye view of the Vegas strip as lights strobed, blinked, or scrolled the names of famous landmarks. Seth, minus his disguise, watched as the other three ate.

"Elvis lives again, but it sucks that the casino wouldn't let us keep our winnings," Vinod remarked. "The whole craps table came up snake eyes."

"Yeah," Rachael said. "At least the other people at the table got to keep theirs, and it's nice that the casino gave us this penthouse for the night."

"But it's still bogus," Vinod replied. "It's not like we were cheating."

"Weren't we though?" Rachael asked.

"Look, it's not our fault that Seth has a supercomputer for a brain," Vinod said.

"I'm not a gambler," Rachael said, "but even *I* know that casinos don't allow players to use computers or other electronic devices while playing any more than they allow card counters. Most don't even allow players to check their smart phones when playing."

"Seth," Joshua remarked, "the number of calculations you had to perform in order to do what you did at the craps table is remarkable."

"It wasn't just me," Seth replied. "I recruited some extra petrins in the collective during my calculations."

"Wait—you can instantaneously recruit their resources for *any* purpose, even gambling?" Vinod asked.

"Yes," Seth replied. "It's one of the benefits of being a collective."

"Amazing," Vinod remarked. "Automatic parallel processing. So the larger the collective grows, the larger the ultimate computing power?"

"That's true. As for rolling the dice, we noted that each of the die didn't weigh the same even though the differences would have been undetectable by the casino. Also, force vectors were involved when throwing the dice, which dictated the angle, speed, and distance I threw them. We performed several billion calculations per second."

"Lucky you're a well-known alien or we'd be in jail instead of a penthouse," Joshua said.

Rachael looked at Seth. "So what do you want to explore next? You've seen some animals and one of Earth's many natural habitats—if you can call this a habitat. What do you want to do tomorrow?"

"I was thinking of exploring more of the flora of the planet," Seth replied.

"Flora?" Joshua asked. "Like a forest?"

"Sure," Seth replied.

Rachael was excited at the thought. "How about we take Seth hiking? I'm sure there are some great hiking trails in the forests surrounding the mountains around Vegas."

"Sounds like a plan," Joshua replied. "We're going to have to rent a car, though. I don't think the convertible would be too happy climbing mountain roads."

Chapter Thirty
The Body Electric

The next morning, Joshua and Rachael sat in the front seat of a rented Jeep Wrangler hard top while Seth sat in the back.

"Where the hell is Vinod?" Joshua asked, impatiently looking at his watch.

"I don't know," Rachael answered. "He said he had to pick up a few things and that he'd meet us here at the car." She glanced at Joshua. "Hey, you want me to drive? You drove all the way to Vegas. Need a break?"

"No, I got it," Joshua answered.

Vinod sauntered up to the car carrying a large duffel bag over his shoulder. He was wearing a rock tee shirt as usual. It was Van Halen with a cover from their *Diver Down* album.

"Where the hell have you been?" Joshua asked. "And what's with the bag?"

"I was at an outfitter store," Vinod answered. "Picked up some rock-climbing gear. I found some killer assents online close to the hiking trail Rachael chose."

Vinod opened the hatch, placed the gear inside, and sat in the back next to Seth.

"I hope you're planning on climbing by yourself," Joshua commented as he checked the directions to their destination on his phone.

"No way," Vinod replied. "I thought we'd *all* go. I'm sure Seth would love it."

Joshua tilted his head and looked at Vinod out the corner of his eye. "Are you out of your mind? There's no way Seth's going rock climbing. He falls, and it may be the end of the sphere."

"The sphere is encased in a protective cavity that's been drop-tested,"

Vinod pointed out.

"I know, but I'm not going to tempt fate," Joshua said. "Even if the sphere were preserved during an accident, we might end up trashing a sixty-million-dollar android. Porter would eviscerate us."

"I'm sure that I can physically make the climb," Seth boasted. "You've already seen how I can handle physics, and my dexterity and stamina are superior. I think I'll be safe as long as I remain tethered."

"That's right, plus he's got thirteen trillion members of the collective to help him navigate any tight spots," Vinod said. "The dude could even handle Everest since he doesn't need food or oxygen. He's a natural on any mountain or hill. You worry too much, Josh."

"Absolutely not," Joshua replied. "I got a lecture from Porter and Williams this morning about the mishap with Seth at the casino yesterday. Porter is royally pissed, and Williams is about as mad as I've ever seen her, which isn't often. They were on the verge of ordering us back to the lab. We're all skating on thin ice here. Guys, we're not taking any more chances—just going hiking so that Seth can learn about the flora. Seth is not climbing. Period. Full stop."

"But the ropes and gear I got are rated for over 2,000 pounds," Vinod protested. "All three-hundred-fifty pounds of Seth should be okay. He can earn his merit badge later."

"I'd like to have the experience," Seth said, "and my actuators and servos are fully up to the task. I have a better sense of equilibrium than humans because of my internal sensors."

"You said you'd honor all safety protocols," Joshua said sternly, "and this is one of my own making. I'm not discussing this any further, Seth. You're not going rock climbing, and neither am I."

"I understand, Joshua," Seth said. "I will, of course, honor all my promises regarding security measures."

"Looks like it's just going to be me and you, Rach," Vinod said, still enthusiastic.

"You're going to have to count me out too," Rachael replied. "I'm afraid of heights."

"Are you serious?" Vinod replied in an irritated voice. "You *love* the outdoors and all that nature stuff."

"I love it alright," she said. "Just not from an altitude of a thousand feet while staring at a rock face."

"I'm the only one here with a sense of adventure," Vinod retorted. "You two are lame with a capital L."

Joshua entered the directions to the hiking trail into his phone and started to back up the Jeep. "Vinod, how about next time you check with us before going off script. The feds are footing the bill for our adventures, and you wasted a lot of money."

Vinod ignored the dig from Joshua. "Whatever. Rach, can you hit the pairing mode on the radio? Need to get the tunes rolling from my phone."

"No Bluetooth," Rachael replied. "Aux cord only."

"Whoa!" Vinod cried. "Stop the car! I have to sit in front so I can plug into the aux. No way we're hitting the road without Radio Bhakti."

"Vinod, sometimes you're a real pain in the ass," Joshua said as he stopped the car. "You know that?"

Rachael and Vinod traded places, Rachael seated in the back with Seth while Vinod rode shotgun as they drove into the mountains east of the city. Around each curve, they saw tall pine trees and brief glimpses of jagged mountains, some snow-capped, in the distance. As they climbed in elevation, however, the temperature dropped, and a drizzle started to fall as Vinod's phone played "The Core" by Eric Clapton.

"The weather's not so hot," Rachael commented, looking out the window. "Maybe we ought to turn back."

"I think we'll be okay," Joshua replied. "We packed some cold weather stuff and rain gear." He periodically glanced in the rearview mirror to make sure the security team's SUV was still in view. The black Escalade trailed them by fifteen yards as they rounded steep bends, continuing to gain altitude.

"Rach," Vinod asked, "how can you be afraid of heights? You've jumped out of airplanes with me."

"Jumping out of a plane is different," Rachael answered. "In free fall, there's nothing nearby to give you perspective, so it's not so scary. You pull the ripcord, and the ground eventually gives your feet a soft kiss. But when you're on the side of a cliff looking down, that's really terrifying. You cling to rock for dear life and have no reserve chute. Nope, two totally different experiences." Rachael looked out of her window, which began to fog. "Josh, it's raining and getting colder. Are you okay driving in these conditions?"

"I'm fine. The Jeep seems to have good traction on this surface. No problem."

"Are you sure? We could turn around at one of the overlooks."

"I'm good to go."

"Yeah," Vinod said. "You guys can't wimp out on *everything*, especially not a little trek in the rain. Might be romantic." He made kissing sounds with his lips.

Seth puckered his lips to imitate the sounds, but Vinod waved off the gesture. "They're not in the mood for fun, bro. Two wet blankets."

The radio transitioned to a new song from Vinod's phone.

"I don't recognize that one," Rachael said.

"The Vinod Bhakti school of classic rock is officially open," he said as the song blared from the speakers. "I'll give you a hint. It's alt rock Canadian-style from the 90s."

"I don't know," Rachael remarked after listening for a few seconds. "Never heard it before."

"Josh?" Seth asked.

"Not a clue."

"It's Our Lady Peace. The song's called 'Starseed' from their debut album *Naveed*." When discussing music, Vinod always made sure to include the title, artist, and album name of any song that he referred to. As a rock music connoisseur, giving anything less would have been sacrilegious. He could even recite liner notes from his favorite vinyl LPs.

"You're really digging deep today," Rachael commented. "Our Lady Peace isn't on my radar even after more than six years of your expert tutelage."

"I'm a rock encyclopedia, Rach, and the biggest names aren't always the best. Foreign, underground, alternative—there are a lot of great vibes out there. I spend a lot of time in stores that sell old vinyl."

Seth's interest was piqued by the song. "What's a starseed?" he asked. "Is it like a von Neumann probe?"

"Who knows man?" Vinod replied. "A lot of rock lyrics are esoteric, just like poetry, but what kind of probe is that? I never heard of it."

His eyes steadily on the road, Joshua explained the concept. "Mathematician John von Neuman hypothesized that self-replicating spacecraft could travel to other solar systems, where they would mine raw materials from moons, asteroids, and gas giants in order to make new probes that could then be sent to other solar systems to start the process all over again. The probe would essentially be a seed factory. The original probe, called the parent, could conceivably stay in the original solar system to perform any number of tasks."

"If that's the case, then there should be such probes all over the galaxy given its age," Vinod said.

"That's why many scientists invoke the Fermi Paradox, which states that no intelligent life exists in the galaxy." Joshua laughed at the notion. "Well, we know that the Fermi Paradox has been blown out of the water thanks to our contact with Petri, right, Seth?"

"Right."

"But Vinod has a point," Joshua said, "which reminds me of a question I've been meaning to ask you, Seth. If the universe contains as much life as you say it does, how come some type of von Neumann probe hasn't come to Earth yet? I mean, surely the idea has occurred to one of the thousands of advanced civilizations that you've made contact with."

"Yeah," Vinod said. "Sending a probe like that would be a piece of cake for a planet a billion years ahead of us, or even a thousand for that matter."

"Redacted," Seth replied.

"Of course," Joshua said with a sigh as he ended his line of questioning.

Minutes later, the Jeep approached a bridge spanning a river with a slow-moving current. The road was wet but had good traction since its temperature was higher than that needed to freeze the rain landing on its surface. The bridge was a different story, however. It was much colder since it was not afforded the same insulation from the cold that the ground beneath an ordinary road provided. Rain had frozen on its surface, a condition that was hard to discern by looking at it from a distance. It simply appeared wet.

The song on the radio transitioned to "The Body Electric" from Rush.

"Seth!" Vinod said excitedly. "A song about an android!"

"Really?" Seth asked.

"Yes, it's about . . ."

Vinod couldn't finish his thought. The Jeep was travelling fifty-eight miles per hour as it rolled onto the bridge. Unexpectedly, it slipped ninety degrees to the left, its tires devoid of traction on the ice. The Jeep's momentum carried it at high speed farther down the bridge, careening sideways.

Joshua slammed on the brakes and turned the wheel hard to the right to try to correct for the skid, but the last-minute maneuver was only partially successful. The Jeep turned forward slightly, its front end pointed at a concrete post that made up part of the railing at the edge of the bridge.

For the first few seconds, the passengers in the Jeep remained silent as the horror of the situation unfolded in slow motion. And then reality hit as the Jeep headed for the railing, events speeding up again.

"Look out!" Rachael shouted as the car accelerated at high speed towards the post.

"Oh, shit!" Vinod cried.

The front of the car hit the post with such velocity that the airbags deployed instantly, but the impact didn't dissipate much of the Jeep's momentum. Its rear end angled upwards steeply, causing it to flip over the front end. The Jeep tumbled over the guardrail at the bridge's edge, fell, and plunged into the icy river below.

Despite its roll, the Jeep landed upright. Four of its windows were smashed, and the vehicle quickly filled with icy water, its human passengers unconscious. Water rapidly filled the cabin, and the Jeep sank beneath the surface towards the river bottom thirty feet below. Within seconds, it landed on sand, rocks, and gravel, sitting crookedly, the passenger-side wheels partially buried.

*   *   *

Seeing the skid of the Jeep, the driver of the Escalade slammed on the brakes while still on ice-free road. Entering the bridge at a much slower speed, the SUV was able to stop at the precise point where the Jeep had breached the guardrail. Three security guards exited the vehicle hurriedly and peered over the railing at the silver-gray water below.

"The water restriction for Seth!" Agent One shouted. "How deep is the river?"

The second agent was already looking up the information on his cell phone. "Nowhere near one hundred feet," he answered. "Maybe thirty-five max."

"Call it in!" The first agent ordered.

Agent Three, already holding his phone, punched a number on his keypad, one that would connect him directly to the office of General Porter.

Breathing hard, Agent One shot a quick look at Agent Two. "Come on! You and me!"

The two agents scrambled down the steep incline—half walking, half sliding—and stood at the water's edge.

"We're going to need divers, and fast!" Agent One cried to his colleague on the bridge. "Have them airlifted in by chopper."

The other agent, having removed his shoes, dove into the water, but resurfaced thirty seconds later.

"I don't see it!" he called out.

His head disappeared a second time, but he surfaced again and swam for shore. "It's too cold in this damn river. I can't get that deep or stay down long enough even if I could."

The first agent put his hands on his hips. "We're screwed."

*   *   *

Seth had suffered an injury which severely crushed the left side of his face and exposed part of his titanium skeleton. His left optic camera was no longer working. When the Jeep landed on the river bottom, he opened his door without hesitation and stepped with urgency to the trunk of the car. He retrieved rope from the bag Vinod had stored and then opened the front passenger door. The airbag was stuck to the ceiling, with air trapped inside.

Seth rapidly retrieved the unconscious bodies of Joshua and Vinod and, working faster than any human, sealed the end of the passenger airbag with rope, careful not to let any air escape. He then removed the inflated white bag from the car and tied it around the bodies of Joshua and Vinod. The buoyancy of the airbag allowed the bodies to float slowly to the surface.

Next, Seth grabbed the driver's airbag, sealed it with rope, and removed it from the car. He tied the sealed bag around Rachael's waist after removing her from the Jeep and stood on the river bottom as he watched her body ascend. With his right optic camera, still functioning perfectly, he noticed that Rachael's airbag had a small tear that allowed air to escape, a steady stream of bubbles emanating from it and rising vertically in the current. Rachael's body started to sink as she was carried downriver.

Seth ran along the river bottom, jumping over the stones that covered it while staying directly beneath Rachael's falling body. His higher density made it relatively easy for him to move through the water. When Rachael's body had sunk low enough for him to reach it with outstretched hands, he grabbed her around the waist and ran as fast as he could towards the river bank. The bottom sloped gently up, with Seth only ten feet from the water's surface when, for the second time in as many days, his electronic tether was activated. He fell to the bottom, lifeless. Rachael's body disengaged from Seth and floated downstream, still submerged as her arms and legs spread wide, her hair floating above her head like a fan.

*   *   *

Joshua lay unconscious in the intensive care unit at University Medical Center in Las Vegas, an endotracheal tube connected to a respirator having been inserted in his throat. A metal bolt measuring intracranial pressure was attached to his skull, its reading displayed on monitors next to his bed. His right arm was wrapped in a long cast extending above his elbow.

A group of physicians, including an intensivist and residents, walked into the room, Joshua's body immobile.

"Status?" the intensivist asked.

"His cerebral edema seems to be resolving," the chief resident remarked, "and his ICP is almost back to normal. We're decreasing his sedation, and we'll probably be able to extubate him in a few hours."

"Okay," the intensivist said. "I'll inform Robert Langdon at NASA. He was very insistent that I call him. He wants to be here when Dr. Andrews wakes up."

The next morning Robert Langdon, Vinod, and Seth sat at Joshua's bedside in the ICU. It had been three weeks since the accident. Vinod had a cast on his left leg and held a pair of crutches. Seth looked perfectly normal. Dina Williams had decided that the accident should not be revealed to the public and had insisted that Seth's head injury be repaired as quickly as possible so as not to cause suspicion. If it became known that android Seth had been involved in a serious accident while with the American personal and security teams, other nations might insist that the alien be released to an authority in another country, citing a lack of precaution on the part of the United States.

Joshua had been extubated and was breathing on his own, but his eyes were still closed. He rolled his head lethargically to the right and left.

"I think he's waking up," Vinod remarked as the group gathered around his bed.

Joshua slowly opened his eyes and tried to focus on the faces in the room. It took him a few minutes to gain enough consciousness to recognize who was present. Over the next several minutes, his memory of driving into the mountains returned.

"What . . . ?" he mumbled.

"Joshua," Langdon said, "you're just waking up. Relax."

Joshua gradually became more aware of his surroundings and started to remember in greater detail how the Jeep had spun out of control. "Accident . . ." he said in a hoarse voice as the faces looming above him came into focus.

"Yes," Langdon replied, producing a weak smile. "You were in an accident, but you're going to be okay."

"Where's Rachael?" he asked, his brows knit as he failed to spot her near the bed.

"Joshua," Langdon replied, "try to rest. You've been through a lot of trauma."

Joshua was becoming more alert with each passing moment. "Where's Rachael?" he repeated, looking about him.

Langdon glanced at the others before answering. "Joshua, she didn't survive the accident."

"What?" Joshua replied, his voice frantic. "No!"

"Seth saved you and Vinod, but he was unable to save Rachael," Landon said. "She drowned in the river."

"Then how did Vinod or I survive?" Joshua's eyes filled with tears. "Tell me!"

"Josh," Seth said, "I tried my best, but I'm sorry. I wasn't able to save her." His voice quivered with human emotion as he spoke.

"You're wrong!" Joshua asked. "Where is she?"

"Josh," Vinod answered, sobbing. "You've been unconscious for twenty-two days. Her funeral was two weeks ago."

Chapter Thirty-One
Request

Joshua returned to his home after being discharged from the hospital, but he was restricted in his movements for the first month due to a broken right forearm that had been surgically repaired with plates. The scar on his forearm was long and would be visible for the remainder of his life. His right hip had been dislocated during the accident and was relocated at the hospital, but it still caused him pain as he walked. His physicians had reassured him that over time, the pain would slowly subside. He was given physical therapy for his injuries, and a home health nurse checked on his progress twice a week.

When he was more mobile, he wandered about his house, and the experience proved physically painful, although his emotional distress was far greater as he surveyed Rachael's laptop, notes, articles, rough drafts, briefcase, and clothing. Her presence was palpable, and even her scent still lingered in every room. For several days, he limped through his home aimlessly, looking at her belongings, not daring to disturb them. The longer he could preserve everything just the way it was, the more his mind tricked him at odd moments into thinking that she might come through the door at any moment. He was able to intellectually grasp the reality of the accident that had taken her life, but emotionally he still drifted through moments of denial until those times when he forced himself to shower, eat, or run an errand.

Seth was back at the lab and underwent daily interviews with the scientific teams, having no contact with the humans he regarded as his closest friends, Joshua and Vinod. Joshua's physicians had ordered him to rest, and Langdon and Williams granted him and Vinod an extended leave from the project. Joshua had learned the details of the accident, and he replayed the events leading up to the Jeep skidding over the bridge over and over again. Rachael had urged him to turn back when the weather had grown poor, and he felt guilty that he hadn't listened to someone who had great insight and was right about so many things.

Josh, it's raining and getting colder. Are you okay driving in these conditions?

I'm fine. The Jeep seems to have good traction on this surface. No problem.

Are you sure? We could turn around at one of the overlooks.

I'm good to go.

"Damn it!" Joshua said out loud to himself one day while at home. He looked at the ceiling. "Rachael, I should have let you drive that day when you asked." He remembered the incident in the Prius when Rachael's quick reflexes had avoided an accident. "Maybe you could have gotten us out of that skid, and even if you hadn't, it'd be you that would be alive, not me."

After two months, Joshua's doctors told him he had recuperated enough to resume normal activity, and he threw a backpack into his Impala and drove to the hills near Berkeley where he and Rachael had often hiked together. The solo trek felt surreal as he forced one foot in front of the other, wincing occasionally from the pain in his hip. He recalled their conversations and fluctuated between smiling and crying. He reached the spot where they'd been when they'd heard the CNN news alert that somebody had hacked into the lab's computer system and revealed the existence of Seth. He slipped out of his backpack, sat, and leaned against his left arm in order to take pressure off his hip.

"Rachael, it's Josh. This may be silly, but I felt for some reason that I could talk to you here because nature was so important to you. I don't know if you can hear me or . . ." He lowered his head and cleared his throat. "You said you believed in God, and if you were right, then maybe you can. It's funny, but after all this time, I still don't know what I believe when it comes to spiritual matters, but suddenly I want to believe in . . . something. As much as I believed in you, that is. Your body was frozen in accordance with your wishes, and I think I now understand what losing Richard must have been like. The thing is, I thought we'd have an entire lifetime together before either of us would be calling the cryo facility on behalf of the other."

Joshua looked at the valley and the surrounding fir trees before resuming.

"You kinda pushed your way into my life when you insisted on interviewing me the first day you showed up at the particle center. I was a rude jerk, but we sure moved past that quickly. You were so cool and

264

confident, and within a day I felt as if I'd known you for years. Now, I long for those days."

He laughed softly. "When we had dinner for the first time at Angelino's, you launched into that persuasive argument that early life—the cell—couldn't have just appeared on its own. You argued for a first cause. And you alluded to things happening for a reason, even the two of us meeting. But here's the deal. If we were destined to meet, why were you taken from me? What kind of God would do that? And now I'm doubting even more than before. I'm pretty sure you'd have an answer, maybe something like there's a big picture that we—that *I*—can't see."

Joshua nodded his head. "Yep, that's exactly what you'd say, and I'd like to believe that, but even if I did, it wouldn't make the pain go away. I admired your faith, but I never quite made it to the same place as you, and yet here I am, hoping that you're listening. I'm a bundle of contradictions right now, and maybe I'm just talking to myself and the valley over there. But this is as close as I can get to you, or the memory of you, or . . . whatever."

With difficulty, Joshua stood and dusted off his jeans. As he did so, he saw a small reflection coming from the ground five yards away. It was where the couple had sat minutes before the news alert. He walked over, knelt slowly, and clawed the dirt with his fingers until producing a slim aluminum digital recorder. His mouth hung open, for he remembered that Rachael carried a similar device wherever she went. She'd told him and Vinod on many occasions that she was always writing, whether in notebooks or in her thoughts, because she was an astute observer. She would point at her head with her index finger and say, "They can't hack this." Was it possible that *this* recorder had belonged to his fiancé? There was only one way to find out.

Hands trembling, he pressed the replay button and closed his eyes. A few seconds of static were followed by the voice of Rachael, but she wasn't talking about research, Seth, or ideas for future articles. The content of the entry was far more personal.

"I'm going hiking with Joshua tomorrow," the voice said. "I can't wait, and it means the world to me that he wants to share this activity." The words were punctuated with a laugh. "He wants to share everything, really, and that's so endearing. He's smart, romantic, and we really click. Always did, even from the first day we met, and then there was that incredible afternoon when Seth started communicating to us in the bat cave. That's when I knew we were meant to be a team. The rest, as they say, is history. So where is it leading?" There was another laugh. "I know, and I hope Josh does too. I'm pretty sure he does."

Josh clicked the device off.

"Oh, my God," he said in a whisper, tears rolling down his cheek. "Rachael, I loved you so much. And yes, we both knew where it was going."

Limping from the stress he'd put on his joints, Joshua started the trek back to his automobile, but stopped midway along the trail, looking at the handheld recording device. He shook his head and broke into a fresh wave of tears.

"To think that the Petrins can make complete and authentic backups of themselves so that they never die. All I have is a digital backup of your voice, Rachael, but it's not the same. It's not your DNA. It's not *you*. But it's something—maybe a piece of your spirit. That's beyond my pay grade."

He placed the digital recorder in his backpack and continued up the trail. He decided that he would listen to other files on the device, but that would come later—maybe months or years down the line. The sound of her voice was precious, but it was also painful.

He turned and glanced behind him, half expecting to see the gorgeous reporter that he'd fallen in love with following his footsteps. She wasn't there and never would be.

*   *   *

Joshua was summoned to the particle center two months later. He knew it was time to get back to work even though it would be hard to function in the very place where he and Rachael had grown so close—and so quickly. But he missed Seth and Vinod, and the request to return to work had been transmitted by Robert Langdon more as an order than a friendly request. He walked into the atrium and was greeted by Charlotte Lloyd with a warm smile and a brief "Welcome back." The gesture was meaningful to Joshua, who was grateful that some things always remained the same. He took an elevator to a conference room on the second floor and found Vinod sitting by himself, feet propped on the table. The two men had talked over the phone but hadn't seen each other since Joshua's stay in the hospital. Vinod knew that Joshua had grown more than a little introspective. Better, he thought, to give him space. He'd resurface when he was ready.

Vinod rose and gave his friend a one-armed hug so as not to stress his arm or hip. "How ya doin', man?"

"Surviving. Just going through the motions." Joshua shrugged. "The pain never seems to let up. How do people get through something like this?"

"I don't think anyone ever really does, at least not losing someone as close as Rachael. You guys were soul mates in the truest sense of the word. It gets better over time, but I think some level of pain is permanent."

"I also have some guilt that I'm dealing with," Joshua said. "I should have turned the Jeep around that day, or I should have let Rachael drive. Things would have been different."

"You're not the only one with guilt," Vinod replied. "Remember that I was the one who asked her to move to the back seat so I could control the radio. She may still be around today if I hadn't done that. But we can't keep doing this to ourselves, Josh. What happened, happened. There was nothing malicious in our actions, but like I said, some level of the pain we are feeling is permanent."

Joshua was silent for several seconds. "I appreciate your honesty, Vinod. And I agree with you. I've been going over all this in my head for months now, and I've come to the same conclusion. And while it may always hurt, I wouldn't want it any other way. She's a part of me. If I ever got over it . . . nah, this is part of the deal. Funny, huh? Petrins use digital technology to hold onto things forever. Endless copies. People, on the other hand, have the human heart."

Vinod flashed Joshua a bittersweet smile. "That's exactly what Rachael would say. And you know what she'd add?"

"What?"

"That maybe the human heart is enough."

Joshua laughed out loud for the first time in months. "You know, you're right. That's *exactly* the way she looked at things. So what about you?" Joshua asked as the two men took adjacent seats at the table. "You're not wearing a concert tee shirt. That's a first."

"I can't, man. It hurts too much. I was always introducing Rachael to a new band, and every shirt I pick out in the morning reminds me of her. She didn't just tolerate my affinity for classic rock—she really got into it."

"Yeah, certain memories are real killers. I'm thinking of selling the Harley. I eventually taught her to ride, and she was getting pretty good. But the memory of her wearing the black leather motorcycle jacket that Rodrigo bought her . . . it's too much."

The men sat in silence, enveloped by memories of Rachael.

"So what's this big pow-wow about?" Joshua asked. "Langdon sounded insistent that I attend."

"I don't know either. I picked up on the same urgency when Williams called."

"Is everything okay with Seth?"

"Pretty much," Vinod answered. "We took him cross-country and let him walk around some cities and national parks. Otherwise, it's been interviews as usual, not that anything revealing has come of them. Everything's—"

"Let me guess," Joshua interrupted. "Redacted."

"Yeah. It seems to be the most important word in his vocabulary. Hardly seems fair. We show him our planet, and he conceals just about everything. I understand that the petrins have a few billion years of development that they can't share, but you would think that Seth could cough up a bit more info once in a while."

Joshua rubbed the well-kept beard that he'd grown in recent weeks. "I suspect that we're pretty low in the pecking order when it comes to civilized planets, but maybe that's not surprising. We've only had radio for about a hundred years, so we're hardly out of the cradle as far as Petri is concerned."

Vinod sat back and folded his arms. "But it's an old cradle, Josh. Life started here about three to four billion years ago, with meteors bombarding Earth when it was relatively young, and it didn't take long for life to appear."

"And?"

"My point is that it almost feels like we're penalized for being technological newbies. Or that there's some great cosmic scheme that we're too dumb to understand. Does that make sense?"

Joshua leaned forward and looked Vinod in the eyes. "More than you know. I've had the same feeling almost from the beginning, and I shared my concerns with Rachael on more than one occasion. Maybe we're paranoid, but I feel that there's one redaction that trumps all the others, one that we're not smart enough to even ask about."

"Maybe we should confront Seth," Vinod suggested.

Joshua shook his head. "Nah. If we're right, he might close down the entire gig. Better to keep the lines of communication open."

"Probably right. Then again, maybe—"

The door to the conference room opened and Seth walked in, flanked by the obligatory security personnel. The detail positioned itself outside the door, which Seth closed as he approached his friends.

"'Sup Josh, 'Sup Vinod," Seth said as he took a seat next to his friends. "Josh, nice to see you again. How are you doing?"

"I'm doing okay," Joshua responded. "Just trying to live with the loss."

"I understand," Seth replied. "Rachael's death has hit all of us, including the collective. We aren't used to death. The wager that the collective had on your engagement and the updates I provided about your romance gave the collective a connection to you both."

"Vinod and I were just discussing survivor's guilt," Joshua replied. "Something the victims of an accident feel when they survive and one of their loved ones doesn't."

"I understand," Seth replied. "Maybe I have some of that too. I've been looking into the physics of what I did at the bottom of the river, but I know that the first airbag could only lift the weight of two humans, so I picked the two closest to the front which were you and Vinod. I didn't realize the smaller driver's airbag had a hole in it. I thought it could lift Rachael. I'm sorry I couldn't do more."

"You did everything you could," Joshua replied. "Vinod and I wouldn't be here without what you did."

"That's right bro," Vinod said as he grasped Seth's hand. "You saved our lives. We're grateful for that."

The door to the conference room opened, and Langdon, Williams, and Porter walked in and seated themselves.

"Good morning, guys," Williams said. "I appreciate your coming in on such short notice."

Williams wasted no time in addressing the room as her head turned towards the android. "Seth, a few months ago you issued a request for us to build you an android body so that you could move about our world freely and interact with both its environment and its inhabitants. Despite misgivings, we granted you that request, and now we have a request of our own."

"And what is that?" Seth asked.

Williams sat back in her chair, twirling the arm of her reading glasses in her right hand after glancing at a folder on the polished surface in front of her.

"As you know," she began, "we've been fighting a viral outbreak for well over a year, and we haven't been able to contain it. We had a private meeting in Washington yesterday with the head of the Centers for Disease Control, and their revelations aren't encouraging. The reason we haven't been able to control our current outbreak is that we're not dealing with Ebola any longer. The current virus may have originated from Ebola, but it has radically mutated. It's not the same strain we saw the last time there was an outbreak. In fact, we don't even know that it's Ebola at all. Its capsid, or outer shell, now resembles the influenza virus, which is highly contagious. This means that besides being transmitted by direct contact, it's stable in the atmosphere, just like influenza, and can be transmitted by just breathing it in, a fact that we didn't know until recently. Unfortunately, this new capsid has also enabled the virus to significantly extend its incubation period."

Joshua appeared unsettled. "So more people are infected but don't know it?"

"Essentially, yes," Williams continued. "Individuals don't start to show symptoms for up to a year even though they're infectious two weeks after exposure."

"And people come into contact with them without thinking they're in any type of danger," Vinod said.

"Exactly. It's really the worst scenario for a virus, something that has a long incubation period, during which time the subject is infectious. It's stable in the atmosphere and highly lethal. The CDC estimates that at this point, ninety-seven percent of the world's population has been exposed even though they're asymptomatic. Random sampling from blood donated at blood banks around the world has confirmed this figure. Current projections show that the other three percent will be exposed within a year. The CDC has developed antiviral medications that will delay death for six to nine months in most individuals once they start showing symptoms, but that's all we can give them."

"And there's no cure," Langdon said. "Not even a vaccine in development that shows the least bit of promise."

"But surely there are some people who are naturally immune to this virus just as there are some who never got HIV," Vinod said.

"Yes," Williams said grimly. "We've identified twenty-two individuals who are completely immune, and extrapolating from this, we estimate there may be about four thousand people worldwide, but this is just conjecture. The rest of us are going to die sooner or later." She paused and looked at those sitting around the table. "And that includes everyone in this room. We've confirmed that we are all infected. Quarantine is not a viable option at this point."

"Four thousand," Joshua said. "That's not enough to continue the species considering that they may be spread all over the planet. Humanity's going to die off."

"That's correct," Porter said. "Our calculations show that there's not enough time to develop a vaccine. Even if we had a promising lead tomorrow, it would take time to test and manufacture a vaccine, and that's forgoing clinical trials that would normally take years."

"None of this has been made public for fear that mass panic might ensue," Williams said.

"You directed your remarks to me when you began speaking," Seth noted. "You alluded to my request to have your engineers construct an android for me."

Williams stared long at Seth, placed her glasses on the table, and clasped her hands. Her face looked tired, and Joshua thought she had no doubt been meeting for weeks with the president and other White House staff, working in conjunction with world leaders and scientists.

"To be candid, Seth," Williams said, "we're painfully aware that you're capable of finding a cure for our viral outbreak given your advanced knowledge of biology and DNA. It would probably be child's play for you to manufacture a vaccine in a very short time." She paused again as her voice, usually steady and calm, faltered for a few seconds. "Would you please help us? The human race and our entire way of life—tens of thousands of years of culture—face extinction. Speaking for myself and the rest of humanity, we believe that saving humans with medicine or a vaccine isn't the same as introducing radical new technologies to our planet. I'm asking you to look at this from the standpoint of what we call humanitarian aid."

Sitting erect, Seth placed his hands on the table. He'd listened patiently and with no display of emotion to Williams' explanation of the crisis and her impassioned plea.

"I'm terribly sorry to hear this news, Ms. Williams. I've come to love humans very much, and I would never willingly want to see any harm come to your world or its inhabitants. As you know, however, introducing new technology into your world would violate our ethics, and I'm afraid that developing a cure *would* introduce new technology to Earth since you yourselves are unable to find it. If I were to help you, my intervention would almost surely destabilize your society, and we can't take that risk."

Porter was frustrated, but he didn't speak with his usual bluster or threatening tone. "Seth we're *already* destabilized, and as the outbreak spreads, the destabilization will grow worse. I don't understand the distinction you're making."

Seth replied quickly, his voice remaining even and measured. "General Porter, if we give you the technology and you save yourselves, you would still possess the technology when the crisis had passed. That technology might be used to engage in genetic testing that could cause irreparable harm to your species. In the end, the technology would kill you as surely as this outbreak will, and we can't be a part of that. The thought of your species' demise saddens us, but we can't be an instrument in the cause of your destruction."

Porter glared at Seth, now more emotional as he spoke. "You've just signed our death warrant."

"If it's your destiny to succumb to the virus, then so be it. Not all civilizations survive. We cannot give you the technology to cure this virus."

The room was silent at Seth's stark comment and evaluation of the most dire crisis to ever face humanity. He was dispassionate despite his proclaimed affinity for humans.

It was Robert Langdon who finally spoke up after several seconds.

"What if you didn't actually *give* us your technology, Seth?" he asked. "What if you just gave us the cure without telling us how you created it?"

"How do you propose we do that?" Seth asked. "What you require is a honing virus. A vaccine wouldn't work since most humans are already infected. A vaccine only works on those who are not already exposed."

"What's a honing virus?" Langdon inquired.

"It's a virus genetically engineered from the ground up to attack a single target. In this case, that target is the mutated Ebola virus. Building such a virus, however, would require a lab on Earth since the virus that is causing your outbreak is only present on your planet. Regrettably, the lab would have to employ technology that you currently don't have, so it's not possible for all of the reasons I've already mentioned."

"Wait," Williams said. "Maybe . . ."

All eyes shifted to the White House chief of staff.

"What if we build a lab to which only *you* have access to. No humans allowed, not even those in this room or anyone on the scientific teams. No security team either. We'll give you whatever materials you need, and you can build any equipment that we may not have. If we guaranteed that you would have absolute security and isolation, would you be willing to manufacture the honing virus? This would allow you to create it without giving us the methods you used to do so."

Seth looked at Joshua after considering the proposal. "I'm not accustomed to death," he said, "because of the backup mechanisms we have on Petri. The death of Rachael affected me profoundly since she was a friend just like Josh and Vinod. Believe me when I say that I can feel your pain. I'm not unsympathetic to the plight you find yourselves in."

"That's not an answer," Porter said.

Seth was silent for several seconds, and Joshua felt certain that the android was communicating with the collective.

"We're considering your request," Seth said at last. "Where could you give me such security and isolation?"

"We could transform the underground test facility into the lab you'd need," Porter replied. "We'll also turn off all surveillance cameras. The elevator is the only entrance in or out, and I'll give you complete control over that as well. We could also modify your security protocols such that as long as you're in the lab, there would not be an electronic tether. We could also allow you to be active even while you are plugged in for recharging so that you could operate continuously."

Seth closed his eyes for no more than a few seconds before responding. "My friends, we've analyzed your situation and have determined that there is a high probability that humans are facing an extinction-level event. As I have said before, we are opposed to the extinction of sentient societies. Therefore, we've decided to help you given the conditions you've set forth. When may we begin?"

There was a palpable sense of relief in the conference room.

*   *   *

A week passed, during which Seth requested equipment that seemed standard for any conventional biology, chemistry, or medical lab, although some of the articles he asked for seemed unorthodox to the scientific teams assigned to deliver the pieces. None of it, of course, represented anything that scientists were unacquainted with, but how Seth might use the equipment was unknown. In a completely refurbished bat cave were standard beakers, funnels, flasks, tubing, syringes and microscopes—electron and regular—as well as microwave ovens, DNA sequencers, refrigerators, and dozens of digital devices that might be used to perform routine blood work and analysis. Seth had also requested numerous chemical elements and compounds that baffled the tech teams, who had also installed a bank of desktop computers loaded with hundreds of software programs on human biology, DNA, diseases, and anatomy. Various electronic devices more suitable for electrical or computer work were also brought to the bat cave, but those who delivered the equipment were not allowed to ask any questions as to how the alien was to employ them or how he might use *any* of the supplies to possibly fashion completely new instruments. The oddest pieces were several fish bowls and household aquariums of different sizes, complete with thermostats and oxygen pumps.

Joshua looked at Vinod when Seth had deemed the lab fully-equipped. "What Seth is about to do reminds me of how you tweaked the interfaces in your home when Rachael and I showed up with the Bowman sphere," Joshua said.

"Yeah, but even *I* can't begin to guess as to how he might use some of this stuff or how he's going to connect it," Vinod said. "And yet he knew exactly what was needed. A honing virus."

"You noticed that too?" Joshua asked. "Williams gave him the stats a week ago in the conference room, and he assessed the situation and found a solution within minutes. If he wanted, he could probably end all disease on Earth."

"Let's ask him," Vinod suggested. "Give him the same guarantees as we did for wiping out Ebola."

Joshua shook his head. "It would completely throw the entire planet out of balance. A cure for everything would send ripples through the economy, population size, the food supply, and eventually through just about every aspect of human life. We couldn't handle it. I think I truly understand the petrins' noninterference directive for the first time. There would be global destabilization."

Vinod mulled over the thought for a minute. "You know, you're right. As an information theorist, I can see how radically so many subsystems of human culture would be affected. So why do think the petrins cut us slack on the Ebola issue?"

"Damn good question, and I don't have the slightest hint of an answer unless they're honing in on a single problem just as they're honing in on a single virus. Maybe it's only because they view the virus as something that could end humanity on Earth."

"True, but the collective is bailing out humanity, and according to Seth, that's strictly verboten. We've had endless sessions with the guy, and I still can't figure out where he's coming from most of the time. Best guess?"

"As Hamlet said," Joshua stated, "'there are more things in heaven and earth, Horatio, than are dreamt of in your philosophy.' As both a writer and someone devoted to science, Rachael quoted it often."

"Meaning?"

"Meaning that there's something that the petrins could tell us but won't, something that lies beyond our wildest speculation."

"Not surprising, dude," Vinod said. "They have a few billion years head start on us."

"Just a hunch, but I don't think it's something about technology per se."

"You're freakin' me out, Josh. You almost sound like Porter."

"I know, and that's what bothers me the most."

*　　　　　*　　　　　*

Langdon, Porter, Seth, Vinod, and Joshua stood in the lab near the elevator door.

"We turned off your electronic tether, and it will remain off for as long as you're down here," Porter said. "Just remember that if you try to leave the lab, it will be automatically reactivated, and you'll be shut off. The elevator will be locked, and only you will be able to unlock it from down here. Call us on the land line if you need anything."

"I won't be trying to leave, general," Seth said. "And I've inspected everything. Your teams have been very thorough."

Langdon reached down and lifted a sealed package from the floor. Mists of carbon dioxide vapor emanated from the dry ice within. It looked like a portable ice chest, but it had the logo of the Centers for Disease Control on it and was locked in a hard-shell case. A label on its side read DANGER: BIOHAZARDOUS MATERIALS.

"These are the latest viral samples from the CDC, just as you requested," Langdon stated. "When do you think we can expect results?"

"That's difficult to say," Seth replied. "I can't predict the strict series of lab protocols I'll have to perform. If things go well, I estimate that I'll have the honing virus in about a month."

"A lot of people will die between now and then," Porter pointed out.

"I can only work so fast even though I don't require sleep," Seth said. "This is a Terran virus that I'm not familiar with."

"Good luck," Joshua said. "We know you'll do your best."

Seth put his arms around Joshua and gave him a hug. "Anything for a friend."

Android Seth turned away and walked to one of the lab tables as the rest got onto the elevator and rode up to the particle center.

"You look uncomfortable, Mitchell," Langdon observed on their ride up.

"I am," the general confessed. "I just did something that I've been against from the very start, which is to leave Seth alone. No tether and no security teams. Makes me damn nervous."

"We didn't have a choice," Langdon said. "The fate of mankind rests on Seth."

"Indeed. Trust me when I say that it's the only reason I did this."

*   *   *

Joshua sat on the edge of his bed in his bedroom about ready to turn in for the night. It had been almost four weeks since Seth had locked himself in the bat cave which had now been converted into a bio lab. Joshua looked at the framed picture of Rachael that he had on his nightstand and the engagement ring he'd given her that night at Angelino's which sat in front of the picture.

Joshua had just finished packing for a week-long vacation to Patagonia that he was taking by himself; he would be leaving in the morning. He and Rachael had always wanted to go there, but this, like many of their plans, had not come to fruition. He touched his fingers to his lips and then to her picture. "Rachael, I'm going to Patagonia tomorrow for some hiking. I'm sure you would have loved it."

Joshua had just fallen asleep when his cell phone rang. He looked at the caller ID, which showed it was the landline from the lab. It had to be Seth, so Joshua hurriedly answered the call.

"Hello?"

"Josh, it's Seth. Can you come down to the lab?"

"Now?"

"Yes, I have something very important to show you."

"Have you got a cure for the virus?"

"That's what I wanted to talk to you about."

"I'll be right there."

Joshua got dressed and drove to the lab. Seth greeted him as he exited the doors of the elevator that lead to the bat cave.

"Sorry to get you out of bed so late," Seth remarked.

"It's okay. You got some good news for me?"

"I hope so, but I need to show you something first. It's over here."

Seth led Joshua to an area in the back of the lab that housed some of the larger aquariums he had requested when the lab was built. He pointed to a large tank filled with a clear gelatinous material.

Joshua walked over to the tank and peered in. Dispersed in the clear material were spherical organisms one inch in diameter and colored a deep green. Small radial appendages emanated from them, which made them look like sea anemones. Joshua stared into the tank in shock. There was no question what the creatures were: petrins.

Chapter Thirty-Two
Gita

—————————————————

"Seth, what's going on?" Joshua asked, becoming concerned as he viewed the dark green creatures in the tank. "How and why are you growing petrins here? We didn't give you permission to do this?"

"The how is fairly simple," Seth replied. "We simply transmitted the code for petrin DNA to the lab via my spookyon, and I started growing them. The petrins you see in the tank are still incubating and won't become fully functional for a few months."

"But *why* are they here? You're not answering my question." Joshua was clearly agitated. Growing petrins had nothing to do with finding a honing virus to eradicate Ebola. "You betrayed our trust and misused much of the extra equipment we provided you."

"*Why* they are here is much more complex," Seth stated, ignoring Joshua's stern rebuff. "Instead of explaining it to you, I'd like to show you. Please follow me."

Seth led Joshua to a table with a thick, soft cushion on it. "Please lie down," he instructed.

Joshua was reluctant to comply. "Seth, I'm confused and somewhat frightened. Why can't you give me a straight answer?"

Things had come to a head. For months, Joshua had given Seth wide latitude despite his constant suspicion that the petrin was holding back vital information from the teams at the lab. Seth's odd behavior at this moment was validation that his suspicion had been well-founded.

"Okay, Seth. Out with it. What's the secret you've been hiding? If we're truly friends, you'll tell me—now."

Seth's tone of voice remained calm. "Josh, you're very perceptive, and I'm sorry I haven't been able to tell you everything, but you'll have to trust me on this. I want to explain to you what is happening, but I can't. I have to *show* you. I promise that nothing bad is going to happen. It will be an experience you'll never forget." Seth's smile appeared genuine. "Please," he added.

Joshua lay on the table, cautiously eyeing the alien.

Seth picked up a tall beaker filled with light blue sand that shimmered and glowed.

"Josh, I'm going to pour this over your head, but it's completely safe. The beaker contains biograins, which are microscopic living cells that will interface with the individual neurons of your cranial nerves and spinal cord. They will allow me to explain to you what's going on. Don't worry—it's not painful."

Joshua was anxious as he stared at Seth's face. "I don't like this," he said. "I've always trusted you, but this doesn't feel right. Biograins? I don't think so. It's—"

Seth poured the biograins onto Joshua's forehead despite his friend's protest. "Don't worry, Josh. Trust me."

The biograins didn't flow like sand, but instead adhered to his skin and slowly engulfed the upper portion of his head. Joshua felt a slight tingling sensation as they entered his dermal layer, and a few moments later his senses, including, sight, hearing, and touch, ceased to function.

*   *   *

"We were always a collective," Seth began.

Seth's voice entered Joshua's consciousness with extreme clarity. He felt that he was awake, and yet he had no sense of his body—no sensory input at all—although his thoughts and memories were intact. He saw only a black void, but the timbre of Seth's voice was crystal clear, as if it were originated within his brain.

Joshua surmised that Seth's words were being injected directly into his auditory nerves via the biograins. Joshua instinctively knew from Seth's opening statement that he was about to receive unredacted information on the origins of petrin civilization.

Seth continued speaking. "In the beginning, we were a unified mind comprised of individuals who worked for a single purpose, although we didn't know at first what that might be. We were simply information encoded on the molecules of a single planet in a physical form that I cannot explain because you would have no frame of reference. Over time, we came to believe that we pre-existed the universe and had been injected into it as pure information. As you know, information is not subject to the physical laws of matter or energy. It was therefore logical to assume that this information had traversed the singularity of the Big Bang."

For Joshua, the ramifications of Seth's statement were staggering. Was Seth indirectly invoking a creator, or perhaps some creative process that his level of intelligence couldn't understand? He wished Rachael were present to listen to Seth's presentation and assess it.

"Billions of years ago, this information evolved into the society on Petri, and we eventually searched the cosmos for others like ourselves—for evidence of other life. Your species has been searching for extraterrestrial life for only eighty years, but we meticulously searched the heavens for thousands of years after our discovery of spookyons, but we found no evidence for it. We were apparently alone. We didn't know why the universe was created or why we were the only life form within it, but the cosmos was vast, and we decided that if life didn't exist elsewhere, we would create it. We would seed the universe with life since we had the technology to do so.

"Our scientists created a microscopic machine that could travel to other planets and replicate itself using the raw materials there. You would consider this machine a von Neumann probe, but in addition to being able to replicate itself, we gave it the ability to adapt to varying environments and improve itself. In essence, we built a machine that could evolve. For us, simply creating a machine that replicates itself and travels across the universe is akin to spreading cancer. In addition to being able to replicate, our machine had to be able to differentiate itself in each new environment it encountered, becoming a variety of new machines in the process, and that is exactly what happened. On Earth, you call this machine the cell, and we engineered it to spread life throughout the universe. Humans were naive to consider evolution to be a natural process—it is not. It is something that we invented." Seth's voice paused before speaking with an inflection Joshua had never heard before, one that conveyed maturity and benign authority. "Some of our cells landed on Earth billions of years ago and evolved into humans. Josh, we are your creators."

Joshua's mind reeled at the statement, but he didn't have time to dwell on its profound significance, for he now saw a close-up image of a cell. It was incredibly vivid and was rendered in three dimensions, complete with nucleus and organelles. The image was projected directly into his visual cortex via his optic nerves and was therefore the clearest image he had ever seen.

Seth continued his startling narrative. "We decided to use the cell to seed life wherever there was fertile ground for our machine. In fact, the cell and the engineering beneath it were so compelling to our own species that we transferred our very existence into DNA-based multi-cellular creatures. We made ourselves self-determinate.

"There was a planet in our solar system whose outer two thirds was made of water. It had a highly elliptical orbit that revolved around our sun every 292 years."

Joshua could see the water world traveling in its orbit around the petrin sun in accelerated time.

"When it was in the portion of the ellipse that brought it close to our star—its perihelion—the heat from our sun caused the water to become liquid, forming a deep ocean that covered the entire planet. When the planet was farthest from our sun—its aphelion—the water froze, resulting in a planet of ice. The planet was therefore caught in an endless cycle of water and ice, slowly shrinking in size as water gradually evaporated into space year after year. During one of its liquid cycles, we seeded it with our invention—cells that replicated and filled the ocean. These cells were different from cells commonly found on Earth in that they were covered with a layer that would protect them from the hazardous rays of space, enabling them to remain dormant for billions of years. They were intended to be space seeds. When the planet moved away from the sun again, the ocean froze, trapping our machines in ice. While it was frozen, we introduced a thermal fusion device into the planetary core that, when detonated, exploded the planet into trillions of pieces that scattered at an incredible velocity in all directions."

Joshua saw the massive explosion of the ice planet, which ejected large boulders of ice into the interplanetary void.

"Some of these pieces are still travelling through space as I speak, destined to land on distant planets. When the pieces approach a star, solar winds evaporate their surfaces and cause trails of ice vapor—what you call comet tails. These tails contain frozen cells that eventually land on other worlds."

Joshua saw a comet traveling through a solar system, its tail showering ice crystals onto the surface of nearby planets. The vision was more vivid than any projection he'd seen at a planetarium.

"Of course, not every comet you see was created by us. We don't have a monopoly on the creation of water, but many comets are part of our seeding process. It's a very efficient method for ensuring that our cells are only released close to stars, meaning that they have a high probability of landing on planets that can harbor life. Many of these cells don't land on planets capable of sustaining life, but those that do usually replicate and evolve just as I've described. A few of our machines reach a point of intelligence that enables them to discover spookyons and eventually contact us. This was the case with Earth."

Joshua thought of his work at the particle center. In actuality, he'd been fulfilling the petrin agenda that had been formulated billions of years earlier. He felt small, insignificant—a pawn.

"Once a species contacts us, we make a determination as to whether its planet will be suitable as a staging area for the creation of additional primordial cells so that we can continue the expansion of life. We make this determination based on the amount of water present on a planet. Those that do not contain sufficient water are left to continue on their evolutionary path without interference from the collective. Those that do contain enough water are used to further our seeding process. The planet is then bioscaped to resemble Petri, with only the three species that inhabit our home world. It therefore becomes a new node for our civilization. In this way, we seed life through the universe while expanding our own civilization. We've spread our lifeform to thousands of nodes without ever physically leaving Petri. These new civilizations are all part of our collective.

"The collective has determined that Earth will become a new node and will be bioscaped since two thirds of Earth is covered with deep oceans. We sowed our seeds on your planet billions of years ago, and we're now ready for the harvest. As I've told you before, we are opposed to extinction, especially of sentient life forms. For planets that we bioscape, we catalog the life of all non-sentient species as data that is stored in our nodes. We then relocate the sentient species to another planet so they can continue to live and thrive."

Live and thrive? Joshua wasn't sure what connotations these words held.

"We have bioscaped a new home for humanity on a planet inside the realm of the collective, and when you wake, you will find yourself on this new world. The reason we want you to see it up close is that you need to understand that it's a true paradise, one engineered from the ground up for humans. You will have three days to explore the planet, after which I will return you to Earth. It's my hope that you can convince humanity how wonderful this world is so that it won't be frightened about being relocated.

"When you wake, you may wonder how you are able to be there. We have used the DNA from your body to clone you on the new world. The clone is your exact twin, with the exception that it has no brain. Your brain, and therefore your mind, is still in your body on Earth. The biograins will relay sensory and motor information from your mind as data to the Bowman sphere inside of me. That data will, in turn, be relayed through a spookyon connection on Petri to a neural nest enclosing a spookyon located in the head of your clone. This neural nest connects directly to the cranial nerves and spinal cord of the clone. Using this method, we are able to transport you to the new planet in a form indistinguishable from your own body. Even though your mind is still on Earth, your existence and reality will be on the new planet. In essence, your mind on Earth will remotely control your clone, but this transition will be completely seamless."

Joshua's vision returned to black.

"Josh, I know you have many questions. Rest assured that when you awaken, I'll answer them for you. In the meantime, welcome to New Eden."

*   *   *

Joshua had the sensation of returning to his body. He felt his hands and feet and knew that he was in a supine position. His vision glowed a deep red that he recognized as the inside of his eyelids. Upon opening his eyes, he saw a strange room and sat up to examine it, turning his head left to right. The room had circular, concave walls and was fifteen feet across. The ceiling was flat and glowed a soft white. The grayish-blue walls of the room were textured, slightly uneven, and had the resemblance of fine tree bark. The walls had three large circular openings, of which the right-most opened into what Joshua assumed was another room. He sat on what could only be described as a couch, which was tan in color and had the feel of soft fur. The floor was flat, slightly textured, and off-white.

Joshua was clothed in grayish-white skin-tight fabric that conformed effortlessly to his own movements. His feet had shoes that were made of the same material on the top sides but were covered in hard rubbery material on the soles.

Joshua peeled back the sleeve of his right forearm and discovered that the scar from his recent surgery was completely gone. Looking up, he heard Seth's voice in his head. "Joshua, can you hear me?"

"Yes," he replied.

"I know that you may be somewhat disoriented but take a moment to get your bearings. I've told you much information that may be shocking."

Seth had told Joshua that his transition to humanity's new home would be seamless, and it was: he had been instantaneously transported to the strange habitat without any sense of movement. He felt completely normal. In fact, the pain from his hip was no longer present, and he felt younger and more virile than he had in years. Dozens of thoughts coursed through his mind as he searched for what questions to ask Seth. Petrins created the cell? Earth was going to be taken over? Humans were to be relocated? How was any of this possible?

"Did you create the virus?" he asked. He knew that the only way that petrin DNA was growing on Earth was because humans had asked for Seth's help in fighting the viral outbreak. Seth's agreement to do this now seemed opportunistic.

"No, obviously your viral outbreak started prior to your communication with us. We had nothing to do with it."

"But it's because of the virus that you were able to transport petrin DNA to Earth. It's because we gave you the lab to use in complete seclusion. What if we had contacted you and there had been no virus?"

"An opportunity would have eventually presented itself," Seth replied. "It always does. Humans are at a precarious stage of their technological evolution. We call this 'the adolescence,' a stage when new technologies and powers are being discovered, but most societies cannot find ways to control them. We've learned that the vast majority of societies—ninety-four percent, to be exact—do not survive this adolescent stage of development. There are many things that can go wrong and wipe out young civilizations. Some succumb to viruses or other infectious outbreaks, while others are destroyed by natural causes they cannot control, such as asteroid strikes, volcanic activity, large solar flares, or gamma ray bursts. Others destroy themselves through warfare shortly after discovering nuclear fission or fusion. Some irreversibly poison their environments, but by far the largest destroyer of sentient civilizations during adolescence is a technology that humans have not yet discovered but which lies in their immediate future— self-determination."

"Self-determination?" Joshua said, remembering the first conversation that he'd had with Seth in Vinod's study. "The ability to manipulate DNA?"

"Yes. When we created the cell and its microscopic inner workings, we never realized that these mechanisms possessed the power of self-destruction. When our creations evolve to intelligence, they invariably have a need to understand their existence—how they themselves work. This need propels them to strive to understand their own genetic makeup and eventually to control and modify it. Once sentient societies discover the secret of DNA, it inevitably leads them on a path to self-destruction."

"Why?" Joshua wasn't following Seth's argument, which seemed presumptuous, even arrogant.

"Because there comes a crossroad, a decision point that divides advanced societies. One path is to preserve the natural order, not manipulate DNA, and to live as natural creatures. The other path is to reform themselves into improved beings who can completely control their bodies. Try to imagine an Earth in which half of the humans are normal and the other half are genetically modified super-humans. The super-humans would be superior in almost every way, possessing immortality, higher intellect, and physical strength. In a world with limited natural resources, these two group would be incompatible with each other, and the situation would lead to a war between the groups—a war unlike anything you've seen, with biologically-engineered weapons that would eventually wipe out both factions. Very few civilizations survive self-determination.

"The collective has found that relocating civilizations to a new world under its guiding influence helps preserve societies and also prevents their self-destruction. This is our plan for humanity. I know that the thought of having Earth being taken over by petrins is not something you would wish for, but in the long run we're trying to preserve your species since it has begun to explore the human genome. It's already on the road to self-determination."

Joshua tried to process what Seth was telling him. He wasn't sure if the alien was being truthful or not. "Why can't humans just shun genetic modification and resolve not to change themselves? It should be *our* decision."

Seth remained patient despite Joshua's challenge. "Many societies have tried to do so, but almost all have failed. The temptation to use genetic modification is too strong. Imagine being able to cure cancer, become immortal, or heal yourself after physical trauma. Most humans would want this ability."

Joshua could see the truth of what Seth was saying. After all, there were whole industries committed to making humans healthier and more youthful. This could easily be accomplished if and when humanity became self-determinate.

"How would you transport humanity here?" Joshua asked. "What would the process be like?"

Seth's voice adopted a reassuring tone. "The process will be gradual, something that will happen over decades. Individual humans will have the choice whether or not to come to New Eden. Those who decide to stay on Earth will be allowed to live out their lives as usual, but they will not be allowed to procreate. For those who decide to come to New Eden, the process will be similar to how I brought you here, but with one significant difference. Their bodies will be cloned, but their minds will be permanently transferred here by encoding the brains of the clones with information contained in their minds on Earth. After this transfer of information is complete, their bodies on Earth will be destroyed. They will not be virtually here such as you are now. They will be in New Eden permanently. Those who come will be allowed to procreate and thrive in order to further the human race, but with the protection of the collective to ensure that they don't destroy themselves. Also, we will transfer all external data on Earth to New Eden—all of your literature, art, books, and even the complete data of your Internet."

Joshua was amazed. The petrins could transport all of human existence, including all information gathered over thousands of years, to a new planet. The idea was sounding less ominous as Seth explained more.

"We feel that New Eden will be a paradise that will suit your needs well. There is absolutely nothing that can harm you here—no predators or poisonous substances. It's my wish that you explore as much of this world as possible over the next three days. If you find anything lacking or want to change something, tell me after your visit and most likely it will be possible.

"It's also important that you get an unbiased view of New Eden. For this reason, you'll be given complete privacy. Neither the collective nor I will monitor you while you're here. You will be left completely to yourself."

"Will Earth be exploded like the ice planet?"

"No, once its oceans are filled with primordial cells and then frozen, we will transport this ice into space and distribute it from there. Earth will be bioscaped as a new node for petrin civilization and the petrins there will join our collective. Do you have any other questions?"

The information Seth had given to Joshua was overwhelming—almost too much to absorb at once. "I don't have any at present, but I'm sure I'll have more later. What you're asking is the very kind of thing General Porter feared all along."

"I'm aware of that, but I wanted to emphasize that we are doing this for your own self-preservation. After I return you to Earth, I'll answer any further questions you may have.

"There's one more thing I need to tell you. Joshua, I consider you my friend. I personally requested something for you from the collective while you're here on New Eden, and they granted my request that you have a companion with whom you can explore the planet. The one I have chosen is in the room to your right."

Joshua's heart suddenly started beating faster. He got up from the couch, walked through the opening on the right, and saw a bed. Lying on top of it, eyes closed, was Rachael.

Chapter Thirty-Three
Alive

Joshua's eyes welled with tears of absolute joy. Was his entire experience of hearing Seth's voice and being transported to New Eden only a dream? If it was, he didn't want to wake up from it. He was overwhelmed with emotion and was able to utter only one word: "How?"

"When Rachael died, her last copy was never destroyed," Seth replied. "As you know, her body was frozen. While in the lab, I created reconnaissance organisms. They were similar to a swarm of insects that flew out of the ventilation system of the lab to Rachael's frozen body. They scanned the neural connections of her brain and catalogued this information, which they brought back to me at the lab. Using this information and her DNA sequence, I was able to grow a human brain in the lab that was encoded with data from Rachael's neural connections. This brain is now interfaced with the biograins, just like yours, and is transmitting its information to her clone via my spookyon connection. Her clone is similar to yours in that it doesn't contain a brain but has a neural nest to transfer this information to her cranial nerves and spinal cord."

"Seth, you've . . . returned Rachael to me?" Joshua said, his voice breaking.

"Yes. Seeing you suffer caused me to suffer as well. I'm not accustomed to this emotion, which is why I restored her life. If you decide to permanently stay on New Eden, the neural nests in each of your clones will be replaced with normal human brains, and you both can live here permanently."

Joshua knew this was no dream. He stared at the motionless body of Rachael for several seconds as he thought of the incredible gift Seth had given him. Rachael didn't move as he walked slowly to the bed, grasped her hand, and gently brushed his tears away with it. "Is she asleep?"

"No, not asleep, but suspended. I'm going to leave you two alone now. When I vacate your mind, she will wake up. Just a note of caution, however. The last memory she will have will be of the accident, so she'll be startled and confused when she wakes."

Joshua swallowed hard to check his emotion. "I understand. Thank you Seth for bringing my Rachael back to me. I . . . uh . . . well . . . thanks."

"You're welcome, Joshua. I'll contact you again in exactly three days. Make good use of your time. Goodbye, my friend."

Eyes wide, Rachael woke up, startled, and sat bolt upright and stared at Joshua.

"Josh, what happened? We were on the bridge and . . . there was an accident and . . ." She looked around the room. "Where are we? Is this a hospital?"

Joshua was at a loss for words. He hugged Rachael tightly as he sobbed more tears of joy.

"Josh, what's the matter? What's happening?"

Putting his arms around her shoulder, Joshua sat next to Rachael to calm her down. He slowly and methodically recounted the story of her death, the spread of Ebola, and the incredible story of how the petrins harvested their creations while spreading their civilization throughout the cosmos. Rachael was disoriented by her surroundings and shocked by the petrin agenda. Most of all, she found it hard to believe that she'd been cloned and virtually resurrected by Seth. She had tears in her eyes when Joshua had finished. She lifted her sleeve and saw that there was no tattoo on her wrist. "I really died in the crash?"

"Yes, and I was devastated more than you can possibly imagine, but we're back together now." He placed his hands on both of her shoulders and turned her to face him. "Seth brought you back to me, and that's all that matters."

"I don't know what to say," she said as she studied the room, still confused. "Josh, is this heaven?"

Joshua laughed. "No. Like I told you—it's a planet to which Seth transported us using cloning, DNA, and spookyon connections. It's a variation of how Seth can inhabit an android body. He wants us to explore the planet for the next three days. He hopes we'll endorse it in order to convince humanity to voluntarily leave Earth. I guess you could say it will be the biggest PR pitch in history."

Rachael was getting her bearings. "Humanity will never accept the idea."

"Don't be so sure. The petrins are offering us . . . well, everything."

Joshua couldn't believe that he and Rachael were sitting on the bed together, inches apart. After months of feeling that he would never see her again, she was present in the body Seth had fashioned—a perfect facsimile. But was it just a mirage—an elaborate trick being playing on him by a far superior intelligence? He had to be sure that this was Rachael—*his* Rachael."

"Rachael, I want to be certain it's really you. I need to ask you a question that only you would know the answer to. Are you okay with that?"

"Of course. Ask anything you want."

"When we were at the restaurant the day we made first contact with Seth, what was the evidence you gave me for the existence of a creator?"

"The cell, and that it couldn't have simply assembled itself."

Joshua grabbed Rachael in a tight embrace as fresh tears filled his eyes. "Rachael, I missed you so much."

Rachael returned his embrace but said nothing as tears ran down her cheeks.

After a few moments, Joshua looked at her and remarked, "You were right, by the way. The cell was a cairn."

"I have my moments," Rachael replied with a smile, looking around the room as she wiped the tears from her face. "And you're telling me that Seth wants to move humanity here? As in *everyone*?"

"He said it's for our own preservation since most societies at our level of development don't survive the period he called adolescence."

"He wants us to explore this place?" Rachael said looking around the room. The walls of the room were circular, with a luminous ceiling and off-white floor. She surmised that it was a bedroom given the fact that they were sitting on a bed with pillows. The room, which had three circular openings, was a sphere with its top and bottom cut off and replaced by the flat ceiling and floor.

"Yes," Joshua replied. "He says we have three days."

"Well, let's explore then," Rachael said as she rose and went to the closed orifice on her right. Joshua followed.

As Rachael touched the circular door, it sprung open from the center, expanding like the iris of a camera and revealing another room, which she and Joshua peered into carefully without crossing the threshold.

"I think it's a bathroom," Rachael said after a brief visual inspection.

A sink sat on a pedestal, and next to the sink was a toilet with no tank. Even though the shapes of the fixtures were recognizable, the material from which they'd been constructed were unfamiliar to Joshua and Rachael.

Their surfaces weren't smooth, but slightly uneven and colored a mottled shade of light brown. To their left was a small rectangular room.

"I think you're right," Joshua said. "That's a sink, but there's no faucet." Joshua walked over to the sink and placed his right hand into the cavity, which caused numerous jets of water to shoot from the edges of the bowl towards its center, where they met and flowed into a drain. "Wow, that's neat." The water stopped when he removed his hand.

Rachael walked to the rectangular room and placed her arm through the entranceway. Thousands of water droplets poured from the lighted ceiling of the room. "The entire ceiling is raining. I think it's a shower," she said. "The water's warm. It's going to be like taking a shower in a spring rain."

"It looks like a lot of fun," Joshua said as he looked at the cascading drops. "Unbelievable technology."

Rachael removed her arm from the shower, and the water stopped instantly. "I feel like Alice in Wonderland," she remarked, "and we're pretty far down the rabbit hole."

They exited the bathroom and returned to the bedroom. The door closed rapidly and silently behind them.

Joshua touched one of the textured gray walls. "I wonder what materials this place is made of. It feels like bark."

Rachael ran her hand along the wall, dug her thumbnail into its surface, and swiped it sideways, revealing a small green patch beneath. "Josh, you're right. It's exactly like the bark of a tree."

Joshua peered closely at the scratch and then slowly surveyed the rest of the room. "My God, I think it's . . ."

"What?"

"I think the wall, the house, and everything in it—the sink, the bed, the lighted ceiling, the floor—is alive!"

"How can that be?" Rachael asked. "I know the petrins are advanced, but that seems a bit farfetched."

"Seth said they bioscaped this planet to be a new home for humans but remember that their technology is completely DNA-based. Everything looks to be organic and made of living materials."

"They certainly look organic, but how could they build a living home?"

"Because they didn't *build* it. They *grew* it."

Rachael looked at Joshua, her mouth agape. "What do you mean they grew it? Like from a seed?"

"Probably. The petrins are masters of DNA. Hell, they invented it. They could've designed this house and then encoded it with DNA to literally grow from a seed planted in the ground. In fact, I'm almost sure of it."

Rachael turned three-hundred-and-sixty degrees. "Damn. We're inside a living organism."

"If it is living, I bet it's also self-reparative. If there was any damage, it could probably heal itself. No maintenance, no upkeep."

"Also, no manufacturing required." Rachael added. "All that's necessary is the information for the home encoded in DNA. The cells would do the rest. Simply amazing."

She walked to the other closed orifice in the room, which was a few feet from the foot of the bed and touched it. The orifice opened quickly, just as the other one had, and bright sunlight streamed through. It was a window that offered Joshua and Rachael a view of the terrain, one that left them speechless, for they saw a world of immense beauty. It was filled with grass fields, orchards, forests, and snow-capped mountains in the distance. The sky was a deep blue, interspersed with fluffy white clouds. The colors of the vegetation were familiar, and the entire scene, including the forest, was landscaped to perfection.

"My God, what a beautiful world!" Rachael exclaimed. "I've never seen a landscape so perfect."

"It's immaculate," Joshua observed. "It seems like there's no plant or blade of grass out of place. Now I know why Seth called this place New Eden. I can't wait to explore it," he said, rubbing the palms of his hands together in anticipation.

They looked through the window, and Rachael touched the clear material with her hand. It was solid but didn't feel like glass or plastic. It was somewhat squishy and became slightly deformed as her fingers pushed against it.

They walked back to the room in which Joshua had awakened. Rachael pressed an orifice in the wall closest to the bedroom, which opened to reveal a window with a view similar to the one they'd seen in the bedroom.

"I wonder how we get out there," Rachael said.

"Well, there's only one portal left," Joshua answered. "Let's try it."

He approached the remaining opening and touched it with his hand. It opened and afforded them an exit to New Eden. He and Rachael stepped outside and gazed at the mesmerizing vista. Adjacent to the exit of their abode was a large orchard with a variety of trees planted in rows, each with fruit hanging from its limbs. Some of the fruit looked familiar, but some looked quite bizarre.

Joshua stepped forward and looked at the outside of their home. "I was right," he remarked. "Our house is living." He pointed to the roof. "It's covered with green leaves."

Rachael glanced at the roof, which had numerous branches sprouting from it, each with dark green leaves. The leaves themselves had a shape that reminded her of aspen leaves, but these were much larger. "Josh, we're going to be staying inside a living organism. Kinda freaks me out." She turned back to the orchard. "Well, we're here to explore, so let's see what's out there."

Joshua and Rachael strode up and down the lanes between the rows of trees in the orchard. Some of them were instantly recognizable. Joshua stood under what looked like an apple tree, picked a piece of fruit, and took a bite. "Definitely an apple," he said while chewing.

Rachael approached an unfamiliar-looking tree with large, reddish-orange grapefruit-sized fruit, one of which she plucked from a low-hanging branch. The outer layer was tough and leathery, and she thought it might be a peel that wasn't meant to be eaten. The fruit in her hand unexpectedly changed color, turning yellow. "Josh, I think it's getting warmer."

Joshua put his hand on the fruit. "It's definitely warm—almost too warm to hold. Are you okay?"

"I'm fine," Rachael replied. "Let me open it." She used her fingernails to peel the leathery skin. Inside was a warm core that emitted a small wisp of vapor. "It smells and tastes good," she said. "Kind of like mac and cheese." She offered Joshua a bite, which he took.

"You're right," he said, "but the texture is different. It's still delicious, though."

"Here, you finish it," Rachael said as she offered Joshua the fruit. "I'm going to sample another one." She walked over to another unfamiliar tree, one that had reddish-brown fruit that was rubbery to the touch. She picked one, and since it didn't have to be peeled, she bit into the pulp. A surprised look covered her face as she examined the interior of the fruit while she chewed. It had a dark red color.

"Josh, it's ahi tuna."

"Fruit that tastes like tuna?"

"No, it doesn't just *taste* like tuna. It *is* tuna."

Joshua stood by her side and also took a bite. There was no question: the inside was definitely meat.

"What happened to your vegetarianism?" Rachael asked with a laugh.

"It's meat, but without a brain."

"How can meat grow on trees?"

"Meat, trees—everything here is made of cells. The petrins are genetic engineers with complete control of DNA. I'm sure they can engineer a tree to grow meat on its branches, and they apparently did."

Joshua and Rachael continued their exploration of the orchard. Further on, they saw trees that looked familiar, although they'd never seen them on Earth. They resembled the nectar trees on Petri, with vines of different colors hanging from pods underneath their leaves. Joshua grabbed a pinkish-colored vine, put the end in his mouth, and drank.

"It's sweet," he said. "Tastes like some kind of fruit juice. Very refreshing."

Rachael took a drink from a grey-colored vine. "I think this is just plain water."

Two vines were multi-colored. One was gray, with maroon stripes encircling it. "I wonder what the deal is with this one," Joshua said as he took a sip. "Whoa, it's red wine, complete with alcohol," he said, clearly pleased as he sipped.

"Looks like Seth thought of everything."

Joshua and Rachael spent the next hour sampling the enormous variety of food and drink in the orchard. There was hot and cold food of all varieties, not to mention an almost endless variety of beverages from the nectar trees. There was even fruit that resembled a warm bread-like substance.

"I'm full," Joshua said. "Let's explore somewhere else."

They walked to a space on the other side of their home and saw rows of shrubs.

"Their leaves look exactly like the ones on top of our house," Rachael noted.

Joshua examined one of the leaves. "You're right. Perhaps they're growing more homes here."

Thousands of shrub-like plants were organized in orderly rows, with wide pathways in between. The shrubs extended almost to the horizon. "It looks like it's going to be a village or small town," Rachael commented. "Can you imagine what it might look like when completed? It will be an orchard of homes."

"Pretty cool."

Rachael's voice betrayed doubt. "And they'll all look the same. Little houses made of ticky-tacky, just like an old song said."

They walked for an hour along the edge of the still-growing village, adjacent to which was a wide meadow covered with grass four inches high that waved gently in the breeze. When they reached the end of the village, they spotted a creek splashing over rocks. Beyond the creek was another orchard. By the bank, Joshua knelt down and dipped his hand in the water.

"It's cold," he said as he scooped water with cupped hands.

"You're not going to drink it, are you?" Rachael asked, her voice incredulous.

"Why not? Seth said that there's nothing dangerous here. Besides, we already ate the fruit, and it didn't harm us."

"But what about bacteria or parasites?"

"I think it's okay," Joshua said before taking a sip. "Perfectly refreshing water. Try it."

Rachael knelt, dipped her hands into the creek, and drank. "Tastes perfectly fine, but bacteria take time to reproduce."

"I don't believe there's any bacteria here."

"Why not? Bacteria are part of *all* biology."

"Because the petrins engineered this ecosystem from the ground up. They may not have needed to create bacteria. Earth's biology needs bacteria for any number of reasons, but this isn't Earth. Everything that's alive here was engineered with a purpose."

"That purpose being?"

"To serve as a home for humanity, just as Seth explained it to me."

Stepping into the flowing water, Joshua and Rachael crossed the creek and stood in the orchard on the other side. The trees were completely different from those next to their house. "It seems like each orchard is unique, with its own variety of food," Rachael said, brushing her hand against leaves and bark.

"It's like an endless buffet, all delicious—and free."

Rachael shot Joshua a cautionary glance. "Nothing is free. There's always a trade-off."

"Don't know what that might be here on New Eden. It's as close to the proverbial free lunch as you can get."

They sat down in the soft grass of the adjacent field for a picnic. Rachael looked at the forest, with snow-capped mountains rising in the distance. "I definitely want to explore that forest," she remarked. "I'd love to hike it."

"It's pretty far away." Joshua saw that the sun was lower, the sky tinged with orange and pink hues. "Let's do that tomorrow. I don't want to travel too far from the house and risk getting lost in the dark."

"Josh, this place is very different from Earth in some respects, and yet I'm amazed at how similar it is in other ways."

"What do you mean?"

"The gravity and the atmosphere seem to be the same as Earth's. I'm guessing the length of the day is also the same."

"I suspect these criteria are things that the petrins looked for when selecting this world for humans. Given the vast reach of the collective, they had thousands of habitable worlds to choose from. God only knows what galaxy we're in."

"God? Is he in this picture too?"

Joshua laughed at the reference but made no reply.

Rachael sat quietly, lost in her thoughts as she twisted soft blades of grass between her fingers.

"What are you thinking about?" Joshua asked.

"It's all still a big shock for me."

"What? New Eden?"

"That, and that I died in the accident on the bridge. It's like a fairy tale." She paused and glanced at Joshua. "Sometimes fairy tales, like those written by the Brothers Grimm, are pretty scary and have terrible endings."

"I guess you didn't really die," Joshua said. "At least not according to the petrin definitions of life and death. I lost you for a while, and I was completely devastated, but you're with me now, and I'm never going to lose you again. I couldn't go through it a second time."

"But I can never go back to Earth. From what you told me, I can only exist on New Eden since Seth replicated only my brain there and nothing else."

"Don't worry. A lot of what you're missing on Earth can be brought here. Seth told me that the petrins can transport virtually all accessible knowledge on Earth to New Eden. And you'll never be without me. I'll make sure of that."

Rachael leaned over and wrapped her arms around Joshua. "This place is really amazing, especially with you here." She sighed deeply, as with resignation. "I guess there are worse places to be stuck."

"Stuck?"

Rachael smiled weakly. "There's no reason to get your hands dirty here. There aren't any challenges. Still, it's got everything, and it sounds like humanity doesn't have much of a choice given the viral outbreak on Earth." She looked around her. "I have to admit that it's quite beautiful."

"Yes, and we still have a couple more days to explore it, but the best part of this paradise, hands down, is you being here." Joshua gave Rachael a passionate kiss, and they lay in the grass, looking at the slow-moving clouds sailing overhead.

"We should head back home," Joshua said after a few minutes. "It looks like the sun is starting to set."

On their walk back, they'd noticed that some of the plants and shrubs exhibited bioluminescence, which made it easy to see their path. The sun had just set, and the first stars were becoming visible when they arrived at the front portal.

They bathed in the warm rain shower of the bathroom and then lay on the bed, gazing out the window. There were numerous stars in the sky, but none were familiar to them. A small glowing arc rose from the horizon as they snuggled.

"What do you think *that* is?" Rachael asked, pointing to the arc.

"Don't know. It's definitely not a moon. It's too fuzzy."

They lay in bed while the arc grew larger and eventually revealed itself to be a spiral galaxy encompassing half the sky, its arms casting a soft glow on the terrain of New Eden. Its light was like that emitted by a full moon in the skies of Earth. They pondered the fact that they were the first two humans to spend the night on a new world. Quite literally, they were Adam and Eve exploring a New Eden.

Chapter Thirty-Four
Just Like Heaven

The next morning, Joshua and Rachael awoke, sat on the couch in the living room, and ate breakfast. A light rain had fallen during the night, covering the trees and grass with thick dew, but the sun had risen over a clear sky. They grabbed their breakfast from the orchard and were better able to determine what a particular fruit would taste like from its outward appearance.

"Looks like a hiking day," Joshua commented.

"I'm excited to see the forest, but this landscape goes on forever. How does Seth expect us to get a good idea of what New Eden is like in just three days?"

"I don't think he expects us to get a complete picture," Joshua responded. "He probably wants us to see what's possible with genetic engineering. He told me that we could request changes if we wanted."

After breakfast—the fruit tasted like bananas, bread, and a beverage that gave them the same clarity as coffee—Joshua and Rachael started on their trek towards the distant forest. They crossed several grass fields and another stream that Joshua surmised was the same one they had crossed the day before, but at an upstream point.

"There are a few things missing from New Eden," Rachael remarked after they'd made it halfway to the forest. "For example, I don't see any insects here."

"That's true, not that I miss being bitten by mosquitoes. Like bacteria, they're probably not needed."

"But there are no birds or animals either, at least none that we've seen. Also, there are no bees, and bees are necessary on Earth for pollination."

"Maybe there's no need for pollination on New Eden," Joshua

remarked.

"Why not?"

"Think about it. The petrins engineered life here from DNA for a specific reason. The flora is obviously how they want it. It's a completely controlled ecosystem. The last thing they would want would be for independent reproduction or mutation to screw up their grand design."

"So you're saying the organisms here don't reproduce?"

"Maybe not in the traditional sense," Joshua said. "Maybe they're immortal like the petrins, or perhaps they reproduce by cloning instead of sexual reproduction, which would preserve their genetic makeup."

"Mitosis but no meiosis," Rachael replied. "Just a theory, I suppose, but a logical one."

The couple continued their walk towards the edge of the forest. In a field close to the edge of the tree line, they saw two enormous brown tree stumps.

"Those seem out of place," Rachael said.

"Yes, strange that everything else has been perfectly manicured, and yet the two stumps mar the otherwise perfect landscape. They stick out like a sore thumb."

"Oh, my God!" Rachael exclaimed as she grabbed Joshua's arm. "I think one of the stumps shifted position."

The stump on the left moved towards them, slowly at first, then faster. It spread out, and what they had mistaken for roots were actually articulated legs, eight in all, four on either side, all of them attached to a central body. Joshua and Rachael now knew what the creatures were.

"They're arachnids!" Joshua exclaimed.

The second arachnid also started moving towards them. Both were large, about the size of a small elephant.

"Josh, I'm scared," Rachael said as the creatures advanced.

"Don't be. Seth told us that nothing here—"

"Yes, that nothing here can harm us, but I'm not a petrin. I have no idea what those things are doing."

The lead arachnid stood and halted in front of Joshua. It was similar to the creatures Seth had shown them during the lab sessions, but these had only two of the snake-like sensory organs emanating from their carapace instead of four, like those from Petri. The carapace itself was also slightly different. Its top surface had the contour of a saddle, and in front of the curved seat was a T-shaped handle made of a white horn-like material. The second arachnid stood beside Rachael.

Standing beside Joshua, the first arachnid bent its front legs and assumed a kneeling position, which brought its body to within inches of the ground.

"What's it doing?" Joshua asked, scratching his head. "Is it trying to fold up again?"

Rachael examined the position of the arachnid. "Josh, I think it wants you to climb on top. It's kneeling, like a camel or elephant that's been trained to carry a rider."

"You may be right. Its top definitely looks like a saddle." Joshua moved towards the creature and carefully touched one of its legs with his fingers.

"Be careful," Rachael said. "It looks harmless, but I'm just going by appearances."

"I'm going to try to climb up," he said after taking a deep breath. "The top of its exoskeleton feels like soft fur."

Joshua placed his foot on one of the creature's legs and lifted his body to the carapace. He then swung his right leg over the top and sat on the arachnid. His hands grabbed the handle, and the creature, as if on cue, stood up from its kneeling position.

"Whoa," Joshua exclaimed from his new perch as the second creature knelt in front of Rachael. "Climb aboard. It's very comfortable. I think they're here to serve us—to help us explore since there's so much ground to cover."

Rachael climbed on top of the second arachnid, which stood up once she was seated, and grabbed the handle.

"Cool," Rachael replied. "Our own transports. Not limo service but suited for the terrain."

"I wonder how you make them move," Joshua said. He rotated the handle to the left, which caused the creature to spin in the same direction. The further he rotated it, the faster it spun. "So much for determining direction, but I'm not sure how to make it go forward." He pushed and pulled on the handle but neither the handle nor the arachnid moved.

Rachael also spun her arachnid left and right. "Neat, but we're pretty high in the air," she said as she leaned left to take a look at the ground. Her creature immediately moved to the left.

"How did you get it to move like that?" Joshua asked.

"I just leaned left," Rachael answered.

Joshua leaned to the right, and his creature moved in that direction. Left, right, forwards, backwards—the arachnid moved in whatever direction Joshua angled his body. "It works like a hover board. You simply lean in the direction you want to go, and they move in that direction. It's like they're trying to keep our center of gravity lined up with theirs."

Rachael followed suit. "The further you lean, the faster they go," she said. "It's very stable since they match their center of gravity with ours. I think it's virtually impossible to fall off."

For several minutes, Joshua and Rachael practiced moving the arachnids around the field adjacent to the forest. Controlling the creatures was intuitive, and in minutes they were controlling the arachnids with ease.

"Let's head into the forest," Joshua said, Rachael following close behind.

The forest consisted of what looked to be evergreen trees with large brown trunks. The floor was covered with grass and ferns.

"It reminds me of the California redwoods," Rachael observed after they had traveled for a few minutes. "I definitely smell pine in the air."

After they'd spent an hour exploring, Joshua said, "Let's see what these things can do." He leaned further forward, and his arachnid sped through the forest, Rachael still following.

He then pushed his creature to go even faster. He estimated that he was skimming over the ground at twenty miles per hour, but the creature avoided obstacles with ease. It dodged trees by shifting left and right, but always tilted its carapace in the direction opposite the shift so that Joshua was never in any danger of falling off.

Sections of the forest floor were uneven, but the creatures navigated these with ease. Their long, articulated legs compensated for the uneven terrain so accurately that Joshua and Rachael felt as if they were floating. The creatures' movements were smooth, without the jerkiness or bounciness associated with riding a horse.

"This is really fun," Rachael said, bringing her creature next to Joshua's as they continued their rapid advance, her hair blown backwards by the breeze.

They rode deeper into the forest at a fast clip, changing directions at will. It was exhilarating. At one point the creatures approached a narrow but deep ravine with a creek at its bottom. The arachnids didn't slow down, but instead leapt into the air and jumped to the other side effortlessly.

"I wish we had some of these on Earth," Joshua shouted to Rachael as the arachnids continued their relentless pace.

Joshua directed his mount towards a steep incline covered with trees. "Let's see what's on top of this hill."

They raced up the hill which had an incline of about forty-five degrees. Even though the creatures were climbing the incline easily, they adjusted their legs such that their carapace remained level.

"It feels like we're moving up a really fast escalator," Rachael remarked.

At the top of the hill, Joshua and Rachael entered a large clearing covered with grass, and they stopped to take a look around. In the distance, Joshua saw an orchard. "Looks like a good place to stop for lunch," he suggested.

"Sure," Rachael replied.

Joshua suddenly moved his arachnid at high speed towards the distant orchard. "First one there gets to pick lunch," he shouted looking back.

Rachael leaned forward and chased Joshua. "Not fair!" she shouted. "You got a head start!"

Joshua leaned forward as far as he could on his arachnid, which was now traveling at forty miles per hour. He had trouble keeping his eyes open as the wind blasted his face, and he turned back to see Rachael close behind. He stuck his tongue out since he was confident he would win the race. When he looked forward again, he was halfway there.

Joshua heard a low rumble and gazed up when he saw a dark shadow pass over him. It was Rachael on her arachnid, which was now flying! She glanced at Joshua from her elevated perch and, tongue out, returned the gesture.

"How did you get it to do that?" Joshua called out as Rachael took the lead.

Rachael's arachnid had changed the configuration of its legs. They were sticking straight out, having spread sideways from its body. The front and rear two legs on either side were joined by transparent membranes that acted as wings. The four wings beat rapidly to move air downwards and backwards. As Rachael passed overhead, he thought to himself *she's riding a dragonfly.* "How?" he shouted.

"Lift the handle!"

Joshua followed her instructions, and the handle clicked into a higher position. He felt the creature getting lower to the ground as its legs grew straight, and clear membranes grew from the center of the body to the tips of its legs. When the membranes reached the tips, the creature leapt into the air and beat its wings rapidly. Joshua was flying.

The arachnid's movements were controlled the same as before now that it was airborne. Joshua could still lean to change the direction of flight, but the handle now moved forward and backward. Moving the handle forward caused the creature to point its front down and move closer to the ground, while pulling it backward caused it to veer up and climb. He chased Rachael, who now had a substantial lead. When he caught up, she was already at the orchard, but her arachnid hovered, its momentum in check.

Joshua leaned back, causing his creature to hover as well.

"You lose," Rachael said. "That's what you get for trying to get a head start."

"These are unbelievable creatures."

"A true testament to the power of genetic engineering."

"I wonder how we get down," Joshua said.

Rachael pushed down on her handle, which caused the creature to drift downwards and shift to its walking configuration. She then let go of the handle, and the creature knelt, allowing Rachael to dismount.

*   *   *

Joshua and Rachael sat on the grass and had a picnic. There was a small field close to the orchard that was covered with a variety of flowers, the fragrance of which filled the air as they ate lunch. The arachnids moved beneath nectars trees in the orchard and drank from vines to replenish their energy. After they had finished their meal, Rachael sat on the grass with Joshua's head in her lap. "Do you know what's amazing?" he asked.

"What?"

"Before we made contact with Seth, humanity saw no evidence for life beyond Earth. In the end, the evidence was there all along, but we just hadn't recognized it."

"How so?"

"How about von Neumann probes? We thought we had no evidence for them, but we ourselves were the probes. We were the evidence of life beyond Earth, but we never realized it."

"I see what you mean," Rachael said. "But by the purest definition, aren't von Neumann probes supposed to replicate and reseed more of the galaxy? We weren't doing that."

"If the Petrins turn Earth into a new node for the collective and blast oceans seeded with primordial cells into space, aren't they doing exactly that? Their timescale may be in the billions of years, but it really does meet the definition."

"I guess so," Rachael said. "Do you know what really amazes me?"

"What?"

"The petrins never physically left their home world and yet have colonized thousands of planets."

"We've always thought of colonizing other planets with space ships, but they didn't use any ships at all. We had tunnel vision once we entered the age of rockets. The petrins were far more ingenious."

"It's all just information, Josh—information transmitted by spookyons. Henry never knew how right he was when he said that information is everything."

"Maybe he *did* know, but I'm sure he knew nothing of petrins."

"Consider this: Seth is able to come to our planet, there's petrin DNA growing on Earth, an entire world is created for humanity, and even my being alive—it's all because of information transmitted via spookyons."

"Feeling philosophical?" Joshua asked.

"Yeah, but it's all true—and a result of information theory."

Joshua thought for a moment about what Rachael had said. "Such a vast universe with incredible energy and matter, but in the end the only thing that counts is how that matter and energy are arranged. Information may be the only thing of significance in the cosmos. Without it, everything else seems meaningless."

"I'm sure Vinod would agree," Rachael replied. "He mentioned something like that when we first met while waiting in line for Henry's lecture. I miss him. I wonder when or if I'm going to see him again."

"I'm sure he'll decide to come here when we tell him what we've seen, although the petrins better provide classic rock or Vinod will thumb his nose at paradise. But he's one of the 103ers after all is said and done. I don't see too many of them turning down the opportunity to come here. Half of all cults think some savior or alien is going to whisk them to paradise on a spaceship or comet." After a few moments of reflection Joshua added, "If information truly is everything, does that lessen your idea of a creator?"

"Not at all," Rachael replied. "*Someone* had to create a universe in which information exists. For that matter, who created the information to begin with?"

"You've remained consistent in your views," Joshua said with a smile. "I've always admired that in you."

Rachael sat quietly for a moment, lost in her thoughts. "There *is* one thing that disturbs me, though."

"What?"

"I was dead, and for all that time before I woke up, there was nothing. No near-death experience, no floating out of my body, no traveling down a tunnel, and no angels or beings of light."

"Are you wondering why you weren't in heaven or some afterlife?"

"Yes. I mean my spirit had to be *somewhere*, right?"

"It wouldn't make sense for you to be in heaven if you could be revived in the mortal world."

"What do you mean?"

"I mean that if the possibility existed that you could be brought back, maybe you weren't actually dead. Seth said that you were in a suspended state, and maybe it wasn't much different from the frozen frog he described.

You still contained life, but you weren't actively living or, as he put it, fulfilling your purpose."

Rachael couldn't suppress a smile. "The Gospel According to Seth. Are you saying that you agree with it? That death is the loss of the last copy?"

"It seems to me that if you want to believe in heaven, then the concept of a last copy makes sense because when the last copy is lost, it's permanently removed and can't be retrieved. Maybe you only go to heaven when your last copy leaves this universe."

Rachael pondered Joshua's last statement, which seemed to assuage her doubts and give her solace. She leaned over and wrapped her arms around him. "I'll make a believer out of you yet, Joshua Andrews."

*   *   *

Joshua and Rachael mounted the arachnids and once again took to the air. They followed the forest, which led to the foothills of the snow-capped mountains. At times they flew low, skimming over the treetops; at other times they flew high in order to get a birds-eye view of New Eden. They reached the foothills of the mountain and followed the forest slopes to higher elevations.

Joshua pointed to a waterfall in the distance, which originated from an outcropping of rock high above and far from the rock face in front of which it fell. As they got close, they realized it was immense in height—over five hundred feet—but was narrow in width. The water evaporated in a mist before it reached the valley below. They flew through the mist as water droplets condensed on top of their heads and shoulders. They positioned their arachnids to hover at the midpoint of the falls between the rock face and the falling water, mist still drifting across their bodies.

"Let's see if the arachnids will fly through it," Joshua said as he commanded his mount directly through the falls.

When the weight of the water hit the creature, the arachnid dropped precipitously in height until it made it through, at which point it regained its flight. Rachael followed Joshua, and the two hovered in front of the falls, soaking wet from the torrent.

"It's warm," Rachael commented.

"*Really* warm," Joshua said. "It must be coming from a geothermal spring."

They followed the falling water to the bottom, where they landed the arachnids and dismounted. The height of the falls caused the water at this lower elevation to be more of a rainy mist than a torrent. They stepped into the center of the falls, their arms outspread.

"It's still warm, but not as warm as it was above," Rachael noted.

"The evaporation on the way down must cool it. It feels like we're in an enormous shower."

They spent a few minutes reveling in the refreshing downpour before getting back on their mounts.

"Our clothes aren't wet at all," Rachael said.

"They're completely hydrophobic," Joshua agreed. "They don't get wet."

"Josh, everything in this world except for the rocks and water is living," Rachael said examining the fabric of her shirt. "Do you think this is some type of living material?"

"I wouldn't doubt it. I can't envision the petrins using synthetic materials when everything is made from DNA."

Back on their arachnids, they rose into the air and followed the waterfall to its precipice. They noted that the water flowed from a cave in the mountain.

"Looks like it comes from an underground spring," Joshua said.

"The mountain must be volcanic and is therefore heating the water."

They flew higher up the mountain and reached the end of the tree line, where the mountain's bare rock was exposed. They hovered and took in their surroundings. The air temperature had dropped considerably.

"Josh, it's getting colder. Should we keep going up?" Rachael asked looking up the mountain. "It's got to be pretty cold where that snow line is."

"I don't think we'll freeze. Otherwise, the petrins wouldn't have left us alone."

As they continued up the mountain, the air grew even colder. Joshua noted that the fabric of his clothing was mutating, becoming thicker and adopting a fur-like texture. "Our clothes are definitely alive," he said.

Rachael's clothing grew thicker too, and her chill slowly dissipated. She also felt heat rising from the carapace of her arachnid. "Josh, the arachnid seems to anticipate our every need."

"Yeah, just like our clothes."

They flew higher still and reached the snowline. The temperature had dropped further, but they were nevertheless comfortable and warm. They soared through a high-altitude valley covered with a thick ice-blue glacier. The glacier gave way to a steep snow-covered incline, which they followed to the summit, where they stopped and dismounted to gain a better view.

The snow was deep, and their legs were buried up to their knees; it was light and fluffy but nevertheless slowed their progress. Now on top of New Eden, the air was crystal clear, and they had a panoramic view of their new world. They looked in the direction from which they'd come and saw the forest that had guided them. At the edge of the horizon, they could just barely make out the village where their home was located. To the right, the mountain beneath the snowline was covered with thick vegetation.

"Looks like there's an ocean over there," Rachael said as she pointed to the right.

Joshua looked to the left and saw more forests and fields, which culminated in a distant red landscape devoid of vegetation. "I think I see a desert," he said.

Rachael walked next to Joshua and wrapped her arms around him as she admired the varied landscape. "Josh, this really *is* a paradise."

"This has to be one of the most beautiful views I've ever seen."

"The sun is getting lower," Rachael said. "It's probably going to set soon, so maybe we should head back."

Suddenly, one of the arachnids, which had remained motionless, shivered.

"What's it doing?" Joshua asked.

The creature leapt into the air, flipped over, and landed in the snow on its back, its legs pointed at the sky.

"I don't know," Rachael remarked. "Is it playing dead?"

The couple moved towards the overturned creature.

"Josh, check out its belly. It looks like the material on our bed at home."

Joshua bent over to examine the creature's new posture. "You're right. It feels exactly the same."

He climbed onto its belly. "Come on," he said as he helped Rachael up with his outstretched hand.

"It's warm," Rachael said moving her hands over the belly of the creature.

The second arachnid now leapt into the air and landed upright on top of the first one. Their legs interlaced, and the combination of the two created a sealed sphere that enclosed Joshua and Rachael. The clear membranes of their wings acted as windows that allowed the couple to see in all directions, and the interior of the newly-created sphere grew warmer as the fabric of their clothing returned to its thinner state.

"Josh, they've created a shelter for us."

"I guess there's no need for us to go home. We can spend the night here."

Joshua and Rachael lay inside the shelter and considered the amazing events of the day. Shortly afterwards, the sky grew dark, and the spiral galaxy rose over the horizon. Thin bioluminescent lines developed on the inner surfaces of the legs of the arachnids, illuminating the habitat with a soft white glow.

Joshua was in absolute bliss and hugged Rachael. "If this isn't heaven, it comes awfully close."

The galaxy became obscured by a bank of clouds, and a light snow started to fall. Joshua and Rachel embraced each other and watched the falling snow before making love on the summit of humanity's new home.

Chapter Thirty-Five
Dome

Joshua and Rachael awoke to rays of bright morning sunlight slanting into their cocoon. The night's snow had been heavy; their shelter having been completely buried, golden light had begun to melt the white drift. Water dripped from the overhead carapace.

"Wow, it looks like we're buried," Rachael said, peeking outside.

"Nice and cozy in here," Joshua commented as he hugged Rachael. "I wonder how we get out—not that I'm in a hurry." He smiled and pulled her closer.

Suddenly, the shelter quivered and shook, causing its inhabitants to gently roll left and right, as if they were in an amusement park ride.

"Whoa," Rachael said. "Is it an earthquake?"

The shaking stopped, and the powdery snow covering the shelter slid off, enabling Joshua and Rachael to see a bright vista underneath the clear morning sky.

"Not an earthquake," Joshua said. "Just the arachnids shaking the snow off."

Cold air swept into the shelter as the interlaced legs of the arachnids separated. The top arachnid jumped off its partner and into the snow with a crunching sound.

"Guess this is our cue to get down," Rachael said as she climbed out, Joshua following her lead. The upside-down arachnid flipped into an upright position, its carapace shedding more snow.

"Our saddles are still snow-covered," Joshua pointed out. "Must have been a really cold night to get such an accumulation."

A few moments later, steam escaped from the top of the carapaces as the remaining snow melted quickly.

"Guess they turned their defrosters on," Rachael laughed.

The saddles were soon warm and dry, and Joshua and Rachael were in the air again, flying down the side of the mountain towards the jungle in the distance. After they descended below the snowline, they followed the swathe of forest for several miles. Beyond this was a patchwork of fields, some with grass, others with orchards, and still others with plants that would eventually become houses for humans.

They stopped in the first orchard they came to for a quick breakfast before taking to the sky again. They cruised over varied ecosystems, from large deciduous woodlands to evergreen forests, as well as rivers, streams, and freshwater lakes. The colors were vivid, with the forests clad in deep green, while the waters presented a silver sheen. Each new scene was a testament to the bioengineering genius of the petrins.

Joshua figured that this side of the mountain was the windward side since there was more vegetation on the slope than the one facing their home. The windward side of the mountains always received copious rainfall since moisture-laden wind, sweeping up the mountain, cooled and caused water to condense and fall as rain.

As they reached a lower elevation, the vegetation turned into a thick rain forest with jungle-like plants and trees, some of which were unfamiliar. The temperature had risen, and the air was more humid. The terrain was still mountainous, with numerous waterfalls spraying mist into the air and surrounding jungle.

Their destination was the ocean they'd seen from the summit the night before. They traveled for several hours over the canopy, occasionally hovering when they saw an interesting tree or waterfall. They soon neared the large body of water, which was rimmed by a pristine sandy-white beach. The water was a crystal blue color that rivaled the waters of the Caribbean. The couple followed the beach line and landed near an adjacent orchard. Surrounding the orchard was thick jungle—mostly shadow—and the beach itself was a mere two hundred feet wide.

Joshua and Rachael selected their lunch from the orchard and sat on the warm sand, gazing at the ocean as the arachnids positioned themselves under nectar trees. It was a tropical paradise in every respect, one they had all to themselves.

"We must have covered a good two hundred miles this morning," Joshua commented, eating a piece of fruit that tasted like a cross between a grape and an apricot.

"And encountered many climate zones along the way," Rachael added. "Everything from snowcapped mountains to a tropical rain forest."

Joshua stretched out and absorbed the warmth of the sun. "Definitely much warmer than last night. Maybe we can go for a swim to cool off after we finish lunch."

"Sounds like a plan," Rachael said while taking a bite of her fruit. "It still amazes me that the petrins can grow food and shelter at will. You need something, and it's just . . . *there.*"

"It's quite pleasant, but it's also highly efficient," Joshua remarked. "Think about it—no need for harvesting natural resources or for manufacturing facilities. The petrins grow whatever they need simply by coding DNA. If humanity decides to come here, there won't be any poverty or starvation. Everyone will have food and shelter in abundance."

"I guess that's true. Everything here literally *does* grow on trees."

After lunch, they strolled up to the water line, and Rachael, bending over, swept her hand through the shallows. "It's warm, like bathwater. Very tropical."

Joshua dipped his hand in the water and tasted it with his finger. "It's fresh water," he said, eyebrows raised. "No salt at all."

"A fresh water ocean?" Rachael said.

"Sure, why not."

"Pretty odd. Salt is an important part of Earth's ecosystem, including its ocean."

Joshua waved off the remark as if shooing away a fly. "The petrins can balance everything perfectly through genetic engineering. The ocean can have any characteristic they choose."

"Right. This is paradise," Rachael said as she started taking off her clothes.

"What are you doing?"

"Somehow I don't think our organic apparel was made for swimming," Rachael said. "Besides, there's no one to see us, and we have the whole planet to ourselves." She looked at Joshua mischievously. "Adam and Eve started out sans fig leaves."

Joshua and Rachael stripped naked and ran into the ocean hand-in-hand. The water wasn't deep, and they waded out a hundred feet until the water lapped at their necks. The ocean was crystal clear, had no fish or vegetation, and had minimal wave crests. Rachael and Joshua embraced, unashamed in a world that was all their own.

"I wonder if there's anything like algae in the water," Rachael said.

"I doubt it. Most of the oxygen here is probably produced by vegetation."

Rachael stood on the soft, sandy bottom and glanced towards the mountain peak where they had spent the night. "It's like a postcard," Rachael admitted.

"Made more beautiful by your presence," Joshua said, kissing her on the lips.

Joshua and Rachael frolicked in the ocean for some time before exiting and donning their clothes. They sauntered along the beach for a distance, his arm around her waist, and encountered another large area where homes were growing.

"Beachfront property," Rachael joked.

"I'm sure these are going to be in demand," Joshua said, mildly amused as he noted that the homes were in various stages of growth.

As they continued their walk, they heard a low rumble behind them, and they turned to see the arachnids flying towards them before landing on the beach, their wings kicking up a cloud of sand.

"Looks like our Ubers have arrived," Rachael said, winking. "Where to next?"

"I want to check out that desert we saw from the mountain."

They got back on their transports and were in the air again, headed towards their next destination.

The desert was on the leeward side of the mountains, so they had to reverse direction. They flew fast, pushed along by the ocean breeze, reaching the other side of the mountain by circumnavigating the base. There were more patchwork fields, but Joshua observed that there were fewer forests and more grasslands, causing him to surmise that the area received less rain than that by the beach. The air was still warm, but less humid.

They rose higher to get a view of the red desert, the fields below giving way to a vast grassland. As they continued, the grassland stopped abruptly in a straight line, beyond which there was no vegetation, only red desert. The sky seemed darker, although they could still see the sun directly overhead. As they approached the division between grassland and desert, the arachnids descended with no command from their riders.

"What's going on?" Joshua asked. "My arachnid is going down, but I didn't direct it to."

"Mine's doing the same thing," Rachael said.

The creatures flew lower and landed on the edge of the grassland. Joshua and Rachael disembarked, walked towards the desert, and stopped at the edge of the fine-grained sand. The dividing line extended to the horizon to both the left and right. The desert consisted only of red sand, rocks, and boulders, with no trace of scrub, cactus, or weeds. It was barren. The sky above was nearly black, and Rachael thought she could see stars.

"Why is it so dark?" Joshua asked. "There's plenty of sunlight here."

"I don't know," Rachael replied, shaking her head. "It's very strange." She crouched and reached out to touch the sand but felt an obstacle. "Hmm. There's some type of barrier here."

Joshua touched the barrier, which was solid and smooth and had a texture similar to glass. "It must be made out of some material that has a refraction index for light similar to that of the atmosphere. I can barely see it, although it seems to have thickness." He ran his hands up, down, left, and right across the wall. "There are no openings in it." He dug a small hole at the edge of the grass. "It extends below the surface. The petrins might as well have put up a no trespassing sign."

"The desert reminds me of a Martian landscape," Rachael said. "The barrier must go high into the air since the arachnids couldn't fly over it."

"I wonder what it's for?" Joshua asked.

Rachael thought for a while and peered at the dim stars overhead, then behind her towards the mountains and blue sky. "Josh, I don't think it's a wall. It's a dome."

"What do you mean?"

"I believe the petrins are terraforming this world, and we've been living inside an enormous dome, the environment of which they've been controlling. They're obviously not finished yet."

Joshua considered what Rachael had said. "You may be right. Maybe there's no atmosphere outside the barrier to scatter the sunlight, which is why the sky is so dark."

"A dome encompassing an entire continent," Rachael said pensively. She stared at the desert for a while, her hands placed high on the walls of the dome. "I think we should head back," she finally said. "It's probably going to get dark soon, and I'd like to sleep in our home tonight."

They mounted the arachnids and flew for several hours before reaching their house a few minutes after the sun had set. During the flight, Rachael said almost nothing, and upon arriving at their home, she sat on the couch and fell silent. When Joshua sat next to her, he saw tears in her eyes.

"What's wrong, Rachael?" Joshua asked, wrapping his arm around her tightly.

Rachael looked directly at Joshua before responding. "Josh, it's just another zoo."

"I'm not following."

"This place—New Eden. It's just another zoo, one meant for humans."

Joshua shook his head, leaned forward, clasped his hands, and braced his arms against his knees. "I don't feel that way at all. It's a paradise, a place specifically designed for humans in the face of insurmountable odds on Earth."

"Oh, it's definitely a paradise alright," Rachael conceded, "but that doesn't make it desirable. Sure, people can live and thrive here with shelter and food *provided* for free, but they won't *be* truly free. They'll always be under the watchful eyes of the collective, unable to do what they want."

Joshua was visibly upset. "But that's exactly what Seth told me this place is for. New Eden is a planet where humans can thrive, and precisely *because* of the oversight of the collective, they won't be in danger of making mistakes that could lead to human extinction."

Rachael frowned, unconvinced. "But maybe humans are happier making mistakes and learning from them. It is, after all, what we've been doing for thousands of years. The irony is that struggle—hard work and even failure—is wired into our DNA, but the petrins, for all their skill at bioengineering, don't understand that. Although this is a wonderful place, humanity isn't meant to live in a bubble. I don't think mankind would ultimately be happy here. Some people would no doubt enjoy luxurious captivity, but most will resist it after a few months or years. I myself don't want to be harvested like some crop. It's insulting, Josh."

Joshua was growing angrier by the minute. "I *love* this place. These past three days have been some of the happiest of my life. I couldn't disagree with you more." He folded his arms defensively and leaned back against the cushion.

Rachael maintained her composure despite Joshua's displeasure. "Do you truly love this place—could you achieve your potential as a scientist here—or would you love it just because you'd be able to spend time with me?"

Joshua hesitated for a moment before answering. "Both."

"You don't seem very sure of yourself," she said. "If we allow Seth to do what he proposes and relocate our species to New Eden, I think we would be doing humanity a grave disservice."

Joshua couldn't believe what he was hearing. Rachael, after all, had been given her life back. She seemed ungrateful and was also reducing humanity's dilemma, one with no solution according to Seth, into a philosophical issue.

"That may be your opinion, and I guess I can see where you're coming from," Joshua stated in a begrudging tone of voice, "but at this moment I don't think we have much of a choice. As you recall, there's already petrin DNA growing on Earth, and humanity is going to be wiped out by a virus. There isn't much we can do at this point. We're at Seth's mercy. We need a cure for the virus, something he's been very evasive about. We have to proceed on the assumption that there's no cure, and if that's the case, billions will die unless they're able to come here."

Rachael sat quietly, looking down at her hands. "That may be factually true, but . . ." She paused and searched for her words. "Yes, much of humanity may be killed by the virus, but I'm sure at least a small number of individuals will survive. Maybe they can be the seeds for a new generation of humans. If we want humanity to be free, sacrifices will have to be made."

"Sacrifices? You're talking about the deaths of billions of people!"

"I know, Josh, but we can't just think of short-term consequences. What we do will affect humanity for thousands of years. I, for one, believe that we shouldn't sacrifice our free will just for the sake of one generation." She looked into Joshua's eyes and stroked his cheek. "I love you, but I can't live in a zoo or consent to the petrins stifling mankind's ability to grow and exercise free will. Thriving and being happy are not the same things as the right to evolve and advance—to carve out our own destiny. The petrins would take that away, but it's what makes us who we are."

Joshua sat still and pondered Rachael's words. They made sense to the scientist in him, but his heart was pulling him in a different direction. "Even if you're right, I really don't see much that we can do given the current situation."

"There isn't something *we* can do." Rachael looked down and grasped Joshua's hand. "But there's something *you* can do," she said quietly.

"What?"

Brushing away tears, Rachael stared back into Joshua's eyes and said nothing.

"What?" Joshua asked again.

"You can break the sphere in Seth."

Tears now also filled Joshua's eyes. "Break the sphere? Why? That's pure insanity, as well as suicide for humanity."

"Josh, if there's one thing we've learned, information is everything, especially for the petrins. The information flow through the sphere is what would allow petrins to develop Earth as a new node for themselves. Breaking the sphere would instantly stop the information flow, and they wouldn't be able to carry out their plan."

"No, Rachael!" Joshua yelled. "That sphere is the only thing keeping you alive. Without it, you couldn't exist."

"I know," Rachael replied, her tone subdued. "But what is the sacrifice of one human, or even billions, if we can save the destiny of *all* humanity."

"Rachael, you can't ask me to do this. It would be akin to murdering

313

you. I simply won't do it. I can't lose you a second time."

Rachael put her arms around Joshua's shoulders. "Josh, it isn't murder. It's sacrifice. This isn't about me or you. It's much bigger than that. You *must* break the sphere. It's the only way out. Think about it objectively, without emotion. Think about it as a scientist. You know I'm right."

"I can't believe this. You're the religious one here. Are you willing to go against the wishes of our creators?"

Rachael was resolute. "They're not *my* creator—not the creator *I* believe in. They may have had a hand in how humans ended up on Earth, but they didn't create the universe. No matter how advanced they are, they're not God even though they've assumed the role of supervising all life in the universe."

"No." Joshua was grasping at straws to find a solution. The prospect of losing Rachael permanently was killing him inside. "How about if I just disconnect the sphere without breaking it. That would stop the information flow."

"But it wouldn't be permanent. Think of all of those 103ers. Seth and the petrins are practically a religion to them. They would demand that the sphere be reattached so that they could speak with Seth. Any mention of the sphere being reconnected would cause huge divisions in humanity that would lead to severe unrest. Josh, you have to break the sphere. You're the only one who possess the knowledge of how to capture spookyons created by the Big Bang, so if you break the sphere, the connection with the petrins would be cut permanently. It's the only way to ensure that Earth will remain under human control. You know in your heart it's the right choice." She placed the palm of her hand on his chest.

"What do you know of my heart?" Joshua asked angrily, brushing away her hand. "You didn't have to endure the loss I felt over the past few months."

"Believe me, I know your heart, Josh, and I know that in the end you would be willing to sacrifice it for the good of humanity."

"I can't." Joshua sobbed as he lay his head in Rachael's lap.

Chapter Thirty-Six
Sacrifice and Empathy

The next morning, Joshua and Rachael lay quietly on their bed, the sun still low in the sky. Rachael faced sideways, her arms wrapped around Joshua, who lay on his back and stared blankly at the ceiling. Their eyes were red from lack of sleep and a night of tears and frustration. They had argued and cried for hours, each holding to their philosophical view on what should be done regarding the petrins' plan for humanity.

"Seth will be back soon," Rachael said, breaking the silence.

"I know. Don't remind me." Joshua's voice betrayed exasperation and futility.

"Josh, I'm tired of arguing. I've made it clear how I feel and what I think you should do, but in the end, I can't force you to do *anything*. You're going to have to make a decision for the entire planet, not just for you and me."

Joshua sighed heavily. "One that's almost impossible to make. You're asking too much of me."

"Josh, my love, don't worry about me. Just know that I love you no matter what you decide."

"I understand," he said, his voice softening as he turned to Rachael. "I love you more than you can know."

He gave her a kiss on the forehead and resumed staring at the ceiling.

A few minutes later, Seth's voice was heard in the minds of Joshua and Rachael. It had been three days to the second since Seth had brought Joshua to New Eden.

"Josh, can you hear me?" Seth asked.

"Yes," Joshua replied, his voice emotionless.

"I hope you enjoyed your time on New Eden."

"Seth, it was truly paradise for me," he said, taking a deep breath to regain his composure. "Thanks."

"Good. I'm glad to hear that. Rachael, did you enjoy it too?"

"Very much, Seth. I want to thank you for allowing me to have this lovely experience."

"You're welcome Rachael. Josh, I'm going to take you back to Earth now. Are you ready to go?"

Joshua turned to his love, whose smile reminded him of their first day together. "Goodbye, Rachael." He smiled weakly as he touched his fingers to his lips and then to hers.

"Goodbye, Joshua." She kissed him tenderly one final time.

"I'm ready," Joshua said, his hands by his side, his body still.

Joshua's senses went dark. He retained his thought processes, but his five senses were now absent. A short time later, he opened his eyes and saw that he was back in the lab, Seth hovering over him like a surgeon over a patient.

"Please lie still," Seth instructed. "I'm removing the biograins from your cranium."

Joshua felt a tingling sensation in his scalp as the biograins exited his skull and flowed into the beaker that Seth had held three days earlier.

"You can sit up now," Seth said, a smile on his robotic face. "But take it easy. Your body has been in a supine condition for seventy-two hours."

Joshua sat up slowly. Every joint in his body was sore, and he spent several minutes stretching as he tried to work out the stiffness. The pain in his hip had returned, and he slowly stood and continued stretching until he was able to take a few tentative steps across the floor of the lab.

"I feel like *I'm* the android," Joshua said, wincing as he took small, mechanical steps.

"Josh, I hope you found New Eden to be a satisfying and stimulating environment. The collective put a lot of resources into creating it. As I told you, we can make adjustments or additions if you found anything missing or not to your liking."

"You did a wonderful job, Seth. It was an amazing place that I enjoyed thoroughly. Rachael and I marveled at your technology, not to mention your foresight in anticipating our every need. It was utterly remarkable."

"If I may ask, what was your favorite part?"

"Rachael," Joshua said, shooting Seth a serious sideways look as he continued his arduous walk.

"I understand," Seth replied. "I know that you may have more questions for me, but I can tell that your body is weak. Please go home and get some rest, and we can talk more in the morning. I want to discuss the best way for you to present New Eden to the rest of humanity."

"Okay." His voice remained flat. Why did Seth need to have such a serious discussion so soon? The petrins had waited billions of years for humanity to evolve. Would a few extra days make a difference? He was emotionally drained.

Seth walked towards the elevator as Joshua, now somewhat limber, followed. They passed the tank with the young petrins, and Joshua noticed that they had grown much larger than when he had last seen them. Seth had already begun work to make Earth the newest node for petrin civilization—the latest outpost for the spread of life through the universe.

Joshua, despite a certain predisposition in his thinking before leaving New Eden, had not made his final decision until now. Looking into the tank, he was now certain of the course he must pursue for the good of Earth. He therefore steeled himself for the task ahead. With Seth in front of him, Joshua raised his wrist and eyed his Apple watch. The battery read four percent. He activated the watch's emergency shutdown procedure for Seth, which immediately halted Seth in his tracks. The android stood motionless, both feet on the ground like a broken attraction at Disneyworld.

Joshua advanced and lifted the back of Seth's shirt carefully and deliberately, placing his thumb on the thumbprint reader in order to gain access to the pressure vessel containing the Bowman sphere. The compartment opened, revealing the sphere that glowed its usual green color. He then extracted the sphere from the vessel, thus extinguishing its glow.

He stared in wonder at the sphere, which had allowed humans to talk to an alien and visit a distant planet without a spacecraft or propulsion—a sphere that could change the life of Rachael and billions on Earth. Overcome with emotion, he held the glass vessel in trembling hands as tears ran down his cheeks. As he gazed at the sphere, he thought of the day when it had almost shattered in the very spot he was standing, only to be saved by the always-alert Rachael. How differently things would have turned out if the sphere had broken that day, he thought. Mankind would have continued its evolutionary trek, albeit one that Seth predicted would quickly become a dead end due to extinction caused by the virus or other societal factors.

Joshua wasn't sure how long he'd been standing in the lab with the Bowman sphere in his hands since it had caused him to experience an almost hypnotic reverie about the times he'd spent with Rachael, Vinod, and Seth in the past year and a half. His thoughts were interrupted by the stark reality of the decision he'd made, one that would determine mankind's fate.

His breathing slowed as he focused his concentration on the sphere and let it slip from his hands. "Goodbye, Rachael. Goodbye, Seth." The sphere hit the ground loudly and smashed into thousands of pieces. The spookyon within was lost for good as it mixed with the molecules of the atmosphere.

Joshua dropped to his knees among the shards of glass and cried uncontrollably, his hands covering his face. He thought of the billions of people infected with the virus and their inevitable death and wondered if humanity would be able to survive after a majority of the population had been decimated. He also pictured Rachael, her now-lifeless body lying on a bed in New Eden. She had made the ultimate sacrifice to ensure free will for humanity. Until the very end, she had shown her trademark tenacity and individuality, adhering to her values and beliefs. Joshua had argued with her, but he knew—in his heart, as she'd said—that her view of humanity's future was the only one she could ever entertain. It was who she'd been. More importantly, it was the woman he'd loved so deeply. And she'd been right.

As Joshua wiped the tears from his eyes, he heard a hissing noise behind him. Startled, he turned his head quickly to see steam rising from the tank containing embryonic petrins. Joshua got up from the floor and peered into the tank. The petrin embryos had dissolved and were nothing more than green, gelatinous puddles at the bottom of the tank. Creatures that modeled their lives around information and membership in a collective, Joshua reasoned, apparently couldn't survive without a connection to that same collective.

Joshua started walking towards the elevator when he was jolted by Seth's voice coming over the speakers in the lab.

"Joshua."

He froze in his tracks, looked to the front of the room, and saw that the projector had been automatically activated with a video of Seth on the main screen.

Seth spoke in android form as the video played. Gone was his urban vernacular and casual humor dating from the early days of contact.

"I programmed this video to be displayed in the event that the connection with the sphere was terminated. You have obviously decided to end your contact with us, and I respect your decision. Perhaps in the future, humanity will decide to contact the collective again, and we look forward to that contact should it occur.

"Joshua, we consider humans to be our children, and parents always want what's best for their children and to protect them. Sometimes children follow a path set by their parents, while other times they choose their own way forward even if that way is hazardous or unclear. But in the end, parents only want their children to be happy. You've made your decision, and I know it must have been agonizing. Believe me when I say that I understand the sacrifice you've made. We want only the best for your species. Like all parents, we don't like to see suffering in our children, but we respect all civilizations that choose to set their own course.

"In the back of the lab you will therefore find a large silver tank filled with fluid that contains the cure for your current viral outbreak—the honing virus that I created. Next to the tank is a flash drive with instructions on how to distribute the virus. The drive also contains a file that is a security key. If humanity ever decides to contact us again, it is imperative that you ask whomever you contact for that key to ensure that you are talking to the collective."

Joshua's eyes welled with tears again at the overwhelming love and compassion Seth and the petrins were showing humanity, a degree of love he wasn't sure that humans themselves had demonstrated over the centuries. Seth's actions would save the lives of billions of people. He had been true to his word, and for that Joshua was profoundly grateful. The petrins would allow humans exactly what Rachael had longed for: the opportunity to succeed or fail on their own merits even if it meant that humans, as Seth thought likely, might cause their extinction for any number of reasons.

The future was now open-ended. Joshua would soon talk to Langdon, Williams, and others, and he would tell them of the perils that mankind faced and the grim predictions that the petrins had made about its future. If necessary, he would take his message straight to the public regardless of the consequences, which might well end his career. He would think long and hard about what he would do next, but he believed that Rachael would have advocated giving mankind a fighting chance by sharing the truth with the entire world. It would be a risky move, but that's what Rachael had lobbied for on New Eden: the right to roll the dice without the guaranteed outcome Seth had demonstrated in Las Vegas. Could they avoid the mistakes predicted by the petrins? He didn't know, but Earth's future had grown far more interesting in the space of just a few days.

Rachael. At least he'd had time to share a few final happy moments with her, time that he never dreamt he would have with his love after the automobile accident. And he'd had time to say goodbye properly. Thanks to Seth, he'd been able to have three blissful days with the woman who had captured his heart one rainy afternoon. But his time on New Eden had been bittersweet. Given the emotional rollercoaster he'd been on, he was glad that Seth had videotaped his message. Trying to speak now would be difficult, for he felt a tightness in his throat—felt that if he tried to speak, his voice would waver and that he'd break down completely.

Seth's video continued. "I've enjoyed my time on Earth, and I thank you for introducing me to your people, your culture, and your planet's many habitats. But my most cherished memories are of the times I shared with you, Rachael, and Vinod. Josh, you are my friend and always will be. I'll miss you deeply. I remember the pain you experienced when Rachael died. Believe me, I felt it too."

Without thinking, Joshua began to speak, his voice shaky. "I know, Seth. And you—you were always a true friend, even when you were playing your cards close to the vest. I always suspected that you were—" Joshua stopped in mid-sentence. He was reacting to a recorded message, but the alien had nevertheless found a permanent place in his heart. He allowed the video to continue.

"One more thing," Seth said. "I've left you a gift. Suffice to say that you can't create a living human brain without an accompanying body to nourish it. Goodbye, my friend."

The video shut off abruptly, and Joshua was puzzled by Seth's final comment. A living human brain? An accompanying body? What was he talking about? Why did Seth have to use a riddle as his final communication? Joshua would never know the answer to his question. He was alone in the lab, and Seth was gone forever, separated from Earth by an incomprehensible interstellar—perhaps intergalactic—distance.

"Josh?"

The voice came from behind him. He wheeled around to see Rachael swinging her legs from a table, standing and walking towards him.

Joshua's eyes opened wide, but his mouth was unable to form any words.

"What am I doing here?" Rachael asked. "I was on New Eden—or was that a dream—but now . . . I'm in the lab?"

I've left you a gift.

"I'll explain it later," Joshua replied, running towards Rachael, whose brain pattern had been injected into a clone via bioengineering. It wasn't a duplicate. It was Rachael, who had come home for good.

Joshua embraced Rachael tightly. "Thank you, Seth," Joshua whispered. "Thank you—my friend."

ABOUT THE AUTHOR

Kishore Tipirneni MD is an orthopedic surgeon who lives in the Phoenix area. He is also a self-taught programmer and serial entrepreneur who in the late 90's developed digital imaging software which became the leading digital imaging solution in the US that was later acquired by Stryker Medical. He owns numerous patents in both the medical and computer science space.

A REQUEST FROM KISHORE

I hope that you enjoyed reading NEW EDEN. It is a story that I've culminated over the years and is my first foray into the literary world. If you enjoyed the novel and want to see a sequel, I have a few requests that will help me in this endeavor.

First, please leave a review in the amazon kindle store. You can do so at this link: https://www.amazon.com/review/create-review?&asin=B07VCGVNLB.

Second, please tell your friends about the book via social medial or other methods. You can use this link to share: https://getbook.at/NewEden

Finally, follow me on twitter @SciFiKish.

Thank you!

Made in the USA
Coppell, TX
01 September 2021